MONKS OF A SEPARATE CLOTH

DARREN SPEEGLE

JOURNALSTONE
YOUR LINK TO ARTIST TALENT

ISBN: 978-1-950305-07-0 (sc)
ISBN: 978-1-950305-08-7 (ebook)
Library of Congress Control Number: 2019943368

First printing edition: September 20, 2019

Printed by JournalStone Publishing in the United States of America.

Cover Design and Layout: Don Noble/Rooster Republic Press
Interior Layout: Lori Michelle
Edited by Scarlett R. Algee
Proofread by Mike Thorn and Scarlett R. Algee

JournalStone Publishing
3205 Sassafras Trail
Carbondale, Illinois 62901

JournalStone books may be ordered through booksellers or by contacting:
JournalStone | www.journalstone.com

PUBLICATION HISTORY

"The Symphony of the Normal" First published in *A Haunting in Germany and Other Stories*, PS Publishing, 2016; reprinted in *Best New Horror 28*, 2018.

"The Horticulturist's Daughter" First printed in *Cemetery Dance* #59, 2008; reprinted in *Cries from the Static*, Raw Dog Screaming Press, 2018.

"Porta Nigra" First published in *Three-lobed Burning Eye* (3LBE) #8, 2001; reprinted in *Gothic Wine*, Aardwolf Press, 2004.

"Lago Di Iniquità" First published in *The Third Alternative* #42, 2005; reprinted in *Cries from the Static*, 2018.

"Chasing Fuseli" First published in *Gothic Wine*, 2004.

"To What We Were and Shall Become Again" Original to this collection.

"Buoyancy" First published in *Gothic Wine*, 2004.

"End of the Line" First published in *Gothic Wine*, 2004.

"A Monk of a Separate Cloth" Original to this collection.

"Der Teufelobstgarten" First published in *Brutarian* #44, 2005; reprinted in *Cries from the Static*, 2018.

"Saudade" First published in *Crimewave* #10: *Now You See Me*, 2008; reprinted in *Cries from the Static*, 2018.

"A House of Webs and Dust" Original to this collection.

"Windows of Alaska" First published in *A Haunting in Germany and Other Stories*, 2016

ADVANCE PRAISE FOR DARREN SPEEGLE

"Darren Speegle's delicious evocation of landscape delivers the reader, quite seamlessly, from places of precisely-evoked geography into landscapes of haunting spiritual menace . . . "—Graham Joyce

"Darren Speegle is a remarkable new writer."—Lucius Shepard

"Speegle's voice and worldview are bizarre and mesmerizing, humane and compelling, and the stories contained in this collection will fry your mind. Bleeding between horror, dark fantasy, science fiction, as well as all things heartbreaking and nerve-wracking, Speegle's stories could best be described—if it's possible to describe them at all, and I'm not sure they should be—as 'the savage cerebral,' something you've not encountered much before. That's because Speegle doesn't write fast enough. You'll agree with that last statement before you're halfway through this exceptional collection."—Gary A. Braunbeck

"Darren Speegle's characters, and their situations—in his often brilliant stories—are brought vibrantly, horrifically to life, because he cares about his characters, the stories he tells through them, and the words he chooses, with such great care, to bring them to the printed page. He's among the best writers I've read; sitting down with his new collection, *Rhapsody*, was a real joy for me both as a reader, and as a writer."—T.M. Wright

"Darren Speegle is a real discovery."—Graham Joyce

"Elegant, sometimes intense and horrific but always finely crafted and devious in the best way, Darren Speegle's stories will delight and entertain fans of dark fantasy."—Jeff VanderMeer

"Fiendish ingenuity."—*Asimov's Science Fiction*

"Elegant and sophisticated; Darren Speegle is one of the most intriguing voices active in genre fiction."—*Cemetery Dance*

"An exquisite collection of literate and evocative stories."—*The Magazine of Fantasy and Science Fiction*

MONKS OF A SEPARATE CLOTH

Table of Contents

THE SYMPHONY OF THE NORMAL

Chi Bay, Alaska
April 2011

A LATE SEASON snowstorm was in the works when we reached the Forest Service's remote cabin on Harrow Mountain. The last leg of the eight-hour hike had been rough, the wind having picked up considerably as we moved along the rim of the ridge, unable to enjoy the one higher-elevation view of Chi Bay the trail offered. At our destination at last, we were shielded from the main of it by the densely wooded slope forming the near wall of the deep valley in which Harrow Lake, white in the downpour, slept in a semi-frozen state. The log cabin, in its snowy mountain setting, painted a fairy-tale picture into which we were vastly relieved to be inserting ourselves before dusk.

As I was still digging out the key they'd issued at the Douglas Valley Ranger Station, Valerie—who'd ducked into the shelter of the porch ahead of me, letting her bag fall in a heap on the weathered planks—announced that the door was unlocked. We made eye contact while she held the turned knob of the still-closed door in her gloved fist, but neither of us said anything. What needed to be said about the place had been said along the way. Our respective positions were clear. She allowed for the possibility that there was some sort of negative energy here. I did not. Still, the door being unlocked wasn't a good sign. A person who could make that kind of oversight could also forget other things, like food. This was Southeast Alaska, and Southeast Alaska had bears, cute black ones and not so cute brown ones. And in April, those bears were hungry.

A leftover can of pork and beans was one thing. What we got when Val pulled the door open was entirely another. The single room of the cabin interior was lived in. Articles of what appeared to be a man's clothing hung from the posts of the wooden bunk. A sleeping bag was bunched around the foot of the lower bed. A backpack stood against the adjacent wall, its various pockets gaping open. Toiletries lay on the rim of a sink that, according to the information the Forest Service personnel had provided along with the key, supplied filtered water from the lake. Every surface in

1

the sparsely furnished room, except for that of the lone chair, was in use. Strewn across the table were metal cooking utensils, a hunting knife, and other miscellaneous gear. The wooden locker stood open, cans of food resting on top of it, carelessly folded clothes stacked within. The chair's emptiness in the cluttered room was a vaguely unsettling comment of some kind.

Valerie had stepped back against the open door to let me have a view as well. I now nudged her into the room, grabbing her pack as I followed, dropping it by the wall after I'd closed the door behind me. Inside, we were greeted by an acrid, slightly rancid smell coming from the fireplace. It was hard to tell how recently it had been used because moisture was collecting in it from the chimney, drawing out the unpleasant odor from the charred stumps and dregs. Beside it rested a stack of collected sticks and mossy logs, possibly another source of the complicated smell. Shrugging off my backpack, I stepped over and knelt on the fireplace's protruding base, noting the hardened meal drippings staining the stone. The smell nearly overpowered me as I reached in and turned the handle that controlled the flue.

"Jesus," I said. "Let's open the windows."

But she was more concerned about the occupant. "Should we be messing with anything, Chad? With someone still around? Did we get the dates wrong?"

"*We* didn't. If anybody did, the Forest Service did. But when I reserved the place, the lady looked at her book and said the gentleman using the cabin would be out Thursday by two. She also said that of the four remote cabins in the Chi Bay area, this is the only one you don't have to get on a long waiting list for. That it often sits empty—no, don't say it, Val. This is the most difficult cabin to get to, that's all. Dude probably thought he could stay a day or two longer without running into anyone. He wouldn't have known we were coming. He was here when I booked."

While talking I'd opened the window that looked on the lake, failing to dodge in time the affront of cold air and needles. I immediately closed the window, then stepped across the room to the one by the bed. As it came open without the blast, Valerie said, "So what do we do?"

"We act like the place is ours, that's what we do. It is, for three days. We have a snowstorm on our hands, babe. Do you really want to wait outside until he gets back? Hope that's soon, because I sure as hell don't want to spend the weekend with him."

"Do you think something might have happened to him? I mean, shouldn't he be inside out of the storm?"

"Jeez, Val. That's kind of a leap, isn't it? He probably went hiking, got caught by surprise."

She was silent. Worrying, I could tell. I went to the fireplace and dug around the ashes with a stick, unearthing a shapeless something that might once have been a vegetable, a piece of blackened meat, and then another chunk of meat, this one raw. It looked like our man had been skewering in here. Yes, here came a survivor now under a half burned log, food partially melted around what was left of the wooden shaft. I fetched an ancient dustpan resting against an equally outdated broom in the corner and, holding my breath, used it to scoop out the food.

"Grab one of the trash bags out of my pack, will you? Middle pocket."

She fished it out and held it open for me. Wrinkling her face as I dumped the contents of the pan, she said, "That's spoiled meat."

"You don't say."

"That means it's been sitting for awhile. He would have used it his first night with no way to keep it. I can't believe he dragged it up here."

"If he came in from the old prison road, he'd have had only a few hours' hike. A brutal one, but that's beside the point."

"The *point*, Chad, is that food's been allowed to spoil. I don't care if it's in the damn fireplace. It's *spoiled*. Where *is* he?"

"Val—"

"Chad, shit."

"For the love of Christ, Valerie, will you just chill out?"

"I can feel it, Chad. Something's wrong. Can I close the window, please?"

"Yeah, go ahead. I'm going to bury this outside."

I didn't give her a chance to object, quickly opening then closing the door behind me. As I stood watching the intensified storm for a moment, I considered how I was going to go about performing the task in this mess without a shovel. I'd left behind the entrenching tool we always took along on camping trips because it was heavy and took up too much space. I'd my hunting knife on my belt, but that seemed insufficient for the job even if I'd been willing to use it. I decided I wasn't going to find anything standing here, so I stepped off the porch into the whirl, heading toward the back where I'd noticed from the trail a decrepit log pavilion housing a log picnic table, the lot built on site with the raw materials of the land. But before I'd even reached the back, I found what I was looking for. Just around the corner, resting against the side of the cabin by a spigot that used the same plumbing as the sink inside was an iron fireplace poker. How weird to find such a tool here. Yes, we had a fireplace, but wouldn't a stick have served the purpose? God knew what our occupant had been up to with that. Probably stabbing at the bear some other act of carelessness had summoned.

Tool in hand, I continued on around behind the cabin, where the trees

3

were denser and the snow bed shallower. Picking up the trail we had come in on, I put some distance between myself and the cabin before selecting a random spot below a spruce tree where I dug the hole, planting the whole bag. It was Valerie who always insisted on the biodegradable products—the bags, the toilet paper, the paper towels. Originally an Alabama boy, my idea of camping was a cooler of beer, a bag of pot, a box of beef sticks, and a sleeping bag. She was a California transplant, and something of a club liberal to boot, and sometimes I thought the only way we found our middle ground in these things was through the necessities of the rugged place where our roads had deposited us. She'd no choice but to shed the bumper sticker mindset—"Global Warming is not just a trend"—and I'd no choice but to can the disregard. Burying your waste, hanging food in trees, skipping the perfumes and loud deodorants, leaving killing grounds undisturbed, all the realities of outdoor Alaska were matters of respect as well as survival. Respect *was* survival. Do unto your environment as you would have it do unto you, or suffer the consequences. It was a simple philosophy that served its purpose. The reward was living to see whether the relationship could grow on external dictates.

As I covered in the hole, a strange sequence happened. It began with the first deposit of the moist, silty earth I'd removed and didn't end until the hole was filled. As I swept the dirt and snow over the edge of the hole, the universe became smaller, the clumps of celestial material I'd dislodged seeming to fall through a deep, yawning shaft rather than into the shallow pit I'd chopped and scooped out of the ground. My attention was initially on my work, so this occurred in my peripheral vision, with the signal taking its time to get to my brain. By the time it did, I was already into my next sweep, which created a sense of fluidity and order in a process that would otherwise have seemed disorderly and random. The small roots I'd mangled while digging, some pulled in half by the poker's hook, seemed to shiver as the dirt showered over them, to shiver and bend downward, opening the way with an organic flourish. As the earth found the bottom, however, my perception returned to normal, but only until the next drop, when the process repeated itself. After about the third deposit, the depth effect was replaced by the perception or illusion of motion. The roots continued to appear to move for a second or two after I looked at them directly. The act of filling in the hole became a repetitive experiment whose result was always the same. In my peripheral vision, as I brushed the material into the hole, the roots writhed. In my direct gaze, they caught me watching a moment too late. It was eerier yet to see the earth, as they were covered, move on top of them. But that only lasted a few seconds, and then the job was done. Filling in the hole had taken about as long as it takes to get the full flavor out of a piece of gum. Weird analogy? Well, the roots had seemed like gum, twisting in and out of shape as they performed their impossible dance.

Pushing snow over the scar I'd left, I caught a whiff of bad air. I looked at the ground near my feet and there was the bag, unburied. I was sure I'd dropped it into the hole—but then, no, I couldn't have. It would have obstructed the perception of depth in so shallow a space. Even pushing it down under the roots with the poker would have left only a few inches of room above. There would have been earth left over. There would have been . . .

I began digging again. Put all my focus on the task itself. When unnatural movement threatened while I was still reopening the hole, I closed my eyes to finish the task. I had to open them once, looking only at the bag as I dropped it in, but as I closed them again, I caught the motion of the bag in free fall, with no boundaries visible around it. Other than for that unaccounted-for second in time, my trick worked as far as the optical side of the thing was concerned. Where I almost came undone, where I almost fled the scene leaving the job incomplete, was in the sonic realm. I don't know whether the universe took exception to my trick, or I'd been so distracted by the visual the first time around that I'd failed to hear the faint screaming of the roots and earth. But I heard them in the rerun, at first only a distant ringing in my head but then with form, with curve and undulation as the cosmos came apart in my very hands. I managed just enough detachment from the experience to whisk the dislocated material back into place; then I was backing away, one foot over the other in the snow, the poker extended before me like a weapon. I heard the cry of a bald eagle passing overhead, the whisper of the wind and snow, my own heartbeat trying to find its place in the symphony of the normal. And as they all came together like clockwork, logic clicked into stride with them, making me my own tenuous master again.

Shaking my head, blaming but not really blaming Val and her superstition for the episode, I headed back to the cabin. I'd the presence of mind to collect an armful of firewood along the way, dumping the bundle on the porch as I arrived. Before entering the cabin I stood at the edge of the porch for a few minutes, watching the wind carry the snow over the lake, aware of its bite but not to the point of conscious discomfort. After ten years in this land, earning my calluses in the fishing industry, the mines, and clearing snowmobile trails before finally landing my manager/bartender gig at the Ghost Town, the elements and I were old acquaintances. I suspected I would go to my grave wondering just what that twenty-year-old college dropout who had gotten on his Harley and taken the long ride north, trading in his bike for a more suitable four-wheel-drive somewhere around Minnesota, had actually been looking for. Had he found it? Did it look like Valerie, who had zeroed in on me among

5

the disenchanted cuts of meat that made up the high side of the four-to-one gender ratio? Three years my junior, she had come here by her own roads, paved by her undergraduate work in marine biology at the University of Southeast Alaska in Juneau. But as with all of us who weren't indigenous or born on Alaskan silt, there were reasons underlying the reasons. We just didn't know what they were.

But it wasn't merely conditioning that kept me standing here exposed to the weather. Oblivious to its sting as I was, I needed the shower of needles to clean off the strange. Valerie had said she could feel it. Something wrong. In spite of myself, so could I. And it wasn't about some drowning in the lake in front of me; or a fatal fall from the slope rearing behind the lake; or a murder-suicide in the structure behind me; or a bear attack that left a ranger dead; or an avalanche that buried a party of four; or any of the other tragedies Valerie had dug up for her case against one remote mountain cabin. It wasn't even about our missing man. Or the fact that we were going to be snowed in here for God knew how long if we didn't take our asses, right now, and head back down to civilization. No, it was about the mechanics behind events, the hidden mechanics of which those underlying reasons I mentioned were a part. It was about the voice that nature normally reserved for itself, but which here, if you got too close, you could hear calling from the edge of reason, from the wriggling mouth of the pit, offering the way into blackness.

⸻

I was surprised to find her sitting in the chair, now out of her wet jacket, a small hardback notebook resembling a ledger open in her hand.

"You've gotta listen to this," she said as I removed my own jacket and sat on the edge of the bunk. I could feel her eyes on me as I began unlacing my boots. She was waiting on an acknowledgment so she would know she had my undivided attention—a habit I couldn't stand.

"Are you in his personal stuff, Valerie? Don't you think we should get a fire started and get out of these wet clothes before we start the full-on invasion of a stranger's privacy? What is that anyway?"

"I don't know. Journal. Research notes. Whatever it is, it's damned compelling. Just listen to this." She let her pause indicate she was entering reading mode. "'The locals have no idea what they have on their hands. Harrow Lake Cabin, which was built by the Forest Service as an outpost and was later made available to the public as a hiker 'remote cabin,' seems to have developed its own reputation as opposed to being guilty by association with the area of Harrow Mountain. Also, local history seems to have left out the tragic and unexplained events that occurred before Chi Bay became a municipality in 1886, some of which date as far back as when white man first brought industry to Southeast Alaska, giving birth to Chi

Bay and settlements like it.'" She licked her finger and with an aching deliberateness flipped the page, the silence during this pause sudden and overwhelming. "'So too has the record somehow forgotten the small mountain tribe from which the name Chi Bay originates, which I wouldn't have thought possible here where the Chi-Ikuk lived. I knew they'd all but disappeared from the broader record, but to discover that no local myths had survived the centuries—this was unreal to me. I've spoken with several of the native Tlingits, and most have never heard of the Chi-Ikuk tribe. Of those few elders whose reactions indicated they had, none were willing to admit it, as though doing so might somehow bring the Chi back from the void.'"

Valerie paused to look up at me. "The void? They sound like the Mayans. If these Chi Indians actually lived here, what could have happened to them?"

I had no answer, though she had my attention now. I watched her flip to another page, scan its contents, then flip again. Her eyebrows knitted as she settled on the current passage. She read with a voice of subdued wonder, turning the page at the appropriate spot with that strangely demonstrative motion of her moistened finger. "'The Chi-Ikuk knew about the fracture. They embraced it. And that's why the Tlingits didn't mix with them. Not that the Chi had any interest in coming down from the mountains, which were spiritual to them, though I suspect they may have wintered at lower elevations, maybe even on some of the uninhabited islands. Again, no independent anthropological record exists. What artifacts might have survived have no doubt been mislabeled as Tlingit or another indigenous group. They seem to have been a people who lived austerely, without ornamentation or tribal motifs, and entirely on their own means. They manufactured nothing that did not contribute directly to their basic human needs, did no trading, and left nothing of their own mark in their wake. It is entirely possible, however, that the tribe is actually a sub-tribe of mystics or the like that broke off at some point in the distant past from the Tlingits, who were all too eager to omit them from the oral and pictorial record. This seems to be a view shared by my trusted source, from whom much of the information I do have came.'"

At this natural pause at the end of a page, I jumped in, telling Valerie to go back, to before the point where she'd started reading the current section. I wanted to know more about this fracture that the Chi-Ikuk embraced.

She flipped back, eyes perusing the material a moment before she read aloud. "'"Of the multiple fractures I and my source in Whitehorse, Canada believe to exist in the world, Alaska's is the most intense, volatile, and potent. Others are active; there is no question of that. But the body and senses are not attuned to them as they are here on Harrow Mountain. Harrow is the one. The one whose particles carry far and wide, to every living soul on earth, touching the places that have waited to be touched. Harrow is the one that will potentially envelop us in darkness.'"

Val's eyes, as she looked at me, gleamed with a sort of dazed awe. "'Us'? Chi Bay? The world? What could he be—"

She lurched mid-sentence. Took impact, as if by some unseen force. Dazed awe became shocked fright as she stared at me, mouth trying to find the words.

"What is it, Val? What's wrong?"

Now her face changed completely as she gave me the strangest look I've ever seen. "What . . . " she struggled. "What *is* it? What's *wrong*?"

"Val, I don't—"

"Let's see, could it be the thunder or avalanche or earthquake or whatever the fuck it was that just rocked the cabin?"

Now it was me staring with my mouth open. "No, Val. No thunder. No avalanche. You're disturbed by what you're reading—"

"The whole fucking cabin, Chad!"

I went to her, placing my hand on her shoulder. She resisted the gesture halfheartedly as I said gently, "Give me the book, Val."

"There was *nothing*?" she said in a whisper.

"Nothing, baby."

"There's something terribly wrong here, Chad. It's not me. I swear to God it's not me."

"Okay, baby. Just please let me see the book."

"No! I want to read you the last couple pages. That was the part I read before you came in. It didn't make any sense then, but now . . . "

"Maybe we should wait, Val. Just cool for a minute."

"No. I'm okay. Go sit down."

"I'll stay here, thanks."

"The sound, Chad. Listening to its echo in my head, it was more like the moaning of a ship's hull, only a hundred times louder. More violent. Like something shifting or wrenching apart."

Her words chilled me. Reason didn't want to believe she'd heard what she thought she had, but instinct wasn't taking the easy way. Hadn't I felt something, too? In her reaction? Did it matter whether it was the reaction or the cause of the reaction that had jolted me? An answer lay in there somewhere, in the *experience* of reality. God, I hoped we never found it. Because finding it, that same instinct told me, would be the catastrophic failure of whatever mechanism kept us pretending that we were comfortably afloat.

She'd started reading again, and my mind had to fall in. I chose to step back and follow the nuances of her face rather than the witchery on the page. "'My Catholic parents, rest their deluded souls, hammered evil and sin into my hands and feet, crucifying me for the flesh and blood of which I was made. I am convinced that all the evil in the world is organic; that nature is God, dust is Christ, and electromagnetism is the Holy Spirit; that all the dark impulses of every living thing, including Mother Nature, originate not in the heart, but in the stress fractures that developed in the primal forge after the product bubbled and spat into shape. Balance is not a philosophy. It is a physical property whose opposite is imbalance. And without it the realm of flesh and blood is unenlightened. The Chi-Ikuk were right to embrace their environment. To not do so is to alienate yourself from your origins, and thus your identity. If there is any mortal sin, it is surely that—to deny what you are for some fantasy of higher thought. I think of random death and murder and torture and rape and escapist suicide and wonder how the pretenders and clingers, the worshipers of their own morally conceived normality, endure. The key is balance. I realize that now. Don't be caught naked and unawares, because then it will compensate for the discrepancy you represent all at once. The same holds true for offering yourself to it as a slave or seizing it like the weapon you will use to slay thirty random people. If you flex like a palm, let it bathe you, let it shake free what is ripe or extraneous, then the mayhem may be averted. The Chi-Ikuk knew that. They did not run rampant among the sea people, or slaughter needlessly. They kept their eye on the prize, which was utter communion with the element. The Chi'i of the Chi, so to speak. Yin and yang. They are here, I can feel it. My Whitehorse source spoke of their relationship with the glacier. That is where I will find them. They whisper to me on the icy wind.'"

Valerie closed the book, reverently. I didn't like the look on her face. Didn't like it at all. "It's stopped snowing," she said softly, looking beyond me, through the window by the door.

I turned, and so it had. Everything a silent white. The trees. The lake. The wide mouths of the avalanche chutes behind the lake. Above the frame, through the wall, I saw the designs these fissures must have drawn during this moment of pre-dusk clarity, symbols so stark they'd make Arthur Gordon Pym speak in tongues. We had to leave, I told myself, looking at the floor, noting absently that I wore only one unlaced boot. There was still time. The snow bed wasn't more than six inches deep at this point. But dusk was on its way. If we took Harrow Trail back the way we'd come—the route to the old prison road was far too treacherous—we'd be hiking all night. If we didn't freeze, we'd miss our footing along one of the ledges. Maybe even plunge, I thought crazily, into the *fracture* itself. Dear God, why hadn't I listened to her?

"We have to go there in the morning," she said.

"Go *where*?" I said feebly, rubbing my face.

"Where he went. The glacier's on the map."

"Valerie, they specifically told us at the Ranger Station not to go near there. People have died. Assuming I were willing, which I absolutely am not, what is it you hope to accomplish?"

I hadn't realized how far she'd retreated until now, as I met her befogged gaze directly. "Balance," she said, causing parts of me to crawl. "Karma. He is a fellow human being. We cannot just leave him, knowing where he has gone."

"We'll hike down tomorrow with the book, give it to the authorities. They'll send out a search team. *We* can't help him, Valerie. Have you even considered the notion that what you're reading might be fiction? That he might be a writer? Or a fucking madman?"

"You know that's not the case."

"*How*? How, Valerie? How the fuck could I know that? Writers sometimes write in the first person. They grab your attention with their words. What about that book says something different?"

"For one, the words are alive. At certain points they squirm on the page. Behind them is a hole. A deep, deep h—"

The door came open, causing my heart to quit as abruptly as her sentence. A tall man in a hunter's jacket and Russian hat stood there.

"Who the devil are you?" he demanded, letting the fireplace poker resting on his shoulder fall down in front of him like a lance. Like I'd held it over the hole I'd dug.

Neither one of us could find the breath for explanation. His patience was three seconds long. When it had expired, he stepped into the room, covering me with the poker, snatched the book from Valerie's hands, snatched the hunting knife from the table, turned, strode back through the door and was gone.

——•——

Dusk had arrived. We were back in the cabin after an unsuccessful attempt to ignore the risk and get out. The storm had started up again almost the moment we walked out the door and had thrown us back, in a lust it hadn't previously shown, within twenty minutes. Though we had weapons at the ready against his potential dementia—our knives; a solid, easily clutched log—neither of us believed it of him. A lot can be learned in a few seconds, and in this case it seemed clear by the man's behavior that he was about his purpose and his purpose only, and as long as we stood out of his way we were of no concern to him. Still, he was a risk we were willing to take only *after* we'd been denied other options. Now, in fresh clothes, surrounded by the cabin's shadows and the gathering warmth of a fire that had taken some time to get going, a quiet had settled over us. In the quiet, words and roots still writhed, holes still gaped, hulls still wrenched, but our mechanisms had taken over, finding the middle space where we nestled in to wait on the intervention of God. There was nothing worthwhile to say or do, and to try was to test what threads of reason remained.

What had needed to be accomplished had been accomplished. We'd collected enough firewood for the night, stacked it around the brief hearth where it now dried. With some prompting, I'd convinced Valerie to join me in a couple of boiled eggs, a Pop Tart, and some trail mix, which we'd washed down with the two beers we'd made space for in our packs. We'd washed up, brushed our teeth, and made sure our bags were ready in case we had to leave in a hurry, never even untying the bedrolls we'd preferred over sleeping bags because of the weight the latter would have added. Instead, we had removed the thin mattress sheathed in a plastic factory cover from the top bunk and placed it on the floor, where we now rested. I'd suggested we use the bunk itself, but Val hadn't relished the thought of being "up there," whatever that meant exactly. I lay propped on my elbow, looking at the map Val had referred to earlier—though not, I hoped, for the reason she had suggested. Valerie sat cross-legged by my legs, watching the black front window, behind which the storm continued to howl with a hellish ferocity. Sleep was a retreat we hadn't yet discussed, though I felt the day's hike in my joints and muscles. I knew she did too, but I wasn't ready to fight that battle just yet. It would catch up to her.

I don't know when precisely I began to notice the physical change in the room, but it was sometime during this period of quiet, idle terror. It was realized not in the discovery sort of way, not with impact, but rather with a slowly dawning awareness, as though the knowledge was already there and had been patiently awaiting our admission. Valerie, I think, came into it around the same time as me, but neither of us said anything until its manifestations were impossible to partake of alone. Nor can I say what preceded what in terms of our senses' reception of the stimuli. But once the experience took hold, "stimulating" assumed a whole new meaning.

For me, the disturbance escalated from a random series of off notes in the symphony of the normal, each a trifle until perceived relatively; then they became contributors to the breakdown of the whole. While the log cabin was a staunch object against the storm, it was by no means sealed tight. The foundation creaked like the iron joints of Valerie's ship hull. The floor moaned, the porch rattled, the chimney whistled, the door pulsated, the windows shrieked at their rubbery seams. The roof was like a drum, amplifying every beat, of which there were many as gusts of wind drove under eaves, among beams, tore limbs from winter-weakened trees, sending them crashing across the roof's slopes. Though the April storm could hardly be called normal, all of this constituted an internally logical symphonic improv. It was the *other* sounds, the sounds that seemed to come from *within* the room, that wrecked the fierce beauty of it, that worked against rather than upon the senses, testing reason, equilibrium, the ability to bend beneath their subtle onslaught. The fleeting patter on the floorboards, the sudden but not so sudden air lock sigh, the flit of unseen wings by the ear, the fade-out of a song that had never been sung, the withering lilt of a bloom that had never whispered open, the hiss of release that stank of the earth's bowels, the shift of microscopic plates, the groan of colliding air particles, the fluff of things that danced among the fire's reflections, the long, elastic drip of magma. And beneath it all, the desperately regular thump of the driving engine, which seemed to reside just outside my own hands, breathing its crude breath on my skin.

Where I *can* find a beginning is in speech. Valerie was the one to provide it, and the beginning her words represented was the beginning of an end that never materialized. Nothing between then and when we found him the next morning had the proportions of time, least of all that harmoniously strange question from Valerie's lips.

"Will they be able to hear us too, Chad?"

I looked up from the pulsing topographical marks of the glacier on the map. "Who? When?"

"Hikers. When they come."

A cold thing came into being inside me. "What hikers? What are you talking about?"

But she had risen and was stepping over to the window, lifting something that had crawled through its crying seam. A tendril from which a leaf, then another, sprang as I watched. She pulled it like a rope and it came easily through the seam, came and kept coming as she wrapped it around her hand, her expression in flickering shadow, unreadable to me. I was still trying to collect the words when her knife was suddenly in her hand and she was chopping wildly at the vine, both she and the vine screaming as it frayed and finally broke beneath her attack. As if dealing with a snake, she half unwound, half ripped the coils from the spool of her hand and hurled the writhing vine into the fire. As the fire leaped in response, the flash illuminated her face, exposing the utter terror written there for an instant before her features fragmented among the winking sparks and reflections. But though the fire's surge had been brief, the flames had not returned to their former melody. They were now crawling along the stone walls of the alcove, out across the log walls surrounding the fireplace, hungrily seeking another taste of such rare fuel, of so validating and affirming an experience in a universe woven of organic material. While I salvaged the composure to observe both the fire's and Valerie's behavior, Val's body language indicated that the flames had consumed her as surely as they had the vine, making her as much a part of the phantasmagoria that dazzled the room as any shadow. Before she had the chance to reach out her hand and commune with the element, I was there, snatching her back out of harm's way. The two of us became entangled and tumbled to the bedding, where over her shoulder I watched the fire whisper back into shape.

Then she was clutching me for life itself and the symphony of disorderly order bled in again and somewhere in the trembling reaches of the night another phantom made its appearance, and its name was sleep.

———•———

We woke multiple times during the night, on each occasion to less noise— from the storm, from its undercurrent, from the nightmares. Occasionally I got up, wresting myself from Val's clinging to place more wood on the fire, always warily, always wondering if we wouldn't be better off out there among the elements where certain death, rather than the agonizing prospect of it, awaited. But as dawn neared and the room remained just a room, I was able to organize my thoughts, to separate the fear from its shadowy source, to begin to appreciate, if not to comprehend, the dimension of our involvement in what was happening. We weren't bystanders, exactly, but neither were we true participants. I'd no idea what had led to past incidents like the murder-suicide that had happened within these very walls a decade or so ago, but in our case we were caught in someone else's affair. Many hikers had been up here through the years without incident, and I believed the same would have been true of us had we come at a different time. I'd no illusions. I didn't cling like some character in a movie to the possibility that it was all a fantasy. I knew beyond doubt that Valerie and I had entered the realm of the supernatural—for lack of a better word—just as I knew that the author of the notes on a lost Alaskan tribe and this "fracture" they had embraced had opened the door. I also felt that I partially understood his need to find himself this way. We all have our paths toward meaning and truth. His lay here in these mountains, with the Chi-Ikuk. The question for Valerie and me was, how far would we let ourselves be pulled along another's path? Did we have a choice now that we were involved? Forget the fact that even if the snow began melting with the rising sun, we would be taking our lives in our hands by attempting the hike down to civilization. Would the thing willingly release us?

I retreated in distaste from this line of thinking. It stank of captivity. Inevitability. The complete absence of personal control. As though I was trying to convince myself to do something that every ounce of me said was our destruction. But even as I recoiled, a relevant passage from the man's notes came back to me, in Val's awed voice. *The key is balance. I realize that now. Don't be caught naked and unawares, because then it will compensate for the discrepancy you represent all at once. The same holds true for offering yourself to it as a slave or seizing it like the weapon you will use to slay thirty random people. If you flex like a palm, let it bathe you, let it shake free what is ripe or extraneous, then the mayhem may be averted.* These words seemed to suggest that contact with the fracture, if not handled as advised, could lead to a psychotic breakdown. God knew what we might carry back with us if we simply fled. Its roots were wriggling inside us now, had spawned nightmares the likes of which I wouldn't have imagined my mind capable. Could we ever be free if we didn't also look into the abyss? Embrace the thing as others had embraced it, at least to the extent that we didn't have to wonder for the rest of our lives, however short that might be, what it was we had fled? Whether we had missed our one opportunity at truth?

Again, I recoiled. How could I even be considering such madness, knowing the fates of others whose presences hadn't agreed, or had agreed too well, with Harrow Mountain? But by now the first strains of dawn were filtering in, and with them came the knowledge of being human, a fundamental equation of which was: that which you flee is that which you confront in hindsight. Maybe it was because of this rule, maybe it was because she was a biologist, that for Valerie there was no question. The first words out of her mouth as she woke to the dawn were, "Have you figured out the best route to the glacier?"

In the end there was no justification for our decision. It was simply the right one.

————•————

It came into view within an hour of departure. In the crook of two adjacent slopes, it flowed downward toward our elevation, trapping that bluest band of the spectrum in the crystal of its body. As we climbed higher, the large pool formed of its melt became visible, extending from the glacier to the left. Swaths in the snow indicated the paths of streams winding down from the pool to Harrow Lake itself, which was the official source of the like-named river along which we had hiked at the beginning of our trek to the cabin. The sky was clear, the morning-after sun bright. Snow dripped from ledges and overhangs as the transformation to slush had begun. We were wet up to the knees of our insufficient weather gear, but neither of us felt cold. Our purpose, though we didn't know what it was, carried us. We spoke only about the path, not what lay behind or in front of it—even now, as the first blood stains began to appear, seeping up through the snow that had covered his tracks. Whether or not in the physics of the world we called normal such a thing could occur, I didn't know. We weren't in such a world, so it was irrelevant. What mattered was that the marks now provided the way.

We climbed to a point above the mouth of the glacier and then worked our way around the right side, eventually descending to the spot where he had entered. It did not surprise us that he had known to come to this specific pocket to chip away at the ice with his tool until the door to the catacomb interiors was opened. We too could feel the energies concentrated here, though we did not leave patches of bloody flesh lying about the entrance for the wolves and bears, should they dare draw so near. I thought I understood what he was doing by removing pieces of himself with his knife, but I could not have articulated it, no more than I could have expressed in words the beauty of the tableaux the Chi-Ikuk had left along the paths they had carved inside the glacier, where the ice would keep them encased for as long as it took the globe's warming processes to reach the hearts of the blue crystal. How the encasing was accomplished was a mystery, as was the meaning behind the symbols that the ends of the roots and vines with which their bodies were entangled drew in the ice around them. Or the order in which they'd been placed along the tunnels, painting their more complex version of the Stations of the Cross, which in their case numbered in the scores.

When we came to him, and the one who had come before him, and the one who had come before her, we knew. These newer offerings were distinguished from the natives not just by the color of their hair and eyes, but also the condition of their bodies, which had been mutilated, eviscerated, the entrails suspended in the ice around them. In the purity of the glacier's light, we knew that eras were involved, that communion of the sort the Chi-Ikuk had achieved was no longer possible. We knew that our man had been wrong to associate his fracture with the primal fire, but right to reference the Industrial Age, a dawn for man, a dawn of modernity. We knew that he'd been selfish to speak so broadly, so eternally of evil, when the demons of his upbringing were his own, not the world's, to bear. We knew that to blame the fracture for anything man did was to cast responsibility off ourselves. We knew these things and we knew where we fit into it all, and knowing, we were in no hurry. We sat in the tunnel with his book, of which there were enough blank pages left, and we quietly finished his notes, Val doing the actual writing in tight lines on the small pages, using the pen he had left beside the other implements—the fireplace poker, his bloody knife. But though our knowledge was secure, it wasn't until we were standing before our mirrors that we finally let ourselves bathe in the impact. For it was then, as we gazed in wonder at our own gutted bodies suspended in their showcases, that the symphony of the normal achieved its finest pitch.

15

THE HORTICULTURIST'S DAUGHTER

HOW DO YOU console an unreachable child? How do you tell her that the one thing that has inspired any emotion in her, the one thing that has penetrated the moroseness that has surrounded her all of her eight years of life, is gone and will not be coming back?

I will never forget the expression on my wife Haley's face when she came out of Jonna's playroom that September morning, her weekend routine of drawing curtains and opening windows having been bluntly interrupted. I will never lose the image of her grasping the door frame for support, tears welling in her eyes as she looked at me, trying to get the words out. I was standing by the hall table, had just gotten off the phone with, coincidentally, the most recent therapist, the one who had suggested getting Jonna the parakeet in the first place. It had been a month, you see, since our last visit, and Jonna had been improving remarkably. Because of the bird.

The bird that—as Haley finally managed to get out the words—was lying on its back in its cage, dead.

———◆———

"We have to make a decision, and quick," Haley said when her crying subsided.

We were in the kitchen now and could see Jonna idly wandering the pebbled path through the flower garden. If there had ever been a place of comfort for her, then it was in the backyard among the flowers and fruit trees, a paradise my wife and I had built around the darkness and pain. Haley liked to think our daughter was attracted to the garden's cheerfulness. I knew it was the gloom seeping between the petals, the leaves of the bowing branches.

"Haley, I'm not sure what decision there is to make."

She turned from the window, anger amplified in her moist eyes: "We've got to do something with the bird, Ray. This will just kill Jonna." She glanced outside again and suddenly grew taut. "Oh no, she's coming. Go and occupy her while I figure something out."

I didn't argue. There was no point. Besides, I hoped to God she did.

I called my daughter's name as I stepped outside to meet her at the mouth of the maze she walked. Once, I had come around the side of the house and caught her in a pile of potting soil I had dumped by the pansies a couple days before. She was eating a worm she had dug out of the black mound. I liked to think that I had embarrassed her. That the reason she paused was because she knew what she was doing was not normal.

The therapist, when told of the incident, had disagreed. "Do you have a lot of birds in your garden?"

"We have quite a few, yes," I said.

"And does Jonna seem to take to them?"

Haley and I looked at each other as though the realization was just dawning.

"Then you must keep her out of the garden," the therapist said.

"Keep her *out*?" Haley echoed, clutching my arm. "After all the work?"

"Clearly, she is imitating behavior she has witnessed. It is not wise . . ."

But this had been the previous therapist. Cheltenham, the nearest population center of any size, had only three that fit our needs, and we were on the third.

I held my hands out to Jonna as we met between the trim edges of grass. She looked up at me with the saddest expression you have ever seen—her regular one. I let my fingers trickle like water and she placed her hands, more by wont than desire, in mine. She was frail as well as morose, a September flower of her own. I spoke to her quietly as I always did, so as not to damage her. "Hey, little golden one."

Her vocabulary—what she was willing to use, anyway—consisted of perhaps a hundred words. I had inadvertently invoked one of them.

"Goldie," she said.

Yes, Goldie, her poor dead parakeet.

"Are you having fun playing outside this morning? Look at the sky, how blue it is."

But she was finished talking now, letting her finger communicate instead. Following it, I was surprised to find Haley emerging from the back door, having already settled on a solution.

"Honeydrop," she announced. "Honeydrop, I have something to tell you. It's about Goldie. She's flown away."

———◆———

It might have worked had Jonna not paused on the way to her playroom to look in the drawer of the hall table, where Haley had stored the bird until she had more time to figure out what to do. Jonna did random things like that, though I could not rule out the suggestion of the eyes, *à la* that memorable scene in Steinbeck's *The Pearl*. How many times have I read to her from my favorite author? In any case, Haley was so stunned by Jonna's action that she could only gasp as the drawer came open.

As always, our beloved daughter did not offer much in the way of expression. She lifted the limp bird in her hands and, stroking its feathers, looked at Haley quizzically but without expectation. I saw that Goldie's head lolled as with a broken neck; its wing lay at a tangential angle, which said so much more than "Goldie's dead."

Haley knelt before Jonna in remorse and contriteness and supplication and reverence. "When I said Goldie had flown away, I meant her soul, Jonna. Goldie is a ghost now. She has left her body and flown away to heaven. Do you understand?"

If Jonna did, she didn't indicate so, the melancholy as entrenched in her face as I had ever seen it. Without a word she turned and stepped into her playroom, where the cage door as well as the room's window lay open to that heaven suggested. Goldie cradled in her hands, she went to the window and looked out on the garden and orchard, suddenly grotesquely plastic against the equally artificial September blue. My wife and I, having agreed long before to let Jonna fulfill her moments, however unidentifiable for us, could do nothing but watch—Haley's hand over her mouth, mine clutching the neck of my tee shirt in a habit that never dies.

This situation of course fell well within the identifiable, but there was nothing we could do but our classic stances as Jonna raised Goldie in her hands as if in offering. Haley and I saw in advance what was to come, yet had no choice but to let matters follow their course, for Jonna's sake.

"Bye," said our daughter as she let Goldie go. There is no language for the way the bird fell out of her hands, striking the windowsill before dropping into the yard below.

"Oh, Jonna," said Haley, rushing to her.

In the face of it all, I somehow maintained the presence of mind to suggest to my wife that we formally bury Goldie. "There is no closure otherwise," I said.

She nodded in affirmation as she clutched our daughter to her breast, bleating, "Honeydrop."

Hands lax by her sides, Honeydrop watched me.

———•———

Honeydrop. Haley had begun calling her that when Jonna was three and the blue of her baby eyes had surrendered to the melanin that gifted her irises with their unique long term hue. Haley rightly equated that hue with the color of a drop of honey pierced by light, and indeed it was a central feature, complemented perfectly by our daughter's whimsical blonde hair and slightly dark complexion. We were still in New York then, and the people on the street would stop to look at our undersized Jonna in the carrier on my back and comment, "How lovely she is. And those eyes, how *unusual*."

Like her mother and maternal grandmother, Jonna was born in the United States and answered England's call later. Haley's American mother had met her British father while on vacation in London, and they'd later wedded and settled in the States. Haley had been born in Virginia and in the course of time met an ex-Airman turned commercial airline pilot in New York City. They had soon left their lives behind, subsisting on his retirement as a fighter squadron commander (veteran of both the first Gulf War and Kosovo) and both their savings—his from his five-year stint with the airline, hers as a standout artist from a rebirthed psychedelic art movement in NYC. Disenchantment with their respective careers had brought them together in some random bar at JFK, where she had confessed that she had always wanted to go back to England and her heritage.

And so they had, settling in the Cotswolds in a little stone house on the outskirts of a hamlet called Abury-on-the-Wold, a peaceful place to continue to raise a five-year-old child with golden eyes and hair and a love of birds that extended beyond pigeons and seagulls and the mocking parrot on the arm of the indigent on the corner.

———•———

I woke in the night and discovered Jonna outside exhuming Goldie.

I had been trapped in one of my recurrent F-16 dreams, in which I fired upon and fired upon, pounded and pounded, the same stretch of long since defaced foreign soil. I woke, as always, before the scream rising within me found escape. I woke hating what I was, even afraid of myself and of what I was capable. Beside me, Haley stirred in her sleep, but she was used to my disturbances and rolled over without waking.

It was an impulse, possibly the same force that had driven Jonna to open the drawer, that made me pull back the curtains and look outside. The night sky was as clear as the day's had been, casting the rolling wold in that wonderful unreal twilight knitted by moon and stars. The movement revealed itself almost immediately, but my eyes had to adjust before I could make the determination that it wasn't an animal out in the garden. As the nature of the figure took shape, I found myself conscious of the scent of my shirt collar in my fist. Sickly sweet, fruity, like the pears that wouldn't make the cut when we harvested our nine trees next week, tossed into their pile at the back of the garden to rot.

Then the creature in the yard became Jonna. My Jonna digging at the grave of her own creature, Goldie.

I stopped in the kitchen to fetch the schnapps from the cupboard. As always I cringed at the sugary buildup around the mouth of the bottle. We make our own schnapps, Haley and I. Or rather, I do. The flower garden is technically hers, the orchard mine, but they are one and the same, really. I smell the flowers on the both of us sometimes, like perfume. The fruit, too, though sometimes I smell it on my own person when we haven't even been working in the garden. Lifting the bottle and taking three deep swallows, I recalled a note I had seen on a bulletin board once at Aviano Air Base, Italy: *Life is a grape. Those brown spots are just a sign of sugar oxidation, resulting in a sweeter, more mature fruit.* I took another swig of the schnapps and stepped outside into the night.

What is her name again? You know her name, my Jonna, with the fleet little hands and the words that come and go as of their own wings. Funny that when I called to her, I called Haley's name. But maybe the word didn't actually come out; maybe it was a fancy of mine. When she wasn't crying, Haley liked to say that my fancies reminded her of her abandoned art. (*Will you leave me, too?* I asked her once. We didn't speak for days after.)

Jonna held the exhumed body in her hands and was kissing it, whispering to it, now letting it go. And so it did, engaging its green and yellow wings (the pet store had commented on the unusual amount of yellow in the wings; hence the name Goldie) and flittering away into the starry night.

As she closed the cigar box, carefully putting it back in the hole, another impulse overcame me and I looked to my bedroom window and saw Haley's face there, stricken with wonder, dark and ripe.

2

How do you console an unreachable child? How do you tell her that the one thing that has inspired any emotion in her, the one thing that has penetrated the moroseness that has surrounded her all of her eight years of life, is gone and will not be coming back?

If you know, please tell me. For I have no expertise in things of emotion and instinct, except as they trail back to me like the worms in Ray's pears. I did not breast feed my daughter for fear that I would poison her. Nor can I do this. Ray will take care of it. My husband will know what to do with this broken bird in its cage. It might as well be Jonna, for all we have given her out of our wretched lives. No, that's not fair to Ray. He at least served something besides his selfish ends. What did I serve, in my LSD-induced flare of a career? I served a scene. I served Haley's art. I served Haley.

Leaving the parakeet where it lies, I gather up the horror of the thing into the package of my mobile soul. But as must be expected in our world, I find Ray on the phone with the child therapist. The hot tears fall, and I rejoice that I can feel anything, an increasing occurrence as the distance between the mother I am and the artist I once was widens with every month, week, day that passes. He puts the phone down and I tell him, in gasps so much as words, that our daughter's only meaningful reference in the world is lying on its back in its cage, dead.

———.———

"We have to make a decision, and quick," I tell him when my crying subsides.

We are in the kitchen now and can see Jonna idly wandering the pebbled path through the flower garden. If there has ever been a place of comfort for her, then it is in the backyard among the flowers and fruit trees, a paradise my husband and I have built around the darkness and pain. Ray likes to think our daughter is attracted to the garden's cheerfulness. I know it's the moroseness lurking beneath the vivid, psychedelic splashes of color. I have seen what she sees. (My agent used to wear a dark purple tee shirt on which was written in lavender: *I was there to hear the tortoise sing.* I never asked him what it meant; all that really mattered was that he had been there.)

Though Ray knows that I'm right about the urgency of the decision, he stalls. I hate him when he is like this. He watches Jonna in the garden with more of the horticulturist's eye than the father's, and seconds, precious seconds, pass unattended. At last the response: "Haley, I'm not sure what decision there is to make."

I turn from the window, anger blooming as starkly as the afterimages of the roses on my retinas. "We've got to do something with the bird, Ray. This will just kill Jonna." But my eyes, my vagrant eyes have returned to the garden. "Oh no, she's coming. Go and occupy her while I figure something out."

He does. Thank God he's finally acknowledged how critical these moments. He calls her name as he steps outside, a warning, a tocsin: but it isn't she eating the worm; the worm this time is eating her. She is one of Ray's pears.

Now what do *I* do? I am the one who found Goldie. The strange mechanics of fate say that I must also unfind her. But how? I cannot just wish her to go away as I did my own (infinitely less real) reference to existence, my excuse of a profession. Or can I? Parakeets have the actual power of flight, whereas professions have only that illusion. I will not see Jonna peel back the garden's layers so far that she looks upon death. Goldie will fly away first.

I open the cage. I open the playroom window. I hold the bird in my hands and realize its neck and one of its wings are broken. *Oh God, Jonna, I know, I know. Please forgive us for all of your suffering.* Hiding Goldie in the first place I find on my way back to the kitchen, I open the back door and the words come as if I'd rehearsed them a thousand times. As if I'd always been the liar:

"Honeydrop. Honeydrop, I have something to tell you. It's about Goldie. She's flown away."

———•———

I hear her voice inside my skull as she walks in front of us. Rather, a voice of my own that I attribute to her; a fine line there, as I used to also hear it from the womb.

Why have you put her in the drawer, mother? You know that I know she is there. Why put yourself through this?

Her wing is broken . . . her neck, Jonna. She was so fragile.

Putting her in a drawer will not mend her. Only flight will mend her.

But she cannot fly, my honeydrop. She will never fly again.

I flew.

So she had. Ray never knew how close to dying she was during that first week. He was aware that there were problems, but I begged the maternity ward staff not to reveal how severe. As far as he knows, she was kept for ten days after delivery because of her size—five pounds and change.

Will you open the drawer for me or will I have to do it?

I warned you then, in the womb, about this world, Jonna. But you wouldn't listen.

She stops at the hall table, looks down at the gilt handle of the drawer. Though I have seen it coming, I can only gasp as she reaches out and pulls the drawer open.

I don't know what to say as she lifts the broken bird in her hands. So I kneel before her in remorse and contriteness and supplication and reverence. "When I said Goldie had flown away, I meant her soul, Jonna. Goldie is a ghost now. She has left her body and flown away to heaven. Do you understand?"

If she does, she doesn't indicate so, the melancholy as entrenched in her face as I have ever seen it. Without a word, verbal or otherwise, she steps into her playroom. I can only watch as she crosses to the open window, raising Goldie in her small hands as if in offering. I see clearly what is to come, yet have no choice but to let matters follow their course, for Jonna's sake.

"Bye," says my daughter as she lets Goldie go. There is no language for the way the bird falls out of her hands, striking the windowsill before dropping into the yard below.

"Oh, Jonna," I say, rushing to her.

Behind me, my husband, the voice of reason, suggests that we formally bury Goldie. "There is no closure otherwise," says he.

THE HORTICULTURIST'S DAUGHTER

One wonders if even a funeral is closure as I clutch my honeydrop to my breast, nodding back at him for lack of anything more.

———•———

Honeydrop. I remember Ray's face the first time I, quite innocently, used the expression. Like most babies, Jonna had blue eyes until age three, when they started developing that unique color and quality for which I had no other description. It might have been the way the word resonated along the bustling New York streets that struck a chord with my husband, but I rather liked the thought that we were going someplace more appropriate to honey and sunshine, more rural.

When I met him you would have thought he was going nowhere. Just like me. He showed up in his pilot's charade and bloodshot eyes from hours on hours of East Coast flights (he did not specify just how many). He preferred European flights, he said; at least you got to rest at the other end. In the bar, with his white shirt and its un-exalting shoulder emblems, he seemed a dead thing. That's what called me, I think. And maybe that's what called him, too. Because I was in my own inglorious outfit and bound for the farthest reaches of nowhere.

He saved me, it is certain. I like to think I saved him, but that is not so certain.

———•———

Ray dreams in the night. In his former vocation he has killed and killed, not face to face, but worse—from a great distance. I can hear the horror in his voice as he talks his squadron through the mission before them, the individual pilots through their trepidation as the targets begin to appear on the radar. I hear it all in the night, with my own radar. Ray there, upon his back and clutching the collar of his tee shirt. The smell about him is different in the night, in the closed bedroom; it is as though he is made of candy.

I am made of candy, dissolved in the saliva of dreams and nightmares. I refer to him because he is all that is left of the active part of me. He *feels* as I will never do again. He pretends that I channel through him, as I in turn pretend our daughter does me, but there is nothing vicarious about any of it. Life is about tides, and reality and perception certainly, but mainly tides. We were swept by them into the most beautiful land on the earth, and though still we dream, and hide, and mourn, Abury-on-the-Wold keeps our souls and is the only thing that matters to us besides our beloved child.

What was her name again? Jonna. Yes, sometimes I forget that she is not just a drop of honey there in the light. There in the light of the moon, with the unburied body of her bird in her hands. Kissing it. Whispering to it. Now letting it go. Now watching it fly on its green and yellow wings away into the night.

3

We found in the local newspaper that the Forestry Commission was doing a bird banding down in Tetbury at the Westonbirt Arboretum. It was Haley, actually, who brought the article to my attention, pointing out that it might be something Jonna would enjoy. When I told her that I had happened upon a bird banding in the Tongass National Forest during an Alaskan cruise I had taken after retiring from the Air Force, she cited that old friend of man's, fate.

"We have to go then, don't we?"

It was well over an hour's drive down to Tetbury, but yeah, we had to go. A bird banding was about more than being close to the birds. It was about interacting with them—on both a personal and biological level—and then letting them go. A prospect that seemed to have been easier for my daughter than my wife during the days since Goldie's funeral.

The information appeared in both the *Gloucestershire Echo* and *The Forester* on the weekend after the loss of Goldie. The event was to happen the following weekend when I'd planned on storing and canning pears, but that could certainly wait as the formula for harvesting pears was imperfect to begin with. Nonetheless, we went ahead with the picking of those fruits that fell from the stem with the slightest twist and pull, and laid them out in the cool barn on shelves lined with the very newspapers that had diverted attention from our orchard of nine trees and its modest yield. Walking back through our farmer's market of gleaned fruit, Haley commented on the lovely smell. Of course it was an association. We weren't back in Sicily on our honeymoon, with the smell of lemons on the breeze. I checked my collar, in case.

———•———

Meanwhile Jonna had stolen an elongated look from beneath the hood of her metaphorical shell. It happened so naturally, so seamlessly, that her whole case might all along have been a question of moods as opposed to anything medical. Not only was she less reticent than usual, her vocabulary increased by uncounted words that week. A simple overview of what a bird banding was all about—compliments of the *Echo* by way of my wife's mouth—set her tongue and honeydrop eyes adance.

"Will I see Goldie?"

Haley looked at me, master of words and situations that I am (in some reality that I have not quite come to terms with). "You will see all kinds of birds," I told Jonna, "and be able to touch them." *And whisper them goodbye.*

"It's okay," my daughter said. "Goldie is home again. She is safe."

I looked at Haley and she at me, and there *were* no words. Just as there had been no discussion about what we both knew we had witnessed.

———•———

We arrived early at the National Arboretum, the parking area near the designated spot vacant except for the Forest Commission vehicle. Seeing it, I was reminded of shuttling from the cruise ship at sunrise to the Mendenhall Glacier in Juneau, Alaska, where I had stumbled upon the uniformed lady unloading her equipment from her wagon. There hadn't been anyone else around then, either—at least not for the bird banding. I'd slipped away from the group snapping pictures of the glacier and waiting for the Visitor's Center to open, curious as to what the uniform was up to. Little did I know that fifteen years later I'd be taking my daughter to see what the morning mist had given up in the Cotswolds of England.

The *Echo*'s in-depth article had detailed that visitors arriving before 7:00 a.m. would stand a better chance of seeing a variety of birds, but that they would have to find the biological technician—named Melissa Henry— on their own. A series of colored markers would lead to the first of the vertically erected nets, then it should be easy to the follow the path from one net to the next. As it turned out, that first net hidden among the beautiful autumn maples wasn't so easy to find, the markers having obviously been placed in a hurry. We didn't care. The September air was slightly crisp, but refreshing. Condensation clung to the foliage and the sky was a patient blue waiting for ribbons of platinum-white to burn off.

When the first net appeared from behind golden leaves, Jonna cried out. "Look! A birdie."

Sure enough, there was a wren caught in the net and looking around in alarm or bewilderment, though not struggling. As we drew close enough to touch it, Haley invited our daughter to do just that. I knew from my own experience that this would not sit well with the tech, but before I could utter my wisdom, Melissa Henry herself appeared—suddenly, and in a high state of excitement.

"No, no. Please," she said, exhaling as from a sprint. "Wait till I'm able to do the round with you. We don't want to cause the birds any more stress than we have to."

The first thing I noticed about Melissa Henry—aside from her being wound a bit tight—was her fingers. They were exactly the fingers of the bird bander in Alaska: rough, with dirty nails clipped to the quick, knuckles swollen as with arthritis or tendonitis. Otherwise she was perfectly presentable, even good-natured behind her aura of urgency. I suspected she would prove gentle as the morning dew when handling the birds.

Jonna seemed to take to her at once (it was as Melissa was extending a hand to our daughter that I observed the knobby tools of her trade).

Actually, *seemed to* drastically understates it. Melissa made more progress with Jonna in her introduction than the hired experts had in all their sessions combined.

"Would you like to see where I do my work?" Melissa asked, smiling down at Jonna.

"Where you let the birds go?" said Jonna.

"Well, yes," the tech said, looking up at Haley and me. "Where we let the birds go. But we don't keep the birds too long after they're caught in the nets. We make some notes then band them and let them fly away again."

"I wish I was a bird," said Jonna.

Melissa's smile grew ever wider as she touched Jonna's face with her hand, "Me too, honeydrop."

Jonna was hers upon those words. That word.

"Follow me, troops. My workstation is back this way."

———•———

We passed three other nets but only one other caught bird before arriving there.

"Looks like a second or third-winter goldfinch," said Melissa, turning to toss Jonna's hair as if to accentuate the *gold*. Jonna, wholly against her nature, was outwardly *delighted* to be a part of it all. Haley's hand found mine, warmer than it had been in days, since that night out of dreams, when what was real escaped both of us in favor of a bird's flight.

To Jonna's evident fascination, the tech had already bagged three birds during a previous round and now pulled one of them out of a canvas tote she had been carrying inside her coat. This one was a song thrush, she told Jonna, as she held the bird delicately in one hand while recording her observations in a notebook with the other. These observations consisted of blowing the feathers below the bird's breast to determine gender, then fanning the wings in her bulbous though expert fingers to locate the stripes that determined age. Even though I had been through the same lessons in another lifetime, I was as fascinated as my daughter. Haley merely watched Jonna for those reactions that must be savored now, on the moment, lest the world collapse tomorrow.

When she finished with the third bird, fixing the band on the colorful blue tit's leg, Melissa let Jonna hold it. "Like this, with the neck between the fingers, but very gently . . . that's right."

"Can I let it go?" Jonna asked.

"You may stroke its feathers first if you like."

Jonna looked at Haley, then me. She held my gaze as she said, "I just want to let it go."

"Of course," Melissa said.

Jonna whispered to it before releasing it. She did not let go of my eyes until the blue tit had disappeared into the foliage.

"Okay," said Melissa. "Shall we do the next round then?"

Haley felt the need to interpret. "Would you like to go see if there are any more birds in the nets, Jonna?"

"Does Daddy want to?" said Jonna.

Caught in my own net, with my collar in my fist: "Sure, honeydrop. But you three go ahead. I need to . . . relieve myself."

———•———

There is literally no description for what it is to live with such moroseness, with such distance, with such failure. It consumes you until all that is left is the memory of what you'd hoped for, the dull realization that what your fanciful optimism has gained you is not salvation, but penance for what you have been and done. And then even those vestigial wisps of thought and feeling begin to succumb to the general numbness. A winter-white calm descends, covering the graveyards of fruits and flowers, stilling the vivid expressions and impressions of life.

But not fully, not ever *fully*. There are moments, beautiful, terrible, majestic moments when emotion finds you again and you lash back against the mocking futility of it all. When you *feel* and you *acknowledge* in one magnificent rush what it is to be abandoned by your God, your dreams, your illusions, your soul, your child. For that instant you are closer to freedom than you have ever been before, but you know it cannot be attained, the instant cannot be *fulfilled* without action, that your chance is already slipping away. So you reach again for the bottle of schnapps, the great prolonger of moments . . .

———•———

Their sounds as they moved up the trail were unreal to me as I took the flask out of my inside coat pocket and drank so deeply that I nearly heaved the gin back up. As I removed the container from my mouth, liquid dribbled down my chin onto my collar. I started to cap the flask but thought better, drinking another long swallow. Smelling sugar, pears, rot in the air.

I stood for a long time with my penis in my hand, nothing delivering itself from me.

Somewhere among the trees, now devoid of mist, now vivid and vivacious in the clear morning, I heard Jonna squeal in happiness. I knew what had come. I knew what had found its way here by migration patterns that could not be measured by summers and winters. I knew what had inspired the moment, that moment which exists separately from waking and sleep even as it calls its servant out of those very wastelands.

I had come when it called then. I did so now. They were one and the same moment as I picked my way along the corridor, brushing aside shadows, pausing a time or two to partake of the bottle again, remembering the spring, when Haley was fresh and beautiful and round with child. Remembering when salvation emerged in the form of a bloody squirming babe.

I came and I saw that the cage incorporated the same basic principles it always did, only was of a different material and configuration and scale. There she was, my Jonna, caught in the mesh and trying to free herself, her arms batting against the fabric, her eyes where they had always been. On me. Always me, as I extended a hand through the open door, seizing the creature in my fist. Hating it for what I could not accomplish. Hating it for what it had. Hating it as I had hated every target that had appeared in front of me, every action of my finger on the joystick, every emotionless look my daughter had given me. Hating it as I did her, with her frail wings and monopoly on expression.

Then withdrawing my hand, green and gold feathers peeping through my gnarled fingers. And her voice, Jonna's, growing more confident with every breath, singing, "Can I let her go?"

4

Jonna fell asleep in Haley's arms on the way back to Abury-on-the-Wold. Her mother had elected to ride with her in the backseat, maybe feeding off Jonna's strange complacence. Maybe afraid of it. A smell accosted me as I drove. I looked back at them through the rearview, but they were ignorant about the subtler things. They were victims as I was. The road stretched before and I thought about pears, and canning, and by turns Steinbeck. I wondered what he would have thought of Kosovo . . .

We arrived home before eleven a.m., but for some reason it seemed more like eleven p.m., perhaps owing in part to the fog that surrounded the vicinity of Abury. I joined Haley in pulling Jonna's curtains and putting our daughter to bed. As seemed appropriate, we were silent as we performed these duties. The suggestion of a smile on Jonna's face spoke all that needed to be spoken.

Haley retired soon after, cuddling up with the pillows on the living room couch.

At two I went in to wake Jonna for lunch. She was not in her room. Her window was wide open, the breath of the wold lapping in. Out beyond the roses and the pear trees, I thought I saw a wind in the mist. But I knew it was only a bird, going wherever birds do.

PORTA NIGRA

AS THE CHRISTMAS lights began to come to life over the cobblestone streets that converged at the Hauptmarkt, Archbishop Stephan von Saar awoke from long sleep. He awoke with a rhyme on his lips, and a stiffness in his wretched body, and the knowledge that it was Advent. He awoke knowing his name, Stephan Wolfgang Muhr, and that this was not the eighteenth century but the dawn of the twenty-first, and that outside the stone walls of his prison the day was giving over to the long December night in the ancient Roman capital of Trier, Germany's oldest city.

I am cursed.

He knew, for he dreamed. With eleven months separating one year's period of Advent from the next, and every hour of these months passed in slumber, it might otherwise have been easy to forget. He dreamed the sort of dreams that men do, strange strains drawn of memory and experience. Yet unlike those that haunt the rest of us, his were of the nature of things as fell within the guidelines of the waking world. The fantastical and the absurd were there, but only as they existed in the realm of reality. Reality, for Stephan von Saar, was intensely ugly, nightmarish in its configurations, and for better than two hundred years, it had been his only domain. He not only failed to find solace in his long sleep, he failed to find fantasy. And so he emerged from those depths without disorientation, which absence was perhaps as poignant in its event as the hunger that seized him almost upon the moment of his awaking.

Cursed, I am a slave.

To rise from his place of unrest he drew upon the unwholesome strength that had been given to him by the same curse which bound him to his cycle. The stone slid with a grinding noise as the tomb was opened and he crawled out of his containment into the whispering hollows of the catacomb, so familiar for their meaningful, meaningless song of clashing morbidity and perpetuity. Above, in the cathedral's cavernous hall, the tourists would be murmuring in reverence and admiration over the lofty ceilings, the great pillars and buttresses, the elaborate eastern chancel and its Baroque treasury, where the Holy Robe was kept. Believers and unbelievers alike drifting from one wonder of architecture to the next, unknowing that one of the tombs below had been opened and a sleeper was coming forth to move among them on the streets of ancient Trier.

Enslaved, I am a predator.

Before resealing the tomb, the archbishop checked the pockets beneath his aging robe, adding to the cloud of dust already surrounding him. Satisfied the keys were there, he returned the lid to its rightful place, then stole from the cellars by way of a passage rarely visited anymore, emerging on the ground floor of the old chapel, which had long been shut off to tourists.

He fell out of the window onto the cobblestone, startling a passerby. The woman would have run, he'd little doubt, but for the daring volume of *Glühwein* that she had consumed. Today's Christmas Market, he knew, not so unlike the days of yore, very much started at the square's center, where the mulled wine was served, and radiated from there. He himself had spat some of it out only last year, after accepting the mute offer of a stranger. The present company would not serve his needs—although so easily obtainable as she stood there regarding him in open wonder—for the hour was yet young. When he lifted his right arm in her direction, she saw the hairy monstrous claw that protruded from his sleeve and moved off hurriedly, *Glühwein* or no in her dark veins.

Predacious, I am by definition without conscience.

Snow had been falling for some time, and continued to fall, its blanket covering every available surface. The Christmas lights formed spiraling designs over the way, arched bridges between the venerable walls that flanked the cobblestone avenue. To his senses the air stank of wine and worse, and this was good, for he would not be smelling so pleasant himself after his slumber. Nevertheless it was in the opposite direction of the square and its throng that he went, and with a nimbleness more befitting a shadow than anything of material makeup. He knew his destination, and it was the ancient Roman gate, where the ticket booth would be preparing to close for the evening.

No matter how many times he saw the blackened monolith that was the *Porta Nigra*, Archbishop Stephan von Saar found himself in awe of it. There it stood in the falling snow, spittle in the face of time and its destructive ways, a testament to man's strength, his fortitude, his defiance. Blackened with the weathers of two thousand years, majestic and mysterious, stood this mighty gate, and never mind that it was no longer attached to the walls that had surrounded ancient Trier, for those walls must only have deferred to this great stonework edifice which the archbishop, for one month out of every year, called home.

And yet I am here.

He would have remained here admiring its architecture and motif, its massive circular towers, the arches of its twin gates and the windows that lined each of the three floors over its inner court, but the hour was failing and the ticket booth would in moments be closed. The rhymer was in the booth, this his fifteenth consecutive Christmas season, and it had been eleven months since von Saar had seen the man's bearded face or heard his rich rolling voice.

As some of us collect coins, the man who sold tickets for entrance to the Black Gate collected nursery rhymes. His collection consisted of both the German and English varieties—which of course, in the essence of it, are but one and the same—and he loved to lavish them upon the little ones in line. This evening was no different, as the archbishop stood along the wall listening.

A mother and daughter were the only ones in line. The little girl, who was three or four years of age, was saying:

"Mommy, he speaks American."

"That's English, sweetie. American is not a language."

"Ah, madam, but of course American is a language," said the ticket man.

The mother did not quite know what to say to that, so she smiled accommodatingly.

"Little Jack Horner sat in his corner, and do you know what he was doing, little lady?"

Little Jack Horner was his favorite. Not only did he collect them, which in itself was a coincidence so perverse that it scarcely affected the archbishop anymore, but Jack Horner, of them all, was his rhyme of choice.

"He was eating his curds and whey?" said the American girl.

"No, as a matter of fact—"

"Wait, I know. He put in his thumb and pulled out a plumb."

"Yes, eventually he did that."

"I think that's scary."

Indeed, thought von Saar as he watched the man dispense the tickets.

When the mother and daughter had disappeared up the stairs that led to the sentry paths, the man pulled a sign announcing the Porta Nigra was closed for the day.

Von Saar stepped up to the window.

The look on the face of the ticket man when he saw who stood there was less a display of recognition than of desolation, seeming to wear like a confession on his otherwise warm features.

It had to be this way. Above all, the ritual. Though innocent in its appearance, this particular ritual could be regarded as almost a sacrament itself.

31

Von Saar held out his hand, his bestial right hand, and a final ticket, without the adornment of words, was issued.

But as the archbishop ascended the stairs, the voice of the ticket man, contrarily anguished and reverential, wafted up to his ears:

"Save us, our Lord . . . save the children."

Don't you know by now? thought von Saar. The little ones are always spared. Sister Inga says it must be so.

He went up to the highest floor, inserting a key in the lock when he arrived at the door within the east tower. For the merest second he thought he saw her standing there, quoting to him of the Bible, and the little children pawing at her feet. But it was only the air, dank and moldering textures mixing with poisonous light filtered in by the slit in the tower wall. And his hunger. His hunger murmuring not only within him, but about from him.

Would they be long? he wondered. The mother and daughter. He lifted his nostrils sniffing for them, but it was no use. The lingering odors of last Advent were still on the air. He would wait till the darkness was saturating; then they would be gone, out of harm's way.

Save us, our Lord . . . save the children.

Meanwhile he would sit in the corner, Little Jack Horner, abhorring the stagnant bouquets of past Christmas pyes. Until—and wasn't it beginning already?—these palpable reminders of what he had turned into became so overwhelming that he found himself unable to refuse them any longer, lowering his face to the floor, tongue hanging from his mouth like a dog's as he proceeded to lick the cold stone surface. And managing somehow to wonder, even as he gave himself to this loathsome act, if a significant portion of the unwholesome perfume didn't actually emanate from his own wretched body. Would he in fact someday turn upon his own flesh in his craving? Would he create his own sort of irony by twisting Sister Inga's already manipulated reference from the Gospels into something even less recognizable? Adding an even darker, viler symbolism to the prospect of abandoning the promised eternal life for the vain wants and desires of the earthly body?

I have committed a grave sin, Sister.

The worst of it was that he could ask himself these questions, that he retained his identity through it all. But such was of course the curse's nature, quite as the unholy allegiance which had bound him to his fate had intended. As Sister Inga, with her very special sense of the ironic, had intended.

In my human vanity and presumption, I have sinned.

He rose from the floor, satisfied that the curtain of night had finally fallen, that he could draw no sustenance from the naked stone and its fading stains. He stepped from the room in the tower testing the air with his nostrils, detecting the faintest trace of the mother and daughter, their passage. From the Platz below, he must have seemed a shadow as he passed by the arched windows that lined the sentry way, a ghostly resident of the haunted interiors of the great Porta Nigra. The locals likely gave it not a second thought. For them, all of ancient Trier's paths were haunted. He emerged from the monolith itself by the alcove that shaded the ticket booth. Drawing the hood of his robe around his face, he told himself he should seek new garments this time around. But he rather suspected he wouldn't go to the trouble. It had only been two decades since he had acquired those he wore.

The avenues of old Trier unrolled before him, less-trodden ways branching off towards destinations unfulfilled. The high towers of the cathedral stood dark and majestic against the deepening sky, lording over this place of mystery, enchantment and unrest. Music drifted from the square, song of pipes and drunken accompaniment. Somewhere in the virgin night a cat cried, the realm of darkness its pleasure as surely as it was the archbishop's disanointing. He remained apart from the main crowd but ever upon the market's fringes, lest the cathedral itself fall completely out of sight, which would not do.

Even as you partake of the flesh, which is the bread, and the blood, which is the drink, you shall be looking upon the cathedral, where the desecration was done.

Oh, Sister, that you had not depended so upon my piety, feeding on me as if I were your own manna. Better you had stayed with that nest of witches from which I rescued you. You should never have known the abbey and its abstemious living, for in the end you were no better than me, wanting more than we are given, and seizing it in your greedy fists at all costs, humility be damned. For wasn't that our downfall, Sister—reaching like the tower of Babel for heaven itself? Never mind the children, never mind their bright eyes upon you as you read to them, for it was to another, higher purpose that you went about your work. Even as you held your *Mother Goose's Melody* before you, reciting as from the Word itself upon the little ones' dazzled ears, you were seeking attainment by pretentious works and deeds. Would that I had never brought that book back with me from England. For you used them, the little children, made them your *disciples* to spread the news of you, the news of you to the mothers and fathers of Trier, to the bishops and cardinals of the Church, to the very highest of the high, even Our Lord on High, Who surely hath cast us both forever into darkness for our vanity and pride. You used them as you used me, although my sin was no lesser for it.

A man stood slumped in the niche of a shop doorway, his inebriation obvious, his eyes only half seeing von Saar as the archbishop passed.

Von Saar's hand began to throb, the pain starting as an ache and then evolving into something more intense, more sinister, as he stopped in his tracks and looked back at the recess whose wall now hid the figure within.

So shall you be cursed with not only a beast's appetite, but a beast's savage hand . . .

He placed himself against the continuous wall that flanked the street, slipping along the glass storefront back in the direction of the drunken figure. Sister Inga's words were not only pulsing in his head, they were on his tongue, bristling to be spoken aloud, announcing his deformity in advance to his victim so that there be no mistake about the nature or mechanics of the thing to come. As he reached the corner, swiveling on his heel to block the entryway, his claw spoke for him, leaping forward to hover above the startled face of the man.

"*Was ist los?*" said the man, as if a casual verbal reaction might somehow mitigate the horror of it.

In spite of the magnificent, overwhelming hunger to which he was enslaved, there was the usual moment of hesitation on the archbishop's part, a moment in which to entertain the thought of first allowing a confession. That it would fall upon the ears of a dark priest was but another blasphemy in a book of them; that it might actually work in some hideously reverse fashion like damning the victim forever was the deciding factor.

Dropping his transmogrified hand to obtain the preferred angle—a lie so quick it stood no chance of being judged—he plunged it into the man's body, upwards beneath the rib cage to seize the heart, retreating with the thundering organ in his grasp. He closed his eyes in simultaneous revulsion and ecstasy as the blood erupted from the wound.

As he sank his teeth into its pulp, he heard the bells of the Abbey of St. Agnes, where rested the bones of Sister Inga, patron saint of hypocrisy. He would go there, he knew. When the feeding was finished, he would go there to place upon her tomb a token of his remembering her, an organ from his victim. For the curse wasn't so thorough that it abolished his every freedom.

He consumed only what he could not endure—or spare the risk—to savor at the site of the kill, then moved swiftly along the shadowed cobblestone streets with his load over his shoulder, back to the Porta Nigra. In his room in the tower, hunched by the narrow sentry window through which he could just make out the spires of the cathedral, he gave the feed the etiquette it deserved. He wiped up after himself with the sleeve of his cloak, now the textured cloth of his tongue, abandoning not a morsel save the spleen, which he thought a fitting gift for his witch at St. Agnes's. As he consumed he felt the lost year returning to his body, the degradation reversing, the tissue and material of him regenerating towards the whole.

The blood vitalized him, made him feel as though it were the year 1790 again, and the aspirations of his virginal body and mind pushing him towards that conclusion which stood alone in time and space, like this mighty Porta Nigra, Black Gate, reality of itself.

When he was done, he lay back not in sleep—for he would not sleep for another four weeks—but in meditation. Next in the broader ritual, the cathedral, where the desecration was done. Perhaps this time . . .

Ah, but that was an illusion.

———◆———

In its peculiar configuration the window to the treasury annex looked like the mouth of a grotto—or perhaps the over-scaled cross section of a piece of hollow quartz. But for that jagged glimpse into the sacred chamber, the treasure it had been built to house might have been some concoction of an overzealous mind. As it was, one had to venture to the back of the chancel, defying the velvet roping that fenced off the area, to look over the lip of the aperture and actually view the glass-encased Robe. Though a security matter and nothing more, this inaccessibility to tourists undoubtedly lent to the relic's mystery in their eyes. The clergy, of course, had their own access, which Archbishop von Saar knew all too well.

He went by way of the chambers below, passing the reliquary, which closed around the same time the Porta Nigra did, and coming to a door for which his pockets provided the key. He hesitated before opening it, remembering the sound of her voice, so full of consternation, self-righteousness, concealed pleasure, finally jealousy—although she would never have admitted it. The door opened into the treasury, and his eyes fell upon the transparent case reflecting the flickering light of surrounding candles. Within it, spread out as for consideration for wear—

Perish thy wicked thoughts, Archbishop von Saar!

—*der Heileger Rock*, the Holy Robe of Christ.

In the cathedral's main hall, the noises of footfalls and whispering voices, the discomforts of children and introspective adults, would be echoing between the great walls. Here in the treasury, no sound save for that of his breathing, breaths which came short, invasive, out of harmony with this sanctum.

It was here he had stood when she had caught him. The very place where ten years prior to his profanation, when she was still about her witching ways, he had made her stand and look, unconcerned that her mere presence might be a sacrilege. Here, at this spot, within this manmade addition to this manmade church where this manmade cloth offered the bridging of gaps which might otherwise have remained impassable.

Or so he had believed.

He had shown her this human remnant of his Lord and she had converted soon after, eventually becoming a nun, then an abbess, then a judge herself, as she caught him, in this very room . . .

Oh Lord, deny me if it be Thy will . . .

With the Robe of Christ upon his shoulders.

What sense, what knowledge, as he had placed it over his back? Power? Assurance? Invincibility? Godliness? No, none of these. Only a robe. A robe and his shame. A robe and his shame and the gasp of her, the abbess, as she beheld the sacrilege he had performed.

Back to the nest she had run, to the witches and those black powers she herself had once shared in employing. Back to the womb for the means of accomplishing her revenge upon him, an action forgivable by her God for the reason that the end justifies the means. Unwilling to accept the same logic of him, who donned the Robe only to know God.

Or something like that.

Archbishop Stephan von Saar stared at the content of the glass case, and he wondered if perhaps this time . . .

But wasn't that an illusion?

He brought his fists above his head, prepared to shatter the case, to put his hands on the cloth once more. Anguishing, he could not bring himself to do the thing.

The abbey was silent, unvisited. The nuns slept. Inga's tomb stood in an alcove appending the chapel, the resting place of a figure of great importance. Paintings decorated the walls, angels and children dancing around the enclosed remains of her, wishing her the best in her heavenly place.

The archbishop placed the organ on the tomb.

"So that we remember *each other*," he said quietly. But he knew the rats would have it before dawn's light.

———•———

As he stepped out into the night, he thought of procuring another companion for the evening. The urge passed as the majestic Roman gate came into view, and he decided he would mingle with the ghosts instead.

LAGO DI INIQUITÀ

"THIS IS THE most beautiful place I've ever seen," came the inevitable words from Lily's mouth. She was posed like the lover she was against the balcony's decorative railing, blouse revealing her midriff, the caressive June air as Italian as it was Alpine.

Her exact sentiment must have been expressed thousands of times, in a variety of different languages, from the balconies and terraces of the mountainside on which the village of Tignale had been built. The words nonetheless sounded recited to me, as if she had consulted my late wife's journal, or ghost, or my own nightmares prior to our departure from the States. I had the brief inexplicable urge to press my palm against the tanned arch of her back, to cause her to have a flutter of doubt about my intentions as I forced her to look at the stone building below.

How had we ended up here, in an apartment so close to the one I had stayed in with my family five years before? Of course there had been that risk when I selected a Tignale location out of the *Tui* vacation rental catalog, but what were the chances we would be within eyesight—indeed practically on top of—the *Rustico Spagnol*? Perhaps subconsciously I had remembered the name of our current spot, *Cottage Mediterraneo*, from the sign on the winding rutted road that led up from the lake. I dared not discuss these thoughts with Lily, for she would call it destiny, a flavor that did not linger well on my tongue.

"I told you you would like it," I said. Past the moment of danger, I placed my hand on the naked skin of her back, rubbing, consciously ignoring that her thong underwear were visible above the low-cut waist of her fashionable pants. In many ways I got along with her *in spite of* her attractive features and figure.

She turned to me, putting her sleeveless arms around my neck. "Yes, you did. Now I'm wondering how you're going to drag me away from here to see Florence and Venice."

It had that effect, the northern part of the Gardasee. Across the lake from us the lushly green slope, punctuated with granite bluffs and medieval church steeples, merely provided the foreground for the snow-capped peaks beyond. Lake Garda itself painted a blue-green glassy serenity, playground to sailing vessels and dinner boats, and the promise of an aesthetically-oriented God.

Lily was further evidence towards that promise, as amazing to my touch and awareness now as she had been the day I found her deliberating over her studies outside my evening philosophy class. I had been more than willing to help her with the question about which she had been waiting to consult Dr. Jessie (whose nickname spoke to an uncanny resemblance to the actress Jessica Lange), though I discovered for my efforts that my younger peer grasped its core meaning better than I did. Her reason for haunting the university after dinnertime was the textbook one; mine, on the other hand, had more to do with loneliness than education.

In a sense, I thought as I smelled Lily's hair, felt the years that separated us against my rough cheek, this trip was like that.

In other ways it was vastly different.

———•———

We did Florence, Venice, and Verona, in that order, during the first three full days of our seven-day vacation. In the presence of Michelangelo's *David* one reassessed one's opinions about the nature of things; all the superlatives, no matter how soulfully or originally uttered, became instant cliché. Lovers' Venice, with its watery streets and sighing bridges, was a much easier distraction. As was Verona, which ensnared one in Roman history rather than the elusive and delicate Renaissance.

Somewhere in the middle lay the dark ages, my real reason for being in Europe again. It wasn't Caesar or da Vinci who'd called me, but a medieval saint named Laguaro, of whom the world at large knew nothing: a wandering monk who had wept tears of olive oil into a secluded Alpine lake in what he termed a *"valle di iniquità"*— valley of iniquity. If he had attained any renown, it was among sinners like myself—us and our victims, our wives and our sons and daughters, wherever they had gone.

While Lily and I didn't often converse about these topics, she knew that demons were in the cards and elected to accompany me anyway. It might have been easier to think she wanted a free trip to Europe, the mildly satisfying company of a widower with a portfolio and a phobia for deeper attachments. But we had grown more than compatible over the last year and a half, such that the strange words had been floating around for months: life, marriage, baby. She had even been crude enough to suggest that this trip was a honeymoon. My soul, my conscience had the same idea, though with peace as the bride.

After hanging out by the pool and doing nothing on the fourth day, I invited Lily to ride up into the Dolomites with me on the fifth. She was duly surprised when I told her I wanted to spend the night in an Alpine village not more than an hour's drive north of the lake. To her credit, when I explained that I had always wanted to do an overnight in the mountains, she pretended to take me at face value.

We took our time, breakfasting on the balcony as we watched the low mist reluctantly give way to the windsurfers and sailors. Although the sky overhead looked promising, I suggested we carry both cool and warm attire. Aside from the fact that Garda created its own weather patterns, we were heading to higher elevations, where I had been surprised before.

Lily kissed me as we squeezed into the rental Fiesta. "You look sexy today, Tim." She always knew when to say what, pulling a smile out of the most subdued expression.

"We're going to need to stop and fill up," I told her as I let the engine idle, warming up the cool interior. "We don't want to be up there without petrol."

Had they had a station in Laguaro? I couldn't remember such details.

———•———

"You've been thinking about Kris and the kids a lot since we've been here," Lily said as we cruised along the narrow shore road, passing in and out of tunnels cut directly out of the rock, cowering from campers and buses compensating over the faded solid line. The occasional vineyards and lemon groves—their stone walls and winter housings often dating to Roman times—passed too quickly for contemplation.

"So I have," I said, keeping my eyes on the wily road.

"It's okay, you know . . . to talk."

"Truly, Lily, I'm not sure what there is to say." I pulled into a service station that sported a coat of arms logo and not even the pretense of a competitive fuel price.

"Say it pisses you off to pay these outrageous prices for gas," Lily said.

"It does, I assure you."

"Say it pisses you off that I ask questions."

"That too."

"Yet you invited me along."

"Yeah." I got out, only to find it was a full service, which I'd somehow missed.

Lily stepped out of the car, immediately engaging the guy in an argument over who was responsible for cleaning the windshield. I didn't care nearly as much as she did as I watched her storm away in the direction of the WC. If I couldn't expect to fill a Fiesta's fuel tank for less than sixty euro—which was seventy plus dollars at the current exchange rate—I certainly shouldn't expect service.

She reemerged in record time, perhaps in an even more incensed mood than when she'd entered. I suspected she had found one of the hole-in-the-floor toilets she so despised, and was about to issue consolatory words when I saw a shape emerge from the men's bathroom behind her.

My heart forgot its cadence as his eyes met mine for a familiar moment before his weathered mustached features dissolved beneath the shadowy brim of his hat. The afterimage remained, like a flash from a dream: the vineyards worker looking forward to (or returning from—it made no difference) another stooped day in the sun. Indeed I *had* dreamed of the stranger, in photographs snapped from around sudden corners, or as he became visible from between rows of luxuriant vines. I had dreamed of that partially detailed face ever since my Italian vacation of five years before, when I had brought my wife and my children.

Then the attendant was asking for my money. Asking for my money at that exact moment, an eventuality so terribly typical of this recurrent experience. When I turned from stuffing the twenty notes in his greasy fist, the other man had vanished into reality—the driver's seat of a car, the restaurant next door, the pedestrian tunnel that led to the other side of the street. I looked in every direction, but he was nowhere to be seen.

As Lily stepped into my sphere, I sensed that the change that visited her was to do with my change, that the stupor, the disorientation had reached out to her like a contagion.

"I hate those fucking toilets," she said, following my eyes around the place. "Goddamn piss splashed up on my legs and there were no towels."

"I'm sorry," I said.

"Next time I'll go outside."

Up in the mountains you can do that. For some, the fluids fall from their bodies as olive oil.

————•————

I tried to explain the tradition to Lily as we drove the twisting roads up into the Dolomites, but my words made little sense even to me.

"Santo Laguaro said that his tears represented the sins of the iniquitous village he had found in the mountain valley. As olive oil can be removed from water without compromising its purity, so can our sins be removed from us. The custom is to pour a drop of olive oil into the *Lago di Iniquità* and reflect on a personal sin."

"And that's actually the name of the lake? They actually gave it that name because of a medieval monk's reference to a 'valley of iniquity?'"

"You'll find it on the map in your door sleeve."

"That's bizarre."

"Nonetheless."

"So why was the village given its Sodom status? What separated it from any other village?"

"I don't think that's ever explained. Maybe it was plague. Isolation. Excessive wine. Who knows."

"What does this have to do with your family, Tim?"

There it was, in fire, the present tense speaking either to the violence involved or to my refusal to let go the memories after a half decade. The question, in all its nakedness, asked: How does any of this figure into a random threesome dying at the hands of a random psychopath, across the Atlantic in America?

To which I have never been able to give a convincing answer, even to myself, with my vineyards worker peeking 'randomly' over my shoulder at my sins. My silence did not disillusion her. She knew innately that to go into the mountains seeking specific answers, rather than simple validation, was folly. The mountains were about answers in the same way that they were not about them; they filled one's body with desire at the second, with cold at the minute. Lily accepted this truth with a wisdom that was greater than me.

As the lake came into view there were no more questions. Shining waterfalls fed down from the peaks rising above the opposite shore, barely disturbing the tranquil surface as they united with the Alpine pool. Like the last time I had driven this road, the structures that came into view at the far end of the oblong body of water seemed out of place. As pristine a picture as they painted, they still seemed an annoyance on the face of nature.

For once in my life I didn't care about money, selecting the hotel with the best view. We unloaded from a street that was like an incision in its meager width, and parked the Fiesta in a pocket of our future memory of the place. Our balcony looked over the sea of my nightmares, with an empty cruet on the table, and a complimentary bottle of wine that might have been a deterrent, or an element of ease.

———•———

We had the restaurant's terrace to ourselves as we lunched afternoon-style on cheese and bread and red wine. When I ended up having to ask the waiter for the oil, he was perturbed, as though by some magic the tradition in which the village was so steeped had evaporated during the last five years. I didn't understand, and demanded to know why there were empty cruets on all the tables then. He forgot English suddenly, looking down on us from aloft before primly striding away. Lily didn't know what to make of his behavior any more than I did.

Though she had questions.

"Did you reflect over a sin back then, Tim? Is that what we're doing here?"

"Yes." The wine was like the mountains in its potentiality. "Yes, I reflected over a sin."

"Do you want to explain?" She sipped, and I saw the grape reds on her face, reflections of her European experience, its unsolicited mysteries.

The sun blazed out of a cloudless sky, counteracting the briskness off the lake. From behind my darkly tinted sunglasses I pondered the strangeness of Lily's presence. Her lips pouted her fashion of sobriety in my lenses, and I wished suddenly that I hadn't brought her here with me. Why had I? Was it fear? The need to fall back on someone?

"You've accused me," I said, "of being torn up with guilt about something I had no control over. Well, I may not have had control, but I do have responsibility. You see, my sin . . . "

"Yes?"

"It had to do with my family."

"Go on," Lily said.

"Garan and Debs were always fighting. They were always being disrespectful to Kris and me. Particularly Debs, who was eleven at the time and felt the world revolved around her. She would hurt Kris with words, with disobedience, with actual physical bullying. Yet when I tried to punish her or her brother, Kris would come to their defense with the tears and blood running down her face. The family credo was dysfunction. I never understood what Kris and I did wrong aside from our differing parenting styles. I guess that was enough."

"Sounds like any middle class family to me," Lily said, watching herself in my shades. Her wisdom had a flavor about it that reminded me, not fondly, of Kris.

"The morning we'd planned to drive up into the Alps," I continued, "we started fighting, all four of us, *loudly*. God knows what the people staying in the neighboring apartments must have thought. In the end Kris did this thing she had a habit of doing, waving her arms in the air like so and telling me I should just go on without them. *Without* them, mind you. We're in the middle of our European vacation, having planned to take a drive into the Alps to hike and picnic and enjoy the scenery, and suddenly I'm going without them.

"I should have waited till everybody cooled, but I didn't. Basically I said fuck the bunch of you, I will go by myself and I will fucking enjoy it."

I paused to drink from my wineglass.

"Still," said Lily. "I've heard worse stories from my mother about my childhood."

I lifted my sunglasses so that she could see my eyes.

"I didn't mean to trivialize, Tim. Really."

"As I drove up the same roads you and I drove this morning, I had thoughts. It wasn't the first time I'd had them. I had thoughts about what it might be like to be alone."

"I'm not sure we haven't all—"

"I thought about what life would look like if my wife and children happened to meet a truck on their way to the supermarket in Tignale. I thought about freedom from burdens."

She grew quiet now, casting a sideways glance at the waiter as he arrived with the small pitcher of olive oil, which he set rudely on the table. As he walked away again, glancing back as if for any conclusion to this apocalyptic inconvenience, Lily said quietly, "And that was the sin you reflected on."

"The waiter," I said. "How old do you think he is?"

"What? I don't know, early thirties."

"I think he waited on me before."

"Didn't you say that you wouldn't normally pay for a place as expensive as this?"

"It was just me the last time I was here. And I hadn't necessarily intended to stay longer than it took to drink a beer."

"But the legend of Saint Laguaro inspired you?"

"Yeah."

"Why is it that I see no legend, no tradition, nothing but your empty cruets?"

"Lily." My voice sounded like the one I had reserved for scolding Garan and Debs.

"Why, Tim?"

I stuck my finger in the only direction it could go. "Ask him."

To my surprise she turned and called: "Excuse me, waiter!"

He stopped in his tracks, stiffening before turning with a slight bow of his head. His face was admirably calm as he approached, but I could taste the steam nonetheless.

"Signora," he said to Lily as he arrived.

"My fiancé here"—she dared me under her brow to contradict her—"tells me that your village has a custom that has to do with the lake. Can you tell me about it?"

What was the purpose of this? I wondered. I wasn't quite sure why she required convincing. Did she think me a lunatic? A *rendered* man searching for reason in the wake—a five year long wake—of his family's death?

"Yes, signora," said the waiter. "The custom involves pouring a drop of olive oil from a vessel such as this into the lake, and to *muse*—this is the word?—about a past sin."

"And what is the purpose of doing this?"

"Surely your *fiancé* has explained this to you."

"Why would you think so? Do you know my fiancé?"

43

"He has been here previously, yes." The waiter seemed uncomfortable in the lenses of my glasses.

"And what makes Tim so memorable to you after five years?"

The waiter turned a quarter turn so that he faced me directly. "He was drunk and loud, signora. When he returned from the lake he wished us to fill his bottle again. This is not okay, to pour *all* of the bottle's contents into the lake. When we did not honor his request, he became . . . angry. We asked him to leave the restaurant, but he refused. Santo Laguaro, he said, belonged to more than our little village. He was correct to say so, but he was bold to assume that Laguaro was his personal saint."

"What do you mean?" Lily said.

Yes, what do you mean, Leonardo?

"Perhaps, signora, you should ask your fiancé."

She looked at me.

"I don't remember," I said, in all my eloquence.

"You do not remember smashing the empty vessel against these tiles that I am now standing on?" said the waiter. "You do not remember telling the guests at another table to look at the shattered glass, to look at 'your family' on the floor?"

"I don't," I said quietly. "I don't."

And yet his words conjured images, thoughts, helped to separate the oil from the water. He had indeed been my waiter, and there had been an empty cruet on my table. That's where it had begun—not at the tourist office or in a brochure. It had started with a question.

Why is there an empty cruet on each of the tables?

From there the tradition sprang, as if for only those customers tortured enough to ask. There had been no advertisements, no volunteered information, only the empty cruet—a bottle, a prop as clear and perceptive as Lily, who knew me better than *I* knew me, better than *Kris* knew me, almost better than *guilt* knew me.

"I'm sorry," I offered the waiter.

He shrugged slightly.

"I'm sorry for assuming Laguaro was my personal saint."

"Was he?" he said.

"More than you know."

———•———

We took the cruet down to the lakeside, Lily holding it like a funeral candle while I wondered why I hadn't brought my jacket like she had. The sun still hung superior over the mountains to our right, but the lake shimmered with an icy brilliance. As we stood on the pebbled shore, I turned to Lily.

"'Fiancé?'" I said.

"Yeah, why not? Could you ever hope for better than me?"

I thought about it as I took the glass candle from her. "Not in multiple lifetimes."

The waves lapped in, cold, clear, snow-born. I sat on the beach, tempting the water with the bottle for a couple minutes until at last I let the drop fall. My eyes closed as the foreign substance struck the water, and I forgot about Lily and Laguaro and the Alps for awhile. Forgot about confessions in favor of the therapeutic breathing of a five o'clock am jog.

Without my mornings I never would have been able to cope with dadhood, nor discovered the meaning of being human. In addition to its skyscrapers and its CNN, Atlanta had its parks and birds, which provided the setting for my regular loop. That morning was no different than any other pleasant spring morning—a diversion, an aviary and a botanical gardens to my senses. I thought nothing of the fact that Kris hadn't been in bed beside me when I woke. She often slept on the couch, where the darkness of her nightmares somehow couldn't reach.

Then I saw the leg protruding from between the bushes, and the cap that Garan always wore, lying by his ankle. The wish that had remained so well submerged now surfacing in blood, the blood of more than a sacrificial boy, for in there with him were his sacrificial sister and his sacrificial mother—and my jogging clothes convenient because of the wiping, the wiping and the strange thin streams from my glands as I dropped among my family and should have died there, there at nowhere. Nowhere in a pool of my graceless fantasies.

As I looked up again from my memories Lily spoke from her eye, the tear like the drop of oil falling from its glass container into the pure melted snow. We both lay back on the pebbled recession as the waning afternoon sun fawned over us as though we were worth it. In my sun dreams I saw Kris, but I couldn't see Debs, because she was never there. I could see Garan, but not his wrecker sister Debs, whom he clutched in his shadow as if he had known bad times were coming.

And then the day began to die.

———·———

"No, I'm going to stay and enjoy this room, thank you." As I looked at Lily's lopsided expression, I knew a serenity, if a cautious one, that I had not known in a long time. Santo Laguaro had knelt with me in prayer, and I almost forgave him because of it.

"Are you *sure*?" she said. But her smile told it all.

We made love and slept in each other's arms, the window open to the gathering chill. Sometime during the night I got up to close off the outside air, and stopped by the balcony window. On the breast of the lake a boat seemed to drip with the light from its lamps, to coalesce with the figures on its deck. I forgot about the chill, making myself comfortable on the balcony, drinking the house wine, smoking one of Lily's cigarettes, then actually sleeping on the chair until the four o'clock came to claim me.

As I pulled back the cover to check on her, I thought I heard a whisper from somewhere. But it was only the vineyards worker, staring back at me from chaos.

"Lily!" I hissed as I covered his face.

She obliged, laughing lightly.

"I'm sorry to have brought you here," I said.

"Don't be. I've my own sins to reflect over."

As she removed the cover completely, revealing her jarring nakedness, I thought that easily could be true. Meanwhile, the vineyards worker had other tales to tend to, other iniquities to reap. We were alone in the room, as we were in the world, lovers among strangers. We clung to each other, sweating and searching for breath, until the light peeped through the cracks in the blinds, and then we talked from faces slashed by dawn about the skewed reality of being.

"You really adored Debs, didn't you?" she said at some point.

"You couldn't imagine what a monster she was. Yeah. I did adore her. I adored them both." With those words I let it come, the anticlimactic flood of tears, no less than *all* of the bottle's contents as Lily held me in her arms and whispered words of meaninglessness and salvation. I drifted off wondering what I was going to do now that I had no more missions to fulfill and no load to cast off my shoulders.

"Coffee," Lily said, holding a cup as she smiled down at me. Where she had gotten it, I didn't know. But her smile was the color of my freedom.

———·———

The Fiesta purred to life under an Alpine blue sky, Lily looking like the goddess she was. There was a lightness about the world that made it subject to the caprice of the wind and weather, the mountains, the man and woman who visited its wonders. And yet, suddenly nothing was shallow to me, not Lily's perfection, nor her company, nor my own fathomless self-absorption that so defined me as a human being.

As we started out of the parking lot, Leonardo our waiter stopped us, presenting an empty vessel to take with us.

"*Grazie*," I told him as I handed the cruet to Lily.

But the face under the brim of the hat, offering a certain *ciao*, wasn't the waiter's.

As I sped away, Lily wanted to know why. But I couldn't say why. We were wrong to invade the mountains, I was wrong to have brought her to Laguaro. I didn't know truth from sanity as I simply wanted to be out of there, down the winding roads to Lake Garda again. We managed to coexist without words as the kilometers coiled up to escort us in our descent. I knew that she wondered about my stability because of her calm . . .

Yet over the next hour or so we managed to find our way along the tunneled paths of the Gardasee to our *Cottage Mediterraneo*, the sun still shining as brightly as it had tomorrow and the next day. The pool would be a welcome diversion, a solvent of sorts for my still shedding layers. Lily went ahead without me, asking me to bring a wine cooler when I was finished in the bathroom. It took a while but eventually I vomited, the confusion as intertwined with my metabolism as Santo Laguaro's oil.

Outside, the sun transformed the lake into a mirror; the warmth felt good on my face as I found assurance in the exoticism of the property's cypress trees, in its palms spilling over walls of stone. But there was no assurance for what I found when I walked onto the pool's deck. The blood trailing along the concrete towards the reclining chair said only for the raw fact of it.

And Lily's eyes still locked upon her visitor peeking from beneath his hat before slipping away to his fields.

CHASING FUSELI

CHILLED, DEJECTED, RESIGNED, I lamented the sound that preceded the train. I'd prayed halfheartedly that by some stroke of fortune the last run of the day had been canceled, that the mist enshrouding the narrow Lauterbrunnen Valley would remain undisturbed until it chose to abandon the rushing mountain stream that was its source. Of course in the dream I wasn't fortunate either. In the dream the train arrived precisely at 9:44, according to the clock that stood above the empty station.

The bundle in my arms, emitting a stench of alcohol, weighed on me. I looked back along the road, locking the image of the wheelbarrow into my memory, a keepsake of this awful night. The wheelbarrow might have been sitting there since last fall, so idle and useless it seemed. My eyes wandered across the stream and up the hillside till they found the lights of the cabin peering out of the mist. I wondered if within those walls the dream kept going, though the cabin was empty. I let my gaze continue up the slope, beyond the sheep pen, above the waterfall, to the snow-covered firs growing at the brink of the sheer cliff. Above the trees, crisply configured against the moonlit night, stood the mighty Jungfrau and Eiger, treasures of the Alps. Just three days ago we had been skiing somewhere up there. But then . . . then the thing had culminated with a ferocity to which even the master's brush mightn't have aspired.

I turned my attention to the station in time to see the train part the fog and come to rest by the desolate platform. A lamp stood by, casting a somber glow over the double metal doors of the first car as my heart—what was left of it—ticktocked in raw, agonizing anticipation.

———•———

Fuseli dreamed.

That was when I knew it was going very, very bad for me. I lucid-dreamed that I was Fuseli dreaming, and it was so viciously real that when I woke I thought for a moment I *was* Fuseli.

"We've got to get you help, Gordon," Dana said to me.

I looked down at my chest, where she had placed her hand. It was moist with sweat. The hand I put over hers trembled.

"Do you want to tell me?" she said.

"Yes. It's better if I tell you."

We were at our Brunnen cabin by then. It was supposed to have been a retreat from the nightmares, from the ghosts in Zurich. "Chasing Fuseli," my wife had once called it. *Ha.* Fuseli was chasing me.

———•———

The corridor seems endless. The canvases that hang on both walls shimmer, as if with fresh paint. The carpet beneath my shoes rolls ahead of me, into darkness. I seem to carry what light there is with me, bringing the oils to life as I come. I recognize the paintings. I have envisioned these scenes, dreamt these scenes, even painted these scenes with my own brush. To my right, three witches point along the corridor toward whatever lies at its end. To my left, Lady Macbeth. Ah, and there she is again, with Banquo and the hags on the heath. And there—there is Thor in the boat of Hymir. And on the other side, Cardinal Beaufort. And there . . . but there seems no end to these creations of mine.

I look down the length of the corridor and frown to see a dim light. I know it is an end at last, but the sight of it stirs something in me, a sense of familiarity and dread. I walk more slowly, considering whether or not I wish to continue, but now the light is moving toward me. Is it someone coming? Is it . . .

It is a door. I tell myself, do not touch it. But I'm dreaming—what harm can be done? A voice within me says, But are you dreaming?

I touch the door. I open it. Oh no, oh my God, my God, I knew but I could not stop myself. The words are caught in my throat. What are you? What are you and why are you torturing my innocent, sweet Anna?

———•———

"And you actually recognized her as Anna?" Dana watched me intently.

"I knew her, Dana. I knew the woman lying on that bed. She was Anna Landolt. It was as though I were watching a scene from my life."

"Which perspective?" she said.

"Detroit. That's the one that haunted him. That's the image *he* saw."

Detroit referred to the Detroit Institute of Art—as opposed to the *Goethemuseum* in Frankfurt, Germany. What I dreamed was not just a nightmare, it was *The Nightmare*, Henry Fuseli's Romantic-era masterpiece, and whether it manifested itself as the first version or the second, there was no escape from it.

"But it makes no sense," Dana said.

"What the hell does?"

"I mean, it being a scene from your life—Fuseli's life. Demons don't exist, Gordon. There was no such scene from Fuseli's life."

No, no escape from it. It had driven us here to Brunnen, and now it

49

seemed our theory about escaping Zurich was misguided. Location had nothing to do with it. To the ragged ends of the earth, it wasn't going to relent.

———·———

I first fell in love with *The Nightmare* when I was dating a girl who worked at a gallery near Purdue University, where both of us were students. I was no connoisseur, just a kid with an unsophisticated, college-taught knowledge of the Arts and a taste for their darker samples. Fuseli's depiction was certainly that. As I told my wife when we got to see the original in Detroit, *The Nightmare* is to painting what *Dracula* is to literature.

Although I came to regard the work as my single favorite artistic piece in any medium, I didn't obsess over it as, in fact, I had with Stoker's novel in my younger years. On the contrary, I might never even have viewed the work if my wife and I hadn't been in Detroit for a writers' conference. Our winding up in Vienna, too, was by pure coincidence. Dana accepted a job with the World Wildlife Fund, and there I found myself, in the very city where Sigmund Freud had hung an engraving of Fuseli's masterpiece in his apartment. It wasn't until a year later, when Dana was transferred to Switzerland, no less than the birthplace of one Johann Heinrich Füssli, aka Henry Fuseli, that I began to wonder . . .

I dreamed of the painting our first night at the hotel in Zurich. On waking I rationalized about associations being at work. Fuseli had been a topic on the drive down from Vienna, when I had noted to my wife the irony of our life's course. She had admitted the coincidences were odd, but that's as far as she would go with it.

"Chasing Fuseli," she said. "Sounds like something out of one of your novels. Or worse yet, those twisted films you watch."

I had rented Bergman's *Hour of the Wolf* recently and Dana had had her own nightmares.

"Well, if I'm chasing Fuseli, I'm doing it backwards through time. But I guess that's the way we chase ghosts."

I thought about this dialogue as I disentangled myself from the cobwebs of my disturbed sleep. It was the dead of night, the November air penetrating the high arched windows of the fourth-floor hotel room, and Dana slept right on through, as if I hadn't just dreamed of Fuseli's nightmarish vision and, indeed, of the artist himself. He was a more squat, malevolent-looking rendition of the man whose face I had managed to memorize along the way, but definitely Fuseli—my dream-sense said so.

Just as the incubus did with the woman in *The Nightmare*, he had been crouching on my wife's belly as she lay sprawled across a bed in the throes of an erotic nightmare. Peering from out of the curtains behind her was the ghastly head of the steed that bore the incubus through the night.

Strangely, as I experienced the horrific image in my dream, my perspective was that of Fuseli's *second* version of the painting, the one that hung in the *Goethemuseum* in Frankfurt, the one that I thought far inferior to its predecessor. I say "strangely," because I never even vaguely referenced the second version when I brought *The Nightmare* to mind. I did know something about the first painting that might have encouraged my imagination's modifications of the image, however.

Fuseli was known to have fallen in love with one Anna Landolt, only to have his heart broken when she rejected his offer of marriage. On the back of the original painting in the Detroit Institute of Art was the portrait of a woman art historians believed to be Anna. Many agreed that if it was indeed she, then the demon haunting the woman in *The Nightmare* might very well have represented Fuseli himself. Because I had always been fascinated by this possibility, it wasn't unreasonable to assume—in a world where dreams made perfect sense—my mind might conceive of his face on the body of the incubus. The thing was, dreams *didn't* make sense.

I thought to wake Dana and tell her all about it, but decided I would be accused, with more sympathy than I could, uh, pardon me, *stomach*, of taking this "Chasing Fuseli" a wee bit far.

The dream graciously proved not the recurring type—not then, that is. Dana and I spent the next few nights making our own startling images. We called it a vacation, though the days were spent looking for a house to rent, getting to know our way around, and, in Dana's case, familiarizing herself with the office and her new duties. Because the WWF's studios were on the skirts of the city, we were able to go rural in our house search, unlike Vienna, where our apartment overlooked the Opera House in the middle of the city. We found a place nine days after our arrival, pulled our stuff out of storage—touring Europe via an outfit like the WWF, which relied wholly on donations and subsidies, you trailered what you had, and you didn't have much—and cozied in among the cattle and sheep.

Between hikes and local bike tours, my exercises of choice, I spent my days writing, and my evenings trading the day's events with my wife, who loved her job every bit as much as I loved mine. Winter came and went, I dreamed tolerable dreams, and in the spring there was a writers' conference in Frankfurt.

Dana teased me, but we went right to the *Goethemuseum*. The "other" view was much better than the cheap prints (and cheaper critics?) had made it out to be. The perspective painted nine years after the first was almost as disturbing, almost as erotic, almost as delicious to the darker tastes. Like most of Fuseli's work, it was somewhat overblown and lacking in subtlety, but God help me, I loved the man for these very merits. As

William Blake said of him, Henry Fuseli was "The only man that e'er I knew/ who did not make me almost spew."

I went home from that conference happy. I had had no expectations, and look what Mr. Fuseli, Romantic that he was, had managed—the quelling of my layman preconceptions.

The night of our return, I dreamed of *The Nightmare* again. The perspective was that of the first version of the painting.

The next night I dreamed. And the next. And the next and next and next. Sometimes I dreamed one version, sometimes the other, sometimes my own variations. It wasn't until the eighth night running that it became so violent, Dana was stirred from her own slumber.

She had heard me in its throes. When I woke, she remembered some of its fiercest parts for me.

"You said you were going to rip the heart out of me and feed it to your horse." Apparently the subject matter of the dream, which I vaguely remembered myself on this occasion, was lost on her.

"I did not say that."

"And you said you were going to dip your paintbrush in my blood."

"Did I actually speak your name?"

"'I'm going to dip my paintbrush in your blood, *Dana*.' Those were your words."

It was crazy, nonsensical, not to mention perverse. Fuseli and the demon seemed interchangeable in my unconscious mind. "God, Dana, I'm sorry."

"No, no. No need. But if any of your future conferences ends up near one of Mr. Fuseli's paintings, we'll skip, mm?"

"What else did I say?"

"You said I was a demon's whore, *your* whore, and I should remember that."

"Jesus."

"Yeah."

It was that night, I think, that I first allowed myself the bizarre notion that I was possessed by Fuseli. Ghost or reincarnation.

I did not speak this to Dana. I never spoke any such thoughts to Dana until the last night in Brunnen, when we sat by the hearth, in the glow of the fire and the cognac.

Dana said something to me, and unbeknownst to us both, the end was beginning.

"Why don't we take a vacation, Gordon? We haven't gone skiing since Austria. They were just talking at the office about how fantastic the skiing is in Switzerland. What do you say?"

"I think that's a great idea, Dana. I do."

A month later we were in the gorgeous Lauterbrunnen Valley.

During that month before we packed up our skis, neither of us commented on the weight I had lost, on my hair seeming to gray and thin, on the haggard face I regarded in the mirror each morning. I entertained the thought that maybe Dana didn't see it, or maybe she attributed it to difficulties I was having with my novel in progress. One day I remarked that I wished I had never quit smoking. That evening she brought a joint home from work, courtesy of the secretary. "It's not tobacco," Dana said, "but maybe it will make you feel better." That was as close as she came to commenting on my condition.

When the day came, and we loaded up the Opel wagon, I found myself feeling better, looking forward to getting out. My hikes and bike tours had diminished to practically nil. I even brought along my laptop, which Dana, under any other circumstances, would have been bitching her head off about. This time, anything that bore a semblance to normalcy was okay. She knew. She knew I had been under a slow, twisting knife, dying from within.

Our journey took us by way of Interlaken, which only served to further brighten my spirits. It was said the water of the sibling mountain lakes was among the purest in the world, the fish that came out of it second to none. Mid-afternoon found us dining by the clear water, in the shadow of the mountains whose snows fed the lakes, and the fillets, as advertised, were the best we had ever tasted. I kissed her over white wine, making my wife of eight years actually blush. It seemed a long time since we had done that—kissed for any reason.

We drove twenty kilometers south through the narrow, deep cut in the Alps that was the Lauterbrunnen Valley. As we approached the village of Brunnen, we watched both slopes for a cabin we had seen only on the Internet. We had to turn around ultimately, so overwhelmed by the beauty of our surrounds that we could not possibly have picked out our little cabin. At the *Bahnhof,* they instructed us how to get there. This side of the big waterfall.

"Not *that* one!" exhaled Dana. "The photo didn't do it justice."

I took her hand, and we passed a face on our way out. It looked like Henry Fuseli's.

That particular injury may have been the hardest to overcome.

As usual I said nothing to Dana. I listened to her go on about the cabin as we drove up the hill. I smiled. I participated as best I could. By the time I engaged the emergency brake, she sensed the change in me.

We unpacked silently. When our eyes happened to meet, I saw the sympathy pouring out of her. It was only a matter of time before that emotion would be joined by fear and confusion and even anger. We are all built to react that way.

It came that night, down in the village, over *Salat* and *Brötchen*, a lighter dinner after the late, satisfying lunch we'd spent.

"You know, Gordon, this . . . whatever it is . . . is beginning to hurt our marriage. I have tried to be patient. I have tried very hard. I don't know what happened earlier, but you're on a path that's not just going to destroy you, but *us* as well. I'm involved, you know. You look in the mirror and feel sorry for yourself, but I—*me*, Gordon—I'm involved too."

"I know," I said stupidly.

"We're here, it's beautiful, it's an absolute wonderland . . . but you . . . you've fucked it up again."

"Again?" I echoed.

"Every time we seem to be making strides."

"You make it sound as if I'm trying to overcome an addiction."

She let her head fall to the side slightly, stared fixedly at me.

"I don't know what's wrong with me," I said. The beer tasted bitter as I tried to clear the dull haze that had followed me from the Bahnhof.

"I don't know what's wrong with you either."

"I'll come out of it."

"Will you?"

Silence reigned for the better part of dinner. The waitress, in her quaint made-for-tourists Swiss outfit, felt the mood. Feeling the mood, her English grew deliberately poor. Her face fell each time she came within ten feet of our table, a chore she tried to avoid even when our glasses sat empty. I almost had to shout for the bill—and *Rechnung* does not sound pleasant off my baby tongue—when it came time to pay.

After settling up, Dana and I strolled the village. The sun set on us as we shopped windows and their baubles. Sounds of merrymaking drifted from a nearby campground. A rollerblader shot by, glancing back at me to show me his straight Fuselian nose by the light of a streetlamp. A net of stars dipped in the deepening liquid of night.

It would be like this each night, wherever we were, only worse.

The next night, as we descended by rail from the slopes, I called my wife *Anna*.

"*What?*" Her mouth was open, and her eyes were inside me, every bit as cold and steely as the knife that always twisted. The train bore at a steep downward angle, gravity playing hell on my body and mass.

"I don't know why I—" I threw up, all over my boots, all over the seat in front of me.

She pitied me. As I looked around, wondering if anyone had heard, if anyone had seen—the seats immediately surrounding ours were empty, perhaps because of the gloom that hung around us—she pulled an extra sweatshirt from her bag and began to mop it up.

"We've got to get you help," she whispered.

"I . . . I had too much to drink."

"You had two beers, Gordon. Three hours ago."

"I'm sorry. I'm sorry, Ann—" Too late. I had done it again.

She hit me in the chest. A terrible taste filled my mouth. A terrible smell filled the air.

We got off at the next stop, though it wasn't the bottom. Dana stuffed the sweatshirt in a garbage receptacle. Faces peered out at me from the train. They all knew. They all had long straight noses and a penchant for drama and symbolism.

Dana wanted to know if I was ready to go back to Zurich. I told her to take the next train down, I wanted to walk for a while. I was backing away as I spoke. She started to protest, but then she let me go.

We were still well above the snow line, so I had a time finding the trail out of the little tourist village where the train had deposited us. Finally I did, and in shin-deep snow, I made my unhurried way down the mountain. When I reached the valley, I was desolate, empty. By the rushing river, at the dead station, I found a bench, curled up and slept.

———•———

I sleep in the night, on a wooden bench. The moon is new, but the stars are countless. The river rushes, foamy and brilliant, music to die by.

My eyes are open as I lie here, and I see someone on the footbridge, coming my way. It doesn't look like a man, but a boy, or perhaps a woman, small and squat, old. What can she want of me as she steps from the bridge, turning in my direction?

What have I to offer an old woman?

But I now recognize it is not a woman. It is not a boy. It is not human. It is stumped and beastly, and horribly grim in the gesture of its claw. It belongs in lower places, not here, not in beautiful Where I am.

Where I am.

It wants something from me, but what have I to offer a demon?

Anna, *it says.* She is mine.

———•———

"What, what—?" I started beneath the flat of her hand.

"You're dreaming again," she said.

"Isn't it cold? Who . . . ?"

"It's Dana."

"Dana. Yes . . . "

"Let me get you something," she said.

"Sleep. Sleep is what I need."

I drift into a corridor. It seems endless. Canvases on both sides shimmer with fresh paint.

"I'm so afraid for you," came the tendril of Dana's voice.

To my right, three witches point along the corridor toward whatever lies at its end. To my left, Lady Macbeth. Ah, and there she is again, with Banquo and the hags on the heath.

"Wake up . . ."

I ignore the voice. I am touching the door. I am opening it. Oh no, oh my God, my God, I knew but I could not stop myself. The words are caught in my throat. What are you? What are you and why are you torturing my innocent, sweet Anna?

"Wake up, wake up. Gordon!"

I started beneath the flat of her hand.

"Are you—?"

"I'm Dana, Gordon."

"I was Fuseli dreaming. I knew I was dreaming, but I knew it as *him*." I looked down at my chest, where she had placed her hand. It was moist with sweat. The hand I put over hers trembled.

"Do you want to tell me?" she said.

She listened, and I told her.

"And you actually recognized her as Anna?"

"I knew her, Dana. I knew the woman lying on that bed. She was Anna Landolt. It was as though I were watching a scene from my life."

"Which perspective?"

I stared. "Which—?"

"Perspective."

"But we haven't discussed my nightmares except that once . . ."

"That once when you said you would dip your paintbrush in my blood."

"Did I speak of . . . perspectives?"

"With your brush you did. Your brush, my blood, in the mirror."

"Did I—"

She showed me her tongue, with the deep teeth marks in it.

"I would never do that to you, Dana . . ."

"Wouldn't you?" she laughed, throwing her head back and letting her tongue loll from her mouth.

I threw the covers off me, rolled off the bed, looked back—

There he was, upon her belly, as she twisted in the erotic nightmare that gripped her.

And yet it was *her* saying, "It makes no sense . . . A scene from your life? . . . Demons don't exist . . ."

———•———

The last day, I woke late. The dream was fresh, unabating. I would carry it with me all day.

"What shall we do today?" she asked cheerfully.

What had I done to make her think the end hadn't arrived? Maybe she knew it was the last day, and was grateful.

Over *Brötchen* and cheese and soft-boiled eggs, we talked about how pleasant life really was, how fortunate we were to be in Europe, and in Switzerland specifically, lovers of nature that we were. How fortunate we were to know their traditional breakfast of *Brötchen* and cheese and soft-boiled eggs.

"I think we should stay close to the homestead today," I said.

"Do you love me?"

"I do, Dana."

"You wouldn't go back to Zurich without me, would you?" She laughed as she said it, but I wondered.

There was a falls a few kilometers south of the village of Brunnen that was touted as carrying a higher volume of water than any other waterfall *within* a mountain in the world. We decided to hike to it, do the ascent through the water-carved rock, and hike back. Once upon a time, that would have spelled paradise to me. Now it spelled the motions of the last day. I told her I loved her four times as we explored the falls.

But still I didn't die.

"Tonight," she shouted over the roar, "I want the richest, most expensive, most sinful dinner we can find." It was Saturday night. All the restaurants would be open.

We took the suggestion of a proprietor and did a place that had appeared in the film *The Eiger Sanction*. The choice, tender portions we received certainly merited that sort of stardom. They served cognac, and we drank cognac. It was the color of Dana's hair.

Night fell during our return. She had insisted I buy a bottle for the road, though the road amounted to but four kilometers. We drank as we walked; the sky grew less clear, a mist evolving of the river-stream that cut the valley.

"You could toss me in, and never have to worry about me again," she said.

"Is that something you've thought about?"

"Maybe." Still laughing, amber laughter.

"Do you think I would do such a thing?"

"I don't know you well enough to know, do I?"

It would be easy, I thought, as I looked at her, half-drunk wife of mine. But I envisioned the incubus hanging from the footbridge to snatch her up as she swept downstream.

When we reached the cabin, we fetched glasses, just for the exercise. Before the hearth we sat, sopping and hopeless, and made short, furious love by the flames. I lamented the sound of its coming even then.

———•———

Chilled, dejected, resigned, I lamented the sound that preceded the train.

The noise of the rusty wheel of the wheelbarrow hung with me. The stench of alcohol was pungent, but that was goodness and mercy, not a forerunner of the abominable act being committed. Little that it mattered. It was 9:44, and she was a demon's whore.

I turned my attention to the station in time to see the train part the fog and come to rest by the desolate platform. A lamp stood by, casting a somber glow over the double metal doors of the first car as my heart—what was left of it—ticktocked in raw, agonizing anticipation.

As the doors parted, wrenching open the night itself, I begged her, without looking down at her face, to forgive me. A dark horse and rider emerged. The bearer of the incubus, eyes aglow, snorted and blew in the misty night. The clop of its hooves, as it majestically bore its inhuman rider toward me, was that of my heartbeat. Within a few feet, the noise stopped.

The incubus and I stared down.

"The whore," the demon gestured.

"Why?" I said, meaning all of it, every bit, the nightmares and the rest.

"My whore!" he lashed.

I stood there with her weight in my arms. "And Fuseli?"

"*Bah*, Fuseli. She was always my whore. He just caught us at it."

"I've loved this woman," I stated.

"You may have loved her, you may have made love to her, but she was never yours." The incubus shook its unseemly head, tapped its chest. "She has always been mine."

"What will you do with her?"

"What do you do with yours, mortal?"

The decision descended on those words. "I look at you, demon, and I find I have at least enough for this one last thing."

And I lunged for the river, my bundle in my arms. As I tossed it, he screamed. But it was a rueful scream, which gave me hope. A last hope.

They rode the river, horse and rider trailing wings of hell, and I started back for the cabin, shoving the wheelbarrow aside as I stepped onto the footbridge.

She was there on the bed as I entered, tossed across the draping sheets in the throes of an erotically violent dream, her hands caressing her breasts, her belly, clutching at the fabric of her gown, moaning a name unspeakably vile to my ears.

Dana for that moment, and then . . .

Gone. The smell of cognac and ashes and sex lingering. Her tongue crawling out of nothing to touch at the residue of my clumsy strokes against her, against my own nightmares, against the devil rider. Whichever perspective he chose.

TO WHAT WE WERE AND SHALL BECOME AGAIN

(To What We Were is set in the world of Gene O'Neill's *White Plague Chronicles)*

I 'M WHITE. Let's start there. I record this as a fifty-one-year-old white man who lived through it as an adolescent, watching his father succumb in pain and anger to the wretched Caucasian-specific contagion that he called God's Own Wrath. "Better," he said, "that the Black Death had entirely wiped out Europe before its kingdoms and countries did the damage they did to the rest of the world." His angle was that white men had fucked indigenous peoples everywhere, bought Africans for labor, cut shit up for sheer amusement, then asked for dessert.

He was a simple man like that. I'm a simple man. I followed his footsteps into employment with Bio-Tek Labs, which entity managed to hang on through the mayhem, in spite of it all, this humble son eventually reaching the level his father had, that of Chief of Laboratory Directed Research and Development, in which capacity I managed to do something that will forever set me apart from the rest of the human species. I found, via a refrigeration section warehouseman, a vial with notes attached. I immediately knew the notes' meaning, though this horrific treasure had somehow madly slipped through the cracks, perhaps with my father's own knowledge—the man I felt I knew could have done such a thing. Just a little bottle: a nothing, really. But I knew what it was. It was an altered, specialized strain of White Plague—perhaps one of a hundred such samples and strains that had otherwise been systematically and thoroughly destroyed among laboratories worldwide—and God forgive me, but I was going to do something with it. No, no forgiveness necessary, God. How about *we* forgive *You* for once.

I liked having it with me as I quit my job and began my wanderings, which is what this record is about. If you're alive, that means something, but I'm not sure what. It's afterlife I've been after, the place where monsters go. And maybe that's where we are now.

Before setting out, I returned to our family home in the Lake Tahoe area of the Sierra Nevadas to touch base with Little Wing, my Washoe girlfriend of several years, and to gather provisions. My father had kept his parents' secluded ranch after moving to Silicon Valley with Bio-Tek Labs, and I'd vacationed there all my life, knew the ins and outs of the surrounding forest, every foot track, every snowmobile track, every horse track. It wasn't so isolated that the tongues of plague hadn't been able to reach it, but it was far enough on the outskirts to provide a new starting point for me. It was home for me—more than San Jose, more than anywhere. The black bears, mule deer, coyotes, raccoons, porcupines, marmots . . . they were my friends. They don't know a Caucasian from a bullet hole in the head. My father championed these animals. He was that, too; a sort of amateur environmentalist. He meant it, too. He'd as soon shoot you as see one of his "pets" harmed. He killed, he did, he was a hunter, but only in season and when overpopulation was an issue. He fished like that too. You never saw anybody so careful about what he did with trout, which was mostly throwing them back into the water after tenderly removing the hooks. He taught me things, the old man. He taught me a lot.

He didn't teach me how to steal the most destructive force on the planet. I did that on my own. But I knew he watched. I knew he approved. I did things for him. As simple as he was, he was a genius in my eyes. He knew something about something. He said things to me before he died. He entrusted his seventeen-year-old son with these brutal adult insights into life.

"This is how it is, Son. It's a trap; there is no way out. It's constructed that way. Go two steps forward and watch a wall materialize before your eyes. That wall is real. Don't listen to your mother. She doesn't see it. It doesn't stand in front of her, and therefore there's nothing to resist on her part. She likes it like a pie—find the freshest fruit, do it up, deliver it to smiles, licking lips, but the wall's not there for her. She doesn't see. She doesn't *want* to see, and that's how it is with her. Learn the word old-fashioned. It has a place."

Yeah, Dad. "I don't think Mom would like to hear you talk that way. She considers herself progressive."

"Progressive?" Dad laughed. "How old are you now? Be careful with terms like that. Your mom doesn't work where I do. She doesn't see what we are capable of."

"I don't know, maybe she's repressed as a woman. That's what she sometimes says."

Which was when it got weird, as it sometimes did, with the old man spilling sugar all over me. "Your mom's the most complete human being in the world, Son. Forget me. I'm a weird scientist."

I liked the weird scientist. He knew some things, Mom notwithstanding.

When the White Plague happened, Dad managed to get us back to the ranch, having concluded that his work in San Jose was a lost cause. I asked him to give it to me straight. It seemed very real to me, the pandemic.

"It's real. It's going to replenish the world through death. We may not survive it.

Be ready, okay?"

"I want to, but I don't know how."

"I don't think we're meant to know that. But Son, listen—your mom's in town right now helping others. She can't survive that. She's likely already contracted it. She's going to die. Do you understand me, Will?"

I didn't, but then I did.

"We all die," he went on. "The question is, is that enough? To die?"

He painted it as an obligation, something that didn't sit well with me at all even in my young years as I watched them put her in the ground, already infected themselves, just performing some ancient ritual. Appealing to some lust for lost life. Civilization was already dead by then— the marauders and Daesh customers with dirty bombs had finished the job. People performed their functions out of habit and guilt.

Was it enough? After years of deliberating, I thought maybe not. I thought maybe acceptance was not enough. Maybe something could be done. Thus, I made decisions in the lab, decisions that would ignite my journey into the Sierras. My parents were both dead by then, but I had the firecracker. The one re-awakening the world perhaps needed. I didn't take my task lightly. I maintained when others hadn't. But I was, let's face it, lord now. A wanderer in the forest, an island in a stream; I was lord god.

———◆———

A thousand times I wanted to cast the vial against a rock, imagined I could see its microscopic contents carried off by the wind, a thousand times I did not. I thought about children. I thought about me as a child, with my buddies, Tony and Tim, black as the ace of spades and little devils like me. I thought about having almost committed myself with the marital question to the Native American woman who had refused to let me go on this mission, whatever it was, alone, in spite of the fact that the strange, misplaced guilt had overtaken my life overtures to her, causing me to back out not once, but two, three times through the years. So many things to think about when you're lord god hauling around the great secret. Oh, how I wanted to do it when some survivor like me said the "others" had done the "black magic" on us.

Little Wing, whose name is Wendy Little Wing Washika (the "Little Wing" part had been as much a Jimi Hendrix reference as an indigenous thing, and I, like her hippie parents, would not call her Wendy, no matter how confusing it might have been to other people), had not hesitated for even a second when I'd told her I had to do something for myself and I would be a while at it, she was free to go her way.

"Whatever it is you have to do, Will, I'm doing it with you."

"Including mounting a horse with whatever provisions you can carry and wandering off into the mountains, the world be damned?"

"Ha! Like I haven't ever wanted to do that. And September now? The best time? Summer going out, no winter to worry about yet? I'm coming, old man." *Old man* was her endearment, which I take as such, though she was seven years my junior.

"Without knowing why?" I asked.

"What's to know, Will? You want to return to where you came from, let's go. I knew what was up when you quit your job."

"You knew I was going wandering off into the Sierras?"

"I knew you were coming to terms with something in this fucked-up world of ours. I knew, I *know* there were things at the lab that made you question yourself as a man and human being."

"Listen, Little Wing—"

"Baby, we're good. You're my love. I've waited all these years tending to my family, who are all dead now, maybe sick of watching everything else die, for you to come back to me permanently, and I'm going with you. Save it for when it's important, 'kay?"

Couldn't believe the kind of partner she was. Had never been able to believe she was real.

So we packed our shit up, grabbed my best horses, and ventured forth.

It wasn't like I had to worry about killing her when I did it. Is there room for sarcasm in such a world?

2

Three days in, dusk settling, we saw fires in the foothills at the end of the valley we were traversing. To my surprise Little Wing said she knew something about it.

"It's a compound, a commune of my people who fled Tahoe before they realized it wasn't us the plague was after. They've lived there ever since. My father spoke to me about it, wanted to go himself. I remembered the place when we were looking at the map earlier. This would be it, I think."

"But you didn't mention it to me."

"What point? Is it our destination?"

"I don't know. We could replenish our water supply. Mix with folk a little. They might have some alcohol to take the nip off the coming night."

She smiled, but that wasn't what her face was saying. "We have alcohol, there's scarcely a nip, and I'm not sure mixing is what you want here, Will."

I was puzzled. "Are you talking about me or them?"

"I'm talking about you." She sighed before continuing, as though this were something she'd been wanting to get off her chest for a long time. "I don't know if you know it, Will, but you're not completely stable. I listen to you in your sleep. I hear things. You're not happy with something. Something about what remains of this world. You threaten to destroy. You literally use words like that—*destroy*. Can I trust you taking a rifle, a handgun, a hunting knife into a populated place where they're bound to look at you like you're from another world?"

This concern on her part was news to me. Not shocking, not the opposite. Rather, her words made me aware of a numbness in me that lived underneath, or at least among, the emotional layers. That I'd not considered it before might have been a byproduct of its very existence.

I regarded her. "You think me capable of harming other people?"

"I'm sorry, but yes, I do."

This seriously troubled me, now that such a thing was out in the open. Even though I carried, usually on my own person, the living equivalent of a nuclear device a thousandfold the power of anything man had made, this troubled me.

"Yet you're with me," I said.

"I love you. I'm with you."

"What else?" I said, eyeing her.

"What else what?"

"What else might I be taking in there, Little Wing?"

"I don't know. You tell me."

I stared at her, but she neither flinched nor expounded, which led me to set the matter aside, for now, for more practical concerns. "Let's move on then, and we'll set up camp after we're past the compound."

It wouldn't play out like that. We were too close. A scout team of three, on horseback, emerged not three minutes after we'd let the discussion go and proceeded. They didn't insist we come with them. While they were armed, they weren't a war party. They didn't present themselves as hostile in any way. Rather, they invited.

Little Wing, with a meaningful glance my way, accepted their invitation in the proper, companionable spirit.

———•———

The encampment, no, the *village*, was an impressive something out here in the middle of nowhere. Even before the local chief, who introduced himself as Low Sun, and his son Moving Water (I resisted such names as anachronistic, even untrue, not like Little Wing) showed us around, we could see the place was completely self-sufficient. Its inhabitants grew crops, raised cows, goats, sheep, and chickens, and had built their log cabins—of which there were perhaps two dozen, including workshops and such—around two vibrant streams. A high waterfall fell from a bluff behind the structures, providing a pool of crystal water in which, we were told, the children liked to bathe. It was a living paradise, at least at this time of year. When winter struck, Low Son said, things grew tougher but still manageable. They'd two engineers among them—one from the Army Corps—as well as skilled tradesmen. They hadn't entered into this lightly.

Prior to this twenty-minute impromptu tour, after the horses had been tied off at the stable and we'd been provided, as "surprise guests" to Shadow Valley, a hot root tea by way of welcome, I'd detected nothing but warmth with a dash of curiosity from the folks who sat out on their sheltered porches, knitting, rocking children, sharing dinner, what have you. It was unreal to me. A movie set. It didn't belong. Now, Wing and I finding ourselves back in the middle of the compound, most of the folks having retired inside, leaving a significant fire burning in a large stone-rimmed pit in an open court between their houses, the place seemed even less real. Night had fully fallen, and the shadows of the flames danced everywhere, beautifully really, but as though expecting more tonight.

We joined Low Sun, his wife Kai, and Moving Water on the hewn-log terrace of their house set distinctly apart from the others and nearest the waterfall. It was here, as we ate fish and vegetables with them—a young, shirtless man with whom Moving Water flirted when he thought we weren't looking, doing the cooking and serving honors—that the conversation became more than a hospitality.

"You'll forgive us for all these formalities," Low Sun said. "They're appearances for the community as much as anything else. We need our people to feel they are a part of the world, even while isolated from it. We don't want folks dwelling on the Collapse. We want them to see that the world goes on, that white men such as yourself, Will, still move freely and comfortably about without some tattoo marking them as abhorrents. The children, it's imperative, see this. Don't get me wrong. You're not the first to have passed this way. Strangers come through from time to time. Our lookouts go out and meet them, to check on who they are and what they're up to, sure, but also because the world, the world we continue to believe in, must not be a world of strangers. If I had my way, we wouldn't teach the Collapse at all in school. But I'm advised against that. Reeks, they tell me, of history. They invoke post-World War II Germany, like that's anything to do with anything. So we do this dance, and our community sees that the world is calm and that people care about one another. It's best. Maybe an example for everywhere."

I'd begun nodding before he finished, the piece of trout hanging on the tines of my fork. "I understand you, Low Sun. If things could be like they are here, it would be something."

Wing, conspicuously, said nothing.

"Are they not?" the chief said, glance alternating between us.

I looked at Little Wing. I wanted to hear what she had to say.

If my gaze made her feel awkward, she didn't show it. "I'm still in Tahoe," she said. "I don't see the wider world. We're okay there. White, black, brown, red, yellow, green. It's Tahoe."

He was interested in that, the chief. "We send our scouts in, we look around, we see. But I'm not sure that what we see is what you see. Tell us."

"Sun," his wife Kai reprimanded. "Maybe she doesn't want to *describe* to you. Maybe our guests would prefer to finish their meals in peace."

"No, no, it's okay," Wing said. "I'm a little alarmed, though, let me be frank, by these concerns about skin color, racism, or anything resembling it. It's been a long time, Chief Low Sun. Will was seventeen when he watched his parents die. He's fifty now. He moved out of Tahoe, eventually replacing his father as head of—"

"I don't think that's what we're talking about here," I interrupted, ignoring any effect on the local thermometer.

"Aren't we?" she persisted. "Chief, you are what, twenty years Will's elder? You were in your late thirties when it was happening. Your perception of it was more realized, and that's what you took with you when you came out here. What you remember is not how it is. Not in towns, close-knit populated places, places that have the resources, the drive and determination, the *togetherness* to recover. In the case of cities, I can't imagine it's much different, not after all this time." She looked at me, hard. "Will could tell you about that better than me."

So it was going to be like this. I was to be confronted in the open get a better psychological fix on me. She cared not one whit about what this commune thought. She respected it, would play happily, but her objective was clear: challenge me, call me out, see what it was that pushed my buttons and brought me out into the wilderness on a mission that had no name outside my destructive nightmares.

The chief wasn't stupid. He sensed the friction in the air. "Relax. Both of you. I'm talking about social discomfort. I did not mention racism. We have no place for even the thought of racism in the Valley."

"My partner has never had a place for racism either," Wing said. "Not when awake."

I flung my plate across the table, not caring in whose lap its contents landed, and stormed away, unimpeded, by the shock of it if nothing else, into the night.

———◆———

Beneath an overhang, I lay curled up in a ball, remembering.

Little Wing had woken me one night. It might have been a year before, might have been a month. "You were having a dream," she said.

"Yeah. I know. It wasn't pleasant."

"Do you remember it?"

"No. I mean maybe, vaguely. No, I don't think so."

"You were talking about dark-skinned people."

"Really? In what sort of way?"

"A . . . a sympathetic way . . . that is, I think."

But I'd lied. I had remembered some of it. I remembered holding something in my hand, my clenching, pulsing fist, looking out from my office window upon the streets of Silicon Valley and thinking one day, one day we will truly all be equal.

If I could have slept and dreamed now, I would have, holding the thing like this in my fist. Just like this, feeling vapors seep through its widening cracks. Feeling people of all colors lift up their faces to breathe in this sweet air. Yet wishing I were someplace else, wishing I was with my father again.

When you're after the catfish, the blood and cheese bait needs to go to the bottom, a couple extra sinkers, maybe three, no float unless you're sure about the depth. I know I've told you to keep the bait moving through the water, but with the cats it should be on the bottom, where their whiskers can tickle it. If they're hungry, they'll scoop it up. You can twitch it here and there if you want, just watch out for snagging the hook on the junk down there. It's tricky. Tahoe is deep, Son, as deep as a lake can get. You have to pick your spots, even from the bank. Most of those spots are already fished. You gotta explore some, not like the lake by the ranch. You have to take your boat and explore the shore. We'll get you a boat one day, after you learn to drive and haul a trailer. But be good to your fish. Always be good to your fish, even the bottom dwellers. If it's a kitten, toss it back in, let it grow, mature. Just like the smallmouth, just like the whitefish, all of them. The trout you can see, you're Ernest Hemingway in the Florida Keys, especially in the tributaries. Go for 'em. Catfish cannot be seen. They live down there in the mud and weed. That's what gives them that taste your mother brings out so well in her recipes.

Wanted to be there with her, too. My mother. Southern girl, transplanted *after* she'd been taught the way of the South. *No, Will, for Christ's sake, nail it through its head to the tree, then cut like I showed you and grab the flaps with the pliers to pull the skin away. It's not a normal fish.*

To What We Were and Shall Become Again

What was a normal fish? I wondered as I shivered in the hole I'd found for myself. What was a normal fish in our depleted sea? I hated thinking, I hated dreaming, I hated memories, I hated it all . . .

Better just to close your eyes. Better to and wait for the dark skins to come get you for some hallucinogenic ritual that you would be wise to participate in before your brain starts to truly drip out of your ears, your spine igniting in a column of fire and your dermis wilting away, exposing the naked monster hiding beneath.

———•———

So it is wished for, so it shall be given.

I hadn't meant it, but as they fed me a tea decidedly unlike the welcome one, trying to talk me up out of the pit in a patient, knowing manner that I understood at first, but then watched dissolve among the motions of them extracting me from my cave and guiding me back to the compound, I did begin to mean it, though I couldn't recall what exactly it was I'd meant to mean.

Washoe people. *Wa she shu.* Sierra Nevadas, vials, peyote parties. No. I wasn't here. I was fishing, taking my mother's commands, peeling off the skin, not a scalp. Had they done that, the Washoe? Did I know? Had I ever bothered to find out? Had I ever asked that woman, the feathered whatever the hell she was thing what she needed from me? How I could help *her*? No, a lord god did not need to ask such things. He had his device, he'd had it before he had found it. He'd known it would come to this.

I could feel it in my hands as they propped me up against something and she came to look me in the eyes a moment before dancing away. All of them dancing. Healing me. Curing me. Casting out the bad spells. Drums beating, half-naked bodies indulging in the rhythms, bare feet trampling the demons into the ground. Tongues of fire lapping at the heavens, the stars spiraling away as they were touched by the flames. Black bears howling at the holes left. Slashing licks of water across my face. Hands touching my flesh, voices moaning over my lost soul, eyes flashing before my own, painted faces daring me to come out of my dreams, to become one again with a world I despised. Little Wing, there at last, cupping my face in her hands, singing something to me, a lullaby.

Night falling again. Into morning.

Chief Low Sun giving me something, A stick, staff, scepter, something whose handle was formed of the skull of a small mammal.

"Take it. It will guide you."

In my other hand, though, I felt nothing, and momentarily panicked. Stumbling back to where my clothes hung—was I nude in the midst of all this?—I found it where it should be among the folds. I'd gripped a cracking ghost. Perhaps I would always find myself clutching the tube's cracking ghost in the end. It was a thought. A fleeting comfort.

3

In the morning I found myself fed, watered, on my horse, which had also been fed and watered, a stick strapped to the saddlebag, Little Wing equally ready for the next part of our journey. I waited until we were out of there before confronting her.

"What the hell happened last night?"

"I don't know what you mean," she said, looking ahead.

"Did it happen? Did that actually happen?"

"Did what happen?"

"You were there," I said. "What the fuck was that?"

She sneered. "Better you concern yourself with what happens next. I've seen it. Will you be able to come to terms with it or will you need my help again?"

"Come to terms with what? What did you see?

"Three silhouettes hanging from a tree in the middle of your wilderness."

"It's not *my* wilderness. How do you know this?"

"I saw it in a vision."

"Then last night *did* happen."

"I don't know. it?"

I closed my eyes. "I thought I had something in my hand while it was happening. Do you know anything about that?"

"You mean the thing I put back in its place? Where it belonged? No, wait. It belongs in a laboratory, doesn't it? Or in some underground silo to be appropriately disposed of. What the fuck did you expect me to do with such a thing?"

"But how did you know?"

"You stupid fool. You're obsessive and meticulous about everything. You make detailed notes and then dream on top of that? How would I not know?"

"But if you knew, why didn't you . . . "

"Bury it so that an act of nature later unearths it? Put it in a stream so it gets dashed against a rock? Take it to the top of a mountain so the ice cracks it and releases its contents? Or no, you're thinking I'd be more creative, do something like burn it in our fire last night. Thinking an ignorant nobody like me could easily start the Collapse again, which would free you from all your ghosts. I know it doesn't burn, man. I know it doesn't just go away. Don't you have to nitro-freeze it or cast it into space or let the descendants of worms that sucked the juices out of Paracelsus or something do it in? What I can't figure out is why fuck your own race again? Haven't you had enough? What guilt can you have? You people suffered, not the rest of us."

Which meant she didn't understand. I'd at least been that careful in my notes, even unconsciously. Good.

About the tableau she was talking about . . .

——•——

Two days further in, and there indeed it was. In a column of sunlight that seemed specifically trained to provide the necessary contrast while simultaneously illuminating the fulfilled prophecy, were three dark shapes suspended in space. Hanged men. Black men. Dead, beginning to rot.

I began to feel what I'd not felt before—an outright rage.

Little Wing smelled it on me, recognized it for the distinct, fully-flowered, unambiguous wrath against my own that it was, and pretended without pretending to approve of what I was experiencing for once.

"If you want to unleash it on yourself, your kind again, I'll concede and somehow go out with you."

I thought that overly simplistic, ironic, contradictory, and dangerous to try on me right now.

"No, baby, this is not going to work like that," I said, feeling the fire in my eyes, my skin, every receptacle and nerve ending and sensor as I looked not on her, but through her.

The question was more important to her than the change in me. "How will it work then?"

Seeing a black canvas before me now, I said, "I'm not sure, but not like that."

"Tell me the rest, right now."

Do pupils dilate or contract when opaque blackness has disrupted their function? I only know they adjust like magic when you're confronted with the only voice that you will listen to. "You want to know? Do you really, really want to know, Wing? This strain was engineered for further destruction. It doesn't know from race or color. Assuming it's viable."

She backed away from me as though I were the agent itself, practically whispering, "And that's why you carry it with you, isn't it? Because of that broader power?" She sought the words. "Are you the fucking *Beast*?"

"Yes. Maybe," I confessed.

She had nothing to say to that, staying back, watching me, though I wasn't watching her now because my returned eyes had found something in the dirt. Tracks. Forget the darkness, forget the emotions, I'd been so focused on the horror of the hanged men, I'd missed that the clearing in which the tree stood was at the end of a dirt road, a service or logging affair that disappeared into the trees to my right.

"Look at this, Wing," I said, in this particular moment now. "These tracks are fresh. They were made since the last rain, I'm sure. I want to follow them."

"Why?" Guardedly. Suspiciously.

"Because I want to know where they lead."

"To what purpose?"

"To the purpose of getting lucky and finding the culprits."

She sneered. "Assuming the tracks don't end at a paved road, what exactly are you going to do with the culprits if you find them?"

"I don't know that. Just indulge me. I have a feeling about this. You have visions, I have feelings. Must be some of the shit from last night, still in my bloodstream and cells."

"Christ. Give me the fucking map so I can make sense of it first."

"I don't think it's on the map."

"Give me the map."

I did. You had to do it her way when you were the Beast.

She studied it for a couple of minutes before saying, "There's something a few miles from here. Looks like it might belong to the Forest Service, I'm not sure what the symbol is. The map's frayed, half the legend's missing. How old is this map, anyway?"

"I don't know. It was my father's."

"Great." She studied it again. "The nearest paved road is five or six miles away. A road off it leads to the location I'm talking about. This road isn't shown, but I'm guessing it branches off that one."

"Enough for me."

"And if there's nothing there?"

"Then we move on. Do you have someplace to be, Little Wing? A train to catch? I'm looking for something, okay? I thought that was understood. Maybe it's there, maybe it's not. But I'm looking for something. I'm in this wilderness for a reason. I want to know what it's like outside, where they're not pretending to rebuild. I'm getting a good taste of it. Aren't you?"

"Fine, let's go."

"Not just yet," I said, covering my face with the bandana that hung around my neck and approaching the three men. My mount didn't seem to mind the stench too much, stepping right into the midst of them. I looked down at the marks in the dirt.

"They did it from the back of a pickup, slung them up, drove the truck forward, leaving them dangling."

Drawing my knife, I stood up in the stirrups, carefully balancing myself with the pommel, reins, could just reach the ropes, cutting the men down one by one.

"All right, let's go," I said. "Better the beasts have them than that miserable indignity. Fuck this world."

To which my wary Wing could only respond with her eyes.

To What We Were and Shall Become Again

As we neared the junction of the two forest roads, a figure appeared ahead of us, a hiker rounding the bend that we would be taking, coming in our direction.

"Easy," I said to Little Wing, reaching, strangely, not for my rifle but for the staff Low Sun had given me. I clutched it below its animal head in my right hand while easing back on the reins slightly, only slowing our progress, with my left.

Wing let her mount's pace match mine, unsnapping the strap of the leather holster she wore at her waist.

"Hello there," the stranger called in a husky male voice, lifting his hands to presumably show us he was a harmless fellow. It seemed awfully odd and yet perfectly natural to me that we should be greeting each other this way, as though we were passers-by on a lonely Old West trail.

I nodded—we were close enough now that he could see the gesture—but I said nothing. Little Wing glanced my way once, but otherwise watched him in her own brand of silence.

"You folks have any cigarettes?" the man said. "If you're going up to the Factory, they're out. They have alcohol. They have the pills. But no smokes. I'm on my way to South Lake Tahoe to see if I can scrounge up some there. You coming from that way? Is the weather good over there? I mean that euphemistically, of course."

Almost upon him now, I brought us to a halt. Waited until he, too, had stopped a short distance in front of us before speaking.

I ignored niceties altogether. "Talk to me about the Factory. I've heard only rumors."

His eyes grew bright in his wildly bearded face. "Oh, man. It's an orgy, that's what it is. A hippie trip like you wouldn't believe. I'm still trying to absorb the experience. Of course that's not its function. You know that, I'm sure."

"What is its function?"

He laughed. "You don't know? You really don't *know*? Well, who am I to spoil it for you. You two trot on up there and have a look for yourself. It ain't what the place was originally, that's for damn sure."

"What was it originally? That's not giving away the surprise, is it?" I said testily.

He seemed to ponder that. "You know, I'm not actually sure. This is National Forest, you know, so it can't have been commercial unless they leased it out for some environmental reason. Like maybe, fertilizer or something? But no, that would seem to be very un-*environmental*, wouldn't it? Who knows, maybe they were pumping out fresh trees for after

71

the fires! They were doing all kinds of crazy shit before the . . . well, you know what I mean. Good question. Maybe you'll find out."

"Maybe we will," I said. "Good day to you, sir." I lightly popped the reins, starting past him.

"What about those cigarettes, partner?"

Little Wing took that one. "Maybe that's what your factory was manufacturing, *partner.*"

And we moved on, glancing back a couple of times in distaste before taking the turn to the left, which led up an initially gradual, then steeper grade, this road clearly better traveled than the previous one. There was no following specific tracks anymore; there were many sets. We were going somewhere that lived, operated in the forest. I'd lost my appetite, but not the need.

Wing and I didn't speak as we ascended. I think we both knew we were arriving somewhere. Someplace meaningful to somebody in our broken world.

God help us, but we'd never have imagined anything like what we found.

———•———

WPS were the letters that greeted us at the gate of this thing that indeed must have once been a factory, judging by the rusted metal structures and chutes that stood before us like a dream out of some demented artist's mind. It wasn't that it didn't look like an ordinary factory; the matter was one of context. The place stood in a forest, a National Forest, was clearly a ruin yet hosted dozens of cars, trucks, and motorcycles—stickers on the tail ends of which widely promoted PROPAGATION BY DESIGN—in the parking area outside its entrance. To say it invoked Kafka was putting it lightly. It belonged in no way in the world we thought we knew, whatever the true nature of that world.

The woman at the gate, eyes glazed to extreme degrees, was no exception. "Let's see your tickets," she said. "Also will need medical certificates. You're arriving by horse. Thought I didn't see you park them over there? That's irregular. Doctor's notes, please. We're not a free-for-all. It's not your personal party, despite what you may have heard. And wait a minute, who is this woman? No dark skins here. This is the White Propagation Society. Are you two lost? What's your business here?"

Looking past her into the property through the sliding electronic fence she monitored, we saw a world, on the outside, of children of all ages, running and playing and laughing in next to nothing besides their birthday suits. Walls beyond. Walls with dark windows.

"I'm Washoe," Wing said to the woman. She pulled out her wallet, opened it, flashing something inside, closed it again. "Would you mind stepping out of your booth, ma'am? We are here on government business and would highly prefer it if your electronics—microphones, surveillance, whatever securities surround your box—were not privy to what we have to say to you."

The woman stared, mouth vacillating between dropping open and unleashing her feelings about this. She settled on, "You must be joking."

"I don't think you want to be in this place," Wing persisted. "I think any woman would not want to be in this place. We can help you. Open the window wider so I can have a better look at you. Have they harmed you? We've dealt with cults like this. We know how it can be."

The woman, having had enough, flung her window open, sticking her head out. "Go ahead and take a look then, you b—"

Wing struck her in the temple with the butt of her handgun, leaving the woman hanging there on the sill. As she reached through the opening, searching for the button, I could only stare at her in admiration.

"Fuck you," she said to me, then click, the mechanism was engaged, the gate was sliding, and we were in.

We ignored the playing children; they ignored us as we bypassed the entrance of the building in front of us for a quieter peek. The windows in the crumbling cinderblock façade revealed nothing. On the side of the structure, however, they were not just untinted open . . .

———•———

It cannot be described, the scene, it was so perverse. The room was full of makeshift beds. And upon the bedrolls and blankets and rotting mattresses, *all* of them, naked, writhing, moaning bodies. Beer and liquor bottles were scattered everywhere, the stench of sweat and sex and alcohol such that we could smell the sickening bouquet through the opening in the wall.

As distinctly as we could hear, as poignantly as we absorbed, so did we take in the words of the obese bald man who sat on a lone chair on a platform at one end of the room, reading from a book in his hands:

. . . and God's admission of His mistake to our late beloved leader, while graceful beyond human conception, did in no way remove us from our responsibilities as His divine children, indeed freeing us in a way we might not have been capable of accomplishing ourselves, in effect bestowing His Own authority upon us, His elite, that we might cast our net across His estates, capturing the hordes of the Enemy, carefully picking out our own precious clear gems from the abhorrent misbalance while submitting the rest to the furnace that burns and will always burn in the name of our blood, of which those purest white stones are constituted, and further render this earth free of corruption, of the disease that a mishap on the part of our God in His enthusiasm to correct matters

unleashed in the wrong name, maybe that of His black son, that one, Lucifer, who has always tried to trick the light with phantasmagoria . . .

"I don't want to be here," Little Wing uttered quietly to me. "I won't believe this is a gathering of human beings. It cannot be. It's their god's dream. It's his way of repenting."

I stared at her. "Wing . . . that's . . . "

She stared back. "Nightmarish?"

"Beyond fucking belief."

"What will you do here, white man?" she said. "How will you end this dream? With a glass capsule? Do you have it in you? Now that you see firsthand what's been burning inside?"

"That's a lie I ferociously resent."

"Yeah? You don't want to go inside and participate?"

I found myself shaking, suddenly and almost uncontrollably.

"Go ahead," she continued unrelentingly. "Do it. You have it in your power."

I felt the tears coming. Rage, fear, knowledge. "I don't know what to do with it, baby. Swallow it? Climb the highest peak in these mountains, swallow it and let the cold take me?"

"Must have been how God felt when he made His mistake."

"Please. I need you, Wing. Don't turn on me."

"I don't turn. People turn. I don't turn. Come, let's get out of here. We'll figure it out."

Would we? Could it be figured out? Was there even a vial? I scarcely knew anymore, the world had turned so crooked.

———•———

As we returned by the road that had led us from the horror of the hanged men, we encountered the bearded hiker again. Without hesitation, Little Wing pulled out her handgun, waited until his smiling face was almost upon us, and shot him. Sadly, she wasn't the best shot, so we had to hear this, "I thought . . . cigarettes, sex . . . sex, cigarettes . . . I had to turn back, man."

Lord God, the children he would be responsible for having seeded.

I dismounted and struck him in the temple with the head of my staff. The animal skull remained intact, was hard, good material, maybe not bone at all, but stone replica. I asked Wing what she thought, but she didn't hear me, or she refused to answer.

"It won't get any easier now, Wing," I muttered. "Not now, with all the cards on the table."

She didn't answer. Nor would she, anytime soon. When we reached the spot where I'd cut down the hanged men, scattering what must have been coyotes by our surprise appearance, she looked at the men's ravaged bodies then fell from the saddle, hanging a minute in the stirrup before her horse did the rest, leaving her a crumpled heap.

I could feel the beating life in her when I checked her pulse, but it was a slow, slow beat, as if the reality of being in this world, and with me at her side, had caused her to retire to safer environs. What else could have caused this collapse? Provisions had held. We had purification tablets for the water we collected. The weather had been kind. No bites. No ingestion of any of the plant life. We'd survived the peyote or whatever it had been. She was simply overcome; there could be no other explanation for it. She'd hidden the strain from me or perhaps—and more likely, considering the tough woman Little Wing was—not recognized the weight of it herself.

I considered doing it then, even before giving her the chance to wake up, and I'm sure I would have done if I hadn't known that Low Sun was as close as a couple of low suns. I wouldn't let her die out here, and certainly not in this spot among casualties of an unfought war when her people were just over the overlapping horizons.

I set up camp, slept with her away from that place, caring for her as best I could at intervals during a mostly sleepless night. Whenever I checked, her heartbeat continued to beat to other drums. The morrow, always the morrow, I told myself between dreams of a world I had known as a boy. A beautiful place, a place of wonder, joy, a father's laughter, a mother's reprimands, Tony and Tim concealing themselves from me behind walls in hide and seek. Cities, vacations, lakes, mysteries less fierce than fertile. Imagining the places I'd go, the things I'd see. The wonders I knew I'd explore.

And her beat always slow, almost accommodating, comforting in its refusal to submit, to succumb to what lay beyond the wilderness that was our world.

Tomorrow, always tomorrow.

4

"I don't know what ails her, nor whether we can help her," said the chief after they'd helped me unload her from her horse, which I'd carefully led back to this place of blankets and hope. "But we will try. Let's pray for a peaceful sleep for her while doing our best."

"She is not at peace," I said, looking at her where she lay on layers of bedding near the fire. "I failed her."

"We fail no one but ourselves, Will. That is the nature of things. If she was not content, she would not have accompanied you to the end."

"The end . . . you think she will die, then?"

"As far as your road goes, I meant."

"You know what I carry with me, then?"

"No," he said. "Nor do I need to."

It was dusk, the early strains of it, that strange twilight before fires drew their frolicking designs across surfaces, before the forest awakened with the calls of unseen creatures. I'd loved this hour during time spent outside the big city, in Tahoe, but I couldn't help but feel it represented something else today. That such a word, the *hour*, could be used as metaphor of that sort disturbed me. A day's cycle was not a life's cycle, even with its storms. Life abided by no laws other the final one. And there was no morning after.

Or was there?

How I so wanted to know the answer to that question. *We all die,* my father had said when the end was near. *The question is, is that enough? To die?* How had he meant that? That our deeds, our reputations, our merits as men should carry on after we were gone? Enough for what exactly? Nature? The cosmos? It had tasted to me, as a young man and beyond, like more than that. Like there were tasks to complete and dying was simply one of them. I'd speculated he might have meant tasks required *after* this life. But no, he'd been about *this* life, his existential questions started and ended in the mortal realm. The answers, perhaps they were found on the other side of the veil, but they only followed the right manner of asking, here and now. He'd been inviting me to take the vial, hadn't he? He'd left it there for me . . .

Something had driven me to ask that warehouseman if everything was okay in his section after the reorganizing I had ordered, going around the warehouse manager in doing it. I had known he would say something about having uncovered something he wasn't sure about, hadn't I? I'd unconsciously retained a clue my father must have dropped. How else to explain it? I thought of Little Wing's mysterious condition. Compared to the set of circumstances, from past actions to the moment, that had placed that vial in my hands, hers were easily fathomable. The naked difference was that I held the world in the balance while she was part of the world so controlled. And yet . . .

As I looked at her, lying there silently, face neither peaceful nor otherwise as her people prepared for the ritual, I knew it was more than that. It wasn't for herself she slept. It was for me, it was for her tribe, it was for all the world's tribes, regardless of color. She slept, I imagined, not in retreat but rather in warning. A coma of an unconscious making, certainly, but a symbol nonetheless. A picture of how everyone would soon look, beating to the slow drum of passage from this world to the next. Looking at her like this, right now, I felt something change in me. A shift in awareness, perspective. She was somewhere between a life I'd distrusted and an afterlife I had dreamed of, but which maybe I was realizing didn't have the answers I was looking for after all.

"Chief?" I said, interrupting him as he oversaw the preparation of the potions, spells, whatever the vapory things were.

"Yes, Will?"

"Will you do something for me? It is a serious matter—I don't ask lightly."

"Of course, if it is within my power."

"Whatever the outcome, whether she can or cannot be saved, I want to build something to her. A small something, a tribute, a monument, I don't know what to call it. I have something that means something to her, very, very much to her. It is not a gift, not a token or memento or anything like that. It's more about her worldview, her love of . . . no, it's not like that either. It's more earthy than that. This is about me fulfilling a promise I should have made to her. I want the thing enshrined in mud or cement or something that protects it from the elements but doesn't break it. It's fragile. It needs a box, preferably one that will last time, then a hard-drying material around it. It's a dangerous thing; its contents must be allowed time to die. Seasons upon seasons, maybe. I don't want her name on the structure, just a statement, which I'm thinking about the wording of now. And I want this done tonight, before I potentially look in her eyes again. Can you do this for me? It is something extremely significant. The physical thing, it's something that you will guard, keep sacred. Can you do it?"

Low Sun's attention was fully on me, the other business in the capable hands of those whose role it was to heal in their society.

"I will certainly do this. Let me find a container for you. I think I know just the thing. Put your item inside it, we will take matters from there." He paused, looking around the immediate area. "We will erect it at that spot, between those trees, where all can keep an eye it. It will be safe until your seasons have passed. May they pass into other, newer, better seasons, many and continuous."

I nodded, *good*, as he assembled and set a team on the project.

————◆————

I asked them to prepare a bed for me beside her when they were finished for the night. They'd intended to take her inside, as apparently such things were done, but without hesitation agreed this was an appropriate, even better alternative, letting the stars keep our company. It had been a long, intense process due to the focus and passion the healers—and all who joined them, which seemed to me to be every adult in the village—put into it. They invited me to participate, in the deeper way, and I declined, saying I would wait for her on this plane. They understood and left me free to observe, pray to my own gods, touch her, talk to her as the spirit hit me, which was often. No matter what Low Sun said, I had indeed failed her, and would not do so again.

When the last of them had said their goodnights—not the healers, who would come and go throughout the night, but the people who had erected the modest body in which my capsule and its vile business were stored—I could see no more than its silhouette from my place by Little Wing, but I knew they'd carefully inscribed the words that had come to me—not as a revelation, but as a slowly dawning truth—while they were at their work. I'm not sure when the other, the more personal knowledge settled in, but it was sometime in the twilight heralding daybreak. When it did, I felt I could finally sleep, but didn't dare miss her eyes when they opened.

And they did. Most natural thing in the world. They fluttered open, moved around for a moment while she got her bearings, settling finally on me.

The words that came out of her mouth were not what I'd anticipated.

"Where is it?" she said in a coarse whisper.

"Easy, baby. Slow. You've been ill."

"Where *is* it?" Still in a whisper.

"I'm not sure—"

Her eyes alive now, afire. "Did you figure out a way to destroy it? Did you do something we'll regret? Where the fuck *is it*?!"

I reached out a hand, but she flung it away. "Tell me *now*."

"It's been taken care of. Don't worry."

Rising to a sitting position: "Taken care of *how*? Can you place the thing in my hands right now or not?"

I didn't know how to convince her. "You needn't worry—it's not our problem anymore."

Rising to her feet now. "*Problem*? Is that how you suddenly see it? I've finally been shown the way, and *now* you consider it a problem?"

"I . . . I don't understand, Wing."

She glared down at me. In slow, measured words, said, "Take me to it."

"Why?"

"I'm thirsty, that's why. My lungs long for good air after the darkness. Oh, if you only knew what I saw there."

"Tell me. You're still coming out of your sleep. You have to relax, let reality come back . . . "

"Reality? *Ha!*"

"Don't do this, Wing. Everything's going to be okay now."

"Everything is *not* going to be okay! You knew this. You had it right. What happened to *you* while I was away?"

I spread my hands in dismay. "I woke up, baby. It's okay now. What happened?"

To What We Were and Shall Become Again

She stared at me so fiercely, I thought I might be subjected, firsthand, to whatever it was she'd found in the darkness.

"Shall I kick you in the teeth?" she said.

I still lay on my back. I hadn't had time to decide how to address—

She kicked me in the teeth. Blood, after a split second of doubt, filled my mouth, pain my head.

She whirled, looking around her, almost instantly found it. "You put it in a mud castle? Is that what you did?" Shrieking with laughter as she left me writhing and shot off in that direction.

Voices made their way in. Shouts. Cries of alarm. Bodies were suddenly everywhere around me. I rose, spitting blood, found her upon the thing, clawing it and kicking it, screaming at it. Sets of hands on her now, pulling her back, throwing her to the ground, leaving what was left of the words that had been inscribed there. I couldn't see them, but they were there, sharp as they had been in my mind.

To what we were and shall become again.

The rest, the message about the species being united against every obstacle, had been torn away.

BUOYANCY

BEEKMAN HAD ALWAYS wanted to set aside his job and existence and hop a plane for the South of France. He wanted to share a hectare of sand with forty thousand people and no way to get out to the surf without stepping over their sweetly oiled bodies; he wanted to put on a funky shirt and sandals, slip a cocktail umbrella behind his ear and wander around Cannes playing indie film director; and he wanted to buy a necktie off a wiry-haired street vendor and strut into the rococo splendor of the Grand Casino in Monte Carlo flashing his passport like James Bond.

Then he got married.

He got married and did what married men do. He put his fantasies behind him. Whether they would have surfaced again when the relationship grew stale, he would never know, for one day, not two years since he and Belinda had spoken their vows, he found himself divorced—through no fault of his own—and with responsibilities to no one. He didn't have any money, but by God, he didn't have any bills either. Belinda had driven off in their one financial responsibility, leaving him with perhaps the most captivating possession of all—unadulterated freedom.

It took some months for the shock to wear off. But as each day passed, the heartache, the injury to his pride, all the emotions associated with learning Belinda had been having an affair, grew more distant. And the old fantasies woke. They woke refreshed. They woke with aspirations toward realization.

It would never happen unless Beekman made it happen, he knew, so he got on the Internet and reserved two weeks in a mini mobile-home at Camping d'Azur on the Gulf of Saint-Tropez. Third-class accommodations helped offset the cost of the plane ticket, also obtained online with his credit card. Mr. Hobson at the electronics store was a circuit board of nerves when he learned how long his best employee would be gone. Too bad. The Mediterranean called, and that, *mon ami*, was that.

Beekman took a Friday afternoon flight, which would put him in France on Saturday morning. He slept through the last third of the flight,

80

chiefly to escape the smell of the European in the seat beside him. In his dream, he looked up from his blackjack table in the Grand Casino to see Mata Hari, in her gold-cupped showgirl attire, passing through shadows. He followed her into the summer night, and rode with her to the church in which Grace Kelly had been laid to rest. Grace, waiting at the door in a gown and long silk gloves, invited them to see the sea. She led the way inside the church, where she removed three wreaths from her grave, then out a side door and onto a beach. As the three of them ran toward the surf she tossed the wreaths out onto the waves. "Life preservers for ghosts," she laughed as they splashed in the icy-green water.

When the pilot woke him, announcing they would be arriving in Nice at nine fifteen AM, local time, Beekman could still smell the salty sea spray. But of course what he was smelling was the primly arrogant man sitting next to him.

Upon deplaning he picked up euros and his rental car without difficulty. His plan had been to take the autobahn rather than the coastal highway, but he felt so invigorated, he opted for the storied drive after all. As the traffic opened up and the wonders of the French Riviera unfolded before him, he was thrilled he had. For while this had been a dream since he was old enough to know what a passport was, he could not have anticipated the sheer beauty.

From its fixtures to its natural features, the Rivieran coast was glorious in every way. Fruit and olive stands filled the air with their odors. Stucco columns and arches stood against a sea and sky whose clarity had only been hinted at by Camping d'Azur. The fiery volcanic outcrops and cliffs were more stunning than Beekman's imagination could ever have conceived. More than once he stopped to experience the grotesquely beautiful projections with his bare feet, the full focus of his senses. Standing on their cusps looking out upon the broad, uninterrupted expanse of blue-green, the sense of escape swelled like a sail in the stout wind. It was all Beekman could do to tear himself away and proceed on.

Camping d'Azur seemed to have more than its share of business. He waited thirty minutes for the golf cart that would take him to his mini mobile-home. When it came, it came with a complimentary bottle of red wine from the Provence Côte d'Azur, which somehow compensated for the campground's congestion. His mini mobile-home was stuck between two others which apparently had been brought in recently, as (thankfully) they hadn't yet been connected. So, if he wanted to stand naked in his own tin can he could do so without bothering much with the windows. His unit was very much like that—a tin can, with a kitchen/eating area, two small sleeping rooms, a toilet, and an attached wooden patio with plastic furniture. He loved it.

He put the bottle of wine in the little refrigerator, unloaded his suitcase, then made both beds (with sheets he had to rent). He tried the bed closest to the front door, quickly passing out of time for the rest of the afternoon.

———•———

He woke regretting that he hadn't picked up any food to put in the fridge. The camp restaurant was expensive, but he bit the bullet, securing a spot overlooking the bay. On the water, sails shone brightly in the sun. On his plate, grilled chicken exhaled sumptuously when he cut into it.

The night wouldn't arrive until after ten, a fact not under-advertised by the brochures he spread before him after cleaning his plate. As he sipped a wine, browsing, occasionally looking out on the bay, a thought slipped in unchecked. Belinda would have liked it here. The thought was quickly discarded, as she had done him. He felt good about his ability to resist such intrusions. He felt good about the world in general.

Stepping out into a lavish breeze, he walked across the parking area to the camp store. He was disappointed but not surprised to find the store closed. An outside stairway led to a second floor and a small Internet café, which the receptionist had pointed out to him when he'd checked in. Seeing the door was open, he decided he would email his folks (who were glad to see him out there courting life after the divorce, but were worried about the psychology involved) and let them know he had arrived safely. Two of the terminals were in use; a young couple huddled at one, while a man in a bright orange flower-print shirt occupied the other. An attractive, dark-haired woman emerged from a door in back.

"*Oui*, Monsieur?"

He asked the price and she told him three euros would cover the first thirty minutes. She led him to a computer near the corner, three seats down from the man with the beach shirt, then withdrew to the back. Beekman typed in his parents' address and had just gotten absorbed in the letter when the orange flowers appeared in the seat next to him. The guy seemed frustrated as he pointed at Beekman's keyboard, mumbling something in a thick accent.

"I'm sorry. I don't speak French," Beekman told him.

The man's expression changed. "Now look here, mate, I don't speak French either. I heard you talking to the lady in English and I thought you might be able to help me figure out these damned European keyboards, is all."

Beekman felt the heat of his embarrassment around his words. "I was lost in what I was doing. Sorry about that. You're Australian?"

The other regarded him from a face stubbled with the beginnings of a goatee, apparently the only sort of beard he could grow. He looked to be in his late twenties and counting backwards. "Yeah. Tyler's the name. Ty to my mates. I'm not used to these keyboards, you?"

"You know, this is just like the one I have at home. You must have the—"

"That bitch."

There went the self-consciousness. "Maybe she didn't realize you weren't European?"

"Bullshit, we've chatted. I complimented her on her pleasing shape first thing."

"Oh?" Beekman laughed. "Do only Aussies do that?" He extended his hand. "I'm Bart Beekman."

Ty backed up, raising his hands. "Never shake, mate. Too much responsibility. Beekman. Beekman's a damned sportin' name. You on holiday?"

Beekman detected a subtle odor coming off him. It might have been cologne. It might have been his breath.

"Yeah," he said. "You?"

"Business. I was supposed to meet with these cork supply people here at the campground, but they didn't show. The boss sent me all the way from Australia, set me up in a caravan, right? Now here I am in the middle of nowhere and can't get in touch with anybody. The contact number they gave me is no good, the supplier isn't listed in the book and when I phone *my* company I get an out of service message. And now I can't even get to my email because the GODDAMNED keys are all out of whack. I hope the bitch heard me."

The young couple certainly had, staring coolly at both of them, as if they were causing the disturbance together. Meanwhile, alarm bells were going off in Beekman's head. The Australian's spiel had the flavor of some kind of scam. Even if this Ty had no such intentions, his *situation* wasn't the sort you wanted to become involved in, particularly while you were vacationing.

"Look, man," Beekman said. "You can have my computer. I'll be off in a couple minutes."

The muscles of the other's face visibly relaxed. "Really, mate?"

"No sweat," Beekman said as he turned and started typing again.

The other kept talking as Beekman keyed in his message. "Maybe I'll see you around. Buy you a beer or something."

Plan on sleeping in in the morning, then maybe hiking a local "cork trail" I found in a brochure. I'll probably head up to Monaco and Monte Carlo on Monday or Tuesday. Anyhow, gotta go, Mom and Dad. Love you both! I'll check mail next week.

Beekman clicked the send button with emphasis. "Should have another fifteen minutes or so," he said as he stood. "Take it easy, Ty." He inched stealthily toward the escape hatch in back.

"You stayin' here at d'Azur?"

Shit. "I'll be up and down the coast sightseeing, so I won't be around much." The timely appearance of the woman saved him. "Oh, there you are, Madame."

"Mademoiselle," she corrected him, looking past him darkly. Ty was in the process of occupying his seat.

"He had trouble with his keyboard," Beekman said. "I told him he could have mine."

Her eyes shifted back. As she accepted the three euros he owed her, she said under her breath, "Be careful, Monsieur."

He nodded slightly. She might have been the Mata Hari. This might have been one of those transactions made in shadowy places. He might have—

"Wish me luck, mate!"

"Luck." As he exited, the wind met him with eager hands and a scent not unlike the one he had detected on Ty.

———•———

A visit to the stretch of beach that belonged to Camping d'Azur proved brief. The wind off the bay was potent, rattling the racks where the rental equipment was stored, shuffling the thatch roof of the boarded-up Tiki bar. As the sun fell behind the other side of the bay, even the most daring and foolish sailors steered their crafts toward home. Beekman silently wished them the best as the five-minute walk back saw the wind reach yet a higher pitch, the campground's banners fluttering before him in heraldic welcoming.

Nonetheless, when he got back to the relative safety of his mini mobile-home he sat out on the patio with the bottle of wine the campground had provided. Damned if a little wind was going to drive him indoors on his first night in France.

Before he was half through the first glass it became necessary to secure the unused plastic chairs against the deck's railing. The gale took on the color of twilight, and the road that ran alongside Beekman's tin can emptied of evening strollers, the old man who figured to be the last of them chasing his checkered cap through the tumult. But as Beekman clutched his bottle in one hand and his glass in the other, bolting himself down in his newly found and strangely exciting solitude, one more person appeared, the wind sucking her top to her shapely figure, lifting her dark hair like a witch's in flight.

Her eyes were no less ominous when they found him. But as she recognized him, which occurrence was mutual, they lost their glare in favor of a glimmer.

"Monsieur," she said, approaching.

"Mademoiselle. What are you doing wandering around in a windstorm?"

"I am returning home."

"Oh, you live here at the campground?"

She reached the railing, nodding as she said over it, "I was not able to explain about the man."

He held up the bottle. "If you'd care to join me . . . ?"

She looked around, her hair a swirling halo to match her surroundings. "Tonight is perhaps not the night for drinking wine outside . . . ?"

"Come inside, then."

There was an awkward moment as the uncertainty arced between them; then she said, "Okay," and stepped around to the deck's gate. He opened it for her with the hand that held the bottle. The wineglass he clutched against his chest, lest it be snatched away to Oz.

Inside, he offered her a seat at the only place he had—the dining table. She sat on the bench side, and he poured her a glass of the Côte d'Azur before occupying the chair across from her. "Is it like this often?" he said, with an inclusive gesture. The seams of the structure whined as if in response.

"Sometimes." She sipped the wine, lips and eyes taking on its cast in the overtly artificial light. She seemed to be contemplating her approach to the item at hand, but then, it might as easily have been her manner.

"Do you have a name?" he said.

While her smile didn't radiate warmth, it did have that potential. "Danielle."

"I'm Bart."

"Beekman," she said, assuming an accent. "'Damned sportin' name, mate.'"

He laughed. "You heard that, did you?"

"It wasn't difficult. Aside from his obnoxious voice, the walls are rather thin. My father designed the place with computers, not loudmouths, in mind."

"Does your family have interest in the campground?"

"My parents are hosts. I've lived here all my life."

"Lucky you," he said, raising his glass.

She met it with a soft clink. "But we're talking about Tyler."

"Tyler. You sound as though you know him."

She turned the fluid in her glass. "Tonight was the third time I have seen him. It was his second visit to the café. He came in last night—wearing that same loud orange shirt—when I was about to close. I hadn't had a customer for hours, and had opened a bottle of wine and put on music, thinking the rest of the evening belonged to me. Then Tyler showed up with his tale of woe and I gave him a terminal. I did not like him from his very first words to me, which were crude and insulting, but the café was officially open and he seemed the type to complain to the office."

She wet her lips again with the wine before going on. "He rambled about his predicament while I watched the clock. I let him use the computer until ten minutes after closing time and then told him he would have to leave. He gave up the terminal, but began flirting with me, asking if he could have some of my wine. He worked in the wine industry, he said, and he enjoyed sampling. As he talked he wandered over to where the bottle sat. I told him he could find a bottle of that very rosé at the camp store in the morning. He asked if he could at least sniff the cork, to which I flatly replied, 'No; please leave.' He did . . . but not without the cork."

She was interrupted by a violent shudder through the tin can, followed by the light's flickering. For a moment they were caught in some twilit other-region, Danielle's dark features becoming even more pronounced in the layers of gray. Beekman extended one hand, palm up, wanting the microfilm while the shadows reigned. Instead, she put her hand in it, and the light overhead brightened intensely. Then a second gust of wind seized the mini mobile-home and the light failed and flourished, failed and flourished, leaving him wondering if her hand had ever been there at all.

"It's not usually this bad," she said, looking around them as the light grew steady again.

"The cork," Beekman said. "What did you mean about the cork?"

"Yes," she said, swallowing the rest of her wine. "I didn't realize it until after he was gone, but he had taken the cork."

"He stole it?" Beekman said as he refreshed her glass. "Weird. Do you think he did it to piss you off?"

"No. I think he has a fixation with cork."

He hesitated in the act of putting the cork top back in the wine bottle. "Really."

"I said I have seen him on three separate occasions. The second time was this morning, at the campground pool, which I walk by every day on my way to work. On one side there is a break in the hedges, where you can look through the fence directly on the pool. Tyler was in the water—rather *on* the water, floating on his back, perfectly still. So still that I could not help but stare. I had no idea he was watching me, as his eyes appeared to be closed, but after a few seconds he said, 'See anything you like?' I asked him how he did it, how he floated so that no part of his body dipped below the surface and without even causing a ripple. 'Cork,' he said. 'Cork and technique, but mostly cork.' I thought he was mocking me, referring to the cork he had stolen. But then he said, 'Was cork that got me here, and cork that'll see me home.'" She stopped to let that sink in.

"I begin to see your concern."

"Yes. But the worst is to come. Tonight, after you left, he did the strangest thing of all. I had to close the door behind you because of the

86

wind. When the young couple left, the door flung out of the man's hand, slamming against the stop. Tyler jumped up, telling me to hold his computer. I asked him what was going on and he told me this was an opportunity to further test his . . . buoyancy. My English is good, but I had to dig for the meaning of that word. He ran out the door and down the stairs, and suddenly I found myself alone and babysitting his computer. You mustn't think ill of me. It was there, and Tyler . . . well, he is no standard cake."

Beekman almost lost the wine in his mouth. "No, I guess not. Go on."

"He had accessed a reply message from his boss. Basically, it said that now he could have all the cork he wanted, rather than continuing to steal from the company's supply. If he wanted a ticket home he could try the embassy in Nice, but don't come back to work. I quickly scrolled down to the original message, where Tyler accused his employer of stranding him here under the pretext of meeting with a potential cork supplier. That is a sad circumstance, to be certain, but Bart, can we blame his employer? Let me tell you what I found when I finished the message and stepped outside to see if he was out there. He was standing in the parking lot with his arms wide, while the wind actually appeared to be blowing him backwards. His feet moved in quick steps but he seemed to be using them only for balance, as though . . . as though he were a mime, *pretending* to be blown backwards, only there was something unreal about it at the same time. He seemed to come off the ground sometimes. It unnerved me."

Beekman was in the process of finding his words when the storm made its presence known again. The light and shadows formed a phantasmagoria. Skin, then eyes made contact before the effects fled on reluctant wings from a precarious normalcy. Beekman tilted the wine bottle on its base, mourning its depleted contents.

"I don't need more," she said.

Again the tin can trembled. Again, the lantern-show, dissolving in a darkness that concealed only some of Mata Hari's secrets as she leaned across the table, eyes closed, all the rest of her open to the untamed night.

He accepted her mouth, and the lights stayed out while the storm excelled till dawn.

———•———

Bart Beekman's Rivieran fantasies also included waking up in the arms of a sexy Frenchwoman, a destiny for which he would not have been willing to use his credit card. When he opened his eyes that morning, reality bathed him in silken petals. The calm was an aftermath, bringing back the tumultuous night by stark contrast. Sunshine poured in through the translucent curtains, bathing the body that lay beside him. Her accent was a mist on Côte d'Azur vineyards as she smiled at him and said, "Morning."

"Morning," he returned. And in his most disinterested voice: "Do you have to go to work today?"

"Today is Sunday."

He refrained from crying out with joy. "Then maybe you will come with me on a hike."

"I like hiking," she said. "But not until we're finished here." She wrapped her legs around him and the storm returned on its own.

She went home to shower and change and met him at the camp store, where he picked up ninety euros' worth of food and drink (including the rosé she had denied Ty). They sat on his patio and ate omelettes, compliments of Danielle. When he asked her how a woman so attractive could make a dish so delicious, he was delighted to see a blush. For if Frenchwomen blushed, then *all* of his fantasies might come alive. That cocktail umbrella behind his ear might be a pen in disguise, ready to tend to the tax issues connected with his enormous winnings at the Grand Casino.

Though the trail was less than five kilometers from the campground, Danielle had never been there. She had seen the brochure in the office, but the cork oaks and fresh goat's cheese and other highlights of the loop were for tourists. Cork oaks were everywhere, and no novelty to locals; goat's cheese was for people who couldn't afford the alternative; and rock formations were covered by the Verdon canyon and the coastal drive. The idea of doing the trail *with him*, however, had much appeal. On those words he was in paradise, thank you Belinda for your indiscretions.

They arrived to an empty parking area, which suited them fine, and started up the hill toward the spot that looked most intriguing—an overlook with a view of the Gulf of Saint-Tropez—with the sun at their backs. The vegetation was sparse on the dusty hillside, loose shingles of slate slipping under their shoes as they climbed. Before they reached the crest, a wooden sign appeared, pointing to the left and a ramshackle farmhouse and barn, where the goat's cheese could be sampled. She laughed when he tried to goad her into going, holding her ground valiantly. He said, "But we've got to have some kind of snack while we're up here." The less than innocuous remark brought whispers in his ear.

At the overlook, with the Gulf stretching in shimmering splendor below them, they crawled out of their shorts and made love on the rock. Moans which had been drowned by the storm last night and stifled by the proximity of vacationing families this morning drew the cries of a bird circling overhead—as if they had already attained the afterlife. When they were done, they sat on the edge of the outcrop, naked, and wondered in contented smiles over whether the goat farmers had heard them. They didn't care. There was nowhere to be. Sails of every color formed a scattered mosaic beneath a sky as *azur* as advertised. The air had a flavor to it that spoke to the soul. It would have been easy to believe that the next state had indeed been attained, except the scent that teased at their senses also teased at their memories.

It was she who said it, to his surprise. "The fragrance—do you smell it—it reminds me of Tyler."

"Me too. It smells like wood."

"Yes. I don't know that I made the connection before, but I think that is exactly what it is."

The wind shifted and the scent left them. Beekman rose, offering his hand to her. "Come on, let's hike."

They shed the distraction and donned their clothes. The downgrade was almost as steep as the slope they had climbed, forcing care as they moved. This side of the hill had more vegetation. Squat trees dotted the slope, becoming more abundant as they neared a stream below. Beekman knew instinctively, and independent of the aroma that returned with force at the valley floor, that these were cork oaks. The bridge that appeared before them seemed to offer the way to that rich experience. A look between them asked if either was particularly ready. As they crossed the wooden span in spite of their instincts, the answer revealed itself.

Ty, in his famed orange shirt, sat on the ground beneath a particularly robust tree, pocketknife in hand, bloated beyond function. The tree's bark had been cut away in chunks, one of which protruded from Ty's mouth, several others of which lay about him like casualties. It was clear what had gone on, but the imagination was its own agent when it came to what his delusion hoped to gain him. Something on the air hinted at *that,* too, and they didn't know if they liked its taste, offering him one and only one chance to ride back with them; and pretending not to notice when he spluttered bits of cork in response, saying, "Was cork that got me here . . . "

They left him, a swollen heap, and returned to the car. Beekman was almost relieved that it was simply a matter of insanity and not a more sinister projection upon the rational world. Danielle wanted to believe that, and went through the motions with Beekman, chatting with him about the scenery as they drove back to the campground, dining with him on his patio without mentioning Tyler, watching him open a bottle of claret without staring at the cork. But as she was about to take the first sip, she suddenly turned to him and said, "Come with me to the office."

"Now? Why?"

"I want to look at the tide tables."

"The tide—?"

"Come." She set her glass down, rose, and stepped off the deck. He followed without questioning her further, experiencing the first stirrings of a peculiar ambivalence as the prospect evolved out of shadows already present.

The tables were posted against the glass. She left a print where she marked the item that mattered. As he memorized the time, his nerve endings hummed at a low steady frequency, the sense of wonder inescapable. On their way back he found himself looking among his fellow campers for any patch of orange, any face among theirs that glowed with attitude. Somehow the not finding him was much better, much more appropriate to the magical land of his fantasies. As they arrived at the tin can the red Bordeaux sat there waiting for them, afire in the low sun. Beekman drank deeply of his.

Except to go the bathroom or the refrigerator, they remained where they sat for the rest of the evening, and beyond. The sky filled with stars while they finished their second bottle; people retired to their caravans and campers and tents; the night took on a beautiful reddish cast. Then, at last, it was time. She held his hand as they went, and that indefinable secondary scent that had teased their reasoning as they looked upon the bloated Tyler now returned, though with a name. It had always had a name for Beekman, first through his imagination, and then through Belinda, as she presented it to him on a plate. *Freedom* was that name, and the Riviera reeked deliriously of it.

The band of beach left by low tide swirled with the depressions in the sand. Over the bay the sky was brilliant with stars. They spotted him immediately, out beyond the shining, murmuring surf, bobbing gently on the icy-red waves. Their feet sank as they walked out into the water, and for a moment, just a moment, they thought they saw him raise his head and wave. But it might have been an illusion. Who could say?

END OF THE LINE

"WHERE DO YOU want to go, sir?" the lady repeated in a tone of perturbation. Her face threatened to follow her voice, forgoing the stark and perfect emptiness that set it apart from all the Edvard Munch expressions in this place.

Brian Culligan looked up once more at the wall, where a diagram of the area's rail system was displayed. Where was he, anyway? Somewhere along the Luxembourg border, at the train station of a sizable village surrounding an impressive medieval fortress. The word *Deutschebahn* was printed above the diagram, verifying that this was the German side of the river separating the two countries.

"How about there?" he said, knowing she could not see where he was pointing. "The main line branches off to follow a smaller river—the Akyll. It ends at a village named Esch. What's there?"

"Nothing," she said.

"That's where I want to be." The other rail paths exceeded the map's edges, suggesting the tracks would carry him on forever, a fugitive in infinity. Esch was an end, at least for one night.

She sold him a ticket, letting her manner show the blatant contempt that her face must not, lest her own certain insanity be exposed. As he stepped away from the counter, a woman twice his age stepped up. The *Guten Tag* she received from the mask was no less cold than the one he had gotten.

The train was waiting at platform three, artsy graffiti sprayed across the side of it. He was beginning to know the trains, which car best suited him, where the toilets were, when to expect the conductor. How long had it been? Five, six months? He had survived the winter now. The numbness of winter carried over, but that was good. He stepped on the grate and into the car, hating the smell of smoke that accosted him, yet lighting up just the same. This was his car. Six years of not smoking—the length of his marriage—gone down the drain. It had been a comfort that they'd had Camels over here. He had never noticed on the trips he and Nina had made to Europe.

There were two people at the head of the car—fortyish like himself, smoking like himself—otherwise it was empty. Culligan sat in back by the window, far from faces. He had his own to keep him company, echoed in the glass, pallid as the day outside. A glance at his watch told him it was ten till three, about departure time. As he put his head back and closed his eyes, a voice came over the intercom verifying what train they were on, where they were going, that they were all visages from Munch's painting, *Anxiety*. The engineer himself would fit that description, delivering folks day after day to their fates.

The train began to move. The conductor appeared sooner than he normally did. Culligan heard the words before the man addressed the couple at the front: *Fahrkarte, bitte*. He had his own ticket ready when the man arrived. The conductor examined it, never making eye contact in his urgency and self-importance, moving on as if there were someplace to go. It occurred to Culligan that they were all as damned as he was.

The train being a local, there would be several stops. He extinguished his cigarette and closed his eyes again, desiring to rest for once without being visited by the events of the day his world met its apocalypse.

———•———

When he stepped into the bathroom that morning of his departure for Orlando, Nina had it steamed up nicely, like they both liked it. Her figure moved like verse behind the shower curtain as she shaved her legs. He knew she was waiting on him, or else both the window and door wouldn't have been closed, allowing the room to turn into a steam bath. They had a sauna, but there was something about the act of getting dirty while getting clean that made the shower so attractive. Warning her in his deepest, sexiest voice, he let his robe drop to the floor and entered.

Beneath the ever present yearning sadness, her blue eyes seemed to express something more immediate as she took his hands in hers. A hope, perhaps? That they were a normal couple about to have an encounter in the shower? She used that word normal as if it were a height to aspire to. It wasn't enough to have a life of leisure and luxury. She wanted some intangible thing he had some time ago quit trying to provide. As to their active physical relationship, it seemed the more intense the encounter, the more sorrowful she was afterwards. And yet if anything, her ability to resist had decreased over the five and a half years of their marriage.

He pulled her close, lightly kissing her neck. But that was as far as he would go before brushing his teeth. He could smell mint toothpaste on her. He could taste last night's Scotch on himself. How much it mattered to her, he didn't know, but he prided himself on being the man a woman desired. He reached behind her for the brush hanging in the rack on the tile wall. They always brushed their teeth in the shower. They shaved in the shower.

They had sex in the shower. It was a protected area; reality was not welcome.

As he cleaned his teeth, she went back to shaving her legs. He watched her, the elegant curve of her calf, her beautiful hands, her toes, and she smiled at the caress of his eyes. She could have her choice of men. Yet she stayed. He was fairly certain she suspected his affairs. Yet she stayed. He sometimes wished he had never asked her to marry him. Such a waste.

"Have you flossed?" he asked.

She shook her head, gracefully raking the last of the shaving cream off her leg and rinsing the razor in the tight jet of water.

"You are a goddess, Nina," he told her as he pulled the dental floss from its plastic dispenser.

She stopped him with her hand as he was about to clip the string. "Pull some more of it out. Let's do it together, with the same length of floss."

———•———

He opened his eyes seconds before the voice announced they were arriving at Griegsheim. A glance at the front of the car revealed the couple had gotten off at one of the previous two stops. Out the window Griegsheim was a dreary place, no romance for all its age and architecture. A lone elderly gentleman boarded, taking a seat near the front.

Culligan lit another cigarette. The ember, as he pulled on it, was Nina's passion.

———•———

"Length?" he said suggestively, placing his hand on her hip and pulling her against him. For a moment he lost himself in the touch of her flesh, the sound of her drawing a breath. Then he gently released her, pulling more floss from the dispenser before clipping it. He let the end of the string hang from his fingers, pulling it lightly over the mound of her breast, her neck, her cheek. She stuck out her tongue to take it in her mouth. He found the other end, wrapping it around his finger. He waited on her lead, following suit when she actually began using the floss in the way it was supposed to be used. They watched each other as they worked the string between their teeth, twirling the used line around their forefingers, steadily pulling out the slack.

As the length of floss grew less and less limp, they were forced to move closer together. She laughed as an abrupt movement on his part caused the string to go taut. She pulled it from her mouth, showing him the blood. He took her hand in his and licked the crimson saliva from her finger, eliciting a soft "mmm" from her lips. His mouth fell on hers and she joined him in the sucking hunger, their eager groping fingers becoming entangled in the twine.

———⸱———

Culligan woke to the face of the conductor. The train was not moving. A smell hung in the air. The conductor's eyes led him to the thigh of his jeans and a blackened hole the size of a dime. The cigarette which had caused it had fallen, died somewhere on the metal floor. The conductor's mouth spouted a stream of German, at the center of it the declaration that this was the end of the line. When Culligan rose, the face retreated. He grabbed his pack and threw it over his shoulder. Another cigarette lit easily. He pulled hard—the ember capturing a different side to Nina's passion for one penetrating moment—then he moved to the door, stepping out into the colorless April afternoon.

The station and village stood in front of him, while a mist obscured the opposite side of the tracks, the sound of its rushing source, the Akyll, merging with that of the train. An iron gate opened onto the broad slab of cement separating the tracks from the station. As he grasped its handle, aware of the slight vibration of the train pulling away, he experienced the momentary sensation of being on the verge of a separate reality, one ruled by a different set of physics. A scan of his surroundings uncovered no immediate sensory evidence to support the feeling, and it dissolved, leaving the cold iron in his hand the prominent impression among the myriad his brain processed.

The station was constructed of red stone blocks, its decorative arches done in bricks. A sign above the door read: *Esch a.d. Akyll.* The elderly man who had boarded at Griegsheim sat on a bench against the wall, watching Culligan walk across the platform. To the right of the station stood houses partially obscured by trees. Beyond, staggered roofs protruded from a hillside forested in firs. The phantom sun hovered just above the crest of the hill, a headlight trapped in impervious fog.

"Hallo," Brian said as he neared the fellow.

The man ignored the greeting, eyes peering out from rims of wrinkly flesh, mouth open as if in a last gasp for life. Culligan considered using one of the cardboard conversational phrases out of the language guide buried in his pack, but decided it wouldn't do any good. If he hadn't witnessed this same skeletal body in these same worn overalls board the train, he would have concluded a statue occupied the bench.

He was about to enter the station when he caught movement in his peripheral vision. The strange sensation returned as his glance landed on the barefooted figure that had emerged from the end of the building. In tee shirt and what resembled pajama bottoms, the man was long-limbed and sinuous in his movements, characteristics doubtless exaggerated by the bizarre balletic dance he was engaged in. Culligan's initial impression

94

was that he was mentally slow, but the longer he observed the gracefulness and fluidity with which the man glided over the cement, his elongated arms grasping at the heavens, the more convinced he was of the need to amend that opinion. The poetry he witnessed was more akin to madness, liquid and archetypal.

A brief glance at the bench revealed that the old man's eyes were still firmly locked on him, as if to remind him that he was the strange one here. He returned his gaze to the ballet artist, who now floated past in his incessant bid to draw down the moon right out of the afternoon sky. Culligan watched him till he passed out of sight around the opposite end of the building. Standing there looking at empty spaces, the weird sensation dulled into slag indistinguishable from his own personal detachment. He stamped out his smoke and entered the station.

In the starkness emphasized by scattered magazines and cigarette butts, he neglected the face on the other side of the ticket window in favor of the sign pointing to the bar. He had found that the locals used the bars at the *Bahnhofs* more than the travelers did, perhaps seeking the sense of randomness and anonymity. It didn't seem to matter whether the station was on the way to somewhere or at a cul-de-sac like Esch. Maybe the bellow of the incoming train reminded people that their village wasn't the last extent of the world.

Today was no different. One glance proved that these fixtures were not travelers. Five people, including the barkeep, occupied the dim, smoky den. Their heads turned in unison as the door closed behind him, leaving him standing there in judgement. Interestingly, the changes that came to the court's thematically stoical aspects seemed different this time, less subtle, momentarily reviving the spent hope in Culligan that one of them would know him somehow, be able to provide the answer to his converging pain and meaninglessness. Alas, among the ranks of the lost the glorious simplicity of existence overcame all such diversions.

The bartender appeared to be in her fifties, a handsome woman with a discernible air of arrogance about her. She made it clear by her expression that she wasn't at all impressed by Culligan. The two men sitting at the bar, over the half-century mark themselves, were decidedly less aloof, their faces blooming with curiosity as they eyed him. The other two customers, a younger couple, sat at a table, expressions incubating in the sphere of a candle that threw useless flickers over amber beers. Culligan dropped his pack by the legs of the nearest stool as he perched there, resting his arms on the bar.

The man two stools down wasted no time in greeting him with a hearty "*Prost*, stranger!" The face of the fellow sitting beyond tried to get around the beer the first man held up in salute. Culligan thought the use of the word *stranger* odd, as he was fairly sure that wasn't the German way of saying it. Maybe it was one of those borrowed expressions. He nodded to them.

The barkeep placed a coaster in front of him and in a voice deep and stately asked what she could get him.

"Scotch," he said, looking her in the eye. Filtered lights above the bar provided what illumination there was. Her features were not softened by it.

As she turned to pour the drink, the two men at the bar continued to be fascinated by the stranger in their midst, their faces blending into one, grinning spectacularly as it gazed back at him. The realization that they were twins struck Culligan as his drink appeared in front of him, a single pebble of ice floating in the liquid. Chuckling, he extended his glass to his identical barmates. The three vessels met, and the barkeep exhaled poison molecules that dissipated harmlessly in the air as she concealed herself behind a newspaper. Culligan grimaced as he took the liquor in, warm to the mouth, hot to the throat and gut.

In English the man who had greeted him asked where he was coming from. The man's graying hair retreated from a distinguished brow. His eyes were a steely discerning blue, almost in contradiction to the warm humor surrounding them.

It didn't surprise Culligan that his origins might bleed through—indeed it had happened on several occasions already—but when only the one word, *Scotch*, had been spoken?

"Well," he said, "I don't really have a *from* point. I'm just traveling around the continent." He paused before adding: "So how did you know?"

The other laughed. "That you are American? The flashy hiking boots were a hint. Then your choice of drinks. I can honestly say that I have never seen that bottle move from its spot back there."

Culligan could accept that explanation, though he was amazed there was any flash left to his hiking boots after a winter of wandering. "Where did you pick up your English?" he said. "It's excellent."

"My wife is British. Once she made me work on the *th* sound for two hours without rest."

"She didn't."

"You haven't met my Mildred. My name is Brecken. Karl. My brother is Klaus. He speaks very little English."

"Brian Culligan. Pleased to meet you both." He gripped their hands in turn.

"This is an odd place to travel *to*," Karl said. "What brought you to Esch, of all the villages on the map? Surely you know this is a dead end."

The question again. It took all forms, but the integrity of it remained forever intact: What are you doing *here*?

While he could never be totally forthcoming in answering that question, a sense of the potential clarity in this random conversation caused him to be more open than he normally would. "I rest better when I'm at the farthest point."

Karl studied him a protracted moment, his brother's face hovering just behind, a reflection upon the edges of reason. The barkeep emerged from behind her paper to apprise herself of the goings on, then sank again beneath the crisp rustle. A jingle of electronic notes sounded from the back of the den, where the couple had begun playing a slot machine. Her hand cupped the back of his head as he fed euros into the contraption's hungry mouth.

Karl turned and spoke in the native tongue to his brother, whose eyes remained on Brian. Brian took another swallow of his now iceless drink before Karl turned back to him.

"We're glad to have you, Brian Culligan. There is only one *Gästezimmer* in the village, as the only overnighters we get are hikers passing through—and then rarely. It happens to belong to my brother and me. You are certainly welcome to it, but before you decide to stay, shall I tell you how I met my wife?"

Brian stared back at him. "You would discourage me from staying?"

"I did not say that. But let me be candid and tell you that for even our own residents, there is little rest here in Esch."

Brian finished his drink and requested another. She didn't even bother with the ice this time, pouring with a contemptuousness to rival that of the woman who had sold Culligan the ticket to this place. Only this time, the contempt wasn't spurred by his *lack* of a compass.

"Yes, tell me how you met your wife, Karl."

"Come, let's sit by the window over there," Karl said.

Picking up his pack, Culligan followed the two of them to a booth with a rather morose view of the village. Beyond an empty parking area, below dwellings whose windows somehow did not convey spring, a nun worked on a patch of decrepit flowers.

"She hasn't performed a nun's duties for some time, though she wears the habit," said Karl. "She's like the village itself, not the same as before."

"What do you mean?" said Culligan.

Before the other had a chance to elaborate, the ballet artist came into view, pulling at the sky as if on the ropes of a bell. The nun looked up from her pruning, demeanor instantly changing. She began shouting at the man, flailing and brandishing her shears. As he glided past in seeming obliviousness to her outburst, she lunged at him with the tool. He deftly sidestepped her and she fell clumsily to her knees, obviously suffering no serious injury as she continued to hurl her complaints at him. To add to the performance, an eerie, woeful sound rose in the background, its source somewhere in the interior of the village, a street or two away. Karl and Klaus looked at each other as it grew by undulations to an awful continuous wailing. A woman's voice, Culligan thought. He found himself pulled into its core of suffering, all too palpable to him. Dogs began to howl, taking up the song from one corner of the village to the other.

This dark festival of the senses was so sudden and engrossing that the reaction of the young man from the slot machine caught Culligan totally off guard. The flash of motion as the fellow threw himself across the bench in the next booth was a split-second precursor to his violent assault of fist and voice on the window and the show it afforded. The barkeep, thoroughly roused from the dead leaves of her communion with the world, fired off a litany of obscenities at the young man.

Karl's voice was a breeze in a windstorm, but Culligan's ears, like the rest of his senses, were alert to any rationalization for what went on. "The event behind all this is the same event that led to my traveling to England and meeting my wife," he said. "Come, let's go to my house. You may or may not wish to stay when you've learned about our village, but at least there we can speak in peace."

The word *event* echoed in Culligan's mind as they passed the livid face of the barkeep charging in the other direction. He looked back to see her advance intercepted by the young woman arriving to the defense of her partner. Weirdly, the image which prevailed, as Culligan followed the others out into the hall, was that of a few moments earlier, when the young woman cupped the back of the young man's head as if to keep it from lolling on its stem.

In the corridor the oddities did not falter, though the commotions outside and in the bar were now tempered by solid walls. The station's entrance was only a few meters from the bar door, but that distance was interrupted. The elderly man from the bench leaned against the wall, letting his mouth gape while the woman Culligan recognized from the ticket window shined a penlight in his throat. When she saw Culligan, she turned the narrow beam on his face.

"*Sie kamen mit den Zug*," she said. "*Haben Sie mein Hans gesehen?*"

He looked at Karl.

"You came in on the train, she says. She wants to know if you've seen her husband, Hans."

Brian looked from Karl to the woman, back again. "This whole village is . . . " He let it fade, not knowing where to go from there. In the ensuing pause the wails and howls outside seemed to grow even fainter. The disturbance in the bar had died down as well.

The woman beckoned him with a finger. In another reality he might have found her a good-looking woman, with her cropped hair and pouty lips, but now she was only a door that he did not wish to look behind.

"She's harmless," said Karl. "Best to appease her, then we'll be on our way."

Culligan didn't know what he expected as he approached the woman, clutching the strap of his pack, a dubious security. One thing he did not expect was to be invited to peer into the throat of the old man. The stench that escaped the fellow had the flavor, however faint, of blood, causing Culligan to release air between his teeth. "What exactly does she want?" he implored Karl. He noticed as he asked the question that Klaus was looking at the gaping hole in the old man's face with something more than disgust.

"It's my Mildred's theory that the throat, the inside of the mouth, the moistness and redness of the gums reminds her of the day she lost her husband."

The day she lost her husband.

"Tell her I can't help her." His words sounded to his ears like they were spoken from inside a drum.

Karl regarded him a moment before turning to her. He emphasized as he spoke, as if to convince her of the fact.

She issued a long mournful moan, exploring Culligan's face with her light. Her free hand came forward to grasp his face. He peered into eyes gray and desolate as she squeezed open his mouth. The light stung like Scotch in his throat and he felt she could see down to the very truth devouring him from within. Then she let go, shoving him away as though he were useless to her.

"Come," Karl said, moving to the door. As he reached for the handle, Culligan clutched his arm.

"But she seemed to be looking for something."

"Her husband. She . . . associates." He pushed open the door onto the parking lot.

The wailing had quit. The ballet artist was nowhere to be seen and the nun had returned to her flowers. The sharp sounds of the shears accompanied the remnants of the dogs' chorus, scattered woofs and whines failing with the afternoon. The breath of the Akyll, expanding over the tracks as if conjured, accentuated the parking lot's desolateness.

The village unfurled before them, closely resembling the last village Culligan had visited, and the one before that, and the one before that. Roofs rose dark and steep, their chimneys releasing the occasional tendril of smoke in anticipation of another cool night. A few people were out, attending to whatever tasks their (Saturday? Sunday?) afternoon called for. Brian endured the strong sense of rehearsing for something that had already happened. He looked from brother to brother, wondering did they somehow know the password out of damnation.

The church bell, in its house of stone, rang as they passed. Culligan's watch said 4:58. Slow. *Kirchstrasse* connected to *Hauptstrasse* and halfway down the ensuing block stood their destination, Karl pointing out the shaded house in advance. Brian noticed the absence of a *Zimmer frei* sign but said nothing, having witnessed firsthand why folk would choose to be entertained elsewhere. As they reached the yard, movement in a second-floor window across the street drew Culligan's eye.

A woman hovered there, an apparition in her paleness, watchful.

"Who is she?" he asked, not knowing why the answer should matter to him.

"That is our Christina," Karl said. He gestured. "Come inside."

The tiled, fan-shaped area inside the front door might well have once served as a lobby. In its center a set of stairs with a carved balustrade ascended to the second floor, where Karl informed Brian the guest room was. A door to the left of the entrance hall led into a dining room with a wide window looking across the front yard. As they sat at a circular wooden table, paying silent homage to the shiny elephantine ashtray resting on the polished surface, it dawned on Brian that he hadn't smoked since before the bar. He fished for a cigarette, found he had been carrying an empty package. Klaus provided one out of his stock. It was wrapped in brown paper and tasted like it smelled.

Karl brought three bottles from the kitchen. "Mildred might have come up with a more suitable alternative for a Scotch drinker, but she isn't in at present. Being German, I simply don't know any refreshment but beer." Culligan found his humor, if such it was, uninspiring. The beer was rich, heavy, it too tasting like it smelled.

"So what did you mean about the lady at the station?" he asked as he set it down, tapped ashes into the grotesque receptacle. "You said she associates."

Karl nodded. "She does indeed. In her mind her husband might have been eaten just like the stuff that fell from the sky."

Stuff that fell from the sky. "What does that mean?"

Karl motioned Klaus, who produced another cigarette, tossing it to his brother across the table. Karl appeared to savor its slightly clove-like flavor before speaking through his exhalation. "Three and a half years ago, on a day much like today—gray, hazy, sunless—an amazing, quite fantastic thing happened here in Esch. I was at my office when it did, so I can only relate what others, including my brother, have described to me. Klaus and I are both doctors. At the time I had a general practice in Bitburg. Klaus worked at the hospital in Trier. He is a surgeon. That day he was on call. He happened to be mowing the front lawn when the stuff began to fall.

"*Red rain*, Mildred refers to it, but it's actually a viscous substance, almost like blood mixed with oil. Esch was not the first place in the world to have experienced the phenomenon. From the Internet I learned of at least two other instances. Mildred, when I sought her out, cited ten more. That is her specialty, you see. She's a parapsychologist, widely known in the field, which is how I came to seek her out. When she heard what I'm telling you now, she dropped everything and came.

"The Red Rain apparently started with a splotch here and there, as though birds had feasted in a patch of red berries and now were depositing their waste on Esch. This occasional, random 'precipitation' went on for a short while, then the whole sky opened up. The stuff fell in a torrent for five minutes or so, then quit entirely. Had people left it alone, it might have done no harm. In fact, in the reports from elsewhere in the world, the stuff fell and then it dried up or washed away, in some cases was consumed by animals, and that was the end of it. Not so here. In Esch, during its fall and even after the fact, *people* ingested it. Not just a few people, but everyone. Evidently, they couldn't help themselves. The compulsion overwhelmed them." He paused, watching Culligan as he took a long pull from his beer.

Culligan stared back, jaw slack, still feeling the penlight's probe, heat on his moist, red tissue.

"The whole village," Karl continued, "went mad. When I arrived home from work, the bedlam was still in full blossom. I'll not waste your time with the descriptions, but know that it was far worse than what you witnessed today. Nearly everyone got through it without serious physical injury, but the mental effects lingered, and continue to linger in one form or another among all who partook of the substance. The kind of incident you witnessed today is fairly common in Esch, although it has been some time since Christina has acted up like that."

Culligan followed his gaze to the window and its view of the house across the street. The second-floor rectangle from which the girl had looked was obscured by the foliage of a tree.

He found Karl's eye. "You mean the girl over there was the source of that . . . *anguish*?"

"You cannot know how appropriate that word," Karl said.

Culligan spotted someone walking along the sidewalk on the other side of the street. He rose and went to the window, identifying the woman as she turned to walk up the path to the house opposite.

"That's the ticket lady from the station. Is Christina related to her?"

"Her daughter," said Karl.

He wouldn't have thought the lady with the cropped hair and pouty lips old enough to have a daughter that age. "How old is Christina?" he asked.

"Let's see, she would be twenty-one. She was not yet eighteen when the Red Rain fell."

As the lady entered the house, Culligan's attention was drawn to a car approaching from the left. The dark Mercedes pulled into Karl's drive. It proved to be his wife returning from her errands.

Mildred was a merry woman, or at least maintained that façade: short of stature, well-fed, strangely agreeable with life in spite of experiencing it within the invisible walls of the loony bin that was Esch. After introducing her to their guest, her husband pulled a chair for her and filled her in on the discussion to that point. Culligan found himself wondering why she would smile knowing Esch lay stretched across a block for a stranger's scrutiny. But it wasn't like that, somehow. It wasn't a secret if you weren't an outsider. How they saw into his soul, he could not say. At this party perhaps all masks were transparent.

She reacted when Karl told her about Christina's episode. She said it wasn't like Christina to express herself during the daylight hours, particularly when it hadn't been invoked. Culligan thought of the activity that had preceded the girls' eerie lamentation, the clash of the nun and the ballet artist, and he wondered what constituted invoking. Mildred turned to him, feeling the need to clench her fist by way of emphasis as she spoke. "There is a logic, an internal logic about it all. Esch's madness is not madness as you think of it. There is an exact point in time and space from which it sprang. Everything else is like the mechanism of a clock working off the instant when it was set in motion."

Brian nodded. "The Red Rain."

She shook her head. "No. You don't follow me. The Red Rain is a result. It is a manifestation of the guilt and anguish suffered by one particular person. I suspect that is the case in every instance of Red Rain, only to various, lesser degrees. For some reason, in this case the pain following the crime was so perfect that everyone, subconsciously of course, was compelled to partake of it."

"Crime?" Culligan said, finding perfection in that one word.

She held him in her gaze. "Yes, Brian, crime."

The word hung there, begging to be expounded upon. When she showed no inclination to do so, Karl offered, "A crime for which she spent two years in a mental hospital and yet continues to pay."

A quiet reigned, Mildred somehow at its epicenter. Culligan had another taste of his beer, waiting for someone to expose the masquerade for what it was. At last Karl made the suggestion that he and Klaus take Brian walking while Mildred prepared dinner. Most of the villagers would be going to Mass, he told his guest. The place would be theirs.

"You'll be staying, then?" Mildred asked Brian, with out-of-place British hospitality.

"I guess I will," he said, as if there had ever been an option.

———•———

Outside, edges dulled as the mist from the Akyll—or steam from Hell below—wove its way through Esch, portending night. In her window, Christina might have been made of the same illusory substance as the fog, her face slipping out of sight just as Culligan made eye contact. The sky deepened, bringing on an unpolished pewter dusk from which the occasional dress or suit emerged, late for church. One such specter stepped right out in front of the three men as they turned a corner. Her eyes shone as she fixed Brian, one finger slowly, slowly rising, as if upon a puppet string.

"What does she want?" he asked Karl, the chill arcing from nerve to nerve.

"I don't know."

"*Ich habe Euch in einen Traum gesehen!*" she said, with intensity.

"What the hell does that mean?" Brian demanded, backing away from her. Backing away from her face, white and maddened and, yes, terrified as it looked back at him.

"She saw you in a dream," Karl said.

Her puppet head jerked towards Karl, then back to Culligan. She spat another string of incomprehensible words and fled across the street into folds, leaving Brian staring dumbly behind her.

Karl explained, "She's one of the ones Mildred refers to as seers. Several of the villagers were affected that way, having experienced dreams and visions almost continually, both night and day, since partaking of the stuff. More than likely Friedrich back at the Bahnhof was in a dream-state when he was beating on the window in the bar. His partner, Elsa, also suffers from being a seer. It's what drew the two of them to each other."

"What did the woman say just now before running off?"

Karl shrugged. "She said she had seen the face rising out of ocean waves."

Culligan's heart forgot its cadence. A sensation like that experienced when looking down from a lofty place started in his groin and expanded through his body. His flesh prickled as if the mist had reached out and begun twining him in its icy tendrils.

Karl placed a hand on Culligan's shoulder as he oversimplified magnificently. "Don't be disturbed. If you give in to those emotions, you might as well have partaken of the substance yourself."

Mightn't he, indeed.

Resisting the impulse to shrug off the other's hand, Culligan motioned with a nod that they lead on. His heart found its rhythm again in the instance of a horrible calm. Karl seemed to give to him and grieve for him simultaneously, offering the way as though it were his responsibility. A woman had once treated Brian that way, a woman whose anonymous face he could never completely recall, a woman who had found him alone on the beach with his pain and his Scotch and tears that he had never let Nina see.

Culligan arrived in Orlando at ten past noon that day. He picked up a rental car at the airport, drove to a brief meeting with Ben Nolan, the executive he'd gotten to know over golf last year. Ben gave him a key to the beach cottage Danler Consulting reserved for out-of-town guests, along with an envious wink when Brian told him about the relaxed weekend he had in mind. It was Saturday and business wouldn't be addressed till Monday, bless Brian's good-hearted and benevolent hosts.

He had been careful not to tell Nina about the free weekend, knowing she would volunteer to join him. As he flew along the expressway, windows down, putting Orlando behind him and the beach in front, he thought about their encounter of only three hours ago. As always, its exquisiteness and intensity had ended in tears, soft, delicate on her face . . .

Jesus, lose such thoughts.

He found a rock station, reception clear over the flat landscape. The mid-September day was cloudless and warm, making him wish he'd had the foresight to reserve a convertible. As the miles passed he concentrated on putting everything but the beach and its mysteries out of mind. Life was uncomplicated when you were rich, despite what the spouse might espouse. He tapped the wheel with his thumb, joined with the voice coming out of the speakers. His tongue began to bleed again from where Nina had bitten it while they were in the throes.

Why hadn't he brought her down with him? Why did his wife sit at home while he drove to a beach cottage for the weekend?

For the life of him, he didn't know.

On the outskirts of town, where the three men turned north along the path of the Akyll, Klaus grew visibly uncomfortable. The fog now permeated everything. Karl announced that the burial place would be the appropriate turnaround point.

"Who is buried there?" Culligan asked.

"Christina's father."

The wall that contained the graveyard came into view first, looking misshapen in the fog. Its configuration changed as they approached, causing Brian to question his eyes, the last vestiges of his sanity. Figures appeared, a teenager and his minions, a glinting blade, slices of blood-meat tossed in the air for mouths to reach out and devour.

Klaus began to shift from leg to leg, blowing in the fog like a beast as he watched them make Red Rain out of the animal organ their leader squeezed in his fist.

"*Bring mich zurück*," he ordered his brother.

Brian clearly understood this sentiment. Klaus wanted to go back.

"But this is where the story begins to makes sense," Karl said to Brian, as if Brian were the one asking to be delivered from here.

Karl's brother pitched his head back and forth, issuing a harrowing sound, opening the faces of the teenagers to his distress. Their leader cut a long strip from the liver and tossed it in a lazy arc towards him. Klaus leapt back, shrieking as it landed wetly at his feet. The laughter of the teenage god and his subjects formed nightmarish shapes in the mist. Klaus loomed among them, peering insanity, yanking the boy off the wall by his throat and shoving the liver in his mouth. The kids scattered in every direction. Karl seized his brother, but his brother shook free, screaming like a demon, giving chase to phantoms. The wall reconfigured into the fast stone construction that it was. "Klaus!" Karl called. When there was no answer the first time, he gave up.

He led Brian into the graveyard, past rows of markers to one specific, flower-drenched spot. The various blossoms and bouquets lay everywhere, covering the slab, and this was doubtless an example of the internal logic of which Mildred had spoken.

"Christina's father," Karl said, clutching Brian suddenly, "found them. He cannot be blamed for his reaction."

Brian shook his head. No.

"Farther up the trail," Karl pointed into the densities, "there is a shrine. Beside it is a bench. Johannes was on his way to his deer blind and a morning hunt when he discovered his daughter and our village priest on the bench. As far as Mildred has been able to determine—from those rare occasions when Christina has revealed herself to my wife—they were engaged in an embrace and no more. She believes they had never engaged in more than that, although they had intense feelings for each other. Johannes of course saw only his daughter in the arms of the priest, before the village had even woken up, and he reacted."

Brian looked at the flowers as he asked what happened.

"He threatened Father Hoffmann with his life," Karl said. "The priest ran, leaving Christina to her father's wrath. The rest is sketchy, but Christina has revealed to Mildred that her father, who had always treated her like a treasure, tore open his shirt and his pants and descended on her, demanding to know if this was what she was looking for. How far he would have gone is impossible to know. Groping for any weapon against his assault, Christina's hand found the cross in the upper alcove of the shrine. She wrenched it from its seat and plunged it into her father's neck."

The petals surrounding the witness's grave became sea foam writhing and hissing deliriously in Brian's ears. "*Bring mich zurück*," he whispered.

———•———

In the night, in a room in a place he was not quite a stranger to, he heard himself scream. It sounded as if it came from a female's vocal organs, but was every bit the match of the pain he bore. He belched and it tasted like Scotch, and beer, and the brandy Mildred had fed him after dinner. Dinner had been pork. Always pork. Germany had become a strange home. Esch was a womb.

He fell asleep again, a cigarette in his hand tossing ashes on the sand, the stars spread out across the vault, the Atlantic licking at the feet of bodies entwined. Bless his good-hearted hosts for providing their client this cottage on the beach; curse the moon and the stars for providing this woman who had wandered upon him as he lay back on his elbows weeping into the incoming tide.

The pain on his lips was the cigarette, or the taste of the shining elephantine ashtray as it wrapped him in its strange embrace. A song in the transforming glass, a siren emerging from the waves, pulling silken twine from her mouth. *Let's do it together*.

And the screams and the screams. And out of the screams, words:

"Are you okay?" Mildred, as she put her hands around his face.

"I never meant to hurt her," he gasped. "I never meant to hurt her."

"Don't worry," she said. "It's only Christina. She's been screaming for the past ten minutes."

"No," he said. "It's me."

He pressed past her to the window. Through the fog she was not invisible.

"Cigarette?" he said, to anyone.

"I'll get you one," Mildred said.

He put on his shoes, he found his way through the mist which had seeped into his very room. As he arrived downstairs, she reached out as if to stay him. But it was only the cigarette. She lit it, and he let out the taste of cloves as he carried it outside with him.

Christina was in the street, hand reaching to him. The world had dissolved in its own breath. She led him along streets, then the stream, past the graveyard, and to the place where her father had found her. She stood there and the waves retreated from her. The shock and emotion filled her face as it seemed to push out from the sea, finding him at his indiscretion, his betrayal, his crime. The girl—had she had a name?—ran, disappearing, leaving Nina's face to hover over the waves as it judged him for what he had done to her. Never had the pain been more perfect than now, as he felt his hands descend on her throat, judge that she was.

Cold landed on his forearm, cold and heat simultaneously as he brought the substance to his nostrils, the tip of his tongue. Christina, in her perfection, was Nina . . . in hers. Another splotch. Then another. Then suddenly the stuff was splitting the fog in long red spikes.

In the distance the streets of Esch stirred to life with the howls of dogs and the cries of madmen and seers waking to their dreams.

A MONK OF A SEPARATE CLOTH

NAMHWAN AND I happened upon the isolated beach by accident. We were trying to get to a cave down around Prachuap Khiri Khan when we hit a wrong turn and found ourselves in this rather beautiful setting between two seaside hills that might as well have been mountains when compared to the surroundings.

Didn't surprise us to find such a place—they were everywhere, after all, in coastal Thailand—but it did strike us that we'd found one so close to home. We couldn't have been forty kilometers out of Pak Nam Pran when we stumbled upon this treasure. We didn't even have to say the words to each other. The cave could wait until another day, or at least until after we'd explored this place a bit. We'd reserved three days for our break, having put up a notice to that effect for the plastic goods shop we ran out of the downstairs of our home, which had been built for the dual living/business purpose.

We parked the motorbike under a roofed but open shelter that stood at the road's end, a brown sign indicating this was public property, welcome and enjoy, please collect your trash on your way out. I'd a few beers on ice in the plastic compartment under the motorbike's seat. We'd also brought along, for potential diversions such as this, some of the salted and sun-dried pork strips Nam was so brilliant at oil-frying to an indescribably perfect texture (as with all her cooking endeavors), a liter of water, an extra pack of smokes for yours truly, and the beach mat and lotion and towel. We were set.

At the end of the shorter strip of beach to the right, rocks big and small were piled around the foot of the hill, presenting opportunities that sang in Nam's eye. Rocks and the pools left among them by the outgoing tide meant crabs. To the left, the same situation, but maybe four times the distance. On that side, however, and starting at the edge of the pavilion, a stone wall ran along the upper part of the beach, containing the visibly abundant coconut palms enjoying the higher ground. The wall had clearly been built to an enterprise of some kind. Resort, I thought, though the beach was awfully quiet for a vacation spot.

"Can you take care of setting us up somewhere in the shade, baby?" I said to Nam, gesturing to the right, where the beach gave over to the grass and trees with no barrier.

"Where you go, Kong?" Her English may have been lacking, but compared to my Thai, it was pure Webster's.

"Just checking out what this wall's all about. What's my name, Namhwan? My actual name."

"Latham Goodwin."

"My first name?"

"Marcus."

"While we're at it, what about my age?"

"Kong," she reproved. "Fifty-four. Too old for me."

"Yet too young to be in black and white. Okay, just making sure you remember."

"You always say like dis and I always tell you same ding. For me, you my Kong. Take a Chang with you, *falang*. I know you need you beer." She stuck out her tongue.

Indeed, as I reciprocated with a kissing gesture. I did as suggested, popping the cap off a half-liter bottle of Elephant and heading in the relevant direction, finding my track among bands of deposited shells in the sandy expanse between the wall and the gently arriving low tide waves. It was around ten in the morning, already warm but with a nice breeze and the occasional fluffy cool-me-downs drifting across otherwise sunny skies. The hint of brine on the air, competing with the scents of the vegetation growing on the other side of the wall—mangos, bananas, papaya; colorful, sweetly aromatic flowers I could not name. It was May. A fine time of year in this part of the Kingdom for the flora. Particularly the fruit. The flowers, due normally in the cooler (relatively speaking) January air, were on board because someone was obviously taking care to ensure that.

And yet, as I'd now walked far enough to see what the wall served, the outdoor caretaking, the gardening seemed all that had been done for the silent resort and its steep-roofed, ornamentally carved, quintessentially Thai bungalows. Nothing moved beyond the wall that didn't whisper. The wind in the fronds was a tale of some reality that didn't exist anymore. The place was a thing of the past, a relic, a fossil, with its rundown wooden buildings, their tightly shut wooden windows. Adding to the sense of abandonment, loss, was the fact that each bungalow stood on tall stilts, the bodies of the structures floating among the leafy boughs of the trees, which once upon a time must have been a selling point, an enticement. Come live in the lower layers of the canopy, among the birds and lizards and benign green snakes. Bathe in what it is to live exotically, among nature—not just you Westerners, you *falangs*, but you Thai folks as well. See how we have given you those comforts you so enjoy? The outdoor grills? The wooden bench swings in their flowery frames? The large circular tables where you can lay out a spread fit for the heartiest, most diverse of appetites? Come out of your cities and explore the real environment. You're welcome one and all.

I'd seen it all before. They were beautiful, these places, and the Thailanders loved such distractions every bit as much as foreigners. But it was rare to find one of these resorts, in such a lovely and secluded setting as this, appealing more to ghosts than those trying to escape them. It puzzled me. Sure, there were always money issues. There were always low tourism years, low travel in general due to chaotic political goings on in Bangkok. But I'd never seen such an example of sheer surrender, the grounds upkeep (some otherwise disinterested contractor's automatic monthly) notwithstanding. Where had the place even come from? I'd seen no sign for it on the main road. Granted, I hadn't been looking, but still. It's not as though they went around uprooting their signs when a venture failed. In rural Thailand everything is left intact, as if for future study, archaeological evidence of its existence. There are no outright ghost resorts. The possibility of life always remains.

Not here, I decided. Definitely not here. And I turned and headed back in the opposite direction to ask Nam what she thought about it.

———•———

She hadn't spoken much since she'd agreed that, yes, it was a ghost resort, and best we just stay away from it. But as we looked for crabs among the rocks at the beach's opposite end, where she'd set up our temporary camp, she suddenly raised up from her picking around to look at me.

"Why falang always do like dis?"

"Like what, baby?"

"Scare Thai people?"

"Baby."

"No. You know I don' like."

"Like what, sweetheart?"

"You do like dis. You know we don' like ghos'."

I sighed, trying to take a hand which she'd already withdrawn. "Nam. Babe. Come on. There are no ghosts, 'kay? We've talked about this."

"I don' believe you."

"That there are no ghosts or that I don't believe in them?"

"No sex for you dis trip."

"Come on. Not again. You know that won't happen."

"Dis time I mean it," she said darkly. "You do like dis, you find nudder Thai woman."

"Baby, it's not me doing anything. The place is vacant, empty. I'm not responsible for that. Whatever I said, I didn't mean to alarm you."

"You say look haunted."

"Not literally, not for real, babe. Just a manner of speaking."

"Don' like. Dis not funny to me."

"Do you want to go?"

"Yeht."

"Yes, you mean. Yesssss."

"*Wah*! You dink joke?"

I'd begun to smile, and now I couldn't keep it in. She glared as I struggled to regather myself. "I'm sorry, babe. I wish you could hear yourself."

"You make fun my English?"

"No! I mean the ghost talk. Oooooooooooh."

"Serious, Kong. Ghos' no joke," though the shadow of a smile touched at her own mouth now. Circumstances required humor sometimes.

"No, sweetheart, you're right. Listen. Let's go over there together and look around, okay? You'll see what I mean then. I wouldn't let you go if there was any danger."

She was suspicious of me, but reluctantly agreed. She liked to bitch about demons, but she also liked to confront them if it meant making me wrong. Because she thought I had power over her, which I assuredly did not. She'd been her own woman long before I'd come along. I was just something she needed to affirm her matronly place. She slapped me around far more than I instructed her. The fears in her were but a glint compared to what she could invoke in you. She was a sorceress, Nam. I loved her just like that. Obsessive as she could be about her Kong, I was her thing.

————◆————

After prowling around the place, on and off its pebbled paths, her Kong making such a show of it she didn't know whether to be disgusted or charmed by him, she said, "We go to store we see before we turn. We ask why no information for dis place."

"So it's not only me seeing that there's no name, no phone number, no nothing in the way of identifying this place?"

"I not say I on your team."

I laughed. "Don't know how you mean that, but I wouldn't imagine you would be."

"I mean what I say. You dink too much. Always dinking."

"Drinking?"

"Dinking!"

"Ah, you mean *thinking*."

"Dinking too."

"Thinking?"

"Dinking!"

Sometimes I thought—no, I *knew*—she did it on purpose. Smart as a wet whip, Namhwan. If I could fuck with her, she could damn well fuck with me too. It was a sort of game we played, like the 'no sex for you' thing she liked to do. I'm not even really sure she believed in her ghosts in this instance. Not anymore. But she'd continue to pretend to until the thing was exhausted.

We left the beach mat where it was, along with some of our stuff. The store was literally just right around the corner, opposite the resort entrance. They were probably missing the business, assuming there had ever been any. But yeah, must have been. The barbecue grills, for one, were blackened from use. There were other signs too, I thought as I drove us to the store. Nam was right. I did think too much. Why did any of this interest us? What was so suspicious about a closed business? What was so sinister about information being removed? The owner didn't want to be bothered. So?

The store was dead. Alive, but dead. No business at all, tucked here under a mango tree watching the occasional passing vehicle. The counter wasn't manned, so I glanced down the few aisles before calling, "Anybody home?"

A response came in Thai from the back somewhere, then a door came open and a woman appeared, apron around her waist.

"*Sawadee ka*," she said with a smile.

I gave her the prayer gesture, bowing slightly. "*Khap*."

"*Sawadee ka*," Nam said before asking her the question in Thai.

The woman gave her a strange, dislocated look. An extraordinary response, if Nam had gotten straight to the subject and hadn't asked the woman to show her what desolation tasted like. For it was like that, a lost, forsaken aspect, as though she'd been completely unmasked and this was who she was beneath. But it was nonetheless a passing thing; the lady resuming her pleasant face, and a dialogue ensued. It ended with the shopkeeper leaning down to look among the contents of a shelf below the counter. She produced an old, dusty card. Nam took it, they talked some more, I purchased a beer from the woman by way of thanks, and we were on our way.

"She was weird," Nam said as we drove back.

"How so?"

"You see how she look?"

"I did. What was with her? She looked like she'd seen a—" I stopped myself before it was too late. Nam wasn't listening anyway. I could feel her behind me on the bike, revisiting the experience, focusing unhealthily on it like she was prone to do.

I parked the bike and we headed to the mat, which Nam had placed in a grassy patch of shade under a tree. "So what did she say?" I asked when I'd settled in with my beer.

Nam still stood, tying an empty plastic bag to a nub of branch protruding from the tree trunk to use for garbage. The lady must have really unsettled her for her to be acting like this, going through some mindless motion, not looking at me.

"Babe?"

"You know what, Kong?" she said, suddenly giving me her full attention.

"What?"

"Let's call dese people and ask if we can stay in bungalow tonight. De lady in shop say she dink people can do. Dey bing key to you."

Surprised, I said, "You serious?"

"Serious."

"But . . . why? What happened to change your mind about the place? Something the lady said?"

"She don' say. She scare, but she don' say. You want to call? If resort I dink dey speak English." She handed me her phone because mine was rarely on or around my person, while she could never be far from Facebook, Candy Crush, and two dozen friends and cousins and such that no doubt took her away from me when I "talk too much."

"The card?" I said.

She removed it from a pocket, looked at it a moment, reading aloud "Sun and Shade Bungalow" before passing it my way.

"Can you read off the number? My glasses are in the bike."

"089—"

"Whoa. Just a sec. Your phone. 'Kay, go ahead."

She read it off. While I waited for the other party to pick up, our eyes met and held. *Are these people actually going to rent us a bungalow?* the gaze asked.

"Hello." A male voice, with the Thai treatment on the last, lingering syllable.

"Uh, yes. Hi. Is this the Sun and Shade?"

"I am the owner of the property, yes. If you are a prospective buyer, you will need to speak with our agent."

"No, no. Beachfront property is a little out of my range. No, I'm a customer. I'd like to rent a bungalow. Are you open for business? My girlfriend and I really love the setting."

A long pause. Followed by: "Where did you get this phone number?"

"From the shop across the street from the bungalows. We were doing the beach and saw your place, but we couldn't find any contact information. The lady at the shop was gracious enough to provide a card."

Another pause. This one shorter, but the gulf no less vast. "Oh, I guess it's time. The doors have been closed for too long. Should talk to Li, my wife, but she's in Bangkok right now. Yes, this will be fine. Price per night is 2000 baht for the ones with air and warm water, the majority of our units; these are the ones on the beach side of the office and former restaurant area. The primitive bungalows, which are the six located deeper in the trees on the other side of the office, are 1200 baht. They have ceiling fans. No amenities."

"Air, please."

"Good. And how many nights?"

"Let me check with Nam."

"One night, baby?"

"One for now. We decide later."

"Sir? One night for now. We'll let you know if we decide to stay over."

"That's fine. Are you at the beach now?"

"I am."

"Okay, I'll meet you at the pavilion in twenty minutes with the keys. You won't be able to move in yet. I'm going to have the cleaning people come. I'll take care of electricity while there. Which bungalow is it you want?"

"One moment . . . Nam, which bungalow do we want?"

"De one close to de beach. Dis side."

"Okay, sir. We'd like the one to the left of the stairs as you look at the resort from the beach. The one that's slightly more isolated and close to the wall, with easy beach access."

"I know the one. Good choice. It's our best. The view of the ocean at night is wonderful from the deck."

He arrived with the key twenty minutes later. I met him in front of his newer model sedan, not bothering with the Thai greeting—other than to nod respectfully—since his English was so good and he had an obvious familiarity with falangs. Instead, I extended my hand, which he firmly shook.

"Daycha," he said.

"Latham. Latham and Namhwan. That accent of yours. Your pronunciation of English words . . . "

"I am half Thai, half Brit."

"Aha."

He looked the part—though I'd never have been able to figure out on my own what that part was. Not Thai enough to be Thai, not falang enough to be falang. The two came together quite well. Perhaps ten years my elder and nearly twice Nam's, he was quite a handsome specimen. And

114

distinguished looking at that, with his neatly trimmed silvery hair, a set of clothes that simply didn't belong in this rural setting in this climate. Loose fitting silver-gray button-down shirt, roomy black slacks, black leather loafers. And a belt. Goodness. An expensive-looking belt, with a fine buckle to shatter the whole illusion of comfort. Had he been sitting around his house like this? Or was this specifically for going out into the nth degree temperatures and humidity? It was hard to get over the belt. Constricted me looking at it. I could almost feel the band of sweat around my waist.

"No need to walk you up and show you around, I presume?" he was saying now.

"No, sir. When can we expect the cleaning to be done?"

"Daycha, please. They're on their way now. About an hour. Place hasn't been used in a while."

I felt odd doing so, for some unknown reason, but the question had to be asked.

"Why is that, Daycha, if you don't mind my asking? This is a beautiful setting. If it's financial, understood and never mind. Not my place to probe into your business."

He regarded me for a moment. Seemed to make a decision then and there, resigning himself to the inevitability of it. "It wasn't economic. There was a tragedy."

I could feel what was coming next, through the nuances in his expression or by some deeper means, and before he could say more, I shook my head, with as little motion as possible but making sure he saw me do it. I wasn't sure precisely where Nam was; she wasn't in my field of view. When I'd gotten up to meet him as he stepped out of his car, she too had stood. When I'd introduced the two of us to him, the man had bowed in her direction, but I wasn't sure she'd ever come out of the pavilion. She didn't normally hang back in these situations, but in this case she knew there was no language barrier and might just be letting me handle business. Wherever she was, she was close enough to hear every word we spoke, because the road ended almost at the pavilion itself. Pray she wasn't close enough to see my message to Daycha.

He saw it, and deftly covered his tracks with a simple addendum. "A family matter. We lost a son."

"Oh, I'm so sorry. I shouldn't have pried."

"Nonsense. Who wouldn't ask such a question when they see the place shut up and stripped of all its information? We had to go black for a time. We felt we had no choice, Li and me."

I nodded. It was all I could do. I was so out of sorts I couldn't find the words.

"Ah, the keys," he said, saving me, both of us, all three of us if you looked at it that way. "Here you are, Latham. This one's for the bungalow, this one the gate you come to as you enter by the road across from the store. You can park your motorbike inside and lock the gate behind you. Let's go ahead and settle up now. That way you can be on your way without bother tomorrow—should you stay only the one night. Just leave the keys under the bedside lamp in the room. Should you stay over, I'll get with you probably the morning of checkout so as not to disturb you folks. Enjoy your visit. I must be off." He gestured at his attire. "No, I don't normally dress like this. I'd rather be strangled by a snake. Business up in Hua Hin."

I chuckled and shook his hand. Good man, Daycha.

———•———

The bungalow, accessed by a short set of wooden stairs, was cozy in its lofty place among the boughs. The deck Daycha had referred to was a wraparound affair, and had been furnished (by the cleaning folks, who'd still been at it after an hour) with a couple plastic chairs and a small wooden table. Inside, the place smelled of air freshener and wood and the natural fragrances the open windows let in. A flat screen TV was mounted to the wall opposite the king-size bed, a DVD player resting on a shelf below it. A refrigerator and microwave, as well a water heater and instant coffee, were provided. The heating unit for the shower was in good working order, as was the air conditioner. The place was quite nice if you didn't mind lizards or the frog sitting outside one of the windows on the sill, the broad frond that had likely gotten it there gently grazing the glass. The trees could have used a bit of trimming, but the abundance added to the charm.

As we sat on the balcony gazing out on the fishing-boat-dotted seascape, much of the afternoon still before us, I asked Nam what she wanted to do.

"Don' know. Swim? Look for crab?"

"Sure. Let's check out the rocks at this end of the beach. Explore a little, then take a dip. We want to get some food to cook out, too. I'm not sure where to find meat around here. Should have asked Daycha about that. That store across the street isn't going to provide anything that isn't canned or a snack. Maybe there's a market in the next village. We'll check it out later."

"I hungry now."

"You're always hungry. We have the pork strips. And didn't you bring leftover fried rice in a container? Where is it, anyway? I didn't see it in the motorbike when I got the beers. Is it in your bag?"

"I eat. Still hungry."

"When did you eat?"

"When you talk to man."

I looked at her. "What man?"

"When you lock gate after parking bike."

"Huh? I didn't talk to anyone."

"Yeah, young guy. I dink he talk to you."

"Where was he? Outside the gate or something? I didn't hear him."

Her face had changed and she was looking at me darkly now. "Why you do like dis, Kong?"

"Like what?"

"Ty to scare me?"

Jesus. Here I was right back where I'd been with Daycha. Having to stop the flow when there wasn't even any blood!

Thinking quickly, I said, "Oh. Oh, right." Rapping myself on the skull with my knuckles. "*That* man. Sorry, I was lost there for a minute. You know me, baby. Getting old."

"You dink beer too early. How many beer you have today?"

"Two or three."

"Tchee, not two. Dink slow. Don' wan' see you dunk early."

"Okay, sweetheart. I be good."

She pursed her lips, not looking at all convinced, but she let it go. When she was hungry, she didn't have time for nonsense.

"Kong, can you get box from my bag?"

"Box . . . you mean the pork? Sure, babe. Wouldn't mind some myself."

Nothing like it, after all. Beer, fried pork strips, and the young man out there talking to you at the gate.

——————◆——————

We nabbed five fairly large crabs (which Nam assured me were edible) from among the rocks at the base of the hill on the resort side of the beach. While Nam kept them contained in a small tidal pool, I went searching for something to put them in, and hopefully to cook them in. When Nam and I had done our snooping around the joint earlier, I'd noticed they had left a lot of equipment stacked on tables on the concrete slab that remained of the restaurant and its kitchen, and thought that the best place to look.

The back area, the kitchen, which had a doorway but no door, was a minor treasure trove of utensils and pots and pans and such. There were even bags of charcoal to aid in the purpose. I grabbed what I thought was a suitable pot, knowing Nam would probably want to come back and sift through the stuff for what she needed, and stepped back out into the vacancy that had been the dining area, meaning to cross the slab and head back to the beach to take care of the crabs. But something caught my eye.

And that something became a larger something.

And that larger something multiplied before my previously blind eyes.

Stains. On the wall. The floor. Tables. Dark, richly dark stains that had no business being in a dining area or any other civilized place. I knew what the stains were. Inside me, in the organs, the vessels, the nerves, the bones, the primal jelly, I knew what they were. The only question here was how I'd been lucky enough for Nam to have missed it during our prowl around. That and . . . *What the fuck happened in this place?*

I backed out of there, not fully trusting my eyes, my senses, my faculties—even while knowing, on a deeper than intuitive level, that what I was experiencing was all too real—and hurried down to the beach and company. Company of Nam, company of crabs, it didn't matter. Anything was better than being alone when a word from a resort owner's mouth became material.

Tragedy. Thank God I'd stopped him before he'd said more.

———•———

Crabs safely breaking each other's claws off in the pot I'd brought, which Nam agreed was fine for the grill, we went for a swim, dodging a few jellyfish as we played, and then decided to go looking for a way up the hill. Nam suggested it, imagining the views for me from an increasingly happy and worry-free perspective, mood, demeanor. I hardly knew what to make of her when I myself was encountering ghosts at every turn now. That I did not believe in ghosts was what saved me. Tragedy, horror . . . I believed in these things. But I also believed in time, and time was an historian. Events happened and got catalogued. Then the present replaced the past and the future the present, and the stains lost their color and material and were merely vestiges. That's what this was. Darkness had happened; darkness had gone.

But when, after several aborted attempts up the hillside, we thought we'd found a suitable path on the resort side where people might have once had an interest, a voice reached our ears from back on the property. A woman's voice. Calling. Calling in Thai.

"You hear, Kong?" Nam .

"Yeah. Is it for us? What is she saying?"

"Stop. Don' go."

"Huh?"

"I don' know. Thai crazy people. I dink it woman from store."

"You can tell that from her yelling?"

"Just feel."

She did that, Nam. Just feel. She meant intuition, I guess. Maybe it was Buddhist, an in with the nature of things. Whatever it was, her feelings were often spot on.

The call came again, closer.

"So what do we do?" I said.

"Just wait. She coming."

And she did. Came running across the beach in our direction waving her hands.

"What the fuck?" I said to Nam.

"I dink she crazy. *Ba*." Tapping her head. "She say danger. Don' know what she mean."

When she arrived on the other side of the rocks separating us, she put her hands on her waist, panting for a few moments before finding her breath and energy and voice. Standing up straight as she said something to Nam in Thai, gesturing out on the water, where one of the fishing boats had come relatively close to the shore, unnoticed or ignored by Nam and me.

Nam listened to her, nodding occasionally, then went off on something of her own. When it was finished, both stood with their hands on their waists looking at each other.

"She say," Nam said to me without taking her eyes off the other, "her husband on boat and he say he see us ty to find way up mountain."

"How could he fucking see that?" I said. "And why is he looking?"

"Bino . . . what you say, these glasses?"

"Binoculars? What? He's spying on us?"

"She say he do what she tell. She ty to help us. Don' go up mountain, she say."

"She doesn't say why?"

"I don' know how to say. She say we . . . wake him again."

"Who?"

"I don' know, you know. She annoy me. I happy before she come."

Confronted by all this shit in a mere few hours? I thought. *Get out of this place, Latham. Why are you doing this to Nam or yourself?*

Because there are no ghosts, that's why! It is an afternoon on a break from work. What the fuck?

The woman now spilling again, practically in a fit. Nam screaming back at her.

I looked up at the hill's deceptively easy slope. No, the *mountain's*. It was in there, was it? Well, that will do. A destination will do.

I turned to the woman engaged with Nam, and said, "You! You go back where you came from. *Now!*"

She seized her hair in her fists and continued to rant.

"She cazy," said Nam, completely off her *r* now. "I don' like her, Kong. I going to hurt her."

I was tempted to let her do it, and I knew she could. She'd once nailed a woman against a restroom wall with hands around her neck for coming into the john after me with a body offer in mind. But I didn't; I wouldn't. I stopped her.

"They're superstitious people, Namhwan. Let them go."

She continued to glare at the still-babbling woman, but my words had eased her a little.

How to get her out now? She'd been bitten. And when bitten, she struck back.

"Come on, babe. Leave her to her . . . episode or whatever the fuck it is. Let's get a shower and go out and find something to cook with the crabs."

"Now she say he will do it all again. He hate his mudder and fadder and will make everyone in village pay dis time. She say it his mudder gene. His fadder found her in show in Bangkok. Her sister and mudder work dere. She say dey freak."

The woman babbled on and on as Nam relayed this, causing a headache to form and instantly expand in my frontal lobe. "Let's go, Nam. Leave her."

As we did, and it became apparent to the woman we'd given up designs on the hill, the stuff spewing from her almost immediately died down, became murmurs, maybe prayers. At the top of the short flight of stairs leading from the beach to the resort, we looked back, but she was gone, mission accomplished.

———◆———

While Nam was in the shower, I went out on the balcony and made the call that must be made.

"Hello, guest," Mr. Sun and Shade answered. "Are the two of you comfortable?"

"Are you still in Hua Hin, Daycha?"

"Yeah, unfortunately. Word to the wise: Don't ever invest in a golf course. What can I do for you?"

"When do you expect to be back? There are some downright disturbing things happening around here that I need to talk to you about."

The long pause that seemed to surround the man set in. Finally: "Disturbing things?"

"The lady from the shop across the street has been running around the place in a rant. But that isn't something I wish to discuss on the phone. Will you be back this evening?"

"No. We'll have to discuss it now."

"Very well. People were murdered in your restaurant. That much is clear from all the blood. It was your son, wasn't it?"

That excruciating pause. "Johnny. We called him Johnny."

"Called? He's dead? I'm sorry to be blunt like that, but this woman seemed to think he was still a threat to people in the village."

"He's dead to us."

"What does that mean? Where is he? Where is he, and what the hell happened here?"

What might have been a sigh. "He can do no one harm anymore. That much was seen to after he killed those poor people. Our *guests*. He believed himself a freak, so he was made a freak. Friends, friends in authority, same friends who were able to cover up the affair since no foreign tourists were staying here at the time, *they* saw to it."

Trying to absorb it. "By *freak*, you mean what?"

"Deformed. Unnatural. An abomination."

"And was he?"

"No, but his maternal grandmother was. We took him as a pubescent boy to see her once, in Bangkok, at a hookah bar next to this perverted theater where she worked. That was as far as she would go into the outside world. As a result of that experience, he developed this delusion about himself. He blamed his mother and me for having produced him, for having let the blood spill out into the world. That's how he referred to it, 'the blood.' He was twisted, but by no means unintelligent. Practically a genius, Johnny. An unbelievable artist. But he shouldn't have been free in the world. We didn't see it coming, but we nevertheless blame ourselves. We could have had him committed. By the time that decision had been made, he'd retreated to his cave in the hilltop. We didn't know about the place at the time. Authorities found it afterward. And inside it, they found him. They didn't want attention on our little piece of Thailand, because they and others have certain interests here. This area is a pipeline, let's just say that. The guests that night were all Thai—ten of them. A sporting fishing party of six, two backpackers, and two locals just eating at the restaurant. This situation could be handled. The cause of it could be handled. They made a call to me to tell me, not ask me, what they were going to do, and I let them. I couldn't stop them, but I didn't try. He wanted to be the horror, let him be the horror. Let him be so hideous he could never again get within the proximity of people without their fleeing at the mere sight of him."

Nam, wrapped in a towel, appeared in the bungalow's open doorway at that precise moment. Had I been looking elsewhere, her voice would have startled the shit out of me, so engrossed I'd been in Daycha's story. "Kong, what you do?"

Had she been inside listening? No, her smile precluded that.

"Just a moment," I said to Daycha. "I'll be in in a sec, baby."

She gave me the odd eye and went back in.

"Is there anything else I should know?" I asked Daycha.

"There's nothing else to know. You can leave the keys where we talked about. I'm sorry to have lost you as a guest."

"I'll notify you when I check out. You've been . . . illuminating."

Inside, Nam was lying on the bed. "Kong," she said. "Sun and cazy people make me tire. Very sleepy. Can I nap while you go out for food?"

"Sure, baby." *Nap as long as you like. It's not as though I don't have other things to do in the meantime.*

———•———

I drove to the next village to try to find something to complement the critters, but alas, there was no market, no fresh vegetables anywhere, not even a papaya salad street vendor. My mind wasn't in it, in any case. Filling the seat compartment with beer, ice, potato chips, and canned stuff from a shop similar to the crazy woman's by the resort, I drove back knowing what must be done next. I didn't know why I had to do it. I just knew that I had to. There was enough daylight left, if I could easily find the cave when I got up there. I thought I could. There had to be a path to a dwelling.

Nam was sleeping soundly when I put the groceries away and stepped out onto the deck to suck a beer down before actually *becoming* the character in the horror movie who didn't grab his girl and run when the chance presented itself. Placing the empty bottle on the railing, I went back inside to give Nam a little nudge, just to make sure. Satisfied, I put on my sandals—thankfully I'd brought the ones with treads, instead of flip-flops—quietly shut and locked the door, and headed forth on my mission to know what that cave contained. If it was a morbid curiosity on my part, I wasn't feeling it. It was something else. I was driven.

I went straight to the path we'd discovered earlier, before the madwoman entered the picture, and started up it at a determined pace. The way was thick with vegetation at times, but I always picked up the trail again when I got through it. Occasionally a sound like that of a snapping twig would cause me to pause and look around, but that too was an obstacle that really wasn't an obstacle. Until . . .

"Kong, will you slow down!"

Oh my God. No way.

"Yeah," she said, coming up behind me. "You dink I don't see you eye when I say I want to nap? I know you come here."

"Baby, go back. This is no place for you."

"I not go back. You know me, Kong."

"Then I'm not going. Come on, let's go back and forget about this."

"No way. Go!" Literally pushing me with her hands.

"I can't have this. What if it's dangerous?"

"I go by myself if you don' come. I not scare."

I opened my hands. "But you don't even know what's happening."

"I hear you on phone, you know. I not stupid. And I see you face when you come back with pot for crab."

"You were showering," I said meekly.

"I not shower. I know you, Kong. Now go."

I grudgingly obeyed, amazed by her yet making myself believe I'd handle her when we got up there.

She refused to let me go into the cave alone. Her behavior was so strange. So . . . accepting. She couldn't have known too much. Only what the woman on the beach had spewed and what I'd said on the phone—murder and blood fairly telling, granted. The other side of the conversation, the story itself, she didn't know. It didn't matter to her. She was in Nam mode, all superstition and fear put aside. She was going to have a taste of this. The madwoman on the beach was still in her. This was her way of saying, *you will not fuck with my mind; I stronger than you.*

The cave wasn't much of a cave, it was more of a deep alcove, and as such, was afforded sufficient light from outside to allow us to see what it contained. Dirty bedding in the rear, fish bones and crab shells scattered everywhere across the floor. Finely detailed self portraits of the disfigured creature that dwelled here all over the walls. It was an unintended museum and shrine unto the freak. It was his temple. It was his record. It bore every signal of him except for the one that mattered most—his actual presence.

I said, as much to myself as to Nam, "Do you think he's lived in the cave recently? How old do you think this stuff is? I'm not getting too much from the smells. Smoke from fires, but how old? The fishy smell isn't overwhelming, if I'm even detecting it."

"I dink he here, Kong."

"But he's not here."

"I dink he still live here."

I stared at her. "And that doesn't frighten you?"

"I tell you I not scare, mean I not scare. Maybe if he ghos'. But he not ghos'. The people he kill, maybe dey ghos', but not him."

Nam feared ghosts when they hadn't manifested themselves. When they began to, in whatever form, she became a force you best get yourself the fucking way out of.

"You want go back down?" she said.

"Yes. Yes I do, Nam. I very much want to go back down. It will be dark soon."

We cooked out like nothing had happened. Boiled the crabs up nice and neat. She cleaned them. Cracked them, pulled the meat out. She liked to do for me. We were real; we were Kong and Nam. Nam and Kong. The rest be damned. I don't know if it was residual excitement, anxiety, or what, but for dessert we had sex. And were in fact in the throes of it in the bungalow—we'd barely made it through the door in our hunger, Nam especially but predictably wild and unhindered tonight—when the screams began.

"I kill dem," Nam hissed. "Ghos'. Why dey can't stay dead?"

"Rest is not possible," came a voice that did not belong in this room.

A second later he—no, *it*—stepped out from the bathroom.

I leapt out of the bed and covered Nam with my body. "What do you want with us? We're not part of your fantasy." My fingers behind me, begging Nam to give something to me, anything to use as a weapon. It couldn't see what was happening back there out of the one eye they'd left it. I could feel her sliding to her right as I moved with her, could taste her finding the stand on that side of the bed, fumbling around for something. The keys Daycha had given us? That would be poetic, but what use against this thing as it now reached its twisted arms out to seize me by the throat? What at last landed in my hand was unexpected, but surely sufficient for the purpose as I swung the beer bottle with all my might, smashing it against the side of the creature's head. Then again and again, broken part by broken part, slashing the monstrosity to shreds.

When I ran out of energy, it slowly straightened, went to the mirror hanging opposite the bathroom door, contemplated itself, beginning to nod.

"Yes. Yes, that's right."

And collapsed in a bloody heap, leaving the admired image still looking back out of the mirror.

DER TEUFELOBSTGARTEN

I T WASN'T MY style to stay at bed-and-breakfasts, being something of a loner and disliking all that intimacy among strangers, but you learn to live with your hang-ups when you have little or no other choice. *Gasthäuser* are as much a part of the German culture as hotels are in America. I suppose I should have simply been glad—as Laura reminded me all too often—that we had cheap rooms available to us in even the most remote places on our cycling tour of central Europe.

By the time we reached the source of the Saar River near Strasbourg, a long day's ride from the edge of the Black Forest, I had actually grown to enjoy immersing in the culture with our routinely polite and domestically gifted hostesses. Having ridden along rivers since we set out from Frankfurt—the Rhine, the Mosel, then the Saar—Laura and I had been averaging ninety kilometers a day with minimal effort. That figure changed significantly when we climbed into the mountains that fed the Saar River. The day we found the farmhouse at the foot of Donon, we had managed forty-five at best.

Laura had just pointed out to me that the map placed us below a Roman temple ruin, elevation 1009 meters, when I spotted a sign in the trunk of the tree beside us. We sat on a deteriorating bench, having stopped to take a breather before tackling the mountain looming in our path. The bright April sun lagged beyond the pasture that the bench overlooked, reflected among the roofs at the near cusp of the landscape. The sign, which depicted a bicycle and a fork and spoon, pointed rustily in that direction. I stood and, licking my fingers, rubbed some of the message back into the present. The price was in deutsche marks, not euros, which completed the mystique.

"You think?" Laura said, not needing to finish.

"I would seriously doubt they still rent rooms," I said. I looked at my watch. "It's nearing seven."

"Can't hurt to try. Worse case, we make the other side of the mountain as it's getting dark. I'm sure there'll be a *Zimmer frei* in the village where people access the Roman ruin."

Our tour went very much like that, Laura asking me my opinion and then settling on her own. Which is how it should have gone, as she had mapped out our route and knew a good deal about the language, geography and culture, having spent six cumulative years in Germany in a military household.

"Lead on," I said.

The cords of her legs were already in motion as she mounted her bike and started up the narrow road. As the view expanded, bringing the resplendent fire of a mountain sunset, thoughts of refuge from the coming night evaporated. The structures sharpened into their configurations, fences stabbing darkly at the sky, roofs sloping in deep humility, as if for their luxurious domain. We rode alongside a fence of electric wire, automobile batteries appearing intermittently, then *immediately* as we reached out, laughing, to touch the containment of animals unseen. The silhouettes in front of us comprised a farm, its current operators probably generations behind the makers of the decrepit sign in the tree.

"I love this place," Laura said, a sentiment with which I couldn't argue as we merged with the rest of the brush strokes in the pastoral scene.

A rock wall surrounded the main house and its grounds. The gate was fashioned from the front halves of two rusted old-fashioned bicycles. If that wasn't enough to make me mend my opinion about the place offering beds, then the laminated lodging info attached to the side of the wall was. Furthermore, the rear of the house, now visible, had a second-floor balcony complete with fresh flowers. The view from there, I imagined, would be fantastic, taking in both the sunset and the mountain. Impulsively my eyes found their way to the top of the steep, thinly wooded slope behind the farm, where I thought I could just make out an unnatural stone shape resembling a pavilion.

We parked our bikes in a rack inside the gate and walked the path's octagonal stones to the door. Before I released the brass knocker a woman's face appeared, her striking blue eyes tempered by expressive age lines. Her white hair was done up in some clever way that Laura would later comment on, and her hand on the doorjamb sported a blue gemstone to match her eyes. In spite of a thin, sad smile, there was a vitality about her that went beyond her welcome.

"*Guten Tag*," she said.

"*Tag*," said Laura. "*Sprechen Sie Englisch?*"

"Oh, a little."

"*Ja. Ich spreche ein bisschen Deutsch.*"

"*Dein Deutsch is sehr gut*," the woman smiled. "Do you wish a room for the night?"

"*Bitte.*"

"*Kommt herein*. We have two rooms with private baths and a view of the valley."

We stepped inside the house inspired—Laura because of the warm welcome, myself because of the unexpected turn of events. My muscles thanked our hostess as they finally relaxed for the day, knowing a bed was near; my senses did the same as they partook of the rustic interior of the farmhouse. A wooden chandelier reminiscent of something found in an upscale hunter's lodge formed the centerpiece of the entry area. The rough stucco walls were hung with woven or otherwise handcrafted pictures. The floor was a richly textured hardwood, as was the carved balustrade leading upstairs. In keeping with the wood theme, the scent of burning cedar seeped in from other parts of the house.

Laura's smile said it all as we ascended the stairs to the guest rooms. The two rooms were identical in nearly every way—traditionally spare but charming—except that the balcony of the second was that much closer to not only the mountain, but also a separate feature that lured the eye. Out in the field beyond the barn and the farm's lone grain silo stood an orchard of some thirty trees—apple trees, I knew at once, because of their twisted frames. In the midst of them grew one that was taller and more grotesque than the others, bearing the glimmer of developed fruit on one of its distorted branches, though it was only April.

I found myself commenting on the loveliness of the view, not specifically naming the fruit trees. But she knew what had evoked my admiration.

"In the village they call it *Der Teufelobstgarten*. The Devil Orchard."

While my imagination bristled, my response was altogether unimaginative. "I can see why."

Maybe it was my taste for the dark, but this time I didn't allow my virgin tourist status to be a factor, plainly accepting the room to our hostess without even a consultatory glance at Laura. When I did cast my eye her way, I saw that my assertiveness had earned me an almost desirous look.

Downstairs, we made introductions, filled out a card, and fielded what was a beautiful question from Helga.

"Do you wish dinner?"

I blinked at Laura. We had planned on eating chili out of a can.

Forty minutes later, with light failing outside, we were sitting down to a table of *Jägerschnitzel*, *Brötchen* (hard bread rolls), *Pommes* (fries), and beer. Helga declined to dine with us, but she proved more than happy to converse. We asked about her family and she told us her husband worked out in the fields till late and her son was away at Heidelberg learning surgery. We told her about our own families, in America and envying our dream of doing Europe our way. The talk went to this and to that, finally landing where I'd hoped it would as our hostess mentioned late spring blossoms.

"So why do the villagers call it Der Teufel Garden?" I asked. It was as pathetically close as I ever came to constructing a phrase in the native tongue.

"The villagers are afraid of *Der Teufelobstgarten*. The site has been a sacred one to some cultures. It has also been a...the word is *grim*?...yes, a grim one."

"What do you mean?" I said, chunk of pork suspended on the tines of my fork.

"The Romans built the temple on Donon because of the energy that is present here." She turned to Laura. "How do you say *Gelehrte* in English? Yes, *scholar*. A Roman scholar named Protus wrote of the Celts . . . condemning this place."

Laura translated the rest because of the obvious strain on Helga's ability. "Apparently," she conveyed, "Druid priests chose this valley as a ritual site because of the energy Helga mentions. But soon after they began performing their ceremonies, they died without apparent cause. Their bodies were found in the spot where the orchard now stands, which is also where their funeral pyres were erected. The Celts believed that the priests fell victim to the same force that had made them choose the site."

Helga went on to explain, with Laura doing an increasingly animated job of translating, about how Protus had witnessed a battle between the Celts and the Romans from atop the mountain where the temple would be built two hundred years later—a battle that resulted in the near total destruction of both the Celtic army and the Roman division with which Protus traveled. He wrote that during the Celts' customary pre-battle clamor of blowing trumpets and banging their swords and shields, they abruptly quit their intimidations, raising their arms to indicate something beyond the Romans. The Romans, believing it a ploy on the foe's part, charged. A fierce bloodbath ensued, with the Celts appearing to try to hack their way through the Roman soldiers without regard for their own defense. Protus later learned that the Celts believed they had seen their Druid priests beckoning to them from a terrace of higher ground. So profoundly were they affected that they never returned for their dead, which spoke volumes for a culture with such elaborate funeral rituals—particularly when it came to their fallen warriors.

A pause preceded Laura's unnecessary footnote that this farmstead occupied that terrace of higher ground. In the succeeding silence, I was about to ask a question that perturbed me when Helga began speaking again. Laura watched her intently before passing yet more history along.

DER TEUFELOBSTGARTEN

"The farm was abandoned during the war, after some sort of skirmish left a party of Nazi soldiers dead. After an SS probe that apparently revealed nothing of substance, no one wanted any part of the place. Helga and her husband picked the farm up for next to nothing after it sat empty for almost two decades. They started renting in sixty-five. Around that same time, they planted the orchard that the villagers despise."

I seized the moment. "The tree in the middle of the orchard. The one that has fruit..."

Helga spouted off a stream of German that did not even attempt to recognize the language barrier. Laura interpreted: "Beneath that tree lies what has been dubbed the *Druid Stein*—or stone. That's where the valley's energy is strongest and what made the Druids choose the place."

I shook my head for lack of a more appropriate gesture. "This is fascinating stuff. Why doesn't she post a new sign on the bike path alluding to the layered history of the area?"

A minor discussion ensued. "They aren't interested in money," Laura finally related. "They much prefer someone perceptive enough to find and follow the sign already there."

"By *they*, you do mean Helga and her husband, right?" I smiled my smile and hoped I wasn't told on.

Laura cast a glance at our hostess, who winked and began gathering up our cleaned plates. She asked if we would like to take a bottle of wine up with us and we told her we would, gladly. As Helga retreated to her environs, Laura and I did the same, pleasantly nibbling at each other's ears as we locked ourselves in. The day and its expenditures dissolved and our intimacies took over. Somewhere between the hour of darkness and total darkness I wanted a cigarette—which Laura, as usual, invited me to enjoy outside.

I stood on the balcony in my boxers, looking out on a night as clear as the day had been. The stone configuration at the top of the mountain stood confirmed in the floodlights that were trained upon it, a tease to motorists and long since disinterested villagers. As I sucked on my Marlboro my eyes fell to the orchard. Its trees were sketched in black wax, darker than all their surrounds, silhouetted even against the ground itself. A half moon hung off to the right, splashing the land in its silvery light. One object captured its radiance more effectively than any other, that fruit so rare, so plump and rare on its jagged branch.

At the foot of the tree I could see the white surface of the *Druid Stein*. I imagined how delightful it would be to sit there smoking my cigarette, submerged in the mystery of the place, knowing the local culture in a way no bed-and-breakfast, of itself, could provide. To venture a taste of the forbidden apple...

129

Something moved out on the skirts of my vision. When I looked I couldn't find it, though I fancied its afterimage to be the right size for Helga's husband, lost abroad in his fields without supper. As soon as I returned my gaze to the tree, the flash occurred again. Even in a hallucinatory context, there was no mistaking it for some manner of passage. I glanced at the moon, wondering if something had disturbed its surface, but my eyes were the only things disturbed, the fragment of motion a ghost on their lenses. The stub of my cigarette arced out into the night, spraying embers like fiery salt.

"Are you coming in?" Laura asked from the spheres of darkness behind me.

I poked my head in, not recognizing any of the outlines. "How would you like to go for a walk?"

"Are you crazy? I'm sticky, if you know what I mean."

"Who cares. It's beautiful out. Let's go exploring."

I couldn't tell, through the darkness, if she was afraid. I suspected not, knowing my Laura who conquered Europe with a pencil on paper. The pause allowed my eyes to adjust, the moonlight to seep in, the magic to re-invert. Laura's breasts came into view, sweetly rounded and milky white below her tan line. I thought of their resemblance to the fruit in the orchard, but of course I had only a glimmer by way of comparison. Which was why I must go there, with or without her, and cup it in my hand.

She opted to join me, with the stipulation that I take her bodily in the spring night.

I thought to deny her presumption, but the refreshed experience of her made me weak.

———•———

The night was magnificently unrestrained as we slipped out the guest door in back. The valley sprawled before us, the temple of Donon a celestial body to complement the moon. *Der Teufelobstgarten* seemed to crawl in place as we approached, its still somewhat stark limbs jabbing angrily at the owls of spring with their shining eyes upon the mice of the field. Among the expressive trees, one rose taller, meaner, more seductively than its fellows, dangling drops of honey for the taker. I asked Laura if she was the taker and she told me she could not be sure. Neither could I as we dared place our bodies on the broad, flat stone beneath. I started a cigarette and she extinguished it against the bark of the tree, drawing me down on top of her. Her gown, translucent in the moonlight, melted around us.

When my pace, or perhaps a quirk in my technique, didn't satisfy her, she positioned herself above me, riding her body against mine as if it were our last encounter. Over her shoulder the bloated apple seemed to dip on its branch, singing with moonlight, begging to be pierced to let its juices flow forth. I felt my tongue reaching upward as Laura won the rest of my body, refusing to release me until I had spent myself inside her. While I experienced the orgasm with her, I could not release everything because a part of me had been captured by the fruit above.

As Laura's eyes hid behind their lids, the apple alone regarded me, a lamp over our pleasures. Again I reached, but it was too high unless I stood. And if I stood I did so above the contented body of the only goddess I had known—until tonight. I closed my eyes and held her, no, clung to her, and the night was linen around us. It was she who withdrew, seeming to fail to see my distraction.

"Aren't you going to have a cigarette?" she said, placing her hands on her thighs.

"Really?"

"Don't you always?"

That's when I heard the distant music of a tractor, presumably Helga's husband working away in the realms below. As I looked that way I was sure I saw wisps of something slipping through fluid layers, but they vanished as soon my eyes found them. I turned back to see if Laura had fallen for optical tricks, instead found her gazing at me. "Cigarette," she reminded me, holding a lit one in her fingers. She must have brought it along with her—behind her ear, perhaps, though I had tasted a different type of retreat there.

I pulled on it, looking up at her.

"If that's not enough, how about this?" She reached above her and grasped the apple. Motion occurred spontaneously in every direction around me, strange light-like shapes emerging from nocturnal folds. Now Laura saw them too, a fact I gleaned as my gaze was torn between the flurried darkness and the apple in her hand. But then she froze, fixing on a point behind me, in the direction of the farm. Her lips parted slightly, her hand—*no, don't do that, Laura*—released the fruit, the gleam of which seemed to intensify as it hung there unplucked.

The surrounding motion quit, darkness becoming only darkness again. "Look," was the word that came out of Laura's mouth, as insubstantial as the shapes still lurking out there, invisibly. I turned to follow her stare and saw at once what commanded it. A single window in the farmhouse was lit up. Silhouetted against it, out on the balcony of the room next to ours, was our hostess Helga. Watching us.

"Jesus, what's happening? How long has she been there?" Laura said.

"It can't have been too long," I said. "We would have seen her."

"It's the apple. When I touched it, it...was it my imagination?"

"No."

"Then something else. An effect of some kind caused by the moonlight—look, she's going in. Jesus Christ, my heart is pounding."

131

She spoke sense—or some semblance of it. I wanted to believe the apple was a disco ball activated by her touch. I wanted to believe it was all about mirrors and reflections. "You're right," I told her. "It had to be illusion."

"There's no other explanation," she said, slowly removing herself from on top of me. I hadn't realized until then how tightly she had been clutching me with her thighs.

We covered ourselves and started back across the field, hand in hand, looking around us, looking back at the tree with its luminous angry fruit. Nothing disturbed the night except shadows. That and the distant, barely audible grumble of a motor.

"Do you hear it?" I asked her.

"I can't hear anything but my heartbeat."

"Come on," I said, turning towards the sound.

"What? Where? I don't want to."

"Just far enough so that we can see what's below. I think I hear a tractor."

"So? Why do we care—"

"Come on." She didn't put up a fight as I pulled her with me, though she kept looking off to her right, where the Devil Orchard flexed its twisted waxen limbs. As we reached the edge of what proved to be a deep slope of more grassland, we had a view that sprawled even in the night, with rolling hills stacked one on the other in progressive shades. Our eyes found the tractor idling in a field, headlights catching its driver digging with his hands in the turned earth in front of the machine. As we watched for a minute or so, he appeared to sift through the soil, finding a glint of something and stuffing it in a bag he wore like an apron.

"What do you suppose he's doing?" Laura said.

"Don't know."

"I want to go back to our room."

"Okay."

The house could not have looked less comforting as we walked along the wall to the gate, wondering which peephole Helga watched from. But as we stepped inside its sturdy framework and the silence of its interiors escorted us to our room, our fears seemed farther and farther away. Laura held me for a long time before I heard her breathe evenly. In that easing music I tried to pass out of time with her, but a persistent gremlin in my system kept me from doing so. I tapped two smokes out of the pack and went out onto the balcony to watch the moon bathe the devil fruit.

I found myself somewhat disappointed when I reached the filter and nothing of report had occurred. I was debating whether to have the second smoke or go to bed when I heard the tractor approaching. The flick of my lighter echoed across the night. Upon lighting the cigarette, I held the flame up to Donon and saw the goddess Diana there. Hadn't Helga said it was *her* temple? The cigarette tasted like a question mark as the sound of the engine drew nearer. When the machine appeared over the lip of the field, the universe had reached a tilted normalcy that flickered among my nerve endings. The tractor turned toward the orchard instead of the house, and I saw the ember in front of my face brighten to unfamiliar degrees.

Helga's husband dropped from the vehicle. As he began to pull the artifacts from his bag and place them on the stone that was probably still wet from his guests' encounter, I had the impression of bones.

———•———

In the morning, as is so often the case, things looked entirely different. Laura joined me on the balcony for my morning puff, and last night need not be visited again as the orchard was only what it was, with actual blossoms breaking out on its branches. We kissed there beneath Donon before donning our cycling clothes and heading down to a wonderfully traditional German breakfast of soft-boiled eggs and *Brötchen* and cheese. When our hostess asked if we had enjoyed visiting the orchard, we could only smile and wonder.

As she saw us off, she apologized for the fact that we never got to meet her husband, who was already out in the fields tilling again. If we took the farm road, which was the easier route around the mountain, we might see him. While we had no practical interest in the drudges of a farmer, we did like the idea of an easier route around the mountain. We entertained only the briefest flutter of doubt when she told us we would save time by crossing the orchard field and picking up the road by the tree line at the base of the mountain.

As we pedaled across the grassy stretch, Laura watched the temple above us, I the orchard. I couldn't be sure without venturing closer, but it appeared as though the rock beneath the tree was vacant. The apple, too, had that look about it as it hung there in the sun, pulpy and bright, unplucked.

SAUDADE

T HERE ARE THINGS we do in this life, crimes we may or may not have committed, that no amount of reflection can shed light upon. Intention can neither be confirmed nor denied. Circumstances cannot be placed back in their proper order. We think we remember what we thought at the time, but can any perspective ever truly be revisited? Can any motive ever truly be known, much less re-known? If not, then regret, remorse, guilt can never truly be applied. We are what we are at any given moment, we do what we do, and the rest is an unsatisfactory record, an analysis without worth, a drive among back roads that deposit us wherever they will.

One such road, a narrow, zigzagging affair that leads up to Tignale above Lago di Garda in Italy, makes no pretenses about its capriciousness. At one turn it might leave you gasping at the beauty of its rugged, foliage-rich setting; at another, hanging in midair over a grove of cypresses or skidding toward the wall of one of the tunnels cut out of the mountain. Where it left me was at the foot of a tiered collection of columned stone structures that vaguely recalled Roman temple pavilions, but whose actual function was lost on the uninformed observer. Particularly one, on that July afternoon, whose preoccupations didn't end with the Opel finally cashing it in after the troubled three-hour trip from Milan.

For a few minutes I just sat there watching the dashboard lights surrender what chi they had left, not bothering to try the ignition, not wondering again whether it was the battery or the alternator, just sitting there thinking about how this situation so coincided with my own journey, my own battle to will it out. Indeed, the car might as well have been me as it merely occupied space in the pull-off, powerless, dead except in the stories of its bones, a fresh relic among the fossils of Lake Garda.

A movement distracted me from rising away out of my body to ride the currents of the surrounding mountains, eternally ashamed of my failure of will but comforted to be done trying. I looked across the road to a point above the pale columns where a woman was descending a set of stairs into the remnants. For a moment her manner and shape were familiar to me, recalling a scene from the first days of my vacation. But I reminded myself that images, like links in the knotted chain of fate, were not to be trusted, and the moment passed—for the short term.

Across the distance of a hundred feet or so she saw me looking, and waved. I reciprocated, knowing that was all I had to offer, a salute, an acknowledgment that we survived in the same world, that our skeletons would mingle when dust had claimed us, and the winds would sing with our unintelligible recollections.

It wasn't until I was out of the car and moving toward her silhouette, framed by the sun burning over the slope that the memory returned, though again only for a salvaged moment in time.

I'd been riding a bike along the Neckar River in Neckargemund, Germany, the sun gone down and the moon, that Renaissance token, risen, saving me from spoiling the shadowy beauty surrounding me with my headlight. My friend Donny was back at the tent, reading by lantern in the tent, fearing a resurgence of the rain that had plagued us for the past two days. I didn't care. In the Nevadan desert rain is a rarity, and when it does fall, it awakens you, doesn't put you inside fluttering the pages of some egoist's remarks. I read, yes, but not as an alternative to experiencing, not as a retreat. I read to know the author. I read to know how the mind works. A fiction author is the best case study around. That's my game as a psychologist, to know the where as to the what. That's why they keep me on the police payroll in Reno, why they recruited a skilled gambler to their ranks. In criminal justice it's the dealer—whether that be the captain or the killer—that takes the final fall, not the player, and that's why we're a perfect match, me and the PD. I was never very good at finishing, and that's what they like, the capitalizing on another's subjectivity.

But tonight, as the bridge came into view, the woman's lifted voice reached my ear, I suppose I *was* reading. Who would be strolling along a footbridge singing her lungs out at this hour? Would the next page tell? Would she be carved out of the night or was she the carver, her tongue the blade? Would I remember her in the future? Was she that lucky or unlucky a hand? I confess to mixing metaphors, but is the page not a card distributed by a crazy, egotistical god? Are lyric and meter not expressions like everything else? This noise of hers was poetry as surely as was a flush at the beshadowed end of the table. As surely as the encoded messages from captain and killer alike. A tease, a promise of something great.

To this day I don't know why when her silhouette came into view, hand carrying the sandals that had at some point in time been carrying her, too heavily, I didn't muster the courage to call up to her, interrupt her song, demand to know if she was simply drunk or if she was enlightened. That she cared not who heard her voice echoing among the bridge's walls only heightened the fascination, to the degree that, yes, she did live on and wasn't that her, there among the Romanesque columns, dark in comparison to the pallid stone, mined out of shadow as opposed to Garda's stony slopes. If the woman who approached me now lifted her head in song, I would return to the lemon Donny had let me borrow and simply mold into its husk, and that would be both all and enough. She didn't, and maybe that, too, was enough.

"*Buongiorno, senora.*"

"*Buongiorno.*"

"Do you speak English?"

"Enough, yes." See? "Are you having car trouble?" She gestured to the broken little scar on the scenery.

"I am."

"Yes, I saw you from the balcony of my hotel. I recognized frustration when you struck the steering wheel with your fists."

"Did I? I thought I just died."

She laughed. Her eyes were the color of her hair, both the perfect complement to her only slightly less dark skin. She wore a skirt about her slim waist, as Italian women tend to do in summer, and a tank top. Her feet were sandaled, her left wrist braceleted. The straps of her bra were visibly transparent. There might have been a shade of blush, a tinge of mascara, earlier, but the heat of the day had worn cosmetics away. We were two people, that was all, joined by the thing that had disrupted our beats.

"Do you have a handy?" she said. I didn't have time to process the European word for cell phone before she added, "No matter, I can call a service for you. Should you end up needing a room, there are two hotels there above the lemon houses. Mine is a nice one. Restaurant, wine, private bath, internet . . . "

"Are you a spokesperson for the company?" I said, hoping she got the joke.

"Didn't you see my commercial?"

"I wish I had. TV's boring these days. But am I so obviously a tourist or passer through that you'd be prompted to suggest a hotel?"

"You have German plates on your car and are speaking English. You could be a businessman, I suppose." She looked at my attire of sleeveless shirt and surf shorts dubiously.

"That's me," I said. "Corporate car and all."

She smiled. A perfect Italian thing among her slightly prominent nose, wondering eyes, suited-to-whatever-expression-emerged mouth. The bones were the only fixed thing about her countenance, supporting her face well, as her frame in general did her undersized breasts, her oversized muscular legs. Her voice, I thought as she issued her next words, had its own infrastructure from which to petal and flesh out with intonations that grazed softly but rippled powerfully.

"Do you recognize me from somewhere?" she said.

"Should I?" Hearing the song carry fully between bridge walls.

"No, but you look like you do."

"Ever been to Baden-Württemberg, Germany?"

"Not that I recall. But I half-wish I had, to inspire such a look."

I don't know why I said it, particularly in this situation, needing help, not a date. "You're inspiration enough as you are."

"Yeah," she smiled. "What sort?"

I vacillated between many poles, finally settling on:

"The only sort."

She didn't say anything, but was not turned away, God forgive me my forwardness.

"So," I said, "you have a phone."

"In my room. You're welcome to use it . . . " She seemed to want to wrap up the sentence, but then abandoned the knot. *I think*. I imagined that's what she'd been thinking.

"Thank you, Miss . . . "

"Elena," she said, offering her hand.

"Darrin."

Now if I could only dredge up the funds the car's fix would require, and see her naïve faith in me through. That ability, as we ascended the stairs she had come down, hinged on the severity of the problem. I made just enough at my Reno PD gig to pay the bills, which included $500 in child support. If it was the battery, I might be able to cover the cost without resorting to my emergency 18%-interest credit card. If it was the alternator, on the other hand, the problem grew more complex. Aside from the expense, how many days would it take to get a part out of Verona or Milan for a fifteen-year-old shitbox a friend had lent me? Two days? Four?

"You have ADAC, I assume," she said over her shoulder.

"Yes. That's why I didn't politely reject my friend Donny's beater when I got a firsthand look at the 'functional car' he'd offered me the use of before I flew over. Said they'd be available to fix whatever needed fixing, that I wouldn't be stuck until the car died. And no sweat if the car did just that. He was tired of having it around anyway. So I guess you could say he just gave it to me to finish off while he finishes up a dissertation over the next couple weeks."

"So you're doing a bit of touring. Been to Italy before?"

"Rome, Pompeii, a few years back."

"Where are you from?"

"Originally, Colorado. Now I'm in Nevada."

"What do you do there?"

"Criminal profiling. I'm a psychologist." I waited for the inevitable "how fascinating" or "like on TV," but neither came. Maybe television was as boring for her as it was for me. Maybe her silence was contempt for psychology or the law. Whatever the case, she was not obliged to reply.

"And yourself?" I said as we paused for a breath at the top of the stairs.

"Ticino, Switzerland. My mother's Italian, my father Swiss. I—is something wrong?"

She'd recalled another memory, a fresher one, one I wasn't keen to revisit.

"I know someone in Lugano," I said. "She says she's half-Swiss, half-Italian. Her husband, a friend of mine, says she's made up the Swiss part to fit in in Switzerland."

"Maybe I'm making up the Swiss part, too. Maybe you're not really a criminal profiler."

"Why would either of us lie?"

"Maybe we're not lying. Maybe we're deluded."

"Deluded? Your English doesn't want at all, does it?"

"I dreamed of moving to America. Put myself to learning all I could."

"Dreamed? Past tense?"

"I don't see myself getting there now. The hotel's a big responsibility, and I can't really see it in anyone else's hands."

"When you said, 'my hotel,' I assumed you meant you were staying there."

"Well . . . I am."

As we resumed walking, I thought about her "deluded" remark. What had it meant? Was it obscure Italian humor? I was about to ask, but she beat me to it.

"You want to know what I meant by saying that maybe we are lying to ourselves. We tend to see ourselves as the mirror depicts us, yes? The left eye is the right eye, so forth. What we really are is quite different from what we think we are. We are always guests at the balls we host. I may think I entertain my patrons, but my patrons in fact entertain me. You may think you have insight into the criminal mind, but the criminal mind actually has insight into you. These lemon houses below us, for instance –"

I'd stopped, gripping my skull, the memory of Lugano a lemon ripened beyond its branch's capacity to support.

"That's very Nietzsche of you," I said between the heels of my palms. "How much are your rooms? You do have soft pillows . . . "

"Sixty euro per night. And yes, of course."

"Consider me booked."

———⁃———

I woke the next morning from dreams of philosophers in summer skirts. I ignored the ringing phone on the stand beside me, as I'd ignored my own cell phone for the past two days. Had she not offered me her phone to call the garage, I'm not sure I could have brought myself to use my own, for fear of who might be waiting in the interim. I didn't want to know who was calling, I didn't want to know anything. When it quit, I turned over, thrusting the pillow over my face. Sleep. There was never enough of it. Not anymore.

A knock at the door. Could I let that go too? Could I muffle the persistence of a call involving so little distance? That's what it was all about, wasn't it? Proximity? The more distance I put between myself and Lugano, the shorter the fall. Now the brink beckoned again, and if I accepted its invitation, maybe it would finally be over.

I didn't bother donning my shorts. I didn't care that I was in my underwear, only that I opened the way upon the depths. And yet, as the door swung open, I found myself surprised to find the space beyond as vacant as advertised. Not even a hand to help pull me down. I stood there looking on the opposite wall of the corridor, perplexed.

"Darrin?" I heard from the vacuum. Then she appeared in the doorway, one hand mussing her hair. "Sorry to wake you, but the garage called. It's the alternator belt. An easy fix, they said. You can pick up the car anytime."

I adjusted. Wiped sleep from my eyes. "What time is it?"

"Nearly nine. Did you not enjoy your dinner?" It seemed a non sequitur until she pointed beyond me to the tray of half-eaten lasagna, bread, salad.

I readjusted, wiped sleep, sleep from my eyes. "It was good. I was just too tired . . . "

"Breakfast is still being served downstairs, but you'd better hurry. Nine o' clock they clear the buffet."

I nodded. "Do I have time to brush my teeth?"

"And put on clothes?" She smiled. "I'll make sure they hold at least some toast and coffee for you."

"Thanks."

When I got downstairs, the buffet was still laid out, though the dining area was empty except for Elena, at a table on which rested a small pot of coffee. I loaded my plate with eggs, salami, bread, and yogurt, and sat at the offered chair opposite her. She poured my coffee, offered milk and sugar, sat back watching my half-delirious "mmm" before I put the mug down to spread butter and marmalade over my bread.

"Join me?" I said as I partook.

"Thanks. I've had mine."

I chewed, suddenly conscious of her gaze, of the fact that I was eating alone, and yet flattered in some weird way by her attention.

"I appreciate your help," I said, wiping my mouth. "Lucky for me a benevolent soul like yourself was on hand."

"We help each other," she shrugged. "That's what this business of life is about, right?"

I paused at my attempt to extract a soft-boiled egg from its shell, then resumed the effort, tapping the hard cocoon too sharply with my spoon. I let the spoon clatter on my plate, said, "I suppose."

"You suppose?"

My next words sounded bizarre even to my own ears. "Are you a friend of Sophia's, is that it? Did Nick call you from Lugano, ask you to look out for me? It was his suggestion, when he learned I wanted to visit Lake Garda after my stay with them, that I find lodging in Tignale, with a mountain view of the lake. Funny you happening to be here . . . "

I could see the shadow bleed into her eyes. "What are you talking about? Who are these people, Sophia and Nick?"

I looked at her, seconds ticking by. "Friends. Never mind."

"What are you running from?"

"Life. Death. If I told you . . . "

"Aren't we all? Running? Tell me."

"I can't. I'm—I mean, I'm sorry." I stood, pulled a fifty-euro bill, the last of my easily accessible money, out of my pocket, dropped it on the table. "That should cover room and breakfast. Thanks for your help."

"It's included."

"What?"

"Breakfast. A taxi to the garage can be too, if you'll just mellow a moment."

"I . . . yes, I could use a taxi."

"Finish your breakfast, have a shower—you look like you need it—and I'll meet you in front of the hotel with my car. You don't mind that sort of taxi, do you? The concerned kind?"

Her hospitality was surreal. "You haven't grown wary of me yet?"

She just looked at me, frowning.

———•———

As we passed the lemon houses she informed me that they had been erected almost four centuries ago, were located variously around the Gardasee, having been part of a productive industry. "I like to think of them," she said, "as four-dimensional photographs. Have you ever heard of the Portuguese word, *Saudade*? It is a nostalgia for something never personally experienced. That's how I feel about the lemon houses. When among them I can smell, taste what they once contained."

I thought about that. I thought about it for a long time. Then we were at the garage and Elena hanging around while they insisted on showing me the old battered belt before letting me pay for the new one. I wasn't sure why she stayed, but I was glad to have her. I was glad to see her embarrassed looks as I caught her glancing at me from outside the garage, was glad to feel my own embarrassment for catching her catching me. Maybe she wasn't here to remind me after all. Maybe she would offer another night's escape, this time in her arms. It was hard not to think such thoughts as we stood by her car again, Elena asking where I would go next, me replying maybe Venice or Florence, I didn't know. When the words came from her lips, they were terribly welcome, like a demon temptress's breath.

"Stay here one more night."

"I would love that—"

"But only if you'll tell me."

"I will," I said, brushing her hair with my lips. The strands in the sunshine smelled of lemon.

———•———

We lay together in her bed, legs entwined, enjoying the afterglow. The guilt I felt for making love to her under false pretenses, for not having told her what I really was, was real, but the moment was even more real, a steady light in the darkest of tunnels. She didn't have to tell me it was time, that what we'd just shared was a sealing of trust, a forging that went beyond animal pleasure. I considered the notion that the philosopher in her had found a specimen in me, a sample of human mystery to probe, to profile, and that she had been willing to pay with her body for my secrets. But I knew this wasn't so. Some deeper part of her had imprinted itself on some deeper part of me. The music of our union had not spent itself in its crescendo, but lingered lazily, not an echo but a protracted chord, a clear vibration going inerrantly on in a vacuum.

Once I started, I was at the mercy of my confession. The words were their own engine, fueled by a necessity of the soul. "I came here on a dime. Before I was a profiler, I was a gambler, an uncannily good one except when it came to the killing stroke, where I failed time and again, accruing a huge amount of debt that I've not even begun to put a dent in. When friends invited me to Europe for some time away, I told them I didn't think it wise to take on the expense. But both my buddy Donny in Germany and Nick in Switzerland insisted, saying they would provide lodging—and in Donny's case, even a set of wheels to get around in. It didn't take much convincing. I've been through a lot over the past couple years, including two rough sociopath cases in succession, and to experience Europe again— it's been ten years—seemed worth the cost of a paycheck or two.

"The trip was going well until I got to Lugano, and the house of my friend Nick and his wife Sophia. I've known them both for several years, but I'm not really sure I ever thought of her as a friend except by extension. But it soon became apparent that since I'd last seen them—how long had it been? a year and a half since they visited me in the States?—that she'd thought *a lot* about me. At first I passed her flirtations off as just that, innocent amusements, minor sport, whatever, but then I began to realize she was seriously attracted to me. Whether Nick noticed anything, I couldn't say, as a lot of it went on behind his back, an intimation over salad chopping in the kitchen, a touch here or there, suggestive remarks. None of it blatant enough to justify a stern response on my part, but enough to make me very uncomfortable. There was no way I was going to betray a friend with his wife, particularly not Nick, who's helped me out of more than one spot in the past. After a couple days of this . . . embarrassment, I begged out of a planned weekend in Lauterbrunnen with them, fabricating a story about having heard from a friend at Como who'd managed to postpone a work engagement in Brazil that would have prevented him from seeing me while I was in Europe. I told them I'd return in a couple days. It was a reasonable story. I do have a number of friends abroad, acquired mainly through the gambling circles. Nick knew this—in fact, that's where I met him. As to Sophia, I hoped she'd take the hint and be cooled off by the time I returned. But things were not to go as devised—not by a long shot. Nick had taken time off work for my visit, but on Friday morning he got a call on some urgent out-of-town business. I was immediately suspicious. For all I knew, Sophia had phoned in a favor from somebody, knowing I wasn't planning to be on the road until about noon."

Elena gently interrupted me at this point, moving her calf against mine. "Friday, three days ago? The day before we met?"

"Yeah, the day before we met," I said, enjoying the glide of her skin, wondering just how much contact she'd want to have fifteen minutes from now when the tale was told. "So, as I'm sure you've guessed, Sophia seized the opportunity. Oh, she was casual enough about it at first, remarking that Lake Como was less than a two hour's drive from Lugano and I might as well hang out at the pool for a bit now that we had a clear day for a change. We could even go for a sail. Yeah, a sail. Did I mention Nick's a finisher? Has the killing stroke? Yeah, he owns a lot of toys, hell, Sophia's probably one of them. Anyway, she wanted me there, and after some resistance on my part, had no scruples about pulling her best card. Her exact words: 'We both know Como's a farce. You don't like me, that's okay, but you owe me.' 'Yeah? How so?' I said, growing angry. She said, 'For convincing Nick to offer you accommodation in this sparkling new house of his. Don't think because we paid you a visit in the States you're his last best pal. Come on!

You live in Reno, for God's sake. Nick would as soon entertain his mother as a—and this is his word—*loser* like you.' My reply to that was disgustingly feeble: 'If that were so, why would he have bothered inviting me? Why take two weeks out of his life, offer his home to a fucking loser like me?' She laughed. 'Because I asked him to, for the love of Christ! What do you think this thing is, Darrin? Where do you think he's gone today? Probably the golf club! I want what I want, he wants what he does, and we don't stand in each other's way. Do you really think he's so dense that our flirtations flitted right by him?' '*Your* flirtations,' I corrected, in a last ditch effort to stop the bleeding.' She wasn't relenting. 'Delude yourself, cowboy, but you were right there with me all the way. You may have been embarrassed. You may have been ashamed. But what you haven't been is unflattered and untempted. Look at me! Look at yourself. Fucking Christ.'

"The 'look at yourself' hit hard, but not nearly so hard as the notion that I may have been receptive to, may have encouraged her flirtations all along. Hadn't I, in fact? If only by letting it go on? I needed a drink, which she fetched like a maid instead of the class-A bitch she was. She wasn't too good to dirty work it, that's for sure. She poured a second vodka on ice for herself, and as the liquor took effect it seemed to temper the air—momentarily.

"'Look,' she said. 'Let's just hang out. You know you're a player, so what's to lose? If you leave me in a puddle of tears, you're a winner. If you leave me in a puddle of something more . . . viscous—' she grinned like a lascivious old man at the playground—'we're both winners. Whattaya say?' 'I say you're a whore,' I said, and stood up to walk out. As I reached the door, not caring about my suitcase, not caring about anything but putting the serpentess behind me, she said something that brought my retreat to a halt.

"Once, at a party, a half-drunk friend of a friend, someone I didn't personally know, made a homophobic joke at my expense, an unclever response to something I'd said. I was alert enough to turn the tables on him, telling him that would have been funny if I weren't gay. Sophia used exactly the same tact. 'That would have been funny,' she said, 'if it weren't true.' I realize now, and probably did then, that it was a designed thing, a sympathy play. Why I fell into it, I can't say, unless it was simply a matter of my having succeeded in insulting her, in penetrating her spheres deeper than she had mine. All I could come up with by way of response, and this with my back to her, was, 'You've such a low opinion of yourself?' The worst of all mistakes, this acknowledgment. I was hers then, for the morning, the afternoon, wherever the day took us. I cursed her, I cursed myself, but that didn't stop me from sucking down the next vodka, and the next. I admit I was charmed by her raw edge, even stimulated, but the game had taken a different turn now and damned if I wasn't going to prove she couldn't make me succumb to her. Short-term surrenders, sure. But long term? She would be paying for her presumption. One way or another.'"

I realized the weight of my words even as I said them. But honesty was at the heart of mine and Elena's game and I wasn't going to shrink because her body had stopped moving.

"That's scary," she said.

The hairs on my arms stirred at the words in spite of my conviction. But I told on, because that's what had to be done. "Sophia and I swam, we sailed, we parasailed, never with more than brief touches. It was like a dance toward delirium. It was like you and me, but without the sense of destiny. The experience would be retrievable after it was finished, but only in the most cursory sense—a sort of landmark between unremembered fucks. Evening brought sekt, champagne, some erotic French short film, reminders of what she considered a determined path. To cap it, this wondrous day, she suggested a place on top of the mountain. We ate strawberries there, ice cream, drank more sekt, but it wasn't until we were heading down again that it all reached the head she was looking for.

"'I want you to stop the car and fuck me,' she told me. We were in her car, not the lemon Donny lent me. Her car, me driving, as if Porsches had always been my choice of transport.

"'When we get back,' I said. 'It's only a—'

"'Now!' she demanded.

"'You won't like it if it's now, Sophia. I promise you won't.'

"'Then again, maybe I will.'

"'Fuck you,' I said.

"'Fuck me? *Fuck me*? I get the words, is that all!' Then she began hitting me in the shoulder, the chest, the head, screaming, 'Let me out of this fucking car! Let me fucking *out*!'

"And you know what? I did. Tired of the whole fucking bash, I did. I stepped around the front of her Porsche, jerked the door open and *let* her out by her hair. She laughed. She laughed and she laughed, and I dropped her there on the shoulder of one of Lugano's steep slopes like so much unwanted baggage and sped away in her sports car, wishing only for another sekt to bring it all back into focus.

"But when I hit the road that led to the Italian border, forced to think about my passport and all that, I also thought of the whore I'd left on the edge of a drop-off, and I'd no choice but to go back. I can't tell you how many twists I had to navigate back up that mountain, but they were many, and the prize at the end an anti-prize, a projection of my own being. I wasn't sure where I'd abandoned her, exactly, but figured I'd find her staggering along the shoulder, nursing her no doubt significant wounds. I was drunk and the country outside my headlights a foggy one. If she'd decided just to sit where I left her, I might easily miss her. So I tried to keep it slow. I say 'tried' because the Porsche was a steed beneath me and I had a mission, though I couldn't really say what that mission was. To fulfill some human obligation? Some devotion to Nick? My own sense of decency? No, none of these, I'm sure. I simply wanted to put the pieces back together, to not leave a wreck behind me that might haunt me later. Yes, that selfish. How I would accomplish the task, I wasn't sure, but I knew I needed to retrieve her from the possibility of falling victim to some other drunk on the road, or a misstep that would land her at the bottom of a cliff. Eventually I decided I must have missed her along the way, and turned around. My feet were angry on the pedals by then. I screeched out of my turnaround, was in the process of rounding a sharp bend when there she was, on my side of the road, facing me. She had no doubt seen me pass and was waiting for me. The sudden sight of her caused me to overcompensate, sending the car into a skid. It was enough. The *thunk* as the car struck her was solid, impressive. I somehow managed to correct the car, braking to a stop before the next turn. I sat there surrounded by blackness, heart pounding, thoughts gone haywire. Minutes I sat there, unsure what to do. Eventually one certain course of action emerged. I had to see what had become of her.

"I turned the car around and slowly approached the point of impact. At this pace I was able to see just how narrow the shoulder, how empty the region beyond it, and I knew she'd gone over the edge. I considered leaving then, saving myself the image that I knew would haunt me for the rest of my days. But I had to see. Call it morbidity. Call it the need for even the feeblest measure of closure, but I had to know. I thought of the smallest things then. Assuming she was visible, how would she appear? Graceful? Broken? Would the headlights glaring out into the vacancy be a detriment or an aid to the onlooker? They proved to be both, taking away my night vision while at the same time providing the glow that divined her silhouette from the darkness of the tree branches among which she sprawled twenty feet or so below. That's the tableau I carry with me, this shadow of a descending bird of prey, wings spread, trapped in leaves. She landed gracefully, I think, as gracefully as one could expect of such a creature."

I let my confession end there, as if to lend it value, validity by a poetic strain. Neither of us said anything for a while. In the silence, the warmth of her leg, her flesh against mine was a dull, awkward pain, one which I knew I could alleviate by repositioning myself, but which I did not want to lose for fear of the cold that would replace it. When at last words came, they came from both of us, simultaneously—

"But the thing is—" Me.

"What did you do then—" Elena.

"Sorry," I muttered. "Go ahead."

"No . . . tell me, what is the thing?"

"Well, maybe it will be better explained if I tell you what I did next. I drove the car back to Nick and Sophia's house, parking it in the garage, rear end to the wall as it had been before we left. I checked the side of the car thoroughly and, finding no damage, no *evidence* of what I had done, I located a vacuum cleaner and thoroughly cleaned the seats and floors, wiped down the steering wheel, the dashboard, the door handles and panels with a cloth, then went upstairs and checked the answering machine to see if Nick had called to say he'd be coming in early—he'd said he didn't expect to return until late yesterday. Then I got my bag, threw it in Donny's car and left. All very mechanical. All very calculated toward fitting those pieces, that wreck back together. Nick's is a secluded house, so I doubted anyone had seen the coming and going. As to people who might have observed us together, or with the car, at the lake, there was nothing I could do about that and so I didn't let it be a distraction from what I *did* have to do. That's where the 'thing' comes in."

I paused to give her the chance to extricate herself from me. When that didn't happen, I wet my lips, preparing to recall to her the comment she'd made about people seeing themselves one way, but actually being another thing entirely. But I couldn't make the words apply, couldn't make sense where there was none, and ended up letting out a terribly succinct, "I think I may be a murderer."

She moved her leg now, a stroke that shocked my nerves then immediately quelled them, the warmth merely having been conveyed to a different spot. "Yesterday," she said, "you romanticized remarks I made by associating them with Nietzsche. I am no philosopher, Darrin, just a lost soul like you. I'm not even sure what I meant at the time. Nietzsche, I can tell you, has nothing to do with anything. I was talking about *me*. About my own deluded course. I don't know who or what I am any more than you know who or what you are. I suspect the same goes for Nietzsche, and, hell, God Himself! We all just hover over the current."

She might have been apologizing for not having the answer I sought, but I sensed more than that. I sensed I wasn't the only one harboring mighty, unanswerable questions. But still we ask them:

"What does that mean, you who are not a philosopher?"

"It means what it does. Nothing. No matter which angle you look at yourself, your life, your dreams from, it's a lie."

"There is no such creature as truth, then?"

"Truth? If you return to the site of the alleged crime, see the bird again

146

by the broad light of day, will that be truth? Will you be suddenly bound to a greater purpose? No, I don't think even Sophia has found truth."

"I didn't say anything about returning to the site."

"Didn't you? You said she was a shadow. That's where we all return. That's where I'll return when your headlights find the next vacancy. You think your story is profound? You should hear mine. Replace sekt with heroin, your whore with my john, your calculated cleaning up with my madness, and then we'll talk about Nietzsche."

But you have a hotel, I wanted to say, a phone to lend, the scent of lemon in your hair. But her response was already there, a perpetual echo in the hovel of her bedchamber. I remembered her description of *saudade*, a nostalgia for something never experienced. Wasn't that what existence was all about? Wanting more? Remembering more? Maybe it is enough just to want, to remember, the solidity of the thing having nothing to do with true value.

I was surprised when she kissed me on my chin, whispered all rights into my stubble. "We'll go," she breathed. "We'll go together."

———•———

We set out the next morning, after soft-boiled eggs and Italian bread and yogurt. As we went we basked in the lemony splash of the sun, not unlike the afterglow of our night's secrets, secrets that now seemed to have absorbed the confessions that followed them. Her hand on my leg was a minor truth in spite of her, and the road in front of us, whizzing with Italian maniacs, not a path to the site of the alleged crime, but a ripple finding its way back to the drop of rain that had created it. What difference, really, our destination, when it is founded in illusion, delusion, glorious madness? And yet, the spell was not without imperfections as we left the *autostrade* for the narrower road that would take us into Switzerland. Each rock face, every bluff and cliff seemed to flash a more arcane band of the spectrum, in turn igniting more primal emotions, ones I might have confused with anxiety, apprehension, had Elena not been there to soothe them as they came. That she displayed no such emotions neither encouraged nor discouraged my acceptance of the terms of her universe. She traveled with me as freely as I did with her, and our onuses our own to bear. Still, the thing that lurked beneath it all gradually unfurled petals of the scent of fear, and the oasis of companionship and mutual acquiescence began to dissolve.

It was when the first sign for Lugano appeared that I relinquished the fantasy of falsity to fear. I tried to hide it—from myself? Elena?—as we found the road Sophie and I (had I ever called her Sophie while she was alive?) had taken, but it would not be unvoiced. The twisting road up the mountain was very much a path to the site of my alleged crime. As the

147

tableau came into full mental view, an alarm went off in my nerves, a terrible screeching recurrence that forced me to pull off the highway into the no zone as I finally gathered in Elena's suggestion that I "answer it."

It was my cell. Yes, too long ignored. Whoever it was, Nick, the police, it was past time I confronted the situation.

"Hello."

"Darrin? It's me, Sophia. Listen, I'm sorry about the way I behaved—"

I let the phone drop.

"Darrin?" Elena said. "Who . . . "

As if answers, suddenly, were so easy.

I pulled onto the road again, my foot heavier on the pedal than it should have been, a weight to rival the silence that had descended over the car. As I rounded the next bend a figure appeared along the left rim of the road, back to me, in the same area, my sense told me, that Sophie— whoever I'd hit—had been. I passed, looking first over my shoulder, then in the rearview, in hopes of seeing her face. But a glare, the curve of the road, would not allow it. Before the next bend I turned around, now finding my tongue again, babbling at Elena beside me, who offered no insights, no consolations, letting me through it alone. The sun was in front of me now, but disappearing behind trees. The face came into view, its hair and eyes darker than its deeply colored skin, its aspect otherwise befogged—though somewhere in there I saw a warmth, a smile of memory, of nostalgia for things never experienced. I braked hard, reaching an arm over to protect Elena. The emptiness beside me was the vacancy out beyond the drop-off. Out there, in headlight-illuminated oblivion.

I got out of the car, went to the brink, and looked down into the abyss. She was still there, the shape in the branches, though her position seemed to have changed, assumed the image of closed wings, as though the bird had not swept down, but crashed. As though the shadow imprinted on my eyes had been lying all along. I found footholds and handholds, roots and irregularities enough to make my way down. The trees were smaller than my memory had them. A smell wafted up from them, a sweet yet sunny smell, a tinge yellowy, fruity. I reached a ledge and stretched out to touch her back, walk my fingers to her hair, pulling gently. "Wake up," I said. "You've had rougher falls. This is nothing, just a couple days' rest from the pain, the places you care not to remember. Open your eyes and maybe the world will have changed. Maybe we can find that other land, that land that *saudade* speaks of." I couldn't be certain in the rippling sunlight, the intoxicating aroma, but I thought I saw the leaves stir.

Somehow—over the course of hours, it seemed—I managed to haul her up to the road. On my shoulder the body made no movements that I could discern, but its flesh was warm against mine. When I reached the car, I lay her gingerly in the seat beside me, squeezing in behind the wheel, starting the engine, uncertain where I was going, but knowing it required urgency.

As I accelerated I heard a horn and a rush of wind as a truck scraped by, its tailgate flinging open in the driver's attempt to right it. Its cargo poured out of the back, causing me to brake into a skid amid the yellow specimens, angling toward the brink. The thought of going there with her, becoming one with her shadow, calmed me as the question of survival hung just so elegantly in front of me. Then, in that instant that is less than an instant, we'd come to a stop, shy of the edge, the woman beside me turning, her lips forming words.

"Where . . . oh yes, I remember . . . someplace pleasant . . . "

A HOUSE OF WEBS AND DUST

PART ONE
A DIRTY HOUSE

I'D SWORN I would never write another "writer" story. That I'd quit my craft before I put out any more material that could be called "introverted" by my editors or critics. But on that October afternoon as I sat on my coat on the crag above the cabin, I found myself doing exactly that. And in the first-person narrative, no less.

The page had always been a mirror for me, a way of understanding the world through myself. The trouble with that was, I could no longer keep up with the threads my brain generated. I knew in some part of me that this was the result of oncoming dementia, yet I kept writing. I kept trying to follow storylines that made sense only within the stream of thought.

I tried to force myself to stop, but my pen just kept scribbling away in the notebook, the story off on its own, irreversible course. I hadn't gone at it with such vigor since—

I'd lost contact with myself, and thus the world. So much so that when I sat at the overlook, my favorite spot for working on my initial drafts, I often forgot to take in the fresh, juniper-scented air, the view of the lake below, even the routine swallow of beer.

—Kay had said goodbye to me a year before.

———◆———

I heard Kay screaming when I pulled up in the drive on the Harley, having returned late as usual from the casino. That the noise had pierced the sound of the engine was almost as telling as the scream itself as I immediately shut off the ignition, dismounted, and rushed toward the cabin's front door—which, I could see by the garage light, was wide open.

I was drunk after a day of close calls wagering on Saturday's college football action, but not so drunk that I hadn't been able to navigate my way up to our isolated home on the California side of southern Lake Tahoe. I was in that danger zone, after the night's losses, where I was just stable enough to be able to focus the otherwise expressionless anger that often simmered in me. You'd never have thought me the gentle and reclusive writer I sought to be as I stormed the doorway, fists tight as springs.

"Kay!" I shouted, searching interiors as dark as her screams had gone.

"Jake!" she cried, appearing out of the shadows and rushing into my arms. "Jacob, I can't take it anymore."

"What, baby? *What?*"

She struck my shoulder as she sobbed against it. Struck it again, and again, with fading force. "If you don't know what, then *who* does, Jake? For Christ's sake, can't we just live a normal life?"

"Okay, Kay. Okay. If this is about my writing again—"

"*You know it is!*" she cried, briefly renewing her assault before regaining control of herself. "They're everywhere, you're your fucking creations. Please, please don't ask me to read your nightmares for you anymore."

"Babe—"

"I mean it, Jake. The gambling, the rest of it I can take. But the stories . . . you pull the both of us in and you don't let us back out."

"Baby, I've told you I don't know where they go. You know before I do."

"Be sober for just once while you're writing, and maybe . . . " But she let it trail away, knowing those were perilous waters.

———•———

"And so, Mr. Shields, without further ado, I would like to present you with the university's highest honorary degree in literature."

"In nightmares, he means," said Kay, winking at me.

"My subconscious speaks and they honor me with sheepskin. Kafka himself would approve."

"Go get your reward, lover. The world needs more of you fearless voices as far as I'm concerned." She joined the rest of the auditorium in applause as I stepped to the podium.

As I accepted my unearned diploma, it seemed almost real to me, this small milestone in my career. Almost made me forget the self-suspicion that had begun to creep in with the reception my latest project had gotten from my own publisher, a damned fine writer in her own right. Or had her words merely been a reflection of what I was already on my way to realizing? *If you were anyone else, I'd have my reservations about this manuscript, Jacob. It's as opaque as it is disturbing to me. But hey, it's not my job to critique it. My job's to get it into the hands of those who will pretend to understand it.*

I caught her eye in the audience as I thanked her during my acceptance speech.

Julia, I'll do better next time, I managed not to say.

———•———

The long nights in bed. The tossing and turning and cracking my knees as I tried to bend and stretch myself into some satisfactory form against Kay's body. Against the maddeningly persistent plot questions, which seemed to

151

always lead back to the same resolution—start the fuck over, man.

Start over. Chase down the unintended tangents, the imposed images, the stray voice, the pseudo-philosophical angle, the obsession with the perceived power of the word *God*. Bring it back home again. Speak from the well, yes, but give the murky output some semblance of clarity. Of logic.

But *why*? I kept asking myself. Is there logic in being? In trying to make sense, rather than simply listening to, the primal voice?

Was there logic in the bottom of a bottle?

That was the sticking point. At forty-one, I was aging now, and the days of the more useful aids, the mind-opening substances, were gone. Left to me was alcohol, which did its diligent duty in wiping out the inhibitions, but at an increasing price. While I liked to believe it simply swept up after the psychoactive drugs of my younger days, gathered the flaked-off brain cells into a little pan where they could be foraged through for some sign of their previous glitter, I knew better. Dementia loved a clean house. It thrived in an environment where it could weave its own cobwebs, accumulate its own dust, create its own sense of terror and loss.

My folly, I reminded myself in my most lucid moments, was in standing in its way. Why shouldn't I be my own janitor? What exactly was wrong with a clean house?

———•———

I looked for Kay everywhere. In South Lake Tahoe, where some of her friends lived. In Carson City, where she'd previously worked and where some of her relatives could be found. In Reno, where the family tree had sprung its branches. Even San Francisco, where her estranged father reputedly lived. All to a dead end.

Not that I'd have imagined it easy, pursuing a former stripper and escort. My own life had taught me that those who "love" you tend to forget you faster than those who truly accept you. But where would she have gone other than to family or friends? Sure, she had the personal account I'd set up for her when she was looking at opening a boutique in town. She had her jewelry, her credit cards, the ready cash she liked to carry around. But she knew as well as anybody that it was a cold, cold world out there. And one that required navigational skills that—despite the penetrating intelligence that had ultimately magnetized me—she hadn't quite mastered at the next level. Top this off with the fact that she was a practical, level-headed individual who'd said her goodbyes to me with a measured, hardly reckless resolve, and I was forced to consider the possibility that she hadn't voluntarily disappeared.

Then someone in her family filed a missing persons report, and the light, inevitably, fell on me.

—·—

"Did you or did you not, Mr. Shields, have an argument with Miss Garner in the parking lot of Harrah's on the day she supposedly said goodbye to you?"

"We did. But it was harmless—"

"Harmless? An argument that preceded her leaving you by only a few hours?"

"Civilized, then."

"Civilized. That sounds like a word that could be associated, by contrast, with violence."

"Objection, your honor!"

"Sustained."

"What was this civilized argument about, Mr. Shields?"

"My spending time away from her."

"Please elaborate."

"She felt that between my writing and sports gambling, I didn't spend enough time with her."

"And what happened after the civilized argument?"

"Your honor. The prosecution is drilling the word into the jury's head."

"Sustained again. Don't try the court's patience, Mr. Stanton. Please answer the question, Mr. Shields."

"Kay went home. I went into the casino."

"When did you leave the casino?"

"About five-thirty."

"That afternoon."

"Yes. I went home to find that Kay had packed her bags. She told me she was leaving me. I wanted her to stay, but she said she had made up her mind and wanted to move on with her life."

"Did you try to stand in her way?"

"Absolutely not."

"Here's where things get a bit sketchy, Mr. Shields. We have accounts of you coming home, but none of Miss Garner leaving your property, though your closest neighbor has testified that he was working in his yard until dark and never saw her distinctive yellow Miata exit the cul-de-sac that accesses both your homes. Indeed, no one seems to have seen her or her vehicle anywhere. How do you explain that?"

"I can't."

"Isn't it true that you have no alibi for that night?"

"After she left, I returned to the casino."

"The casino whose sports book had, by your own admission to police, closed when the west coast games went off the board?"

"The blackjack tables are open all night."

"Yes. So you told the detectives when you later amended your original statement. Why did you do that exactly, Mr. Shields? Why bother? Surely you realized it only made you look more guilty."

"I'd nothing to hide."

"And what did you tell them when they asked why you'd changed your story?"

"That when drinking's involved, things sometimes don't come back to me immediately."

"You were drinking hard that night, weren't you, Mr. Shields? You'd lost a lot of money and you were numbing the pain with alcohol?"

"I suppose so."

"The police first questioned you a week after Miss Garner was reported missing. Several more weeks went by before you were interviewed a second time. Given these significant intervals and your testimony that when drinking's involved, things sometimes don't come back to you immediately, might it be possible that you will yet remember murdering your partner?"

"No. I loved Kay. I would never—"

"You *loved* her? Past tense? We don't have a body, Mr. Shields. Surely you haven't given up hope, have you?"

"I will never give up hope."

"Yes, I'm sure the jury is quite convinced of that—"

"Objection!"

"Withdrawn. I can't imagine what overcame me, your honor."

"Counsel, rid yourself of the sarcasm before I do."

"Yes, ma'am. Back to your alibi, Mr. Shields. You say you were playing blackjack. How is it that no one on the casino floor remembers the local drunken celebrity being at the tables that night?"

"I don't know . . . they're busy on a Saturday night? Look, I'm not what you're looking for—"

"*What* we're looking for? You'll so blatantly play up the dubious testimony of the so-called doctor the defense presented earlier? You're clearly not outside of yourself, Mr. Shields. No more than you were when you killed your partner in cold blood."

"Objection!"

"Mr. Holmes put his client on the stand, your honor."

"Sustained. Approach the bench, counselors."

———·———

Sustained. It was a word I'd hold onto for a long time after the trial was finished. "Sustained" bore more weight than "not guilty" as far I was concerned. A judge was like a publisher; her word merited more than a jury's, even one that had exonerated me of all charges.

A long time. Time enough to see a threatened civil suit dissolve before it ever materialized. Time enough to consider and reconsider the degree of one's own involvement in the tragedy of one's life. To explore, through the only mode available, the sort of evidence that could not be sifted through by prosecutors or brought into a court of law. To reconfirm that the source of Kay's terror had been as real as the screams I'd come home to on that last sensible night.

What followed in the week I had left with her was the stuff of utter madness. My pen was the wand. The lone juniper tree rooting in the rocky crevices of the overhang was the twisted staff in whose knots and gnarls the terrors took shape.

———◆———

I woke to the smell of coffee, done Kay's exquisite way with Kay's carefully selected boutique product. Fresh Columbian beans delivered to the door. Not for her, but for me, as though I cared about such things. If she'd looked closely she would have seen that I accepted her tokens simply to make her happy. But she was blinded by the perceived role . . . and yes, in spite of our circumstances, love.

I'd never questioned the validity of our relationship. In the early days Kay probably had, but those days were long gone now. We'd lived lives upon lives together, as all artists and their partners do. Survived storms and failed compasses and shipwrecks. For all the ill it had brought on us, my writing had also bound us more securely than any ring, and all the more so because of her participation in my creations as my first reader. Every emotion that sprang forth between us had its roots, in one way or another, in the words and pictures and meanings and perceptions, the *art*, for better or worse, that we both had to deal with on a daily basis. We weren't unique, but we were twain souls in our rarity. If I'd been asked to cut off an ear to prove it, I'd have referred the doubter to the bulging envelope in the outgoing mail, and then defied them to name the addressor's gender.

Enter a withered-looking Kay, last night having taken an obvious toll on her. She'd fallen asleep with the screams still echoing through the cabin, and I'd fallen away with her, the alcohol finally putting them to rest for me. What had it been about anyway? I remembered pulling up on my bike, hearing her distress, her accusations, but where did these things belong in the sunny mosaic of a late Sunday morning? Among the rectangles of light on the floor, the familiar scents of java and kitchen cleaner and incense-cedar in the air? What was this strange and distant thing we called "last night"? Could you bathe in it? Inhale it?

"A hundred dollars," she said.

"A hundred dollars?"

"A hundred dollars if you can tell me what we were fighting about last night."

"Fighting? We weren't fighting, were we?"

"I was fighting. You were drunk."

"I love you too."

She put her arms around my neck. "I'm scared, Jake. I mean like waking up scared. I got up, had a cigarette, made coffee and tidied up a bit as usual this morning, but my fingers were literally trembling the whole time. I had to use two hands to hold my coffee cup. Look, they're still not completely steady."

I saw that she wasn't exaggerating. I wanted to blame it on the caffeine in her system, the lack of sleep, the remnant emotions, but I knew there was more to it than that. This wasn't the first morning after. It wasn't the first time she'd responded fearfully to the material I'd printed out for her to read after transferring it from the notebook to the computer. But the instances had dramatically increased lately. The past two weeks had been a minor whirlwind of emotion for the both of us as I poured myself into what had turned out to be a more ambitious project than expected. I usually waited until the draft was complete to show it to her, but for some reason I'd insisted on giving her the latest work in sections.

She took my silence as an invite to pursue the matter more deeply, which she knew I couldn't stomach first thing in the morning. "I'm seeing them, Jake. Out of the corners of my eyes. In the shadows, in the light, everywhere. Do you wonder why the door was open when you came home last night? Because I couldn't stand being closed in with your monsters. I can't do it anymore, baby. I feel the same way you describe yourself as feeling in the story . . . like I'm splintering."

"It's fiction, Kay—"

"It is *not* fiction. It never was, Jake. They're your nightmares. Your own naked, unmitigated truth. I used to applaud you for it, for telling the story others were afraid to tell. The story of the self, the soul. But Jake, I've come to realize that the soul is a black, black place and its story should not ever be told. To tell it is to give shape and dimension and *solidity* to its secrets. I know it's art, and that art and truth should be synonymous, but not when it comes directly out of the primal cinders. That's the last sacred place left, don't you understand? It *has* to remain taboo. Otherwise we're all damned."

I'd poured my coffee as she spoke, blown on it, sipped it, blown on it again. They were actions, habits, routine motions, nothing to do with the realities of the specific moment. The heat of the cup could not be converted into something usable against the chill inspired by Kay's words.

"Damned?" I said. "I'm damned because I write what I feel?"

"No, no, no, no, *no*, man. Only for you is it that simple. You've broken through the barriers, you're able to pull these horrors out of your primordial well at will. But what about what you subject the rest of us to? We still have our barriers. We're still complex creatures."

"So I've *devolved* now? I'm sub-human?"

She looked at me defiantly. "You're less complicated, yes."

I bit back whatever it was that wanted to throat. "Explain."

"You've let your experiences go. You've lost touch with what we think of as humanity. There is no outside world anymore. You live within yourself, and it's a dreadful place."

I'd heard it all from the hyenas about the kill. The professional critics, the editors, the readership, all those who'd sniffed out something while reading my work that threatened to expose them for the raw animals they were. A couple publications had even had psychologists weigh in on my most recent books. I'd listened to them. I'd cried and gnashed in the dark at their words. I'd cared so, so much about what I was in others' eyes, hung on to that first and last writerly flaw, the ego.

"They've torn me to shreds, Kay. Layer by layer, they've taken my identity away from me. The core is all I have left. Even the conceit's gone. I don't care about my audience anymore. I care about hanging on to some semblance of what made me human. God, Kay, admittedly the reception, the adulation fed me. But probing myself for truth was what always kept me in the fold."

She gently took my coffee cup out of my hand, set it aside. "I know, Jake. I know exactly what you've been going through in the vanity sense. I'm a former whore, remember? Not a crack whore, not a heroin whore, but a whore who once, during her career, had some flash, some meaning, some novelty—if only to myself. I broke down, broke apart, and you came along to pick up the pieces. I'm trying to pick up yours now. Do you understand that? I shudder at your nightmares, but I'm shuddering for the both of us. I want you back. I want life to be safe again."

I turned away, but not before she saw the tear fall.

"Jake, let me help you find that humanity again. I did it once, with your help. Let me do the same for you."

As though the two things were equal.

———•———

It was Kay, not me, who suggested I go back to my favorite spot and put an end to my descents. Take in the view, the air, Lake Tahoe itself. Remember how hard you worked to get here. Remember your reference in *The Land Beyond Beauty* to Samuel Clemens' description of the lake: *As it lay there with the shadows of the mountains brilliantly photographed upon its still surface I thought it must surely be the fairest picture the whole earth affords.*

Kay such a fair picture of persuasion, herself, that I'd bought into her ideal of living outward as I climbed through the pines to the craggy overlook, notebook in hand. "Start with the story's title," she'd said. "Don't call it 'A Clean House.' Call it 'A Dirty House.' Give it that human distinction."

It made sense. Temples and humans. What could be a dirtier combination?

But as the juniper appeared, lone twisted thing bearing its testimony there on the rock, I began to doubt the legitimacy of choosing. Paths were what they were as they wound out of the soul. You caught them where you could and they took you where they would. There were no roads less taken. There were arteries and the blood flowing through them. That's all. Two roads diverged on an endlessly red path. Black, if you quit looking at it from your strange, un-Kay-like perspective; if you managed to hold on to the "dirty" idea in your confusion. Bless you, Kay, for saving me with your contradictions. For allowing me to forget myself again.

The various holes in the mine were so black, you never knew how far you'd ventured. Nor by what passage. Ascending was its own unwinding nightmare as you realized the beer was finished and you'd have to go back to the cabin, maybe even into town for replenishment. There was so much more to tell, to unravel, but you knew it couldn't happen now that the last bottle was empty. If only Kay understood. If only she could provide the service I most needed her for: delivering reinforcements against the fragmenting epiphanies. Instead I felt every shard and nail as it sliced through my brain matter.

"Jake. *Jake*," I heard through the noise.

"Baby?"

"It's me, sweetheart. You fell asleep up here."

"What time is it?"

"About six. You've been up here for several hours. I was getting a little worried. You okay?"

"The tree . . ."

"Tree?"

"The juniper."

"Yeah?"

"You don't . . . see anything odd about it?" I had risen to a sitting position, almost bringing myself to look at the tree.

"Come on, babe. You've drunk too much after last night."

"Last night?"

"Never mind. I'll take care of you."

The tree. It meant something to me, but damned if I could recall what as Kay helped me to my feet.

"Wait . . . my notebook," I said, nodding to where it lay open on the rock.

"No worries," she said, bending to pick it up.

Her body motion indicated she was simply going to close it and have us back down to the cabin, but her eyes, as they passed over the opposing pages, interfered with that too-neat result.

"Jesus, Jake . . ."

'Jesus, Jake' to you too. Had you brought me another beer, we might not being going wherever it is we're going.

"I see what you mean now about the tree."

I automatically motioned for the notebook, but then, as I saw the sketch I'd made of the tree, I turned away, not wanting to remember.

"Jake . . . " she said in a slightly broken voice. "This is scary."

"They're only faces. I was trying to . . . " *What? Bring them to life?*

But her attention was fully on the tree now. Searching, sketching, perhaps even —

"Jake, let's get out of here. *Now.*"

A beer. That's all I'd asked.

———·———

She did a rare thing that night and drank with me. While I was prepared for the usual resistance, she took the offered glass without even an allusion to the guilty needs of an alcoholic like me. She'd other things on her mind, clearly, as she sipped, tinkled the ice, sipped again. I waited until the Crown had begun to insulate her against the core and its horrors before I inquired about earlier.

"Kay, I have to ask . . . did you see something when we were at the overlook?"

She made music of the ice in her glass, watching the cubes gradually dissolve. "I'm seeing things everywhere."

"But in the juniper tree—"

"Yes, all right? Faces. Pictures. Moving tattoos. Bradbury would be proud of you."

"But did you actually *see* them? I have to know . . . "

"Why? To determine whether you're sane or not? You care suddenly?" But it was without vehemence. She seemed rather to lament our circumstances, in the warm embrace of the whisky.

"I know I'm not whole, Kay. This life has taken its toll."

"What utter bullshit," she said gently, almost kindly, as she got up and fetched the bottle from the kitchen.

I silently watched her refill her glass.

She offered me the bottle. As I placed my hand around it, she continued to hold it firm in her grasp. "Listen to me, Jake," she said, eyes simmering as they looked into me. "Dementia is personal. The pit is another thing entirely. *Do you dare doubt the fact?*"

With the last, her eyes abruptly ignited, causing me to recoil, clutching at air, at shadows, anything to slow what might have become a spinning free-fall had she not as suddenly reverted to something normal again, as though the incident had never happened.

"Kay," I said, sucking sweet breath out of the vacuum. "You're scaring me."

"*I'm* scaring *you*? Wow, that's a first. I should revel in such power."

How I recovered so quickly, I can't say. But I was able to fix, with all my attention, on that one word. "*Power*, Kay? Really? It's like that?"

"I've been your thing for a long time now, Jake. Don't pretend not to know that. You needed someone to authenticate your creations. In a way, yeah, to confirm your sanity. Or whatever applies. I suspect your mental diagnosis doesn't matter when you've gone this far. When you've—what the fuck was that?"

"What?"

"*That.* You don't hear it?"

"What, for Christ's sake?"

"It's coming from the bedroom."

"I don't hear anything."

"Liar," she said, looking through dilated eyes at the wall behind her.

"What the hell, Kay—"

The wall warped, sank inward, became a writhing hole of faces, pictures, moving tattoos.

Kay's eyes were on fire again as she engaged me. "*Look at them!*" she screamed. "Look what we've brought up into the world!"

———•———

I awoke with my heart thundering in my chest. I felt around me, searched the darkness through closed lids—as if forced blindness could protect me from Kay's smoldering embers.

"*Do you dare doubt the fact, you fucking black-core introvert?*"

———•———

In my dreams I'd go places. Graveyards, where she would be prowling in her short skirt. Pulling bottles of beer from between her legs. Laughing when they became writhing staffs. Tossing them at me. Crying when they wouldn't return. Seeing things in the twilight mist. "Fuck me," she'd call. "Fill me with your bloated, living sap. Father truth in me. Let me bring more fearless voices into the world. I love a clean house, I love a dirty one. It never mattered, did it?"

On the eve of the eve of her departure, I told her I needed to do some soul searching and took the bike up into the hills. She wanted to come, but I told her I had to do it alone. I parked at a familiar place not so far from home and watched the lake for a long time before coming to terms with myself. When I'd done so, I found the best road down to a tucked-away body of water I knew, parked my bike among the trees by an overgrown, long-unused boat ramp, and hiked back in the direction of home along the Forest Service trail.

A feed off a conduit of the main trail accessed my property at the overlook. As always, I took the mostly hidden artery with care, not wanting to do boot maintenance on what most hikers would dismiss as a deer path. So far this minor bit of anti-service, along with some rearranging of the vines and underbrush at the access point, had, as far as I knew, kept potential trespassers away.

Until this evening.

As the thicket opened up to the rocky terrace, I saw a figure in the gathering twilight. A hunched, seated lump below the juniper tree, facing in the direction of the valley—though the lake itself could not have been visible from where the figure sat, far from the overhang's rim. I immediately stopped, weighing this image against a sudden onslaught of other images. I managed somehow not to panic as I removed my backpack, and from it the flask, and drank as deeply as I'd ever drunk before, even from the well of my nightmares.

"That you can begin to think such a thing is something," came the voice of my trespasser, who never turned, never moved in his dwarflike bundle.

"What . . . ?"

"You tried that in trial, didn't you? The 'what' defense? The prosecutor laughed at you then. I laugh at you now. *What*, exactly, are *you*, as you come creeping up on us like this? You made your decision, didn't you? We're your things, all of us. Kay included."

I stepped cautiously forward, heard the twig break like glass beneath my boot. "I am not responsible. I tap something older than myself. You know that."

"*I* know that? We mutually understand your dementia, do we? Imagine waking up in someone else's dream—would you understand?"

"Yet you reference Kay. Some trial that hasn't happened."

"*She* can't wake up in someone else's dream? Didn't she prove otherwise when she left the brothel in Carson City? No, of course not. Because you forged her, too. She burned and screamed and melted into shape. But to be that thing."

I'd stepped out on the shelf now, the juniper rising starkly above me. "You're not real. That's the issue you, not Kay, must face."

Finally, and with excruciating slowness, he turned, opening his cowl to reveal a face that I knew only too, too well, having seen it in every photograph that had ever pretended to capture what I was. "Is that so, Jake?"

I lunged, but it was only that, a lunge off a cliff that promised no bottom, no relief from the guests it entertained.

Which, in effect, validated everything to come.

———◆———

I descended to find the back door and all the windows on that side of the house open. Don't be boxed in with them, I wished her lovingly. We're all shadows about this business, ducking in and out, unrestrained.

Watch me now, the slithering demon, as I come down the chimney, opening my maw wide. Never mind the words. They're only a soft, ash-smelling precursor.

She clung to that as she smashed out her cigarette and welcomed me into her arms again.

———◆———

I had this feeling, as I awoke on the eve of her departure, that she was dead. I hadn't yet rolled over on the mattress to check on her; it was just this sense, born out of instinct, unremembered dreams, déjà vu . . . a knowledge, really. A secret knowledge.

Still, the absence of her was a thing I was unprepared for as I swept my hand without resistance across the space she normally occupied. Where the premonition left off, a sick, hollow feeling took over as I rose from the bed and turned on the light, scanning the room for what I knew was not there: my last contact with a world I had tried and failed to make sense of. There was no use calling. She wouldn't answer, ever again. The hole was too deep. The breath that came out of it too polluted to offer any possibility —

"Morning, lover," I heard from the bedroom door.

Dare I turn? Dare I look upon the face I had scribed in the trunk of the tree?

"Fresh eggs and bacon . . . and a piece of mail you might like."

"From who?" I was barely able to articulate.

"Julia. She loves your latest. Calls it a 'frenzy' that should appeal to all appetites."

"That so?"

"Look at me, baby. The past is behind us, okay? We're taking the Miata out today, remember? Putting a little distance between ourselves and the cabin. 'Doing it up on four wheels,' as I believe you said. Dig in. The whole

Sierra Nevada awaits."

INTERLUDE
A CLEAN HOUSE

After a time of reclusion, of hiding from the suspicious eyes of the locals and writing for naught but my wretched need to do so, I made a clean break. A traditional housecleaning, if you will. While it didn't last forever, it did serve the purpose of buoying me for a time.

It was my publisher Julia, of all people, who secured the gig for me. Her brother had been working in Iraq for a defense contracting company, making six figures a year as a logistics coordinator. He'd spoken to his recruiter about me, citing experience that Julia must have cobbled together out of one of my older bios, which had been intended to paint me as a regular joe who'd done his blue collar time in warehouses and such during his younger, pre-fame days.

But Julia's reasons for stepping in went beyond the money, which she knew I was beginning to desperately need after a string of unsuccessful books. In Iraq, you couldn't drink. It was General Order Number One. Oh, there was the shit the Turkish truck drivers brought in, as I would later see firsthand. But who needed it when they were over there working twelve to fourteen hours a day, seven days a week? Julia's brother, Bob, explained it all very well for me. Only the losers risk their fat paychecks dicking around with contraband, he said. I hadn't asked about contraband. He'd volunteered the information. Which meant Julia had volunteered information about me to him.

I can't say I didn't lose a lot of sleep—of what precious little I got anymore—making the decision. I detested help. I cringed at the thought of looking back feeling I owed people something. The hazard aspect of it, the being bombarded by mortars on whatever camp I landed at, I could handle. The lifestyle, the living in a tent or containerized housing unit with a roommate or roommates, this I could do for a period of time. Hell, I could even suffer through on the drastically limited writing time. But the rehab part—what else could you call it?—that was fucking tough.

In the end, though, I gave myself up.

I held out my hands and said, "Cuff me. I did it."

What had I really done, though? Kept the primal fire aflame? What did that even mean? Aren't we allowed to look deeper than our personal experiences, which we rarely understand anyway? People believed I had slain a woman. They believed I had descended into madness. Did they know the meaning of any of this? Did they absorb it as well as perceive it? If they had, surely they would have seen that it was they who were detached. They who were out of touch with their universe. I mean, what the fuck happened to entropy? To original logic?

Didn't I have this right as I went through their tests at the company's deployment center? Then, on my second tour, through the dreaded CONUS Replacement Center at Ft. Benning? A lot of the contractors had to go through there, as well as military personnel who were deploying without their units. Before we boarded our respective flights to the war zone, we were each required to visit the chaplain. I don't know what he said to the others, but to me he asked a simple question:

Do you have God?

No, I stated flatly.

He smiled, Well, you better get some.

———•———

I survived in Iraq through three tours, not least because I took my money and lavished it on my dying other body during my R&Rs. I loved and hated the place, and in my ambivalence, made some peace with myself. There were simpler things on the horizon now. Everything didn't end and begin in the tips of my fingers, my ten tentacles reaching up out of my soul. There was blood and death always at the edge of vision. Other, even less palatable things clearly within the scope. I stopped writing about it when military investigators came around on orders from God knows where. *C.I.D.*, I called that last story, but never sent it out. I was taken by my environs by then. The desert had me.

The Iraqis say breathing the dust cleanses the body.

That and more, I think.

For what is the body, old or new, but the house?

Cleansed, it is a temple. Not before.

Would Buddha, for example, allow you to walk in shoes on his sacred property?

Hello, then, the next chapter in my life.

PART TWO
A SICKLY HOUSE

Time had slipped me by as I plugged away on the keyboard at my latest project. I'd just finished with the first chapter of whatever it was I was writing—a memoir disguised as a novel?—when I glanced at the laptop's clock. To my surprise it was almost midnight. I'd been at it for a good two hours since I'd last checked the time. Strange, this writing thing. It literally swept you away.

I turned off the laptop, heading immediately to the bathroom to relieve myself of the three beers I'd drunk without a break. As I watched my piss turn the water in the bowl an unhealthy-looking color, I reminded myself to keep hydrated. That had been a mantra in Iraq and Kuwait, where you often didn't realize you were dehydrating until you started feeling the cramps. Thailand's climate was a far cry from the Middle East's. It was more humid, yes, but in terms of raw temperatures, the two couldn't be compared. Still, as stingy as Janya was about the air conditioning, I should have known better than to not have a bottle of water on the desk.

Where was she, anyway? She was usually back from the shop by eleven. With the Buddhist holiday rush having ended yesterday, she had been expecting a lull. There were still some European tourists hanging around, getting what little sunshine they could out of Hua Hin in mid-August, but they weren't exactly banging down the door to buy Thai cell phones. Today should have been the usually slow Monday.

I didn't really worry, though. Aside from the fact that I had a liter and a half of Leo in my system, Janya was known to surprise me at times. Bringing home soggy tacos from the Mexican restaurant by the market or stopping to pick up an out-of-our-price-range Heineken for me was her way of showing remorse for having kept me to so tight a budget lately. Or, when it was that time of the month, for having subjected me to the pissy beast she could be when not coddled properly. She'd nothing to apologize for in either case. I was the one who continued to pretend we had money, though I'd been out of work for four months. I who needed that semblance of normalcy when the defense contracting gigs that had kept me afloat for years had dried up to the point that I wondered if I hadn't been blacklisted or something.

She saw through my illusions with the sharpest eye. If I complained that two hundred baht was a mere six bucks, U.S., she was on me like a cat. No playing the know-it-all *farang* with Janya. She'd shred you for your former lifestyle and then dare you to bring up the value of the baht again while she showed you the mortgage, the lease on the shop, and her day's earnings all in the same deft spread. I'd grown, through the months of my unemployment, to cherish her for this, but could have strangled her for always bringing it back to my attention. Not only was I an old dog trying to learn new tricks (from a woman who, at twenty-nine, was eighteen years my junior), I was a *guilty* old dog for not having accepted a side offer to Afghanistan when a military-imposed reduction in force saw the last contracting company I worked for lay off eight of us civilians in Kuwait. I'd had the attitude that I had done my three war-zone tours in Iraq and wasn't going back to another place where I had to do bunker calls in forty-pound body armor and wait through dust storms to get out on R&R. Four months later, if you ask Janya, I still wasn't humbled.

But those were other issues. Right now, as I fetched my cell from where it had been charging in the bedroom, I just wanted to know that she was okay. That she hadn't taken one too many rides on her motorbike without a helmet, trusted one too many strangers —

A knock sounded at the door.

I froze, phone in hand, looking through the bedroom wall in that direction. Janya never knocked. If I hadn't already heard her drive up on the motorbike and unlocked the door for her, she called through the screen windows. We *never* had callers. Not since we'd left our leased house in a row of abutting houses in the city. She had no family here, having moved down from Bangkok with me after we'd decided to start a business in more relaxed environs. I certainly had no people here, beyond the occasional acquaintance I'd let myself make along the way. While I'd committed to purchasing a house with Janya, it had been with the future in mind. I was still a virtual transient as I waited on the next job.

You're overreacting, I told myself. How many R&Rs did you spend in this country before deciding to set up here? Anything goes in Thailand, remember? Always expect the unexpected.

Yet I couldn't escape the feeling, as I walked through the living room to the front door, that the unexpected, this time around, had all the flavor of bad news. The metalwork windows were perpetually open, leaving only screens between myself and the shadowy visitor on the porch. I sensed the figure was a man, though his stature was small even by Thai standards. That was about as much as I could glean from within the partially lit interiors of the house. That he was aware of my approach, though, was certain.

"Who is it?" I said, a fresh whisper crawling along my skin as I opened the inner screen door but hesitated before unlocking the last defense against my visitor.

"Sir, I must speak with you," came the masculine Thai voice. "It's about your wife."

The chill became a shiver as I stood there, holding the knob in my fist. "I don't have a wife. Who are you looking for?"

"Yes, of course. Clearly you are not Thai. I'm here about Janya Saowaluk. This is her residence?"

As though he'd only seen her ID. Jesus, what had happened? "Just tell me your business, man."

There was a pause. A horrible, agonizing lapse before he spoke again. "I am sorry to be the one to inform you, sir, but Ms. Saowaluk—"

The sound of a motorbike, not just any motorbike but her *specific* one, with its distinct gravelly signature, cut him short. Stepping impulsively to my right to look through the window, I saw the headlights sweep through the darkness, for a split second capturing his profile as he looked back in that direction, mouth slightly open but seeming to grin at the same time. On automatic pilot now, I threw open the door, expecting to hit the stranger with it while I covered his reaction with my raised fist . . . but it was already too late. He'd shot out into the night, the sound of laughter trailing behind him.

Janya sat frozen on the still-running bike in the drive, hand on the key, looking over her shoulder into the darkness. The motorbike's lights now piercing the side of the house, at an angle to me. When she turned, we met each other's eyes.

I will never forget the perfect English that came out of her at that moment. "What the fuck was *that*?"

Not because he'd fled. Not because he'd been there one moment and then hadn't the next. But because of his face: a sunken, wrinkly, corrupt sack of age and lost humanity.

———◆———

We'd talked about it, had concluded he was a thing that couldn't be concluded. He'd looked shrunken, destitute, homeless, wild. Yet he'd known her name. We were private people. She was. I was. We liked to keep it close to home. We didn't have the social networking accounts or the butterfly personalities. We did our thing, liked it that way, and that was it.

Leave it to me to risk a lover's ire by delving deeper. "You're absolutely sure you didn't give our address to any of your customers or fellow shopkeepers?"

"What do you mean to say?" she said darkly. We were back to her imperfect English and my nonexistent Thai. *What do you mean to say* meant *What are you implying*?

"Nothing. God, Janya. It's not always about the Sunshine Bar, okay?"

The Sunshine Bar was where I'd met her, and she had, ahem, *worked* there.

"Two months I worked there! For my family. What do you do for yours?"

While she knew that in my country parents rarely expected support from their children until they were unable to support themselves, it was nonetheless a condemnation of me.

"Baby, I'm just trying to get to the bottom of this," I said. "I worry about you, you know? Creeps running around out here at night? We moved out of the city to avoid just this thing."

"You moved so you would have a yard and could garden in the sun."

"I moved because you hated the beach, Miss Umbrella. It's my fault you don't want to be brown?"

"I'm not brown," she threatened.

"Golden."

"No sex for you for ten days."

"Again? Last time it lasted only three, if you'll recall."

"This time ten."

I held up a hand. "All right, Janya. Whatever makes you right. But listen, sweetheart, this is not a joke. That cat was a freak, and we are a little isolated out here. Yes, I like that we are. But we still need to take precautions."

"Blah, blah. You fucking Americans," she said, smiling.

We'd watched Monty Python a week before. She'd found it a delicious source for teases at my expense. "All right, all right," I said.

She stuck her tongue out at me.

With things back to normal, I shifted to a lighter topic. "So why were you late anyway?"

"You know those little blue sleeping pills you like . . . "

"You got some?"

"Tom came back from a visa run to Myanmar with her Ivory Coast football boyfriend. She was mad that he got them, so I met her to take some of the bottle. I'll let you have two."

"How many do you have?"

"Two for one night, okay?"

"These are Valium, right?"

"I don't know names, Jake. You know that."

"Let me look."

She smiled. "You forgot about my safety already?"

I was all in, but then I wasn't for once. She was right. "Actually, no I haven't, Jan. Let's wait a little on the blue pills. I need to know who you talked to tonight, last night, the night before. I'm very, very serious. We don't joke when it comes to Jake and Janya, okay? Grab a beer, sit down, let's smooth it out."

That's what she wanted. A strength in myself that translated to a strong commitment to her—on her terms. I gladly gave it when it was within my power to do so. Other times, I was just a man looking for a job. She knew all this of course, and toyed with me as women inevitably do. Before, I'd hated them for it. With her, I sacrificed, and almost willingly.

———•———

"No," she said, sipping, always sipping of a bottle I'd finish.

"Nobody freaky or scary, or who just didn't seem to belong?"

She grew quiet for a moment. A sign to me. "You know," she said. "There are a lot of people, they come late to the market."

"Yeah . . . "

"They are not always nice. It's the—what do you call it—nature of business?"

"Go on."

"Last week, on Buddha Day, we all closed late. I was going back to the bike and there was this guy . . . I couldn't see him. He was in the dark area outside the building."

"The shadow."

"He was watching me. Small guy. Old, maybe. I thought he was a tramp."

"Yes?"

"He was burning the Buddha sticks, you know?"

"The incense."

"The incense, yes. But not like I put in the shop with the roses and the flower jewelry, as you always call it."

"Right, the ornaments."

"He just burned them in his hand. And smiled and threw one at me when I drove by."

"That's the kind of thing I'm looking for, Janya. Do you think he could possibly be our man?"

"I don't like this, 'our man.'"

"I don't mean it like that. Is he the same man who was here tonight?"

"I don't know. Maybe. He was . . . what's your word again? Creepy?"

I nodded. That was exactly the word. And I'd kill a motherfucker who made her say it more than once.

"And you'd never seen him before? Don't know where he came from? Nothing?"

"He was a stranger."

"Okay. Here's what we're going to do. I'll go to work with you and hang around the market to see if he shows up again. We'll go home together. Hell, we'll go everywhere together until we've decided he's not in our lives anymore. If we do encounter him, be warned, I will deal with him harshly. No police, no calls. Do you understand? If we never see him again, all the better."

She silently agreed to those terms. She hated the police for reasons I didn't want to know.

No need for any tranquilizers tonight. After checking the locks, showering, eating some leftover fried rice, checking the locks again, and making love, we were out.

———•———

The reason I didn't normally sleep so well was the same reason I was given to routine disturbing dreams—the alcohol. When I didn't work, and when I worried about the fact that I was living on borrowed time on a shop that just barely paid for the bills and the extended visas, I tended to drown my misery in the 5% beer I kept around the house. Janya and I had a sort of unspoken understanding. I got a hundred and fifty baht a day for my beer and cigarettes and she got the satisfaction of knowing she controlled my input and that while on her budget, I couldn't quite get drunk enough to run off to the bar as I'd been known to do when I was still sucking on the tit of the handsome severance the Kuwaiti government required companies operating on their turf to give their laid-off employees.

I mourned that $16,000 more than you can imagine. I mourned what I'd spent on the drunken forays and I mourned what was tied up in the shop and house. The latter was tolerable as long I kept faith that one day I'd be back in the desert making the six figures again. But the wild nights . . . those had been inexcusable. Granted, I hadn't been sure about Janya until I'd hit the proverbial rock bottom and let her rescue me. But Christ, to spend what your average Thai did in a month on a couple days of unremembered sin? And before that, before the Janyas and the Malis and the Nams of the Asian heaven-on-the-cheap I'd discovered, there were the trips to Ibiza, San Tropez, Mykonos, Monte Carlo. What the fuck had I been thinking, spending three and four hundred dollars a night on hotels? And three to four times that on drugs or gambling or whatever suited me that particular night?

So much for my housecleaning, right? Ironic, looking back on a passage I'd written in a work (or was it my journal?) six years before:

That was the sticking point. At forty-one, I was aging now, and the days of the more useful aids, the mind-opening substances, were gone. Left to me was alcohol, which did its diligent duty in wiping out the inhibitions, but at an increasing price. While I liked to believe it simply swept up after the psychoactive drugs of my younger days, gathered the flaked-off brain cells into a little pan where they could be foraged through for some sign of their previous glitter, I knew better.

I'd been a fool not to come to Thailand when the fat, used-up truck drivers I'd worked with in Iraq had touted their little hell as the next best thing to the virgin-infested paradise promised the Allah-loving bad guys if they took out a couple infidels along the way. I'd thought my fellow contractors a certain breed of predator. The sort that blinded the young and pretty with the money they dished out from their old and ugly hands. Never mind that said money balanced things out to everyone's favor (she got the life, he got the lay) because it was still a transaction and who wanted a girl like that—again?

Then I'd gotten a personal taste of that Asia fever and discovered that, lo and behold, Thai women were just American women who left less to the imagination. They suffered like the home girls. They gave it back like the home girls. They dogged you like the dog you were like the home girls. And they were smart like the home girls! The only things that separated the two species of animal, as far as I could tell, were a few kilograms of flesh, a bit of fabric, and a spray or two of pretense. Okay, and maybe some humility. Thai girls at least knew who they were.

Then along comes Janya, who suffered and inflicted and dogged with absolute love—even when you didn't have money and continued to insist upon the three Leos every night. Was it even possible to price that? So far, the answer was no. She did her bitching and controlling, but only in doses, and when it was out of her, she retracted her claws and curled up into the sweetest kitten you've ever had the pleasure of petting. Though I had my moments, I was also truly in love with her. All she'd have had to do was seriously demand I stop, and the turbulence over the drinking would have ended. But she didn't. Not really. Not when she brought home the tranquilizers to make her man happy.

I found them while she was still sleeping the next morning. I wasn't so much looking for them—okay, I lie. The edge was still on, I'd had nightmares about the monster at the door, and there was her bag, open to God and everybody. The digging in her bag was not a violation. God knew she'd perused my wallet enough back when I controlled the money. But to do so out of need . . . that was the bad thing. I smoked out of need, I drank out of need, now I sought the pills out of need. When what I really fucking needed was a job, or at least the self-confidence of knowing there was one on the horizon. I was broken after the months. She knew this maybe better than me. And maybe that, in reality, was why her bag was open in the first place.

I found them in a cellophane pouch. Twelve of them. I popped the safe two, knowing that if she looked, she could overlook that. I then went to the laptop and began writing again. It was slow at first but then the tale began to move, barely hesitating when a sunken, wrinkly wretch made his entrance. So many possibilities in a real, live protagonist. I let the idea of him flow, I let it overtake the memoir aspect of the story and turn it into something else—a vision, maybe?

Dementia loved a clean house. It thrived in an environment where it could weave its own cobwebs, accumulate its own dust, create its own sense of terror and loss. My folly, I reminded myself in my most lucid moments, was in standing in its way. Why shouldn't I be my own janitor? What exactly was wrong with a clean house?

What indeed, as I heard the bedroom door open.

"Morn," she murmured as she passed me on the way to the bathroom.

"Morning," I echoed without turning from the screen.

But the spell was broken now. I'd set up my desk by the backdoor so that I could blow my smoke, with the aid of a fan, outside. The bathroom was on the other side of the wall I faced, such that I could hear, in my imagination at least, every drop that came out of her. These might as well have been seconds off the clock, which as usual I hadn't looked at until now. I'd awoken at eight-thirty, begun writing at nine or so. It was eleven-fifteen when Janya emerged from the bedroom, smiling as she always did in her wild-haired post-sleep delirium, just grateful that my dreams had not destroyed her. If she'd ever counted the pills, it never came out. I was a charmer in my tranquilized state and she the willing snake.

We did the egg and tomato sandwiches, watching a little Thai-subtitled English-language TV on the Universal cable channel. We touched a little on last night, but with a freer attitude. Boogie men, after all, belonged to the shadows. When she showered, I popped two more Valium, reminding myself not to let the ease of living interfere with its responsibilities. Thankfully, I'm a high-tolerance guy. I reminded her as she got ready that I was going with her. She liked this. She liked my being there for her.

"Well, are you going to shower?" she said.

I was, and I did. And when I stepped out, she was there for me too, with kisses.

I rode passenger as we took the motorbike into town, enjoying the wind in my hair.

———◦———

I didn't like to sit in the shop with her. It wasn't just that I knew next to nothing about cell phones (having not been allowed one in Iraq, where third party nationals had been known to lend out their phones' coordinates for insurgent missile strikes). I was skeptical about how Thais took seeing the obvious owner of the shop, the farang, on the premises. Janya said I was wrong, that they didn't care to whom they gave their money, but I remained unconvinced after having spent a few days selling phones with Janya when the shop opened. Nothing I could put my finger on, really, but a perception had stayed with me.

So I hit the Mexican restaurant nearby, admittedly capitalizing on the fact that I had to be somewhere in Janya's eyes, and being somewhere meant spending a little something. That the restaurant was on the side of the market where she parked the motorbike had been a point I didn't have to sell.

The first beer, as I chatted with the heavily tattooed wife of the Scandinavian who owned the place, put me in a zone of no pain. When the second came, I was still diddling over the burrito, almost understanding what it was that made it so un-Mexican. Chili instead of jalapeno? Beans that hadn't been fried in fat? Shell that had the faintest taste of freezer burn? I couldn't quite place it as I managed, meanwhile, to remember my mission, and let my eyes wander the perimeter of the market, focusing on the area where the motorbike was parked.

I didn't expect anything at this hour. The market's indoor shops, of which ours was one, opened around five and closed around ten. Dusk came along about eight, maybe a bit earlier. I could sit here and sip beers for only so long before the sleepy came creeping over me, which would be a bad, bad thing in terms of both my purpose and my ability to get sex from Jan anytime within the next month. I gave it three beers, the last a small one, and then, around seven o'clock, paid my bill and walked through the market to its bathroom. Why I didn't go in the restaurant, I don't know, unless it was the premonition that had begun crawling over me a half hour before. I was dull to external stimuli, but apparently susceptible to subtler, less attributable things. Case in point, the sudden foreboding that hit me as I walked through the bathroom door.

The interiors consisted of four urinals and two stalls, the nearest of which was open. There was one man at a urinal, but he was just shaking out the last drops as I entered. Zipping up, he left the place to me and whoever occupied the far stall. I can't say the foreboding solidified into a fear, because the bathroom was open and at any moment we might be joined by another of the many who wandered the market. Still, there was a thickness to the air that had nothing to do with the facility's function. I could taste it in my mouth. A taste not of waste, but of real, choking *waste*. I don't know how I separated the two, but I did. As I stood at the urinal, I knew that he was here—in all his corruption.

It was too late to cut my business short. The bodily function was automatic, required no willful extraction, and tolerated no attempt to squeeze off my bladder, if such a thing was even possible in my tranquilized state. No, I would see the matter through, double meaning very definitely intended, and woe to him for interrupting a man's life. I was that numb. That utterly relaxed in spite of the shadows that crept over me, one wave upon the other. Indeed, the waves themselves buoyed me. I rocked for him, so to speak. I rocked on my heels and pissed forever and still he didn't come out of the stall and I didn't care one way or the other, because I was ready for him in some Valium land that he'd desecrated.

A last drop, almost gonorrhea dark to my medicine-y eyes. And the stall door opened. I pulled my flapless surf shorts up over my bundle and faced him.

Only it wasn't a him, but a her. And she wasn't wrinkly, but smooth like semi-hardened honey. And her face wasn't a stranger's, but my own Janya's.

For a moment, a strange dull moment in time . . .

Then she seemed to collapse upon herself, reemerging again as what *he* was. A vile sac of spent flesh. I didn't think about what I did next, I just did it . . . I rushed him, hands poised to choke the life out of him. But as they descended upon what should have been flesh, they met each other instead, with a taste in the skin of crumbling, decaying matter.

As I withdrew, still not shocked, not yet, the material of him seemed to blossom again, carrying words on its dry, whispering petals:

Vacate the house.

"Sir, are you okay?" came a voice from some other world.

Vacate the house or become one with its fate.

"Let me help you—"

But the shock had arrived now and I heard no more.

————•————

I awoke from stranger dreams than usual to a hospital room. I knew it by its smell before I opened my eyes. When I did, sweet Janya was there to greet me.

"Hey baby," she said softly. "How are you feeling?"

"Thirsty."

"Here. The nurse said you would be."

"What . . . happened?"

"You collapsed in the bathroom at the market. Thankfully, there was a man there to help you. When the medics arrived, I came to see what was going on. I couldn't believe it was you." Her eyes glistened, as though she'd been battling tears.

"What's wrong with me?"

"You have a very bad infection. Severe . . . is that the word? Your kidney. They said you could have died."

"From a kidney infection? No. I don't believe that."

"You Americans," she smiled. A tear sneaking from her eye. "Let me tell you something, isn't that what you all say?"

"But I feel . . . " How did I feel? Numb?

"You've been asleep for two days, Jake. They've been feeding you through those things in your arms."

I looked, and sure enough, I was on tubes.

"But I still don't—" I cut it off, regaining full memory at that specific moment. *Oh Christ*, I thought. *Oh Lord Jesus.*

"What, baby? What's wrong?"

She was clearly alarmed, but I couldn't stop myself. "When you came . . . when you saw that it was me . . . did you see anyone else? Anyone who shouldn't have been there?"

She stared at me, uncomprehending for a moment. Then her face underwent a change. "You *saw him again*?"

"He was there. In the bathroom. I don't know how to explain it. He was there and then he wasn't. I'm sorry. I shouldn't be talking about this now."

"No, you shouldn't," came a fresh voice. As I looked that way, finding a white woman in nurse attire, she continued, "Good morning, Mr. Shields. Welcome back. Let's try not to overdo ourselves right now, okay? You've been rather serious for a little while now."

She spoke with a British accent, which neither encouraged nor discouraged me.

"How serious?" I said.

"Deadly serious," she said bluntly.

"From a kidney infection?"

"That's only where it started."

"Meaning?"

"Your whole lower digestive system was on fire. I'm surprised you were able to walk around, much less do your bodily duties."

"I'd no idea."

"Do you drink, Mr. Shields? Take the occasional tranquilizer?"

I looked at Janya.

"They needed to know."

The nurse said, "A good recipe for aggravating while numbing the aggravation."

"The pills I rarely take. And I don't drink when I wake up," I said.

"No, but it's in your system. The infection's symptoms probably came to you in the form of your thinking you needing another drink, but this isn't an exact science. Hell, I personally had never seen a case like yours. The doctor says it happens, but I doubt very seriously he's ever seen such a thing. You're an anomaly, in other words. Ever wanted to be special? You're special now."

I smiled humorlessly. "Will I be okay?"

"You will. A couple days, you'll be back home. Lay off the stuff you know is bad for you and I doubt we'll see you again."

"You doubt?"

Yet another new voice as a Thai man in a white coat entered the room. "None of us doubt. You'll be fine, Mr. Shields." He cast the nurse a glance, and with a slight nod my way, she exited.

"I'm Doctor Kwa, your physician," the man said, extending his hand to me.

I shook it with my free hand, and looked at him.

He sat down on the edge of the bed. "Look, we don't really know much about this thing, except that it's responded well to antibiotics. In my expert opinion, that's enough. The tissue isn't inflamed anymore. Everything's functioning normally. Miss Bertra's enthusiasm for sobriety is commendable, but it's not relevant in your case. Your liver function is fine. Your kidney looks good, outside of the current problem. I don't want you to leave here scared, because there's really no need to be. You're a grown man and know your limits. Enjoy yourself with those in mind and you'll be fine. I'm really quite amazed by your body's ability to recover so quickly and efficiently. Keep doing whatever it is you're doing, minus, perhaps, the Valium. They're as over-prescribed as antidepressants and will only lead to higher tolerance levels, which is never good."

Janya jumped in at just that right time, nose that she was, "And the alcohol? That's not a problem?"

"I see no evidence of abuse. Look, my wife and I drink a bottle of wine a night. The heart loves us for it. If it becomes a bottle and a half, that's a problem, okay?"

I could have hugged him for loving me like he did.

Until I saw him fold inward, sucking out of what he'd pretended to be into what he truly was.

———•———

I awoke from stranger dreams than usual to a hospital room. I knew it by its smell before I opened my eyes. When I did, sweet Janya was there to greet me.

"Hey baby," she said softly. "How are you feeling?"

"Thirsty."

"Here. The nurse said you would be."

"What . . . happened?"

She hesitated. "You don't remember waking up before?"

"I . . . I'm not sure . . . "

When I finally got my bearings, I learned from her that the nurse had been there, but the doctor had not.

I felt somehow relieved by this.

Because in the interim, in some interim, I had begun to remember who I was. Not in the personality sense—even the idea of that was out of date now—but in terms of the flesh in which I was clothed. I'd thought myself transcended. Above what it was I'd so long pretended to be. And yet, without my bodily house, what was I? It had given me my escapes, my forays; it had given me my regular blood pressure checks, my cholesterol counts, my drug tests, all the things that made me a legitimate human number during my contracting tours. To know the body that was the house that could be a temple, if only in my imagination, was a something that mattered to me suddenly. I didn't want it infected, inflamed, sickly, even as I, philosophically, lamented what it was, and theoretically continued to doubt its existence. It was real to me again. Dying and living and dying again didn't appeal when there was at least the shred of something there to hang onto.

Janya was that. She knew nothing about the things I'd been through, not really, yet she showed up every day for work, sometimes even within a smile. She was a living, breathing, ignorant thing, forever welcome in my house.

Vacate the house or become one with its fate.

The words hit me broadside while I was still assimilating the magic and miracle of being there in the hospital room with her.

"Jake?"

"Yeah, I'm okay, babe."

If she saw that I was masking a stricken expression, she didn't let on. Instead, she seemed to introvert, to go to some other place as her eyes wandered over my face. "You know, I was dreaming while you were asleep. There was this girl, a white girl, and she was . . . I don't know . . . falling away from you? You were standing over her and she was afraid because you had something in your hand. You were going to kill her, I think, but before it happened she said something to you, and I almost thought it would stop then. Do you want to know what she said?"

I don't, do I? I mean it's not necessary, is it? "Why are we talking about this, Janya?"

She seemed not to hear. For her it was a dream that stank of reality. For me it was something that smelled sweetly of dream.

"'I see it now,' she said. 'You are one of them. The ugly, small one —'"

"Please stop, Janya."

She seemed to come to herself, letting her eyes focus on me again. "I'm sorry. It was just . . . so strange." She licked her lips. "You killed her. While I watched."

"I didn't kill anybody. Please, I'm not up to this."

"No, you're right."

"But listen, I had my own experience. Only it wasn't a dream."

Her ears perked up.

"The little old man, he said something . . . "

"Old man?"

"The wrinkled old man. In the bathroom?"

She looked at me with a reluctant, "Baby . . . "

"What? What do you want to say?"

"He's a fantasy. The doctor—"

"Doctor? You said he hadn't been here since . . . "

She was clearly confused. "Of course he has. You talked to him about Iraq."

"What?"

She seemed shy to say it, but said it nonetheless. "We have to look at everything, remember?"

I didn't, wouldn't, indeed couldn't respond, as it occurred to me that maybe I was still drugged. Do they do that for infections? Do they dose you out of your own house?

———•———

There's that and then there's the other. The other is always less acceptable on the rational side, but might in fact satisfy the physical side quite well. I learned that there, in the place I knew as Thailand. People had talked to me about it. People who had fattened themselves on the world enough to know that the drugs were no match for the thing called dementia. Oh, they hadn't used the words exactly, but we all knew what was up.

The guy was sitting on the street beside the hospital entrance, head hidden by the brim of his wide straw hat, donation plate between his crossed legs. Janya wanted to go around him as we walked to where she'd parked the motorbike, but I asked her to let me give him something. It would be a good token, a good luck charm for us as we put my medical problem behind us and got on with our lives.

She didn't put up a fight, though every single baht counted now that I'd driven us further into poverty. I let a few coins tinkle into his pan, following his own lead by placing my palms together in the Buddhist way and bowing. It should have been done then but for the words he let from beneath his hat, in English:

"What room?"

"What?"

"What room did they have you in?"

"406. Why?"

"That's the fourth floor, that's why."

"Come on," Janya said. "I told you not to give money to these people."

I ignored her. "And the fourth floor is special?"

He lifted his head enough to let me see his pinched mouth as he said, "You know it is. It's where they release you from when they've decided they've met their obligation."

"Which is?"

His lips were like shriveled worms as they laughed, "To warn you, of course! Leave the premises. Vacate the bloody house."

Janya had taken my wrist by then, jerking me away from just one more street oracle paying out his penance for former lives.

I didn't tell her I understood him better than I did the next guy, who in this case happened to be a taxi driver.

"Two hundred baht! Anywhere in Hua Hin!"

Six U.S. dollars to take you back home.

"No thanks, brother. I've got my gal for that."

To which she didn't respond as she hand-led me to the bike, motioning me to mount it quickly, as though she was escorting me to some safer place.

PART THREE
A HOUSE OF ORDER

We'd come to terms. She didn't suggest it, and I didn't give her the opportunity. My writing was my life now. And I kept at it night and day, with medicines only my liver and kidneys knew the names of. A job offer had come and gone, one that required a secret clearance, which in turn required an acceptable credit score and a clean drug test. I was down to looking for positions that fed on outcasts like me. I rarely bothered to look anymore, except when Janya insisted on it.

And well that she did, for one day that rare defense contracting job came along. It required only an SF85, which I'd secured before without a hitch and thought I could do so again, since my bills were less than six months late and the company wasn't in so great a hurry to have my urinalysis that I didn't have time to wash my system out with vinegar. It was the first light of day we had seen in a while, if you could even call it that from within the cave I inhabited.

But I knew my duty, if only automatically. I kept up an email dialogue with the recruiter, and the HR rep, as I scanned and emailed my documents, got a clearance from a dentist, passed the piss test which I'd put off until the last, and generally did and said all the right things in my pursuit of a job whose title I'd forgotten somewhere along the way. My application was in the hands of security now, which left me free to return to my previous pursuits for the week or so it normally took them to get my plane ticket to me.

A week, a month, a year . . . I didn't know as I plunged back into it, pumping out material that was no longer even close to sellable. Janya rarely interrupted me and when she did, it was always with an apology. In lovemaking, too, she was often very delicate, as though I could be broken so easily. Gratefully, we didn't do it so often anymore. I hadn't the taste for it, really, except when she was one of my monsters. Then it was a tsunami that almost smothered the both of us in its intensity. That she liked these occasions was secondary. We both knew which way the tide went after. Love itself was a recession anymore. A falling into Jake's fathomless hole.

Then one day the plane ticket arrived. Because I lived overseas, I was to bypass orientation in Texas in favor of the Dubai processing center. A sliver of what I'd been before latched on to this. I'd been to Dubai too many times traveling through the Middle East. A couple weeks there was a sweat-free experience. You could indulge, you could pretend it wasn't the gateway to the End. Where was I going this time anyway? Oh yes, Afghanistan. What a playground that would be. Ah well, it was what it was as I printed out the electronic ticket and held it up for Janya's approval.

"You're sure you're ready for this?" she said.

"Darling, I live on the challenges."

She didn't seem so convinced as she prepared to go to work, remembering to blow me the customary kiss only after she'd mounted the bike. "Start packing, okay?" she called through the screens that separated us. "I'll help when I get home so we can have a free day tomorrow."

Now that I'd been cleared by the company, I was on the medicine again, including the beer, farewelling myself in that delirious way. Today was Thursday. Saturday I was off to the Middle East. With some luck, I might never wake up by then.

It certainly seemed as if I wouldn't as I ignored her suggestion that I get the packing out of the way, and immersed myself in my writing again. At the end of the last session I had wrapped up the section I'd been working on with my standard three asterisks. This left a blank canvas in front of me. Because I liked a blank canvas, I couldn't be bothered to reread the vaguely remembered words I'd written previously. All I had to do was find a shadow, a shape, an image from which to draw inspiration. This afternoon that came from my favorite tree on the property, which was clearly visible through the backdoor, which was open as usual to let my cigarette smoke out.

It was a mango tree. A handsome specimen with its thick trunk unfolding in long strong branches, a boy's paradise for climbing. Its rich dark-green canopy stretched across nearly the width of the backyard, providing cool shade for the wandering imagination. Mine did that now, slipping easily from the mango's shadow to those of the coconut palms at the back of the yard, through the wooden fence and out over the canal that ran behind the property, where the lotus blossoms and cattails whispered with my passage; across the sandy terrain and the coils of barbed wire, the pits from misspent mortar rounds, up over the rocky shelves through the evergreens to a naked crag from which a single tree grew distorted against a wind that sang of experiences I had known or would know.

"Jake. Jake!" I heard through the noise.

"Baby?"

"It's me, sweetheart. You fell asleep up here."

"What time is it?"

"About six. You've been up here for several hours. I was getting a little worried. You okay?"

"The tree . . . "

"Tree?"

"The juniper."

"Yeah?"

"You don't . . . see anything odd about it?" I had risen to a sitting position, almost bringing myself to look at the tree.

"Come on, babe. You've drunk too much after last night."

"Last night?"

"Never mind. I'll take care of you."

The tree. It meant something to me, but damned if I could recall what as Kay helped me to my feet.

"Wait . . . my notebook," I said, nodding to where it lay open on the rock.

"No worries," she said, bending to pick it up.

Her body motion indicated she was simply going to close it and have us back down to the cabin, but her eyes, as they passed over the opposing pages, interfered with that too-neat result.

"Jesus, Jake . . . "

'Jesus, Jake' to you too. Had you brought me another beer, we might not being going wherever it is we're going.

"I see what you mean now about the tree."

I automatically motioned for the notebook, but then, as I saw the sketch I'd made of the tree, I turned away, not wanting to remember.

"Jake . . . " she said in a slightly broken voice. "This is scary."

"They're only faces. I was trying to . . . " What? Bring them to life?

But her attention was fully on the tree now. Searching, sketching, perhaps even —

"Jake, let's get out of here. Now!"

The words flowed so perfectly, I couldn't have imagined them ever stopping. My fingers fluttered across the keyboard as if I knew what I was doing. As if I had been doing this since before the last of us had emerged from the cave to behold the wreckage of civilization on the horizon. Since before the shriveled one had risen up out of the flames to warn us of it.

Listen and you could still hear the beat of the drum. See his shade playing on the wall. Hear her screams as he enacted it. Smell the blood of her as she confessed that what she was an abomination against original order. Listen to the beat —

Thump. Thump. Thump.

We didn't need a clock then. We had our drum. We had our flickers and flutters and the whole phantasmagoria of motion to show the passage of time. Just listen . . . watch . . .

Thump. Thump.

"Who goes there!"

181

Thump. "Sir, I must speak to you."
"Speak, man!"
"I come to serve an eviction notice."
"What time is it?"
"*Time to vacate the house or become one with its fate.*"
See?

———•———

It's theatrics, nothing more. Look around my dusty, cobwebby theater and you'll know I'm right. They act you up, then they act you out of what it was that interested them. I love a life. I do. But when was it ever more than this incarnation of theirs? This vision of what it is to be human? Are we so easily molded as we sigh, get up from our truths, and walk to the door? Open it to find the bloody imprints of the fist on the outside of it? Next, I'll be scouring Thailand for my lost Janya.

It is infinitely more difficult to write the words, *The End*, than it is to write the words, *Part One: A Dirty House.* Yet that's exactly what I did that Thursday night before I got up from my desk, rather proud of myself, and went to the bedroom to begin packing. I popped some more pills and cracked another beer before settling into it, but when I did, it was a breeze. What did I have but a few articles of clothing, some hardware, the toiletries, the documents, and a laptop, which would go into its separate bag at the end? Everything else was intangible: the Skype password, the bank account numbers, the informational this and that, the memories. Puff stuff. Blow on it and it was gone.

Within thirty minutes, I was done with everything but the laptop, and lay back on the bed to enjoy some music from my thumb drive. The gal should be along shortly now. Close the eyes and touch the manhood. Remember her that way beneath the lights. Amid the props. Within the frame. Don't look at the clock. That's what they do when they're scared. When they're gifted again. When the true fire has become a memory within them.

WINDOWS OF ALASKA

SOMETIMES, IN SOUTHEAST ALASKA, when it's spring and the air is warming and the snow is melting and you're out there hiking or mountain biking or whatever it is you do in the way of immersing yourself in your environment, it feels like the universe is coming apart at the seams. No sooner have you gotten over the jolt of the earth shifting beneath you than the avalanche itself comes thundering down one of the fissures in the mountainside; the bear, ornery with hunger after its long nap, rumbles out of the brittle branches in your path; the helicopter, blades chopping madly, crests the right hand ridge and angles into the valley you're exploring, looking for some missing soul whose last contact with civilization was by cell phone when he told a loved one not to worry, he saw what looked like the roofs of houses through the trees below. During these times the raw innate silence of the wilderness is so utter that every interruption, natural or otherwise, fixed or random, seems an affront. There is no symphonic continuity between the rushing streams, the crashing waterfalls, the buzzing sea planes, the splitting glacial ice, the screaming bald eagles. Even the steady, saturating drizzle, which is a constant outside that desperately anticipated annual window in late April or May, cannot dampen the shocks.

But during that three or four week window—wow. When the whole subtropical rain forest finally quits dripping and the insect-ridden bogs left by the melted snows begin the process of evaporation, it's then that the music becomes music. For while nothing else has changed really—the avalanche chutes are still ripe for thunder, the bears have only gotten closer to sea level and civilization—the vision of mountain, sky, and sea softens the silence, so that it absorbs rather than resists the blows against it. The whole archipelago undergoes a transformation as the towns and villages perched in scattered pockets along the Inside Passage's mountainous shores wake up as from a dream, the cautious joining the hardcore in partaking of this perpetual frontier they call home. The window is the residents' secret, an Alaskan truth they are loath to share. Let the tourists that come in by the droves on the cruise ships continue to think summer's the magical time. Summer, when the rains pick up again, the temperatures drop, and the mists obscure the sights tourists have longed to see. Of course, even if the tourists knew about the window, they couldn't plan their calendars around it because it shifts on an annual basis, is shorter or longer this year than the last, depending on Mother Nature's mood. They could only hope that the season's first cruises happened to coincide with it.

Southeast Alaska, maker of its own rules, painter of its own pictures. The fact that my return from Iraq corresponded with the arrival of this cherished time says something for fate, particularly since this happened to be the year the universe came apart *within* the window.

As I crossed the berm that had been built up from the sea floor to serve as a bridge to the island, I wondered what I was getting myself into. The bridge was only usable at low tide, presumably because it hadn't been practical to build a berm that accounted for tide swings of up to twenty feet, not for this island of only two residences. This meant I was going to have to time my comings and goings, which I knew was only the first of the inconveniences I'd been facing out here, three miles from the next residential area and twice that from the nearest store. There were always repairs to be made, because the elements were always at work. The constant salt wear, the silt infiltration, the October winds tearing down branches or uprooting trees, the ravens wrenching up roof tiles, the snow and ice accumulations, the wash-outs from the rains. A long list, the trials of Alaska living.

The opposite of that, though—as the weathered Wrangler I'd picked up the day before cleared the bridge and followed the crushed gravel road to the right, around the perimeter of the island—was this beauty that unfolded in front of me. In the Chi Bay area, the beauty never stopped unfolding, no matter which direction you went. But out here, immersed in the Sitka spruces and Douglas firs, literally on top of the sea, you didn't have the luxury of establishing objective distance, of regarding the scenery from an outside perspective, because you were so enmeshed in the environment. It was like being in a state of constant breathlessness, and if someone on the other end of your mobile had asked you to describe your surroundings, you'd have had to really concentrate to separate your senses from the experience to complete the exercise.

Take the view that was even now opening up on the passenger side of the vehicle. The boulder-strewn slate beach in the foreground, the ocean waves restlessly filling the constrained space between Raven Island, the chunk of ground I now called home, and the longer, narrower Gull Island, whose feathery inhabitants, as every local mariner knew, whirled and screeched at all hours, including now. Beyond Gull Island, on a far larger body of land that stretched across a good part of the horizon, stood the mighty Chilkats, snow-capped peaks stabbing at the cloudless sky. Unlike the vista as seen from back on the highway, the jagged line of mountains didn't form a backdrop to the foreground. Viewed from here, inside the scene, it was as integral a part of the picture as the bounding porpoise I caught in my periphery just before the trees obstructed the view again.

"Raven Island," I said aloud as the road rose and curved inland to avoid a rocky terrace that the agent had told me made for the island's best fishing spot. The stream that helped give the spot that distinction now passing under the road, little more than a trickle this late in the season, with the hills of the island's southern side free of snow. I didn't like the name Raven Island. Hated it, in fact. I could understand how they'd seen fit to give the island a designation for geographical reference, but the name was too obvious, like something out of Bronte or a Vincent Price movie. The adolescent in me hoped that one day my fellow Chinos, as the locals drolly called themselves, might refer to it by my name. I had no right, really, to let that prideful sense of ownership creep in; it wasn't my island, after all. Still, when you've been in a war zone for seven years earning a six-figure salary as a civilian contractor, have been extremely lucky with your investments and are able, because you've had no one to take care of but yourself for a while, to put your money into something you dreamed in your youth of owning, then you deserve a little pride. Having purchased the place after only one brief visit at the tail end of an R&R, I'd never been told how much land belonged to Raven's other "recluse," but I owned thirty acres and that was a kingdom to me. It still stunned me, though, that the military brat had come back to the very place that had sent his angst over the top and into the rabid throes of rebellion.

Speaking of that other resident—as my new home at last came into view—I wondered what he'd think of me arriving here with ideas. With changing things in mind. In my mind's eye I could see the sign posted above the generous window of my spacious A-frame house, the letters made of the imitation tusks and bones of the beast referred to: The Mastodon. It wouldn't be just a bar or coffee shop. Or a hideaway for small parties or events. Or a consignment shop for the sort of goods only the native Tlingits could provide, by virtue of their legal freedom to hunt animals that were off-limits to the rest of us and to own prehistoric artifacts they found on their land. If I could justify my ideas on paper, my establishment would be a combination of these things and more. I had a guest house at my disposal—there it was, coming into the picture now—which was set a decent distance apart from the main house and was more than sufficient for my lifestyle. Bedroom, kitchen, bathroom, deck overlooking the bay . . . What more did I need? I'd likely open the

Mastodon for six months out of the year, May to October, let hired help run the day to day operations. The tourists would be my bread and butter, while the valley residents, with their Alaskan sense of aesthetics, would bring the occasional high-end purchase—humpback jawbone, mammoth tusk, that sort of thing. Hopefully. To be honest, I didn't know exactly what was legal trade and what was not. I'd simply worked as a teenager in a picture framing shop where they occasionally had such things on offer. But I'd get with the chamber of commerce or whatever agency handled such things in this isolated pocket of twenty thousand people and figure it all out. Assuming, of course, my ideas ever bore more than sprouts. While I may have scored on the stock market, I'd never owned a business in my life. And there was of course that other resident to consider.

On impulse, I corrected the motion of turning into the drive that led behind the house to a partially sheltered concrete parking pad and boat ramp, and kept going, following the road on around the curve of the island. Martha, the agent, hadn't specified where the other residence was located. While I'd done some beer- and marijuana-blurred fishing with friends in the area of Gull Island back before my mother decreed that this was decidedly not what she'd envisioned for retirement and forced the old man to haul us back to Europe, I'd paid no attention to Raven's signs of occupancy. I didn't give a fuck about anything by then. I'd dug living in Baumholder and Heidelberg, Germany, had tolerated Anchorage because I knew it was my father's last duty station. But then to see us actually stay in Alaska after he'd consigned the colonel insignia to a self-worship shrine in the glass-front bookcase in the study? That had been the last straw for me. By the time we went back to Europe, where my parents eventually settled for good in the south of France, the cleft between us was too wide to bridge even at low tide.

Now here I was, looking for something that had been taken from me in Chi Bay, Alaska. Would I find it at the residence I felt the inexplicable need to see right now, before even stepping foot in my own home as its official owner?

Two giant ravens, fighting over what might have been a clump of nesting material, appeared in front of the Jeep for a moment before breaking apart and flapping away. The storm of black wings caused my mind to slip its dreams and focus in on the act of driving. The needle of the speedometer vibrated at forty. Too fast for this little road on which two vehicles would have a hard time getting by each other even at creeping speeds. I slowed, rounding a right bend. The rocky beach briefly presented itself through the trees, then went the way of the ravens. The way I would go if I failed to get the Mastodon kicked off and had to live in joint isolation with the island's other inhabitant. Why was it suddenly so important, knowing about the other resident? I hadn't asked questions when Martha mentioned the old man in passing. Had I merely been showing Alaskan etiquette, respecting the integrity of privacy as she was obviously doing by offering no more than a by the way, you share the island with a reclusive retiree? All I knew was that the interest had bloomed, and its petals were quickly becoming the petals of anxiety. A feeling I hadn't known with such intensity in a long time, since well before Iraq, when Tatiana and I were nearing the end of our brief but oh-so-full journey. Had it really been almost twenty years?

My thoughts were on currents, fluttering in my mind. Through an opening—the same opening I had just driven past—I recognized something. Something that didn't exactly fit the picture, and yet at the same time belonged there among the boulders, against the sea. At the first opportunity I turned the Wrangler around and headed back in that direction. The proportions had filled out before I brought the vehicle to a stop at the opening, observing the partially visible wall of the stone structure beyond an elephantine rock formation. I eased forward to get a better view, and an open window appeared. In the window sat what appeared to be a teenage girl, looking back at me.

For a moment, the merest moment, I thought it was her. Here. Impossibly. In the flesh. As my body went cold, I knew she could feel the change too because I saw it in her face. Its striking features seemed to wither, rather than widen, in recognition. To turn a darker shade of beautiful within their frame of unruly black hair. But while the moment eased for me, with the emergence of this face bleeding through the one I had imposed, it traveled through her like a shock wave, causing her to abandon her seat and disappear into the shadows of the building's interior. I was somewhat stunned still, unsure what to do. As I shut off the engine and placed my hand on the door handle, I caught the motion of her blouse billowing in the sea breeze. She'd exited the other side of the house—was it a house?—and was moving away down the beach, delicately negotiating the scattered stones in her sandaled feet.

She paused once to look back in my direction, and something about the captured motion, about the way her peasant blouse clung to her breasts, the abandon with which her gypsy hair blew across her face, caused the mercury to plummet again. *Dear God*, I thought. *Oh dear God.*

———·———

Funny about time. When I think of seven years in the context of the Iraqi desert, it seems like an eternity. When I think of the same period in relation to Tatiana, it seems like no time at all, as if it's gone by in an instant and we were together only yesterday, whirling in an ecstasy haze across Europe. What would she have thought of this place, I wondered as I gazed out on the Alaska scenery from my kitchen window that afternoon. But I knew the answer. She would not have liked it here. She would not have liked the mountains and their jagged teeth. She would not have liked the loneliness she saw in people's faces. She would have had an appreciation for the raw struggle, the spirit of the frontier, but she would not have liked it. Not Tatiana, who died on those long drives between oases. Who dried up in those beds that did not dance with the reflections of the glitzy European nights she liked. Things might have gone differently if that irresistible urge to go from one party to the next—St. Tropez, Nice, Barcelona, finally Ibiza— had been psychological. But it wasn't. It was inborn. Amsterdam hadn't done it to her. The so-called city of freedom had simply been the first beacon in the wilderness. That's what I continued to tell myself, anyway. Otherwise there was no justification for what happened.

I'd been unable to shake the image of the girl at the stone house. Sitting at her window waiting for some surprise to emerge from the forest. Frozen in balletic beauty on the beach. Nor could I dissociate her with Tatiana. I had tried to keep busy after putting away the groceries I'd bought, unpacking my luggage, and eating a light lunch, but the utilities had been taken care, the phone line activated, the place entirely furnished, down to the extra toilet paper on the bathroom shelves. And there were only so many adjustments you could make to the décor when the hired decorator, obviously at the top of her creative game with the free license you'd given her, had done such a marvelous job toning down all the rich, dark wood with accents and contrasts you'd never have considered. The extent of my involvement had been writing the checks. Otherwise it had been her show, from the selection of art and furniture to the handling of the deliverymen, supplying beer, she told me, while making them move the same articles over and over again until those pieces were in the spot where they divinely belonged. The house was spotless, too. No fingerprint needing removing from any window or mirror. No surface needed dusting or sweeping. The porcelain and marble in the bathrooms sparkled like a commercial. After going carefully through the whole house, dreaming a little of the native art I'd hang on the wood-panel wall behind the elegant staircase that led from the middle of the living area to the columned gallery upstairs, I had sat out on the deck for awhile, watching the ducks play in the tidal pond, the porpoises pursue each other through the rough waters between the two islands, the occasional boat pass by. But not really watching any of it. Just as I didn't really watch anything now, at the kitchen window. I'd arrived at this spot, I suppose, because she had been at a window. By looking through the glass from the inside, maybe I could see what she saw. Maybe I could begin to understand.

My cell phone roused me from my wanderings. It was Martha, with a bit of information she'd apparently learned between this morning and now. Or not. I'd a suspicion she might start finding excuses to call, as she'd done with emails when I was in Iraq.

"Joel, the landscapers will be over tomorrow morning to finish up if that's cool by you."

"Sure, the nettles always need pruning." It was a joke between us—hell, between all Alaskans—a joke that had sprung spontaneously into being when she brought up landscaping the wilds surrounding my yard on my previous visit. The soil and environment weren't exactly a horticulturist's dream. Nor did any self-respecting local harbor the Joneses attitude.

"Ha-ha. The Douglases on the drive side need trimming. Couple hours, then they're out of your hair. Anyway, what do you care, it's included in the price. Gotta girlfriend already?"

It was by no means the first flirt, and while I'd no doubt she was flirtatious by nature, I'd the strong vibe that these weren't of the totally casual or in-the-line-of-duty sort.

"As a matter of fact, yes."

"What?"

"Joshing. But I did see someone of the female persuasion this morning when I took a short drive around this side of the island. Does the neighbor you mentioned live in the stone house?"

"Stone house?" She seemed momentarily at a loss. "Oh, you mean that little building on the beach near the edge of your property? Actually, it may be *on* your property. I'd almost forgotten it was there, the property was overpriced for so long and no prospective buyers to show around. And you with your time constraints, not letting me show you the whole shebang. As I recall, you said spruces are spruces and firs, firs. But is that building a house? I guess I thought it was a utility shed or something. No, Mr. Brown lives on the other side of the island. How old was this someone of the female persuasion?"

I didn't answer immediately. The question transported me back to Amsterdam, to the alleys behind the Red Light alleys, where the vision of Tatiana, so ethereally graceful she might have been poured into her erotic dance, inspired a comment from my girlfriend Brecken that would ultimately follow me across three continents, counting this desolate corner of America where I'd hoped to finally forget their brutal sting. *Jesus*, the words rang with a tocsin's clarity, *she can't be over fifteen.*

As a reward for patiently waiting me out on the line, I gave Martha the tried and true answer, the answer I'd used in Tatiana's case to try to convince myself. Here, it was at least partially truthful. Whatever the hell truth was.

"I'm not sure. Anywhere from fifteen to eighteen. I couldn't see her well. She was inside, at the window."

189

"Inside the stone building? That sounds like kids having some kicks. Maybe she came in with others by boat. It wouldn't be the first time a group of Chi-nagers cured their boredom by trespassing. What else is there to do on a Sunday morning other than go to church?"

"I'm sure it was just her."

"You know what? Mr. Brown has a granddaughter who visits from somewhere in the lower forty-eight. It was probably her. Would any states have spring break this late?"

"Late April? I don't think so."

"Still."

There wasn't anything to say to that, so I assured her I'd no concerns about either the girl or the landscapers and excused myself to some errands. Switching the phone off, I got a bottle of amber from the fridge and sat up on the kitchen counter sipping it for a while. Looked out the window and saw a man creep up in a Jeep Wrangler, hands clutching the wheel as he leaned slightly forward in his seat peering at me. A shadow passing over his features, masking something bad, something spoiled and corrupted. I felt my own face wither at the prospect that I had done that to him, turned him into a leering accuser, someone who could easily catch up to me if I just gave him a chance, paused to pick up one of the broken bottles littering the sticky Ibiza alley, offered it jagged end out, like an admission of guilt.

But he hadn't always accused, had he? Those eyes that had gazed at me from the crowd in Lucifer's had been different. They'd been filled with real enchantment. That and loneliness. The loneliness that only we, the lost, can know. Which was why when he came back, minus the blonde I would learn had deployed to Kuwait for the first Gulf War's push into Iraq, I went with him. I'd like to have met Brecken. She wasn't your typical bimbo. She knew what she wanted out of the world. I made him tell me about her, which he didn't like it but did anyway, because it was me asking. The language barrier had made it somewhat difficult, but I'd learned some English since arriving in the Netherlands from Bulgaria, and was able to piece things together. He'd returned to Heidelberg, Germany five months before I met him, his parents basing themselves in familiar environs while looking for the retirement spot that would suit the both of them and not just the mighty big-game hunter his father fancied himself to be. Neither his Dad nor his Mom had liked Brecken, because she was older than him by four years and they felt she was robbing the cradle. But for Joey (how it secretly delights him when I call him that), the age difference, the military fatigues she filled out so well, the Military Police band she wore on her upper arm had all been aphrodisiac. And he didn't care what his parents thought, after the years they'd stolen from him. After saving enough money from the job he'd landed at the American army base, he moved into his own apartment, never bothering to tell them where it was or how he could be reached. He and Brecken were free to be who they were, the rest of the world be damned. Even the military didn't judge. It set rules for Brecken, which she and her fellow soldiers broke routinely, but it didn't judge. The machine doesn't judge. It just grinds and uses fuel. Joey taught me that.

It was Brecken who introduced him to Amsterdam, six weeks before she went to Iraq. On first arriving in Heidelberg, she'd been dragged to sin city by three of the other MPS in her unit, who swore that she was going to be "broken in" like the rest of the newbies, female or not. Despite her insistence that she had a beau who provided all she needed, they didn't give up trying to break her until after they had deposited her in front of the showcase sporting the most beautiful man she'd ever seen and she still hadn't budged. The beau had found out about her trip to Amsterdam, which left the way open for Joey, who found her in The Cave a month later, dancing by herself in her bare feet on the congested dance floor, to remixed Hendrix. But that was after she'd taken one more trip to Amsterdam with the guys in her unit, succumbing to peer pressure this time and partaking of the forbidden fruit. It wasn't her fleshly appetites she'd fed, though. *Ecstasy*, she told Joey before carrying on the cycle with him as the newbie, had deeper implications than the carnal. I laughed at that later, in Ibiza, when the two of us were swirling in the drug's crystal embrace, because their first ecstasy trip had been spent going from show to perverse show, even as deep into the grime as Lucifer's, on that magical night of that strange summer where paths diverged. Joey and I heading for the Mediterranean lights, while she went plunging into the Iraqi night. I don't know where the unraveling began, at the news of her death or before, when two wayward souls found each other in the back alleys of Red Light Amsterdam. I was there for both events, and each was a sweet, sweet premonition in a godless, soulless world.

Who is who in such a world? Whose beer is it you're drinking? Whose kitchen counter are you sitting on? Whose keys have you been rattling as you look out the window on the majestic lie fading back in, taking its proper place in the order of things? Who are you considering rescuing from the cold? Does it matter, so long as you have the cold to hold on to, to assure yourself of your reality?

———•———

Something was different about the afternoon when I stepped outside, intending to cross to the Wrangler parked outside the carport, but instead pausing to take in the change in the air, the disturbance to the April sublimity. I couldn't put my finger on it at first. The sky remained free of clouds, providing a rich contrast to the snowy Chilkats. Gull Island's

191

denizens were no less active than they'd been this morning, swarming like bees about the hive, raising the pitch of their discordant chorus when a pair of bald eagles ventured too near. The waters were still rough. The breeze still snatched whimsically at the clothing. The sun still shone brightly, though from a position closer to the horizon. What was it, then?

Clarity. That's the word that hit me as my eyes made their second slow sweep of the dome I seemed to be standing in. The contrasts were too sharp, and yet somehow they were not sharp enough. The hues and textures were both deeper and shallower than they should have been. Was it perspective? Did my senses overcompensate as my mind adjusted to what it thought it perceived? Or was reality itself in doubt? For minutes I stood there trying to digest what I was filtering through my eyes, ears, nose, mouth, and skin. Stood there until the edges began to soften, to threaten the integrity of the exercise. It was then, when the fixed contours of landscape and sea were suppressed, that the subtler details emerged.

The first was on Gull Island where, at the base of the whirling fray concentrated at the near end of the island, a light amber-colored mist separated itself from the flutter, a ghostly, vaporous cloud kicked up like dust by the birds' wings. As I tried to make sense of this, removing my sunglasses and peering beneath the visor of my hand, the next detail bled through. This one was aural in nature, existing at the ragged edges of the gulls' screeches. And once it found its way to my ears, it lost all semblance of subtlety. Terror was at the core of it. Terror and anguish. Undivided, these twin emotions turned the birds' cacophony into the risen chorus of hell. But there was an even more deeply encoded message. It didn't lay the nerves and veins open like the cries of the damned, but it was there nonetheless, its steady siren having only needed to find its way to my consciousness. I could smell and taste the acrid, peppery, shrill bite of it, which I associated directly and without thought with the mist. The air shimmered with it. The fibers in my nose and nerve endings vibrated with it. On my taste buds, it was the coppery vestige of a paranoia-fraught acid trip. *Warning*. That's what it was. That first crack in a window that made a couple weeks in spring seem like a fleeting illusion.

I closed my eyes, letting the cold teeth of the keys in my clenched fist divert my attention from the sensory onslaught. When I moved, I kept my eyes on the cement beneath me, closing the distance to the Jeep in long purposeful strides. As I sat in the driver's seat with my hands on the wheel, the carport blocking the view, the doors and windows of the vehicle muting the noise, other sights, scents, tastes, and sounds made a bid on the space left behind. For a moment I despaired. Knowing I hadn't the will to fight my memories. Knowing they would drag me into depths too dark to escape from. Soul-carrying cries and strange amber mists were things I could eventually find a way to justify; that night in Ibiza I could not. But then I was turning the key in the ignition and submerging myself in the tremor of the engine; and the memories, save for the taunting echoes, withdrew.

————•————

She wasn't to be found when I went back, parking in a weedy, long unused pocket in the trees beside the grotesquely shaped boulder. She was not on the beach, so far as I could see before it curved out of sight in both directions. Nor was she in the stone structure, which was open to the elements, splintered door resting against the inside wall, a single window gaping from each side as if to offer the four winds a place to conspire. The building, with its three-room floor plan, was rather like a house, but there was nothing to indicate that anyone had ever resided there. No stripped-out plumbing in the bathroom-sized room, no holes where electrical outlets or fixtures had been. With its tile floor and interior stone-shingle walls, it might have been one of those Roman villas that Brecken and I had visited among the leafing vineyards of the Mosel River valley. Funny that the two of us, who mutually loved to do that sort of thing, never got out of Germany except to Amsterdam, while Tatiana and I, who could have partied anywhere really, went whirling across the coasts of France and Spain, pausing to take in a castle ruin or medieval town only when I suggested it.

I gave the place only a cursory look-over, though according to Martha, the building might well belong to me. The girl was my focus, and I knew if I didn't find out who she was, I'd be useless. So instead of returning to the house to wonder with another beer or two before night fell and I turned on the flat screen to a baseball game or MTV to drown out the urge to step outside and see what sort of clarity the dusk had brought with it, I went in the direction of the original destination, the island's other residence. At no point, incidentally, not when I was looking for the girl or driving along the shore, did I look at Gull Island. It sang eerily, eventually distantly, through the Wrangler's open windows, but I was somehow able to keep it out of context. With a purpose, I could do that. Without one, I'd never have made it beyond the stone building.

Martha had told me that this was the only road that would take you from one side of the island to the other, so I knew it led eventually to the house, or to a feed to the house. The drive was shorter than I'd have imagined, however, probably because I'd still been in my teens when I last observed the island's entire length, which could only be viewed by boat because of the hilly, heavily vegetated terrain along the highway. In five minutes at an easy pace, I was at the rickety mailbox, which must have been from a previous time, because on the mainland side of the bridge there were two boxes. A couple minutes later I was up the small hill, parking next to Mr. Brown's Explorer, thinking: Why would the house be up here when the beach is down there, particularly with the winters that fell on Chi Bay at times? Then I saw the incredible view, the lookout platform from which descended a wooden flight of stairs. I didn't have to walk to the railing to know the stairs led to a boathouse and a recreation area equipped with a grill, picnic table, lounge chairs, probably a skinning block. This was Alaska, where they still mined for gold, and always at a sacrifice. More power to you, Mr. Brown.

The house itself was not unlike my own, perhaps a bit smaller, the facade of its A frame mostly glass, through which plenty of wood was visible. There was no sign of life within, but there was a buzzing from behind the place. My next move was an iffy one by Alaska standards, but I went ahead and took the liberty of walking back there uninvited, hoping that Mr. Brown's hospitable side was the better of his private one. I rounded the back of the place cautiously, recognizing the buzz as that of an electric saw. I needn't have worried, because he saw me from the open bay of his workshop well in advance, averting any disaster. Shadow prevented me from reading his face, but his body posture, as he shut off his table saw and removed his safety glasses and gloves, suggested a friendly disposition. He was a big man, at least two hundred eighty pounds worth, belly getting in the way as he wiped the sawdust from the front of his beige coveralls. As he approached me out of the shadow, his ruddy features were opened in a smile. From a distance, he looked to be in his mid fifties, but I added a decade to that assessment when the wisdom around his eyes became apparent. I liked him before either of us had spoken a word.

"Hullo there," he said.

There was a trace of the lower forty-eight in his accent. Texas, if I'd had to guess. Not all that unusual; many of us non-natives were transplants. The northern reigned, however. No mistaking it for anything else, though my mom would have reminded me of the time we met our first Alaskan, a Juneau woman, while on vacation. I'd remarked in the lady's presence and to my mother's slight embarrassment that she sounded just like those people in *Fargo*, which movie my parents had grudgingly let me watch with them the night before.

"Afternoon, sir. Hope you don't mind my popping up like this. Heard you at it back here. Martha suggested you lived alone, so I didn't see any point ringing the bell."

"Not a-tall. Not a-tall. Martha, you say? Brezinski? You must be my neighbor then."

"Joel Copa. Just moved in today."

His hand was extended before he arrived. I met its strong grip equally.

"Ned Brown," he said. "Pleasure to make your acquaintance. I was beginning to think that house was going to stay vacant forever. Owner's in San Francisco, I'm sure Martha told you. Businessman. Raven Island was his spring getaway. I considered buying the place myself, but it was . . . um, a little out of my range."

I laughed. "Overpriced, you mean. Apparently, the price dropped considerably before I entered the picture. I was able to whittle it down from there."

"Well, I'm glad you did. Wasn't me had the bright idea, but my daughter and son-in-law. What the hell am I going to do with a whole island? Plenty of room right here for their family of three. 'Course, they'd tell you it's cramped. That place of theirs in Seattle is obnoxious, it's so damned big. But I haven't seen as much of them since my granddaughter turned old enough to travel alone. Don't expect to see as much of Casey either, with college just around the corner. Hell, they oughtta be thanking you too, Joel, because it would have been their inheritance paying for it!"

We shared a laugh on that. For me, not just because it was funny. I could feel the tension leave my muscles, the tightness of the years slowly dissolve, as though I'd needed this one last test of endurance to finally let it all go. He hadn't said it yet, but I knew. I knew Casey was visiting right now, probably on an extended weekend, considering Seattle was relatively close, and the only reason she'd run when she'd seen me was because she had thought she and her grandfather were alone out here. I surprised her, that was all. Scared her probably, with the face I must have presented. But to be sure:

"So that must have been Casey I saw on the beach earlier, over by the stone building on the edge of my property?"

"Hell she doing over there? That girl, she loves to wander. But I guess I was the same at her age. Couldn't get enough of the outdoors. I'll have to keep a closer leash on her now that we've got a neighbor."

My body fluttered with the release. I literally swooned, feeling as if I was falling through a fabulous updraft. Maintaining a conversational tone took all my delivered soul could muster. "Not on my account, Ned. I don't hold a shotgun over my property. She's welcome to wander where she likes." And as a therapeutic afterthought, since I was free to think as I liked now without fear of consequence: "Lovely girl, by the way. I spent some time in Europe and thought she might have been from over there somewhere, with that black hair, those unusual features."

For a second I thought I saw a shadow cross his face, as though he didn't know how to take this. But then it was replaced by a smile as open as the gaze with which I'd met and survived his suspicion.

He said, "Gypsy girl, I call her. Her mom hates that nickname. I'm an annoying old bastard, what can I say."

195

Suddenly, it was I who was momentarily thrown off pace. By that one word. Tatiana hadn't just looked the part of the gypsy—she'd been one. Distant Indian roots, communal living, exile status in a still unenlightened society. Not Bulgarian society, specifically, but that of humankind. She would have been at least surreptitiously persecuted wherever she happened to reside. In Amsterdam, they didn't persecute. They gave haven, either physically or ideologically, to the persecuted (just ask the likes of Galileo or Newton, whose heads the Church had wanted on pikes for their heretical suggestions). So went the fantasy Tatiana, young and full of misplaced hope, had contrived for herself.

Ned Brown and I talked for a few more minutes, about the weather, duck hunting, doing a couple beers and some halibut fishing sometime. We were welcome to stop by the other's house anytime and we'd generally look after each other because it was us bachelors, by divorce in his case, against the world. I was careful not to talk about my plans for my house with him at this early stage in our acquaintanceship, and maybe I would rethink the bar and events and go with just the art gallery, opening the doors for limited hours or by appointment. For there was something to be said for privacy and solitude, there really was, when you could finally live with yourself again.

——•——

The sun had dipped below the mountainous horizon as I drove along the beach again. The mixed scents of sea and evergreen, the latter rather a misnomer in this part of the world, found my nostrils through the open windows of the Jeep. Through breaks in the trees I could see Gull Island, but not the end, where a mist had spawned with no apparent source. Had that been my imagination? Had the color been a trick of the sunlight on the water? Whatever the cause, it had been an aberration, either of nature or the mind, and it was certainly nothing to worry about now that the universe had been set right again. Now that I'd faced my demon, which had turned out to be no more sinister than a harmless wanderer whose wild windblown hair, whose ease with the elements, whose enjoyment of the peaceful sanctuary she'd discovered, merely represented her freedom from the constraints of the lower forty-eight. I felt a tinge of regret that I hadn't been able to talk to her. To partake of the purity Tatiana had lost before I came along. There were other days, sure, but in that moment there would have been magic, as I discovered her for her and let the unwholesome thoughts and memories go with the wind.

It was a regret I should have been content with, rather than slowing when I neared that point, and at the last moment pulling into the pocket in the trees beside the elephantine formation that hid the stone structure like an uncertainly glimpsed secret. For what good could come of breathing the aroma of her passage? Of having another look at the active end of Gull Island? Other days were always safer days. Life taught you that. But here I was, stepping out into the last strains of this particularly unstable day, wanting more, something to continue to comfort me in my sleep. Because the days are also ephemeral, along with all that occurs within them. If a taste can possibly be replenished, then you must replenish it—now, while the opportunity exists. Tatiana taught me that.

Which was why upon leaving Barcelona, I took her to Ibiza Island, Spain, self-styled party capital of the world, where all were welcome, regardless of age, creed, color, or income level, so long as you had a high-limit credit card that some American bank had been fool enough to give you. Something told me I shouldn't. She'd been sick recently, body no doubt purging itself of all the chemicals and partying. But more importantly, her Amsterdam face was returning with increasing frequency. Yet I booked us, God help me. She wanted it. She wanted someplace where they wouldn't look at us. Where *we* could look at *them* for a change. Ibiza is such a place, oh indeed, with its psychedelic costumes, its glittery wonder-struck faces, its spontaneous raves and boat parties, its high-energy extravaganzas of light and sound and hedonism that are its clubs. In our room that last night in Barcelona, we also looked past Ibiza to Oktoberfest. Summer was ending and it was just around the corner. Munich would be a sort of homecoming, the last party of the year, then we'd work through the fall and winter until Carnival, which we'd do in Italy. She'd hinted about easy ways in which she could provide money, but I'd not wanted to believe what I was hearing.

I caught myself at my thoughts while they were still picking up momentum in the upper loops of their spiral, and was able to bring the now in again. Without realizing I was doing so, I'd wandered down to the surf and was looking at Gull Island, though it hadn't come into focus until this moment. Time had passed, more than I would have imagined possible, such that the twilight was deep enough to pull out the luminous quality of the mist, which gathered in force now about the island's rim. As I followed its path across the better part of the island's visible shoreline, it was suddenly not a sinister thing to my sensibilities, but a sad one. Its color was that of the first beer of Oktoberfest, held to the light in toast. The amber dream we'd never gotten to partake of. What was it they said in Germany? *Leben, Liebe, und Lust?* Life, love, and lust. It would have been fitting if it had all ended in the country that had invented such poetry.

Some instinct made me turn then, in the only relevant direction, and there, on a lower ledge of the elephantine rock, tucked up near the side of the building that faced the sea where I wouldn't have noticed her, sat the girl, watching me. The jolt I'd experienced on our first encounter didn't happen this time, though the feeling of intimate familiarity was there just the same. There was a ballooning inside me, a kind of breathful breathlessness, but then it was quietly contracted, leaving an absence of both hope and despair. It wasn't a going through the motions, the walking toward the patient figure she was this time. It was more a soft contentment, as though this was how it was supposed to go, how it should have gone the first time, had we but listened rather than reacted. What would she say to me? How could anything either of us had to say be expressed in words? She was so beautiful in the twilight. So young. So womanly in her clinging peasant blouse, her jeans and bare feet. *Jesus, she can't be over fifteen.* Who was Brecken to judge? At least Tatiana had had the balls to say it to my face. God, she was beautiful, sitting here in front of me, painted toe drawing designs in the silt.

"Hi," I said, stopping a short distance from where she sat, trying not to openly partake of her. My mind was able to separate the two of them, even distinguish the ways that Casey did not resemble Tatiana, but the similarities were powerful, aphrodisiac, although I'd never had such tendencies outside a nineteen-year-old's enchantment with a girl four years his junior. Had I left something else in that alley in Ibiza Town? Carrying back a hole that had waited till now, twenty years later, to be filled?

"Hi." She hesitated, as though gathering the courage to say more. "Listen, about earlier. I don't know why I reacted like that. The way you looked at me, it was like I'd spooked you. What's the word for someone from the past who shows up unexpectedly, like a ghost?"

The word seemed to come on the waves washing in behind me. "Revenant?"

"Yeah, that's it. It was like that for me too. Ever been to Spain, by any chance?"

As I stared at her, it was all I could do to keep that face that saw ghosts from presenting itself again. "What would make you say that?"

"I don't know. Just a vibe, I guess. I was there last summer. I thought maybe . . . " She seemed to realize how ridiculous her words must sound and dismissed the thought with a slight wave of her hand. "Never mind."

"No, no. Please. What about Spain?"

She looked at me, looked in my eyes, seeing something for a moment. Something more intimate than recognition, I thought. The same glimmering something that I observed in her own gaze before reason regained its tenuous hold. "Something made me connect you to that trip somehow," she said. "Which doesn't make any sense, because I was so focused while there that I didn't have time for meeting people. Other than the people I had to see, I mean. And I could never forget them. They helped me put the puzzle together."

"Puzzle?" The lump that had started with her mention of Europe had grown into a tumor. Swallowing didn't help. I'd no saliva.

She looked at the ground, the circle she was tracing over and over again. Letting my own eyes drift, I saw her sandals off to the side, one lying across the other. Noticing their presence meant I was free, at least for now, of the physical captivation. But this fresh spell she'd put me under was worse. Whatever this was, it reduced sexual energy to so much dirty residue. As she raised her eyes again, shyly, self-consciously, mine were there to meet them.

She said, "I didn't mean to open up this door into my personal life. I don't even know you."

"I'm Joel, your grandfather's new neighbor. I live in the house you come to soon after crossing the bridge. I was on my way to introduce myself to Ned when I saw you. You're Casey, I presume."

Her smile, slow in coming, slightly crooked, was the loveliest thing I'd ever seen. "I guess we're not strangers then, are we?"

I don't know how, Casey, but we're definitely not strangers.

"Nope. So go ahead. I want to hear what would cause you to ignore an interesting devil like me."

She laughed, and it, too, was superlative. "Well, it started on my birthday. My parents took me out to eat at this quiet place where they told me something about myself that shocked me. I don't know how I'd never guessed, but once it was out there, it was like I'd always known. They'd made the decision to wait till my eighteenth birthday to tell me. I don't know why. I—"

"Your eighteenth?"

"Yes. I turn nineteen next month. The same age my real mom was when she died. She's the reason I went to Europe. To find out—"

This time it wasn't me who cut her off. Not directly anyway. She'd seen the impact of her words. It must have been like looking in the mirror for her, the news causing the same powerful reverberations in me that it had in her. I knew everything in that instant of crystal clarity. The whole purpose of my otherwise wretched existence was shown to me in violent but liberating relief.

"You must excuse me, Casey," I spilled out, then turned and took several strides in the direction of the waves before stopping to suck long breaths of precious air into my lungs. A sudden thirst also gripped me as I stood there with my back to Alaska's gypsy girl. The thirst I'd known sometimes in the desert when I'd had a couple cups of coffee before the temperature soared to a hundred and forty degrees, taking what moisture the caffeine hadn't already absorbed. The same powerful thirst I'd known as I watched Tatiana crawl backward in the alley, hand over hand, face up and looking at me, feet sliding in a trail of blood that flowed from both our bodies. Only this latter thirst had now been quenched, twenty years later, by the water of revelation. In knowing Tatiana still existed, that the two of us still endured in this new form, barriers constructed of guilt, shame, fear, and despair came tumbling down, revealing at least the possibility that the deed committed had been one of defense, not a willful attempt at murder.

But redemption wasn't the point here. It's the scene in the alley that mattered. Whatever the degree of intent, that's where the story truly began. Not at the moment of eye contact in Lucifer's. Not when I returned to Amsterdam for Tatiana. Not even at conception or the specific bodily union that had led to it. The story had begun that night in that sticky alley in Ibiza Town where everything came to a head. My loathing of Tatiana for what she was. My loathing of myself for exploiting her as surely as her employers in Lucifer's had. My shame at robbing a cradle that now proved not to have been a cradle at all. I'd believed the lie that Tatiana had let me believe. She'd thought that's what I wanted, that my sweet nothings about her youthful beauty, about her baby soft skin, her innocence, were part of some fantasy for me. It was all deception, wasn't it, Tatiana? From that inviting look you gave me from your stage in Lucifer's, to that last night in Barcelona when you deftly covered your suggestion that we whore you out through the winter; to that even blacker night in Ibiza when I stood behind you watching you apply your makeup in the bathroom mirror and you told me through a shining mask of ecstasy and sangria not to worry, you chose me over the world. But I still forgave you. When you pressed your ass against my groin, Amsterdam eyes luridly staring back at me from the glass, I lifted the Spanish skirt I'd bought for you and forgave you like I'd never forgiven you before. The last thing you said to me as we stepped out into the party had been the seal of fate. "Thanks for saving me, Joey."

I must have stood there for a while, for when I opened my eyes night had fallen. The tears flowed as I gazed out on the bay, the moon hovering just over the rim of the Chilkats, igniting the snowy caps. I looked for the glow of the mist, but it was gone, Gull Island but a dark shape in the dusk. I didn't want to turn, for fear that Casey might still be there, face as intense as her mother's had been whenever Tatiana had tried to divine something out of me. How could I explain? How could I tell her that she had been saved from the wretched life she would have known with Tatiana and me by an act of violence by her father's own hand? An act I'd thought had left Tatiana dead and myself with no choice but to flee? An act that had set into motion the realignment of the stars that had brought my daughter and me together almost twenty years later? I couldn't. It was that simple. To tell her would be to take away the freedom fate had been gracious enough to deal out in the aftermath. I could only hope that she continued to visit Raven Island for as long as I survived these rocky waters of life.

I turned, finally. And she was still there. As I slowly approached her, her moonlit face was not intense as I'd imagined, but softly concerned.

Before she could put her concern into some sort of language, I said, "I'm sorry for breaking down on you. Thing is, you've helped me put a puzzle of my own together. I once knew someone who looked like you, had that same wild hair, those dark eyes. She was adopted too. Only her adopter didn't take care of her as yours obviously have."

She regarded me for a few seconds, maybe understanding that I referred to myself, maybe seeing that glimmering something again. But then she nodded, seeming to have reconciled with herself, at least for now, that the familiarity between us was some quirk of the stars.

I should probably have called it an evening, said something foolish like *your grandfather must be wondering where you are.* But there was one question that couldn't wait until tomorrow, or whenever I could convince her to meet me again.

"How did your mother die, Casey?"

Her response was unencumbered, that of someone who had come to terms with the matter. "An overdose."

I thought about that. As the night continued to deepen around us, I thought about that with not a little regret.

"Was anyone there for her?" I said, not caring that I risked another probing gaze with the question.

"Some of the older hospital staff remembered the dying girl whose baby had to be removed from the womb, but no one really knew her. Except maybe one person. She had a new tattoo on her breast when she was brought into the hospital, a heart over her heart." She placed her hand on her right breast, as if she was the one wearing the tattoo. "The words *Loving you Joey* circled it. I was never able to find out who Joey was. But I like to fantasize they were two wild souls crazy in love and I was their lovechild."

My tear ducts all dried up, it was only a matter of maintaining facial and vocal composure as I offered her gently, "I'm sure they were, Casey. I'm sure they were."

———•———

I'd offered to give her a ride, but she wanted to walk home along the beach. Though neither of us said it, driving up in my Jeep at nine o'clock in the evening might not be the best idea from an appearances standpoint. Then again, Ned might be glad to have somebody helping him look after his wanderer of a granddaughter, considering it was spring and the bears were coming down from the high places to feed on the skunk flower and other new growth around shore. We'd parted with an embrace that was only awkward because it was so natural and spontaneous, and I leaned against the elephant stone and watched her go, a vision in the moonlight, meeting her trickling finger wave not once but twice before she eventually blended in with the rocks among which she moved with a gypsy dancer's grace. I stayed there a while longer, admiring the silhouettes of the mountains, contemplating the black, oddly quiet ship that was Gull Island, enjoying the caress of the salty breeze on the cheek Casey had kissed. Then I headed up to the Jeep, as relaxed and happy as I'd felt in a long, long time.

As I was about to open the door, I saw twin shafts of light cutting through the trees and darkness from the direction of Ned's house. For a moment, inexplicably, I struggled with a foreboding. The sense that this wasn't going to go well. That Ned had somehow gleaned out of the ether that we were together, and in a way that was too intimate for strangers, and came with a gun in the seat beside him. But I was able to regroup before the sound of the tires on gravel reached my ears, attributing the momentary lapse of reason to residual guilt. Yesterday, I would not have been so quick to recover. Tomorrow, there would likely have been nothing to recover from, the self-deficiencies of two decades as a fugitive from myself literally healing at a steroidal pace. When the Explorer cleared the last bend, I was waiting by the door of the Jeep, prepared to nod, chat, salute, field questions, whatever big boy had. What I was not prepared for, as he braked at the sight of my vehicle, was a passenger in the front seat beside him.

As both doors came open, Ned offered a warm, "Hey neighbor. Glad we ran into you. Casey and I were just on our way into town. She got home just after you—"

He never finished because she'd come around the front of the SUV into view now, her strong, spiky-haired figure reflected like the revenant she wasn't in my astonished eyes. I acted on the instant, turning and running to the beach, out across the slate in the direction she'd gone. But I knew as I groped for a name to call that no matter how far I ran I wouldn't find her. She was an echo that had never been left, a draft existing on the hope of life, a girl who might have been, had her father but cut a little less deeply and her mother fulfilled her end of the bargain by surviving long enough to see the wish legitimized.

ABOUT THE AUTHOR

Darren Speegle is the author of the novels *Artifacts* and *The Third Twin*, as well as several short story collections. His short fiction has appeared in numerous venues, including *Analog*, *Clarkesworld*, *Best New Horror*, *Cemetery Dance*, *Subterranean Magazine*, and *Subterranean: Tales of Dark Fantasy*. He has edited two anthologies with author/editor Michael Bailey: *Adam's Ladder* and the upcoming dark science fiction project *Prisms*. Darren's stories are often set in exotic or interesting places where he has lived (Germany, Alaska, Southeast Asia) or otherwise explored (broader Europe). Between gigs as a contractor in the Middle East, Darren resides in Thailand. When not writing, he enjoys outdoor activities like hiking and biking.